Joanne Harris was b[...] [...] mother and English [...] [...] at Cambridge University [...] now lives in Yorkshire where she teaches French at a boys' grammar school. *The Evil Seed* is her first novel, but she has been writing stories since she was a child. Joanne Harris is married and has seven cats.

The Evil Seed

Joanne Harris

WARNER BOOKS

A *Warner* Book

First published in Great Britain in 1992
by Warner Books

A CIP catalogue record for this book
is available from the British Library.

ISBN 0 7515 0008 9

Photoset in North Wales by
Derek Doyle & Associates, Mold, Clwyd.
Printed and bound in Great Britain by
Richard Clay Ltd, Bungay, Suffolk.

Warner Books
A Division of
Little, Brown and Company (UK) Limited
165 Great Dover Street
London SE1 4YA

She is older than the rocks among which she sits: like the vampire, she has been dead many times, and learned the secrets of the grave; and has been a diver in deep seas, and keeps their fallen day about her, and has trafficked for strange webs with Eastern merchants; and as Leda, was the mother of Helen of Troy, and as Saint Anne, was the mother of Mary: and all this has been to her but the sound of lyres and flutes, and lives only in the delicacy with which it has moulded the changing lineaments, and tinged the eyelids and hands.

Walter Pater: *Mona Lisa*

Part One
The Beggar Maid

Son, raise not up thine eyes to look on a lovely woman, rouged and antimonied. Desire her not in thy heart. For if thou shouldst give her all thy riches, thou dost get nothing the more out of her; but art condemned by God and by mankind. For she is like unto a sepulchre which is fair on the upper side, and below is full of the rottenness and bones of the dead.

Apocrypha: Proverbs of Ahikar

Introduction

Larger than life, face and hands startlingly pale in a canvas as dark and narrow as a coffin, eyes fathomless as the Underworld and lips touched with blood, Proserpine seems to watch some object beyond the canvas in a mournful reverie. She holds the orb of the pomegranate, forgotten, against her breast, its golden perfection marred by the slash of crimson which bisects it, indicating that she has eaten, and thereby forfeited her soul. Doomed to remain for half the year in the Underworld, she broods, pale lady of death, watching for the reflections of the far-away sun which flickers palely on the ivy-crusted walls.

Or so we are led to believe.

But she is a woman of many faces, this Queen of the Underworld; therein lies her power and her glamour. The fruit she holds is living, red as her lips at its centre, red as a heart. Pale as incense she stands, and the square of light which frames her lovely, brooding face does not touch her skin; she shines with her own lambency, her pose weary as the ages, yet filled with the strength of her invulnerability. Her eyes never meet yours, and yet they never cease to fix a certain point just beyond your left shoulder; some other man, perhaps, doomed to the terrible bliss of her love, some other chosen man. The fruit is a gift to the chosen one;

3

who knows what appetites, what ecstasies lie within that crimson flesh? What unearthly delights wait in those seeds to be born?

From *The Blessed Damozel*, Daniel Holmes

Prologue

There's rosemary, that's for remembrance;
pray love, remember.

Hamlet, 4.4

Fulbourn Hospital, Cambridge, *October 1977*

When I was a child, I had a lot of toys; my parents were
rich and could afford them, I suppose, even in those
days, but the one which I always remembered was the
train. Not a clockwork train, or even one of those
which you can pull behind you, but the real thing,
speeding through countryside of its own, trailing a
plume of white steam behind it, racing faster and faster
towards a destination which always seemed to elude
it. It was a spinning-top, painted red on the bottom
half and made of a kind of clear celluloid on top,
beneath which a whole world glowed and spun like a
jewel, little hedges and houses and the edge of a
painted circle of sky so clean and blue that it nearly
hurt you to look at it too long; but best of all when you
pumped the little handle ('always be careful with that
handle, Danny, never spin your top too hard'), the
train would come puffing bravely into view, like a
dragon trapped under glass and shrunk to minuscule
size by some cunning magician, coming slowly at first,
then faster and faster until the houses and trees
blurred into nothingness around it, the whine of the

5

top lost in the triumphant scream of the engine-whistle, as if the little train was itself singing with the fierce joy of being almost . . . so nearly . . . there.

Mother, of course, said that to spin the top too hard might break it (and I always took care, just in case that might be true), but I think there was a suspicion in my mind that she was wrong. I must have thought (and I see no reason to disbelieve it now, especially after what has happened, and is still happening) that one day, if I was careless, if I let my attention wander even for a moment, then the train might finally reach its mysterious, impossible destination like a snake eating itself, tail first, and come bursting, monstrous, into the real world, all fires blazing, steel throwing sparks into the quiet of the playroom, to come for me in fury at its long imprisonment. And maybe some of my pleasure was knowing that I had it trapped, that it could never escape because I was too careful, and that I could watch it when I liked, its sky, its hedges, its mad race through the world all mine, to set into motion when I liked, to stop when I liked, because I was careful, because I was clever.

But then again, maybe I never thought that. I don't remember being a fanciful child; I was certainly not morbid. Rosemary did that to me; did it to all of us, I suppose; it was the way she was. She made us all into children again, myself included, looming over us like the wicked witch in the gingerbread house, ourselves little gingerbread men running around in circles, like little trains under celluloid as she watched and smiled and pumped the handle to set her wheels in motion.

My mind is wandering; a bad sign, like the lines around my eyes and the thin patch at the top of my head, a sign of age, of oncoming death, like the shadow of a skull in a pretty girl's face, but there again, Rosemary's doing, not mine. When the priest said, 'Dust to dust', I looked up and thought I saw her again, just for a moment, leaning against the

6

hawthorn-tree with a smile in her eyes. If she had looked at me, I think I would have screamed. But she looked at Robert instead.

Robert was white, his face hollow and haunted beneath his hat, but not, I think, because he saw her. No, I am sure I was the only one who saw her, and only for a moment, you understand; a change in the light, a movement, and I would have missed her. But I didn't. And that, more than anything, is why I am writing to you now, to you, my future beyond the grave, to tell you about myself and Robert and Rosemary . . . especially about Rosemary. Because she remembers, you see. She remembers.

One

Cambridge, *April 1947*
Fulbourn Hospital, *September 1977*

It was a beautiful day, crisp and Autumn-clear, the ground bright with leaves and the sky as round and as blue as the sky beneath which the little train had raced so many years ago. There were not many people: myself, Robert, a handful of others, all in black, their faces a pale unfinished blur in the sunlight. Only Robert's stands out in my memory, his eyes brown-shadowed, his cheekbones horribly prominent, his mouth drawn down bitterly, his hands clenching and unclenching the fabric of his coat, leaving starlike creases in the flannel. Grief had caricatured his face delicately and cruelly, accentuating the weakness, the bewilderment, like the face of a sick child denied some anticipated treat. It hurt me to look at him.

'White flowers only', the advertisement in the *Cambridge News* had said, and there were hundreds of them; lilies and roses and great shaggy overblown chrysanthemums, lining the grave and the path and crowning the coffin as it was lowered into the ground. Their scent was mesmeric, but the earthy, dark smell from the grave was even stronger, and as the priest spoke the final words of the service I backed away from that open hole as a man retreats from the side of a cliff, feeling wretched that I could not help Robert but also strangely light-headed. Maybe it was the flowers.

He had chosen a lovely plot for her; right at the back of the third churchyard, up against the wall and beneath the combined branches of a hawthorn-tree and a shady yew. The death-tree stood arm-in-arm with the life-tree, their bright berries seeming to mock the grief of the mourner, as if they had been in league with the sweetness of the day to bedeck themselves in their most joyful colours to celebrate her passing. But it would be beautiful in summer, I thought to myself, shady and green and silent. This year, the hemlock and the tall weeds had been cleared away for the funeral but they would grow back.

(. . . *grow back*)

The thought disturbed me in some strange subliminal way, but I could not think why. Let them grow, after all, let them invade that quiet place, overgrow the grave and the stone and the memory of Rosemary for ever; let flowers grow from her eyes that she be blind. If only Robert had not insisted upon remembering, I thought helplessly. If only this could be the end, if only she could be forgotten. But he loved her, of course. Perhaps I did too.

It was spring when I first met her, beside the weir at Magdalene Bridge, and for once I was up early, on my way to meet Robert at a tea-shop before we went to the library. I was twenty-five, a graduate student at the University; I was writing a doctorate paper on the Pre-Raphaelites (a much-maligned school of painting at the time, which I hoped to bring back into fashion), and I loved it there. I existed in an abstract, hermetic world of books and absolutes; the rarefied atmosphere of Cambridge suited my withdrawn, obsessive personality. The stones and cobbles of the university town rested quiet, as they had done for centuries, never-changing; an ideal backdrop for my studies and a retreat for myself from the bewildering advances of the modern world. I lived in the past and was happy there.

I had one good friend, a very nice lodging over by Grantchester way, and a comfortable allowance from my father, which supplemented my grant from the faculty. I had always expected that when my doctorate was finished I would be able to join the University as a full-time lecturer (in fact I already gave lectures on a fairly regular basis, and my tutor at Pembroke, Doctor Shakeshafte, had high hopes for me in that domain). My life was all planned out as neatly and precisely as the gardens and lawns of Cambridge, and it never occurred to me to question the plan, or to hope for something more.

On that particular day, with the bright morning sun reflecting great dazzling panels of gold from the mullioned windows of Magdalene College, and after one of the worst winters on record, a faint scent of long hoped-for greenery at last in the frosty air, I was feeling on top of the world. As I quickened my step to cross the bridge, I was just beginning to sing a popular song to myself when I heard a sound below me and I stopped.

I suppose that was where it started, for me, anyway, and sometimes I wonder what would have happened if I had ignored the sound and run across the bridge for dear life without looking back, but I don't expect there was any question of that in my mind. She had it too well planned out. You see, it was the sound, unmistakably, of someone jumping into the river.

It was spring, as I said, and the Cam was at its highest. The weir rushed and snarled less than a hundred yards away, and anyone who fell in at that point was likely to be caught in the sluice and drowned almost instantly. That was why punting was strictly forbidden beyond the bridge; not that anyone would have been fool enough to try it anyway. For a moment I was still, squinting over the parapet for the log or the broken punt or the piece of floating debris which must have caused the sound; then I saw her, a pale blur of a

11

face over some kind of a pale dress ballooning out around her, dark hollows for eyes, her mouth a dark 'O' of despair, every feature a blur, as if she were already half a fathom under.

'Hey!' I called, or some other foolish thing, and I saw her head tilt into the rushing water like a tired child's into a pillow. No call, no wave, nothing. For a frozen instant, I may have imagined that I was hallucinating, so unreal was she, Ophelia-like on the weedy brown river. Then the realization hit me that this was no accident, no dream, but a suicide, some poor desperate woman half a minute from a cold and muddy death, with only me to see her or to save her. And so I came running, as, I suppose, she knew I would, stripping off my coat and jacket and shoes and socks willy-nilly as I ran along the bank, my glasses slipping from my nose, panting and shouting; 'Wait! Hey! Miss! Young lady!' without drawing even a glance from her. I jumped in close to the bank, a few yards downstream from her as she drifted slowly towards me, bracing myself for the shock of the cold water. My bare feet touched mud and slime at the bed of the river, but at least I was not out of my depth. I reached for her. My hands brushed the floating material of her dress and clenched like a vice. The flimsy fabric ripped but by then I had a good grip on the girl, who seemed to be only half-conscious, and with all my strength I held onto her as I tried to fight my way back to the bridge. I don't know how long it took me, or how I managed to do it; I was not a man of action then, nor am I now, but I suppose that in those days I had youth and ignorance on my side, and somehow I managed to use the uneven brick shoring of the river-bank to pull us both out of the mainstream and towards safe, still water. I know I hauled her out first and myself after her and that for a while I had to lie on the bank, my breath coming in great, tearing gasps and my nose bleeding a little before I could even look at her. She was lying as I had left her, her head

12

thrown back and her arms flung wide, but her eyelids were fluttering and her breathing, though too rapid, was regular. My first thought was that she must be cold, and I retrieved my coat, the first in a line of randomly discarded garments along the side of the river, and wrapped it clumsily around her shoulders, somehow a little embarrassed to touch her now that she was out of immediate danger, as if she might be angry at my familiarity.

My second thought, quite simply, was amazement at how lovely she was.

There was no lack of beautiful women in Cambridge in those days; you saw them at parties or at the theatre or at balls, walking arm-in-arm with their young men in the gardens or punting on the Cam, but this one, as soon as I saw her, seemed as different to them as if she had come from another century. She was slim, pale, her skin almost bluish, like very fine china, the blue veins of her eyelids very much in evidence under skin so thin that I could almost see the eye beneath. Her cheekbones were high, the modelling of her face delicate and pre-cise, the mouth full, pale, tragic. Her hair was enmeshed with weeds and almost black with water, although I guessed that when it was dry, it would be red. But her beauty was not really any of these things; it was lam-bent, like bright sunlight seen through a dark curtain, ardent, arrogant and yet somehow pathetic too, as if it had looked upon ugliness too often, only to become still more beautiful in the process. She was one of those women, I knew then, who are at their most lovely in rags; maybe King Cophetua had thought that too, the first time he looked upon the beggar maid. Then her eyes opened, a deep grey, almost lavender, blank at first, then fixing on my face with a wildness which wrenched at my heart.

'I'm not dead?' she whispered.

'No, you're not,' I said, trying, foolishly, to be com-forting. 'Everything will be all right now.'

13

Well, she wasn't dead; nothing could have been more true than that, at least. But things were far from being all right, then, or ever again.

Two

Cambridge, *April 1990*

The tabby jumped onto Alice's knee, as if to remind her that she had been sitting in that chair doing nothing for nearly half an hour now and that it might be time she decided to do some work. She stroked Cat and kissed the top of her furry head before she put her down on the floor.

Alice was thirtyish but looked younger, with intelligent, laughing brown eyes and short, curling brown hair. She wore glasses with thin wire frames which suited her, and favoured baggy sweat-shirts and T-shirts to camouflage her plump figure. Her vivid face was pleasant though not pretty, but her smile as she leaned over to play with the tabby was almost enough to give the illusion of beauty.

Cat mewed and rolled over to play, a splash of vivid colours in the patch of sunshine, paws frantically kicking the air. Alice grinned and glanced at her sketch-pad, which showed the lively outline of a sleeping cat, firm, economical pencil strokes for the body and paws, markings and facial details half filled in with brown ink.

Not a bad one, that, she thought, especially as it took no less than a miracle to get Cat to keep still for even a minute. But it wasn't real work; it had been six months since she had painted anything worthwhile, and it was time to begin in earnest again. Last year she had had quite a successful exhibition at Kettle's Yard which had resulted in a nice fat contract to illustrate a series of children's folk-tales, but since then, the ideas seemed to have run temporarily dry and it didn't look as if she was going to have very much to exhibit this year. Well, that was how things went, thought Alice; her pictures – the good ones, that was, took time and thought, and the ideas either came or they didn't. There was no point worrying about all that now; it would only slow things down even more. She glanced at the three official-looking envelopes tacked to her notice-board (even at a distance, she could read the flowery 'RED ROSE ROMANCES' logo across one of them), and sighed. That was where the money came from, she thought dryly. The women's magazines. The 'tru-life' dramas. They were the reason she wasn't still sharing a flat with two other students at the rough end of Mill Road and claiming Income Support. A sudden wave of fierce resentment washed over her at the thought, and she stood up abruptly to face the window. Was this what she was reduced to doing? Sentimental line-drawings for pulp romances? She deserved so much better than that. 'Celtic Tales' had been her first really exciting project since her 'Spirit of Adventure' exhibition at Kettle's Yard in 1989, and after that . . . She shrugged. Forget it, she told herself. There was no point sitting indoors feeling resentful.

She pulled on a navy sweat-shirt and tucked it into her jeans, then slipped on a pair of old, scuffed trainers. She tacked the half-finished sketch onto the notice-board, filled the cats' saucer with milk and water, picked an apple from the fruit dish and stepped out into the sunny street, locking the door behind her. The warmth and the combined scents of wallflowers and magnolia hit her with a sudden wave of well-being, and she took a deep breath of the pleasant air. It was warmer than she had expected; the house in Gwydir Street had no central heating and was always cool. In spring and summer it tended to be much warmer outside than in. She bit into her apple and began to walk down the street into the town.

She made her way, without hurrying, into the centre of Cambridge, and spent an hour or so looking at the shops and galleries. It occurred to her that it had been some time since she had walked to Cambridge; she seemed to avoid the crowds nowadays. Strange, thought Alice. Why, when she and Joe . . . But it might be better not to think about Joe. Better not to remember him too clearly, not to imagine him standing beside her, squinting into the shop-windows with his hands in his pockets.

Better not to remember him at all.

Suddenly, she felt depressed again. It was thinking about Joe, she decided, that was all. That and the heat and the Cambridge crowds with their cameras and their College scarves and their brittle camaraderie. What she needed was a little rest, maybe a cup of tea.

As it happened, she was standing at the corner of her favourite tea-shop (a rogue flash of self-critical insight told her that the fact might not have been purely coincidental, but she ignored it pointedly), and she pushed open the glass doors and went in, managed to find a window-seat, began to order Earl Grey, and ended up, unaccountably, ordering hot chocolate with cream and a large slice of chocolate fudge cake instead. Something in Alice responded well to chocolate.

The Copper Kettle was a good place because no one ever bothered you. Alice had been accustomed in her student days to spend hours there, usually in a window-seat if she could get one, drinking Earl Grey (the Philistines' way, with milk) or hot chocolate with cream, watching the endless flow of people go past the window in a pleasant, timeless daydream. Sitting in the same window watching the same street with the smell of chocolate and old leather in the smoky air,

Alice looked down King's Parade, the Senate House reflecting the sunlight from its clean white stones, King's warm golden façade and floating spires, and to her far left, the red brick walls of Catz glowing behind its tall railings. The light in Cambridge was different to anywhere else Alice had ever seen; cool light, even on a warm day, light which was oddly Northern, rarefied, shifting like a Dali landscape over the restless spires, the sleeping gardens. Such a beautiful town, thought Alice, a town for dreaming, for slumber. Even the students had a strange abstraction, despite their animated talk, their colour, their parties, their love affairs; as if in spite of all their activity they knew themselves to be nothing but the dreams of those wise half-wakened old stones. Ever-young and ever-beautiful, every year the students came, pitiable yet invincible in the transience of their youth and beauty.

Watching them, Alice felt so old. She remembered herself, slimmer and with long untamed hair, wearing cut-off jeans and baggy pullovers, Indian skirts and beads. Riding her bicycle in the rain and laughing. Painting in winter with gloves to protect her hands. Sneaking over the gate at night to be with Joe. She tried to remember. Had they felt it then, that sense of destiny? The brevity of their time rushing past? That terrible awareness of death?

Remembering those days, Alice closed her eyes, still not quite easy, and tried to think of nothing.

Suddenly, in the muted hubbub of the crowded tea-shop, she recognized a voice and her eyes snapped open in surprise, something tightening like a wire inside her heart, in spite of herself. She knew that voice well, with its pronounced Northern accent, and remembered sitting there in the Copper Kettle listening to Joe talking to her about his many enthusiasms; Jaco Pastorius and Roy Harper, and how Marxism was going to change the world . . .

She looked round, wondering whether she had

18

imagined it. She had not seen him for a long time, had not wanted to see him, though he had been so anxious, almost touchingly eager to remain friends. Ridiculous that she should still feel that sorry little jump of the heart; ridiculous that she should still look round, furtively, as if it were him. And even if it were, what of it? He would most probably be here with some girl.

She had almost persuaded herself that she had been wrong, that it had not been his voice at all, when she caught sight of him. He was sitting at a round table in a darker corner of the room, his familiar face bent at a familiar angle which denoted attentiveness, a cigarette cupped in one hand, shoulders bent, black hair falling messily over a narrow face, round wire glasses never quite managing to hide the piercing, intent gaze behind them. So he had started smoking again, Alice thought inconsequentially, remembering the smell of his cigarettes, how it used to get everywhere, in his clothes, his hair . . . The memory shifted uneasily.

She hazarded another glance, felt her heart sink. No, of course he was not alone. There was a girl with him and, though much of her face was in shadow, Alice could guess at a slim, small, graceful frame, the emphasized curve of a perfect collar-bone beneath the outsize square-cut neck of a thick creamy pullover, a halo of bright-red hair. Well, she thought with unwonted savagery, what did she expect? So he had found someone else. So what? So nothing. It was what she had wanted, after all.

She caught the sound of his voice again as she pushed back her chair to go, and the wire in her heart twisted again.

She could not distinguish actual words, but the tone was enough. Smoke from the carelessly held cigarette obscured his face, giving his features a disturbing transparency, but in the semi-darkness she could guess his smile.

A memory, long-stored in Alice's mind, flipped over

19

like a dead leaf in the wind. Suddenly the little tea-shop was hardly crowded enough and averting her head so as not to catch his eye, Alice fled into the sunlight, tight-lipped and hating herself for caring, but caring anyway. Impelled by an anger she dared not admit even to herself she quickened her pace, making her way further out of the town, and three-quarters of an hour later she found that without meaning to she had come as far as Grantchester, five miles out of Cambridge. Her face was flushed, her eyes bright, but Joe was almost forgotten again.

There was a church in front of her – St Mary's. A little round tower rising up from the cool green trees. She took a breath; the scent of wallflowers filled her – wallflowers and greenery allowed to run riot. She looked around. It was not a place she had been to before, despite many visits to Grantchester in her student days, but there was an atmosphere there, not unpleasant, but of quiescence, timelessness ... moments frozen in time, like the Sleeping Beauty's enchanted garden. The grass in front of the church was neatly cut, the graves and monuments well kept and orderly. Around the church and its grounds, ivy-covered in places, stood a curving, solid-looking old wall. A little path twisted here and there between headstones and monuments, touching this one and that one, gently, like a friend. Alice followed the path a little way, reading the gravestones. Some of them were even older than she expected: under a tree she found one dated 1690, though most of the others seemed more recent. On reaching the other side of the church, Alice found the path leading her into the second churchyard, even more enclosed than the first, shaded by cedars and apple trees. A red squirrel skittered across the path and over the wall. Alice followed it. At the end of the path there was an arch, with a door set into the arch, half open, looking onto a third graveyard; the more modern one this, sheltered from the road by the same wall which ran around the whole church grounds, this third churchyard still half empty.

It sometimes happens that some destiny leads people, in moments of great importance, to where they need to be; at other times, events touch each other like threads in a woven fabric, one picture overlapping another, the rough binding at the back of the tapestry joined together so that heroine bleeds onto villain, sea and sky merge in uneasy union, clean edges break up and become strange and disquieting boundaries to the other side. Whichever way she tried to look at it afterwards, Alice was sure that it was at that moment that it happened, that from the moment she set eyes on that door, all her movements were accountable, all her thoughts a completion of something much greater, much older. The Tailor of Gloucester in Beatrix Potter's little book had lost everything for the sake of one strand of cherry-coloured silk; for want of a thread a whole coat, embroidered and quilted and fit for a king, could not be finished. And looking back at events later, when the pattern of things began at last to emerge, Alice always imagined, in her mind's eye, the long strand of silk leading to that little wooden door, leading her onto the other side of the picture, where no rules applied, and where the Sleeping Beauty was preparing to awaken.

But of course, no such thoughts clouded her mind just then; they came later, with Ginny and Joe; only a sense of peace and a quiet pleasure in the still warm air as she pushed the door and went into the hidden churchyard. The graves there were beautifully tended, planted with shrubs and herbs and flowering trees. A couple of the headstones were crooked, half hidden in the long grass at the back of the plot, but there was no sense of desolation about the place, only an air of dignity, as of tired old people sitting down in the grass, mindful of the brittleness of their old bones. A couple of the graves were marked with flowers, lovingly planted, perhaps by some relative; yes, it was a good place. Two trees stood at the very back of the garden, a hawthorn in bloom, and a dark yew in stark contrast, shadowing a grave half hidden by rampant vegetation. She wondered whose grave that was, almost overgrown with long, ripe weeds, so beautifully and almost consciously framed by the two trees. She went to look.

There was no headstone, she saw, and there did not seem to be any name, but from its frail elegance she fancied that it was a woman's grave. A simple, almost modernist sculpture topped the slab, though at first glance there was no date. A gate, half open, allowed to swing loosely on its hinges, with an inscription on the outside:

Something inside me remembers and will not forget.

Just that. The words were compelling, charged with meaning and certainty. '*Something inside me remembers . . .*' There was something oddly arrogant about that phrase, something almost threatening. The remainder of the inscription was hidden. Experimentally, Alice pulled at the clinging ivy, trying to dislodge it. The roots were long, but dry, and they came free easily enough, leaving pale scars in the decaying stone, but the inscription began to appear, at the foot of the slab. It was faint – the stone was greenish and friable, but she could decipher it. It was more modern than the state of the grave might have suggested, and read:

Rosemary Virginia Ashley
? – August 1948

Alice searched for some other detail; whether Rosemary had been married, what she died of, who the passionate lover or husband had been who promised never to forget her, but there was nothing more. Tantalized, and yet somehow half satisfied, as if too many details might have spoiled the effect, Alice began to cover up the inscription, replacing the ivy where she had found it; it would be cruel, she felt, to leave Rosemary's grave so open, like a wound, for everyone to see.

Her mind was wandering as she replaced the trailing ivy, and, for a moment, she did not even notice the thin, shiny piece of metal which brushed her fingers from beneath the leaves. At first, she thought it was the ring-pull from a Coke can; it was light, and had the same uneven sharpness at the edges, but as she picked it up to look at it, she saw that it was longer, and older. There was a hole in one end, as if it had once been attached to something, and there was moss clinging to one surface, but even then, Alice could read the inscription:

> Rosemary
> For Remembrance

Alice felt her heart beat faster. Surely this could be no coincidence! This tag had been hers, Rosemary's, placed on her grave when she was buried. Maybe tied onto some wreath or plant left there. Somehow, just finding that little piece of metal made everything all the more real, all the more sad. It was the only thing left. The find was as poignant as finding a lock of the dead girl's hair. Alice replaced the last piece of ivy, straightened the crushed hemlock-stems by the graveside . . . hesitated. She wondered for a moment whether to throw the tag back onto the gravestone, then she shrugged and hid it in her pocket, without thinking what she was doing, without considering the impli-cations; just as the cat had hidden the final twist of cherry-coloured silk from the Tailor of Gloucester.

As soon as she got home, Alice made a cup of tea, took it to her workroom (a table, a stool, an easel, a window facing North, a record player and a messy stack of albums), dragged a thick watercolour pad out of an overflowing cupboard and began to draw. The idea had come to her full-blown, had followed her home from Grantchester, had refused to let her be, and now it was growing, line by line, light and precise on the paper, gaining a depth as the lines grew thicker, gaining shadow, sunlight, greenery.

A girl's figure, thin-shouldered, but with a pure half-profile half hidden in a tumbling mass of hair, barefoot and dressed in a straight, severe shift like a hospital robe. She was sitting on the ground, hugging her knees, her head tilted away from the viewer at an odd, childish angle. Around her, long grass, flowers and lush weeds; in the background, two half-defined trees and a sketched-in figure, possibly male, stooping slightly under the tree branches. Alice stepped back a pace to look at the finished sketch and smiled, liking it. It was deliberately Pre-Raphaelite in composition; the ordered disorder of the undergrowth contrasting with the quiescence of the girl, shrouded in her mystery, watching the river with that curious childlike intentness, while the ill-defined figure in the background watched or waited.

She took a gulp of cold tea and began to think about colour. Then she put a record by Tangerine Dream onto the turntable and quickly, deftly, began to ink in the colours. Green, grey, a splash of reflection in the water . . . the girl's dress white, undefined – she could airbrush that in later – the hair red and cloudy, one bright spray of colour in a composition which was dreamy, unreal, pure as an Annunciation. Yes, she thought with satisfaction; it was good. As good as anything she had ever done before; but then again, she often thought that in the heat of the moment, and it might not turn out to be anything out of the ordinary at all.

The light dimmed; Alice turned on the spotlights and carried on working. Side one of the record played twice before she noticed and turned it over, the other side three times. Once or twice she heard a mewing at her door, indicating that the cats felt that they should be fed; once she heard the telephone and ignored it. Acrylics replaced inks, she carefully painted on and peeled off masking gum while airbrushing the triangle of sky, the water, the girl's dress, replaced her thin acrylic brush for an even thinner one, adding detail to the leaves, the grass, the texture of the girl's hair; then she stepped back, dropped her brushes, and gave a wide, admiring grin.

'Wow!' said Alice.

There was no doubt about it; it was good. Better than good, it was perfect. It was just simple enough to reproduce beautifully as a poster or the cover of a book, classic enough to hang in an airy gallery, peaceful enough to grace a church altar. Never had inks and acrylic produced such pure colours for her before; never had Alice managed a composition which had had quite the same intensity. You *had* to look at it; even Alice found herself speculating about who the girl was, what she was doing, thinking who the figure in the background was.

She looked at the picture for a long time before she took the brush again and signed it. Then, after a moment's hesitation, in her delicate, precise calligraphy, she wrote the name of the picture underneath her own;

Remembrance: The Madness of Ophelia

By now she was exhausted; looking at her watch, she realized with something of a shock that it was almost ten o'clock, and that she had worked through half the afternoon and most of the evening, but it was a good exhaustion, as if working had cleansed her of all her worries and negative thoughts. Already, her mind was racing. Maybe, after such a long time without painting anything worthwhile, she had hit a new lode of creation within herself; maybe there would be more Ophelia paintings, maybe a whole series of them which would be exhibited at Kettle's Yard that summer. The ideas spun like carnival wheels in her mind, and she went happily to the kitchen, ravenously hungry all of a sudden, slammed two frozen pizzas under the grill, fed the cats, made some tea and closed her eyes to enjoy the rest of the evening alone.

One

Cambridge, *December 1947*
Fulbourn Hospital, *October 1977*

After the funeral, I never thought to come back to Grantchester churchyard; as if, by my presence, I might fill that quiet place with unquiet ghosts and murmurings. If she rested easy, then so much the better but, thought I, I was not going to be the one to watch over her rest. In the nervous and despondent state in which her passing had left me, I saw her often; at least, I thought I did. A girl in black, profile slightly averted, stepping into a cab, a girl in the rain, face hidden beneath a dark umbrella, once, a girl walking by the river, red hair fiery-bright beneath a pale scarf. No, I was not haunted, but she mocked me, touching every part of my life with her delicate, spidery hand, walking with me wherever I went.

Or so I thought. I think I fell ill at that time; the doctor told me that overwork and overworry had led to a poverty of the blood, prescribed a rich diet with plenty of red wine, advised me to stop working for a week or two. I made my own secret diagnosis, took the doctor's advice concerning the wine a little too literally, contracted pneumonia and nearly died.

When I resumed interest in life a couple of months later (my landlady had nursed me lovingly throughout my illness in a sweet half-life free from troubles or disturbing realities), it was already too late; Robert had

27

been dead for more than two weeks, buried in the same churchyard as Rosemary while I slept and tossed and whined, thinking of myself as usual, when he needed me most. Not that the act really surprised me, when I came to think about it; the moment I saw her watching him the day of the funeral, I should have guessed that that was what she had in mind. Her smile was possessive, protective, indulgent, horribly knowing. In the same way does the Blessed Damozel in Rossetti's painting look down upon her tormented, stricken lover; patiently, silently, with the hint of a smile. I could never look at that picture afterwards without a shudder, for though I could never see any physical resemblance to Rosemary in it, there was something – something in the smile, perhaps, or maybe simply the witchlike outsizedness of the blessed lady in comparison to her doomed lover that reminded me too sharply of her. I wrote a book, fifteen years later, a rewriting of my dissertation paper on the Pre-Raphaelites, in which I examined Rossetti's fascination for beautiful witchlike women: I dedicated it on paper to my College art lecturer, but I knew that I wrote it for Rosemary, to Rosemary, about Rosemary. I called it 'The Blessed Damozel'. I believe it still sells.

It took me five days of wretched guilt and self-loathing before I went to Robert's graveside. By that time the wreaths and ribbons had been removed and all that was left was the little mound of earth and some shrubs in a stone trough at the foot of the grave. Small green plants, no flowers. There was a label on the thin stem of one of the shrubs, one of those metal tags you see on the stems of prize rose-bushes at garden shows, and I flipped it over to read it.

Rosemary
For Remembrance

I think I kept my calm well enough then, despite the

28

first onrush of panic which threatened to overwhelm me. I had seen too much to be terrified by a cheap practical joke. I already knew she was there. It would take more than that to hurt me; in fact, I foolishly thought that with Robert gone, I had nothing else to fear. For myself, I thought, I could live even with her incessant, cruelly delicate haunting. She was gone, I said to myself, gone, buried, forgotten. I laid my little bunch of mistletoe and holly at the head of the grave and turned to go.

Poor Robert.

Suddenly, I felt her there, her presence filling the calm of the bright, frosty churchyard. And her hate. And with her hate, amusement. The scent of rosemary wafted up from the little row of shrubs in front of me, warmed by the slanting rays of the winter sun, sweet, earthy and pungently nostalgic, the scent of country kitchens, drawers filled with clean white linen, country girls combing rosemary vinegar through their long hair. I was absolutely convinced that if I were to look up I would see her there, the faery's child, head tilted slightly to one side, watching me from beneath her heavy, hooded eyelids, face pale and tragic mouth curling in something not quite like a smile . . . I was so convinced that she was there that for a moment I actually saw her standing there in the shade of the hawthorn-tree, then she was only a jumble of light and shade on the bare path, where a patch of brown and frozen weeds nodded almost imperceptibly over a gravestone I had never noticed before.

For a moment I stared stupidly. It was a simple enough idea, a flat stone set into the mossy ground with a small cast-iron sculpture rising above it, maybe two feet high. A frame, like a door-frame, with a kind of crest on the top, within which stood what looked to me like a little door or gate, set against the frame with hinges. As I looked, a gust of wind pushed against the little gate and it blew open with a tiny sound, then clicked shut as the wind released it. At the head of the grave was a shallow stone trough, in which a few small green shrubs nodded and whispered.

Of course. This must be her grave; this the remembrance Robert had spoken of. His idea. I don't know why I went to look at it then; I should have known that it would do no good to my peace of mind to probe the wound further, but it may be that I wanted to know what had been in my friend's mind before his suicide, as if my penance before Rosemary's grave might help his poor tortured soul to rest. Maybe I felt guilt. Because I killed her, you know, or at least, I did the best I could, but I don't think so. I went for the same reason the young girl looks into Bluebeard's chamber, for the same reason the two children go to the gingerbread house, that the young fisherman lets the genie out of the bottle . . . You know. You all know. God save you all from proving it.

I read the inscription, of course. After all, that was what it was there for. And I don't regret it, really I don't. All it did was to bring things out into the open. It told me nothing I didn't already know.

Rosemary Virginia Ashley
? – 1948
Something inside me remembers and will not forget

Something inside me remembers . . . I don't think I could ever forget those words, even if I had read them only once, and I came there often after that, not able to help myself, fascinated and repelled and terrified all at once. Something inside me remembers . . . but only I could really understand that message. Everyone else took it as a message from Robert, another proof of his undying love for his wife, his lovely wife.

Ha! I knew better than that. Robert was not maudlin. He was weak perhaps, but not maudlin. He may have died a little when Rosemary was buried, but he would not have laid his broken heart open like that for lovers to gawp at as they took their romantic walks in Grantchester churchyard. He was a practical man, and practical men are the ones who suffer the most from love, when it comes their way. And whatever the evidence, I know he didn't commit suicide. That was a message for me from her. A defiant cry from beyond the grave. She isn't dead, and she wants me to know it. She's waiting, that's all, waiting her chance. She has all the time in the world. And she still remembers.

But I'm not afraid. I'm safe. I still have my final trick to play, the last card which will keep me safe. And do you know what my last card is? It's you, friend. You don't believe me? You will. As you read this diary you'll hate me, despise me, but you won't disbelieve me. It's all right, you don't have to do it all at once; put the book away in a drawer, forget it for a while, for years if you like, but you'll come back; I know you will. You'll come back sooner or later, because she's here; she's waiting. For me, for you. So be careful.

When the time comes, much may depend upon which way I turn you.

Two

Cambridge, *April 1990*

Alice was restless. She ate her late meal, nibbled her way through most of a packet of biscuits and turned the television on. A black-and-white film, a chat-show, a Russian cartoon . . . she turned it off.

She made some tea, sat down, let the tea go cold, poured it down the sink, put on a jazz record, played it twice without hearing it, took it off.

Then she reached for the letter from her contact at Red Rose Romances and tried to awaken some interest in the job they had offered her. It was a fairly easy assignment, as they went; twenty line-drawings for a teen romance called *Tomboy Tanya*. A selection of quotations had been chosen for Alice to illustrate, and she flicked through them half-heartedly, filled the waste-basket with half-finished sketches, made some more tea, drank it this time, filled the cats' bowls with a mixture of bread and tinned cat-food, washed some dishes, and finally admitted to herself that it was seeing that girl, that was all, seeing that girl with Joe, hearing his voice so unexpectedly, that had rattled her.

Not that it meant anything, no. That was all over now. She did what she wanted, led the life she wanted, couldn't have the best of both worlds, independence and someone to cling to. Didn't want anyone to cling to. She had tried that and it didn't work. End of topic.

But the topic refused to be ousted. The memory buzzed infuriatingly around in her head (*something inside me remembers*) as she busied herself around her front room, tidying the pleasantly messy jumble of cushions, plants and rugs which filled it (*something inside me . . .*), picking up a week's-worth of empty tea- and coffee-mugs and piling them in the sink. That was one of the advantages of living alone, she thought as she (*. . . remembers*) dried mugs and hung them on the mug-tree. No one to tell you what to do, when to tidy up, no one to ask where she was going, where she'd been. She was free. She did as she pleased.

And yet tonight, it felt lonely. Just for tonight, it might be good to hear the phone ring. A fleeting query from her subconscious (*something inside me remembers . . .*); but who *would* remember her if she disappeared tomorrow? Her mother, keeping the faith for her vanished ones two hundred miles away? Her contact at Red Rose Romances? The only friends she had had were also Joe's friends; she had lost them when she lost Joe. And while times had been good, she had not felt the need for anyone outside him. Damn. A sudden rage at herself overpowered Alice. Why couldn't she let it go? (*Something inside me . . .*) Part of it was seeing that gravestone, she decided; the inexplicable sense of *envy* for the dead girl whose lover would not forget.

She considered ringing up her mother in Leeds, the only person outside her work from whom she ever received phone calls, then she shrugged and sat down again. No. Mother was far too shrewd in her bluff Northern way to fail to detect her depression. It would be nice to hear her voice, but ringing her would simply open the doorway to all the usual reproaches and criticisms and enquiries: 'When are you going to come and visit us again?' 'Have you got a steady job yet?' (as if what Alice was doing for a living were some kind of a hobby in preparation for 'real work'). 'Are you sure you're looking after yourself down there?'

Poor Mother, thought Alice, Mother who had grown harder and sharper with the years after the cancer finally got Dad, Mother whose sweetness had become buried under all the extra flesh she had put on since she turned fifty, and who always spoke in the same careful code, never quite saying what she meant, perhaps never quite finding the words.

She had been bright once: black-and-white photographs showed a dark, narrow-waisted girl with a lovely smile, arm-in-arm with the handsome young man Dad had been before he lost his hair so early. She had been romantic enough to call her little girl Alice after Alice in Wonderland. 'Because,' she said, 'you had just the same kind of wide astonished eyes.' But now she was a disappointed fat woman, coarsened and faded not by grief but by the constant erosion of joyless days passing; and the worst of it was that, some day, Alice was terribly afraid that she might look into the mirror and see her mother's face staring out at her.

Alice sighed and looked at the clock. Half past twelve. She supposed she ought to go to bed soon, but didn't feel tired. She reached across to the bookshelf, chose a paperback at random, hoping to put herself to sleep by reading a few pages. There might be some leftover chocolate ice-cream in the ice-box, she thought; she couldn't remember. She went to the fridge to check, thinking vaguely that she was eating too much nowadays and that she ought to try and cut down. She suppressed the image of her mother, sitting in the lounge in their old house soon after Dad died, eating packets of crisps with a blank-eyed, ferocious energy.

Bottles clinked inside the fridge door, and the four cats materialized, seemingly from nowhere, to investigate the promise of milk. Alice felt the warm, wriggling bodies around her legs and felt herself relax a little.

Rogue memories of Joe. Joe in the upstairs bedroom practising endless riffs on his guitar, frightening the cats. Joe frowning over a pile of manuscript paper and an overflowing ashtray. Joe at the head of a peace demonstration carrying a big banner with 'Bum the Bomb'. Joe arguing with a policeman, Alice tugging at his arm. Joe rolling a joint one-handed, Joe frowning over one of Alice's paintings, saying: 'The lines are too weak. It doesn't stand out at a distance.'

Alice: 'It's perfectly all right, you Philistine. It's supposed to look ethereal, like a Rackham.'

Alice sneaking back to her studio later that night to change the picture and sharpen the lines.

Joe playing in his first band at a May Ball, blind drunk, but never a wrong note.

The binges; making love on an unmade bed with dozens of wine bottles and chocolate wrappers and pizza-boxes piled up on the floor. The quarrels, screaming at each other in Joe's music-room as Alice found success and Joe didn't. His jealousy, his sudden flashes of bitterness at everything, the band which never managed to get a contract, never having enough money, never having been given a chance. As they grew older, watching the students come and go, knowing that the whole world belonged to *them* and finally having to accept that he was ten years older and that a new generation had sprung up beneath him. Youngsters who were strong and beautiful and who knew where they were going. The new materialists, who wore the right clothes. Who went to see the right bands. And with that realization came a kind of helplessness and a kind of anger, against the kids, the Government, all the bloodsuckers who were killing him by degrees. He used to sing a song by Leonard Cohen called 'Chelsea Hotel', and when he got to the line, 'Clenching your fists for the ones like us who are oppressed by the figures of beauty', he would grit his teeth and glare into the audience as if he hated them all. Some days he did.

Friends, friends, thought Alice. If only he had

known how to be friends. If only he hadn't been so afraid. But it wasn't that easy. Intimacy had brought possessiveness, and Joe was not the only one to feel oppression in all its forms. Alice rebelled. An ultimatum was set; her freedom or Joe. She frowned, remembering. She should never have had to choose.

Still, the choice was made now. The regrets were few. She checked the ice-box. The chocolate ice-cream was there after all, and that helped a lot.

Then the phone rang.

Alice started, moved to get up then sat down again. Suddenly, she didn't want to know who it was. The phone kept ringing, chirping, its sweet electronic voice trilling tirelessly into the still air. Cat jumped onto the table and nosed the receiver curiously. Alice waited another minute, then she gave in. It takes a lot of self-control not to answer a persistently ringing phone, she thought bitterly as she put down her plate and loped across the room; probably a wrong number, but she still had to know.

It was Joe.

'Hello? Alice?' his voice was distant and a bit breathless, so that she had difficulty placing it. 'It's me. Joe.' The memory of his voice locked into place with a jolt, like changing gears on an old bicycle.

'Oh, hello!' said Alice, trying to sound non-committal, angry at her failure.

'How are you?' she continued, more in control now; seeing him, then thinking about him, and now hearing his voice on the phone for the first time in over three years gave her a strange sensation, something like dizziness, as if a long-stopped wheel had suddenly begun to turn.

'I'm fine.' His voice was slightly unsteady, as it sometimes was when he was particularly excited or angry; Alice, straining over the poor line, could not tell which.

'Still playing the blues?' she asked, stalling for time and automatically slipping into the old pattern of their conversations, that light, brittle humour which masked so much intensity.

'That's me, the mean guitar machine, man.'

A pause.

'What about you, Al? I saw your book. It was pretty good. Kids' stuff, but still . . . I always knew you'd make it, you know. And I saw your exhibition. You'll be at the RA next time I look.' He gave a little laugh which tugged at her heart. 'I see you still have that trouble with outlines, though.'

'Flattery still gets you anywhere, Joe.'

He laughed again, a little ruefully. 'Me, I've got a new band, "Fiddle the Dole". We've been going for near to a year, now. Electric folk, covers and original songs. We play the Wheatsheaf every Saturday. You should come to listen to us some day. We're good.' A pause. 'Remember the Wheatsheaf? It's as near to "back-to-the-roots" as you can get in a place like Cambridge – sawdust on the floor, broken bottles on the stage. Really classy. It takes me right back, I tell you, to the times when I was on the road with the first band. Bacon sandwiches at the Greasy Spoon, the van breaking down on the M1 with all the gear in the back on the way to a gig – the day the lead guitarist died just before we were due to come on stage and we stuffed him with kapok and took him on anyway – his ex-girlfriend said afterwards that he'd never played so well . . .' Joe paused again, took a deep breath.

'Hey, I'm sorry, Al. Mouth gets the better of me sometimes, you know. How're you doing?'

'Fine, Joe. Yes, I'm—'

'Jess told me about your bit of trouble . . . Are you OK now? I was—'

'You talked to my mother?' Sharpness creeping into her voice. 'When?'

'Hey, relax. I met her by accident. We were playing

38

the University in Leeds. She said you'd been ill. She was just trying to find out how you were.'

'Well, I wasn't ill.' Alice tried not to sound snappish. 'Mother doesn't know what she's talking about.' Trying to lighten her tone. 'Like *Rolling Stone*, I just went out of circulation for a while.'

'Well, I'm back here to stay now,' went on Joe. 'I've got a flat on Maid's Causeway, I told the landlady I was a grad. student and she believed me. She's deaf as a post, and lets the band practise in her cellar. She says she likes Irish music because she's a lapsed Catholic. Just as long as she doesn't listen to any of the lyrics. You know, Al, we've decided we don't want to be famous; we don't want to be part of the star system. I've turned down contracts from Virgin, EMI, Polydor . . . Just yesterday I had Richard Branson on the phone again – you know, I'm going to have to go ex-directory, because he won't take no for an answer. I told him, "Man, I'm not going to prostitute my art for money . . . I'm staying honest but poor." And you know what? He didn't believe me.'

Alice smiled in spite of herself. 'That bad, eh?' she asked.

He made a non-committal sound. 'Could be better,' he admitted. 'What's the point of staying artistically pure if no one wants to contaminate you in the first place? Still, we manage all right on Income Support, and once we start playing the College circuit, you never know, we might begin to get a hard little core of discerning followers. The kind that throw full cans at you instead of empty ones.'

No, he hadn't changed, thought Alice. There was still that self-mockery, that subtle resentment which had characterized him years ago. Already, she felt half stifled by it.

'Joe . . .' she began, searching for the right words. 'Have you phoned me up to canvass for your next gig, or is there another reason? It has been a very long time.

And it's . . .' (she looked at her watch) '. . . nearly a quarter to one. Why now?'

When he did not answer, she continued; 'It isn't that I'm not happy to hear how you're doing, but . . .'

'Does there have to be a reason?' His voice was tense, almost aggressive. 'You always did try to find hidden meanings in everything. Why don't you loosen up a bit? I felt like calling up, that's all. Maybe we could meet, go for a walk, have a pizza, or something. God forbid, you might even want to see me play.'

The sneer, if it had been there at all, was gone from his voice, and the idea suddenly seemed very attractive to Alice. A pause, during which she looked out of the window at the magnolia nodding in the orange street-light and tried to stem the memories. Then Joe continued, in a strange, light voice; 'Any romances in the offing, Al? You've not gone and married the boy next door while I've been away?'

'*You* were the boy next door,' said Alice flippantly. 'What about you? Have you found the L-word yet? Rich sugar-mummy to take you in hand? Does she play the cello? You always fantasized about a girl who could play the cello.'

'No, she doesn't play the cello,' said Joe, with a low laugh, 'and she isn't a rich sugar-mummy. But . . .' Underneath the light tone Alice thought she could hear anxiety mingled with exhilaration. 'I met her at a gig, Al. Quite by accident. You'd never have expected her to come to a gig in a dive like the Sluice . . . you know the place, don't you? They drink the beer, then they eat the glass. Anyway, there was this girl there, sitting right at the front, all by herself, and watching me all the time. Did you ever hear of anyone going to see a gig and watching the bass player all the time? The lead singer, yes. That's Martin, the pretty one with the long blond hair and that kind of fetching undernourished look. But me? She just never took her eyes off me, all through the gig. I went to the bar to get a beer

40

and, God help me, she watched me all the way there as well. It made me feel weird, I can tell you. As if she could see right through me. So I kept looking away, right? Thinking, pretty soon she'll get bored and move off. But she never did. And so I took another look at her, and I went in for a closer look after the set. And she was waiting, as if it was . . . yeh, well . . . the rest, as they say, is history.'

'Oh?' said Alice, trying to take in what she had heard. She was beginning to feel she understood. This phone call, after all this time . . . A complex feeling overwhelmed her; something like regret, but a little like relief.

'I'm glad,' she said simply, realizing that she meant it.

'So am I, Alice,' he said. 'I reckon I was a bit nervous about telling you. I was . . .'

'You don't have to be. I'm glad, Joe. Friends, remember?' His answering laugh was unsteady, a little incoherent, and she could tell that he was moved.

'God, I'm relieved!' he admitted.

'So am I. At last I don't have to spend my life looking over my shoulder expecting to see you in pursuit.'

Good laughter together. Alice held the moment to her, that warmth, knowing that in some way for Joe it was an exorcism of her, of their wild and bad years, of what he still thought of as her rejection of him. She felt a sudden rush of unpossessive, uncomplicated love for him, sad Joe hiding his isolation behind a wall of facetiousness, Joe who only needed to be needed and wanted and clung to before he could blossom. She hoped that this girl would be the right one for him now, hoped that she would like electric folk music, would want babies and marriage and all the things which Joe had wanted, and Alice had given up in the name of her freedom.

Something cold and hard and lonely inside her melted and disappeared, and the relief she felt was like a blessing.

'So,' said Alice (and was the fierce twist of the heart she felt pride or regret?). 'Tell me about her. What's she like?'

'She's different, Alice. She's different from any other girl I've ever met. She likes Virginia Woolf and Egyptian art and chamber music . . . would you believe that I could fall for a girl who likes chamber music? She sings . . . really beautifully. A kind of cross between Karen Carpenter and Maddy Prior. I'm trying to find a place for her in the band . . . or so I told Martin . . . He nearly jumped out of his fake leopard-skin pants with shock. She looks a bit like a cross between Suzanne Vega and Kate Bush, and . . . I suppose I'd better translate that into aesthetic terms you can relate to. You're so square you probably don't get all this technical jargon . . .'

'Watch it,' warned Alice.

'She has a kind of Rossetti-ish hair, and a Burne-Jones-ish face . . . and . . .'

'She sounds like a woman of many aspects. I suppose she has a Morris beard as well?' said Alice with a sour grin.

'Ahh . . . the artist speaks. Why don't you find out for yourself? You'll have to meet her; that's mostly why I phoned in the first place.'

The reality of it was like a shower of cold water. Alice hesitated in mid-answer, off-balance. She shook herself mentally. What was wrong? (*Something inside me . . . remembers.*) Wasn't she ready?

'Sure, some day.' Neutrally.

'You mean "some day" spelt N-E-V-E-R,' said Joe.

'Listen . . . I—'

'I want you two to meet up and get to know each other. She hasn't got any friends, and neither have you. You'd be good for each other. You have a lot in common.' A pause, even his silence laden with mischief. 'Apart from me, of course.'

He hadn't changed at all, thought Alice. He was still

42

the same impulsive Joe, so certain that all obstacles, even those of the heart, were easy to overcome. The sudden depression behind the thought was engulfed in a salt wave of nostalgia which somehow found its way behind her eyes, running down her cheeks along channels of its own. For a moment, Alice was choked by regret more poignant than she could bear, then, with an effort, she shrugged it off, almost in control again.

'I'd love to meet her,' she said, fiercely suppressing the ache beneath her breastbone. 'I think it's a fine idea. And I'd love to see you again, too. I've lost touch with too many old friends to let this one pass me by.' She wiped the stupid tears from her face with an angry gesture, trying hard to keep her tone light and even. 'How about meeting you both in town sometime tomorrow? Or maybe I could come and hear your band next time you play. Does . . .' she broke off in mid-question. 'You mutt, you never even told me her name.'

Joe laughed.

'Didn't I? Hey, you can't expect me to think of everything. It's Virginia, Virginia Mae Ashley, but she likes to be called Ginny. She says Virginia Mae's too much of a mouthful for someone like her. Do you still like pizza? We could go for a pizza somewhere if you like. The band doesn't play again till Tuesday, but we could go out, see a film, if there's something on. How does that sound?'

'That sounds fine.'

'What about you? You sound a bit down. You OK?'

'Of course I am. I'm just a bit tired. It's late, you know.'

'Yes . . . ah . . . I'll get off in a minute. Let you get some sleep. There's just one more thing, but the fact of it is that . . . I'm in a bit of a quandary here, and normally, you know I wouldn't ask you, but . . . well . . . Ginny's new to Cambridge, and she doesn't have

43

very much money . . . I wondered if you'd mind putting her up?'

'Joe—'

'Tell me straightaway if you think I'm out of line,' he interrupted, 'but it would only be for a day or two, and if you've got room . . . I can't offer her a place in my digs because the landlady wouldn't allow it . . . We're looking for a flat or something, but you know how hard it is to get something decent in Cambridge at this time of year, when all the good places have been snapped up by the students or the tourists. It would only be for a little while, maybe just a few days, while we find somewhere else, and failing that, I've got a friend who lives in Grantchester who's going off to the States for a month at the end of this week, and he says we can use his house as a stopgap, so even if the worst comes to the worst it would only be till the end of the week.' He stopped. 'Alice? What do you think?'

Alice sighed inwardly. That was Joe all over, she thought, with some sour amusement. He had always been irresponsible, always demanding, prey to wild and reckless enthusiasms, which he expected Alice to share (or to finance) . . .

'I suppose it'll be all right,' she said wearily, as he had known she would. 'Where is she staying now?'

'Nowhere yet,' replied Joe. 'She's just come out of Fulbourn.'

'Fulbourn?'

'They've offered to put her up for a while, but I hate the idea of her having to stay in that rotten place any longer than she has to. Just looking round there's enough to give anyone terminal depression.'

'Oh, no. Are you serious?' You never really knew with Joe; years earlier, when they had been good friends, before intimacy had come to take their friendship away, Alice would have been able to say: 'Fulbourn? Well, she must be a nutcase if she sees anything in you,' but here, the link between them was still too distant, still too fraught with bad memories, to allow more than a momentary easing of the tension.

'You mean . . . Was she a patient?'

Joe tutted. 'Honestly, I knew how you'd react. There's nothing wrong with it, you know, one person in three has a breakdown at some time or other. Your mother told me that you were pretty close to it yourself, when you went through that bad patch of yours, so don't try to make it sound as if she—'

'Don't be silly. That wasn't what I meant. What I meant was . . .' Searching for the right words. 'How stable is she?'

Joe's answer sounded a little cold; Alice wondered whether she had overstepped the mark. After all, what claim on Joe's private life could she have now?

'I think that's a tad personal, don't you?' His voice softened, as if he too were conscious of the abruptness of his reply.

'It's not that I don't want to tell you about it, Al,' he said apologetically, 'but after all, it's Ginny's private life we're talking about here. I don't think I should have the right to tell people about her private life without asking her first, and I'm not sure how much she wants people to know about what happened to her. I only told you about Fulbourn so that you'd know to be careful of what you say and how you talk to her. She's still very vulnerable, you know.'

So am I, thought Alice, but let it pass.

'Al? You don't mind, do you? I mean . . .'

What the hell? thought Alice.

'I don't mind.'

'Good.' The relief in his voice was apparent. 'Besides, she's perfectly normal. You'd never think that her life had been touched by so much crap, that she'd seen so much. She's only eighteen, you know, she's got everything to live for. You'll love her, Al. Everyone loves her.'

He broke off for a moment, laughed quietly to

himself. 'I think this is it, Al. You know, the L-word. I really think so. It's funny, isn't it? I never used to think that I'd feel this way; I thought that there was only room in my life for the music, playing and grafting and getting bottled off stage and getting my demo tapes sent back and going without food so that I could buy guitar strings . . . you know, all in the hope that one day all the graft would pay off. And in a funny way, it has. If I hadn't played the Sluice, I wouldn't have met Ginny. God knows what she was doing in the Sluice in the first place. Thank God she was. And ever since then she's been bringing me luck. Everything's been looking up for me.'

Alice was silent for a long time. She hated the idea. More than hated it. Not because she loved Joe any more, she assured herself, but because it was all wrong. It wasn't like Joe to talk like this, to think like this . . . it wasn't Joe at all. Joe only cared for himself and his music and his ambitions; Joe was charming, likeable, amusing, but underneath, he was unscrupulously selfish. He didn't put himself out for anyone, didn't really consider what other people might be feeling . . . he was usually too much involved with his own enthusiasms. And he never mentioned what he called 'the L-word' – she had thought he never would.

But Joe was a friend . . . had been, anyway, and she had behaved badly, as she always did when a good friendship went the bad way into intimacy. Maybe this was her chance to make up for that, at least. And more than that, she was conscious of a desire to see him again, to talk to him, to remake their old, comfortable companionship. When he had laughed with her, laughed with the good laughter of old times recalled and recaptured, she had felt warmed, and had known that it was the friendship she missed coming back, and that she would do what she could to keep it, even if it meant putting up Joe's Virginia Ashley. She gave an unwilling laugh.

'Sounds good to me,' she said (and would he ever guess, she thought, the courage which went into those simple words?).

'I think I'll enjoy having her here. I never had many girlfriends, you know, and so I missed out in some important ways. There's plenty of room in my house for her. I can even put you up too, if you like. I'd be glad to have you both.'

As she spoke the words, they were almost true. The last of the old resentment melted, and Alice felt an easy warmth, an impulsive liking for this girl Ginny, whom she had never met. It was so good to feel the rift beginning to close at last, as if the sourness and emptiness had been there all this time, half felt but in disguise, touching everything with cold like the magic mirror in the story of the Snow Queen, making everything ugly and silent . . . Alice realized that Joe was talking.

'So we could meet here, if that's all right,' he was saying. 'We'll have tea or something, then we'll go and have a pizza, or see a film, or both. Does that sound good?'

'That's fine.'

Alice must have hesitated for an instant, because Joe picked up on it at once. Trust Joe.

'Hey, Alice? Is that "fine" spelt F-I-N-E or C-R-A-P? Speak to me, Alice.' His voice was a little concerned, despite the mockery, and Alice replied too quickly, in a bright voice, perhaps fearing that if she did not, that warmth might evaporate. She was conscious of the sharp edge of resentment again, cold and precise.

'I'll look forward to it, Joe. Keep playing those blues, hey?'

'Hang in there. I'll be round at about six. I tell you, things are going to be just great. You won't be disappointed.'

47

One

I don't suppose there was anything I could have done
to avert what she had planned; as I said, she was very
clever, and she knew my failings only too well; when I
hauled her, dripping, into the cab with my coat flung
protectively around her shoulders, myself only half
dressed, with my shoes and hat and tie still abandoned
by the edge of the Cam, she must have smiled to
herself, as such creatures may. She must have smiled
through the veils of her lavender eyes as I hastened to
revive her with my little flask of brandy, panting
around her like an eager dog, murmuring inane
rubbish into her attentive ears. There was nowhere to
take her except to Grantchester and my landlady's
house, nothing to do but to take her in (she was
shivering now and could walk shakily from the cab to
the door of the house), to explain as best I could and to
watch helplessly as she was whisked away upstairs by
a concerned and clucking Mrs Brown to an unknowa-
ble and half-defined realm of hot water and soft
pillows. Lucky that she was such a kind, easy-going
old soul; other, more suspicious landladies might have
treated my strange visitor with less consideration; but
Mrs Brown was by far the best woman in my long and
varied experience; she provided sympathy, attention,
and tea – her all-purpose cure-all, then left Rosemary

in the best bedroom, threatened me with the direst consequences if I were to disturb the young lady, and retired to her business, supremely unruffled, as if I brought drowned ladies to the house every day of the week. Bless her.

Left on her own in the best spare room, her bright hair washed and wearing one of Mrs Brown's starched linen nightdresses, I imagine Rosemary must have laughed. There's no way I could have known, of course; I was downstairs, and Mrs Brown would never have dreamed of letting me into the young lady's bedroom: but all the same, I think she laughed. I'm sure she did.

I spent the rest of that day in a kind of haze. I did not dare leave the house in case some new development arose; in case the girl disappeared or came downstairs to thank her knight-errant, and I was not there. Her face haunted me; the memory of her silent floating on the water filled me with terror and elation. I spent the long enchanted hours lying in my room, reliving those dreamlike instants again and again, my ears tuned to the slightest sound from that secret, silent room in which she slept, my heart bursting with a kind of music. Mrs Brown came and went with cheerful, concerned efficiency. A vase of early cherry-blossom found its way into the sleeping girl's room, then a number of patchwork cushions; then, at about half past four, a tray of tea and biscuits. At five Mrs Brown announced that the young lady might like to get up and have some hot soup; and at six I found myself sitting at the dinner-table, shaking with a kind of sick anticipation, staring at the extra place set by my landlady, my head feverish and my hands clenched out of sight in my lap.

I was love-lorn, I suppose; what young man would not have been? She had stepped out of a fairy-tale for me, a white Ophelia borne from nowhere on a muddy wave and a whisper of morning. The threat of scandal, the riot of speculation which might have arisen later from the society of which I was a part did not even enter my mind; for me, Rosemary might have been new-born there and then, like Venus from the wave. And it was with these thoughts in mind that I waited feverishly for my first glimpse of her, half afraid to look, as if I might see some hitherto unsuspected flaw in her perfection, some humdrum taint of reason behind her magnificent, absurd appearance in my life. I need not have worried. A quick mothlike sound on the stairs, a clip of high heels, and suddenly, she was there, her features, blurred by the movement of light and shade in the passageway, coming into abrupt relief as she stopped in front of the window. Her hair was a nimbus of flame in the sunlight, her figure trim and slight in a straight, woollen dress supplied by Mrs Brown. Her face was pale, her hands clasped childishly in front of her, her eyes lost and haunted, but even then, I think that she was the most beautiful woman I have ever seen. Even then. Even now.

She looked at me silently for a while, then turned slantways against the sunshine, so that I caught a flutter of fathomless aquamarine from her hooded eyes. Her hair was so bright that it threw coppery reflections onto a cheekbone, the curve of her neck.

'To be alive,' she said quietly, turning to me again, her voice hoarse and sweet, like scratched silver. 'What little difference between being alive and not. Don't you think?' I think I just stared at her, not knowing what to say, not thinking.

'To be alive,' she repeated, 'such a brief mystery, too short to understand. The thing to have is power. Power is everything and lasts forever.'

There I had it; the creed of Rosemary Ashley, but, like a fool, I just gaped, offered pity where none was needed, impulsively stretched out my hand towards her (the sunlight bled it white) and said:

'Don't talk. Try to eat something. You're among

51

friends now.'

Her strange gaze fixed me for an instant.

'Friends,' she said, almost blankly.

'I pulled you out of the river,' I said, trying not to sound too pleased with myself. 'However bad things are, the river can't help. Believe me, Miss. I'm your friend now, if you'll have me – if you'll trust me. The river isn't any answer . . . Whatever it is . . . not that.'

I think that somewhere in my mind there might have been a suspicion of something tawdry; some slinking tale of seduction and abandonment, but whatever it was, was banished as soon as I looked into her eyes. She was innocent, I could have sworn she was innocent, staked my life on it, as, in a way, I suppose I did. It shone through her like a searchlight, reflecting a million facets in her pure, violet gaze.

I thought she was innocent. Later I learned to know her better. I think I was as helpless as you, and I think she knew it. Because it was not innocence which streamed from every part of her, piercing her transparent skin and shining from her lilac eyes.

I think it was power.

Three

Cambridge, *April 1990*

He closed his book petulantly and went to the window
again. It was raining now; the light from the street fell
in great corrugated sheets against the thick glass of the
window and bounced from the window-sill with a
sound like shrapnel. It was half past two in the
morning, and still she did not come.

He went to the drinks cabinet and poured himself a
whisky. He didn't really like the stuff, though he
would never have admitted it to anyone, but it was
what *she* drank: whisky, no ice; and he was still
adolescent enough to want to drink it for her sake, as if
the dry, gagging taste could somehow bring her closer
to him. He swallowed, made an involuntary face, then
downed the whole glassful, slamming the glass back
onto the table in front of him in a way he imagined
might have impressed *her*, if she had been there to see
him.

But she did not come. Where was she? A movement
from outside caught his eye, and he squinted through
the window again; was that a figure in the courtyard
below, the gleam of a plastic mackintosh in the
lamplight? He fumbled with the catch of the window,
pushed it open, regardless of the rain pouring in over
his shirt-cuffs.

'Over here!' he shouted through the crashing of the
overflow pipe, and the figure halted, looked up. He

caught a brief glimpse of the pale oval of her face above the shiny black collar, saw her nod, and the familiar thrill always occasioned by her presence overcame him again, a starburst of adrenalin which began somewhere in the region of his stomach and expanded in thin, prickly lines towards the palms of his hands and the soles of his feet; a delight which was partly compounded of lust and wonder and a kind of fearful *insignificance*, as if she were so much more powerful, more knowing than he was; as if she were the carnival-wheel which he rode in the whistling night, his heart beating like a trapped bird's, his breath a silent scream as he fell in endless terror and ecstasy towards her without ever touching her; and she as pure and remote and oblivious of his touch as the earth is oblivious of the life which walks upon it. Making love to her never changed her; she renewed her chastity like the moon, every time; only he was defiled.

Her footsteps sounded on the stairs. He poured himself another glass of whisky and drank half of it at once, afraid she might see his trembling hands. She was not kind, his lady; she knew his weaknesses and laughed at them. Sometimes, in his moments of lucidity, he wondered why he needed her so, knowing as he did that all she had ever offered him were the joys of fear and humiliation and the dark exhilaration of the fairground, rank with the scent of sweat and the beast which was himself. She had no love for him. They had nothing in common, never talked like friends. And yet, her step on the landing, quick and light as a cat's, set his pulses racing, his head spinning, and he ran to open the door as eager as a schoolboy.

So slim, so frail; even now she never ceased to amaze him, that so much perversity could be contained in such a thin white vessel. She stood before him in the semi-darkness, sensing the chaos of his feelings, mocking him. She was wearing the black plastic raincoat, tightly belted at the waist, the collar

54

turned up to frame her face. She had pushed back her hood, and the thick curls of her pale red hair spilled out onto her shoulders. Her mouth was very red; he felt dizzy with his proximity to her, felt as if he were falling towards that mouth, saw the lips part very slightly to allow him to fall . . . She untied the belt of her raincoat, shrugged it open; dropped the coat onto the floor of the landing where it lay in a pool of rain, smiled. She was naked under the raincoat, her body opalescent in the reflected light from the street-lamps, her hair a wild cascade, her eyes, her lips, the tips of her breasts, the dark delta of her pubic hair like holes in that pallid body, holes from which cables of mystic night winched him closer and closer to her, powerless in the face of her irresistible attraction.

'Not here . . .' he mumbled. 'Never know . . . the porter . . . the others . . .'

He stooped to pick up her raincoat; caught the scent of chypre and rain from her body, caught a dizzying glimpse of waterdrops on a slim thigh, and stumbled in his eagerness. She gave a low laugh of contempt.

'My little gentleman,' she murmured. 'So much concern . . .'

She stepped lightly into the room, shedding her low shoes at the door, as graceful and as unconcerned of her nakedness as if she had been fully clothed. He shut the door hastily; not even lust could blind him to the possible consequences if she were seen; he did have his position to maintain after all; he had to be discreet. He hung up her raincoat by the sink, where the water could drip without harming the carpet, turned, almost afraid now that everything was ready.

She was sitting in his armchair, legs crossed, hands clenched wantonly in her hair, and smiling. Despite himself, he began to tremble, and he turned away to hide the movement.

'Drink?' His mouth was dry as he topped up his own glass.

55

'Whisky, no ice,' she said, and as he poured, he was suddenly certain that she was laughing at him, knowing as she did (and he never doubted she did) that she had complete power over him in body and in mind, that hers were the strings which set him dancing, that with her, *he* was always the whore.

'There,' he said, handing her the glass, thankful that at least his hands had stopped trembling now.

He watched her drink, both small hands cupped round the outsized glass, and yet she drank the filthy, oily stuff as if it were water, in quick little gulps, the thin reed of her throat moving up and down as she drank like a swan's. Just another of her tricks, he thought with some bitterness. Didn't he know them all by now? Surely he had been taken in by them enough times already.

Strange and appalling, the power she wielded over him. She was only a woman, after all, almost a child; he had picked her up out of the gutter; she had been half dead with starvation, half poisoned with cheap gin and forbidden drugs, he had settled her in a nice little apartment where nobody would ask any questions . . . he had spent more than half his generous study grant on her, on her clothes, her lodging, her pills and powders, her doctors and therapists . . . had asked nothing more of her than this, this little comfort. She had been everything to him, the guttersnipe, damn it, he had *loved* her. She should have belonged to him body and soul.

But she was perverse, mocking him, sensing his crippled and shameful appetites and satisfying them, yes, but for a price.

'Are you brave enough yet?' Her voice roused him out of his bitter reverie. 'You stink of whisky. Have you managed to drown your bourgeois scruples?'

He cringed.

'There's no harm in a little drink,' he said, hating the weak note of defensiveness in his voice. 'You're partial

56

enough to it yourself.'

She laughed.

'You don't think I could bear you to touch me otherwise, do you?' she said. 'I may be your whore, but that doesn't mean that your professorial ministrations are anything other than repulsive to me. Still, you've paid me well for my time, so I expect you can do what you like with it.'

'Damn you, you've a wicked tongue,' he gasped.

'That's why you want me,' she said, stretching out on the chair like a cat. 'You like to be punished. I know you intellectuals. I've had enough of them in my time, you know.'

'Your time!'

'Don't raise your voice,' she said mischievously. 'Remember the porter, the others.'

'Damn them!' he snapped. 'How old are you anyway? Seventeen?' He tried to laugh.

'Older than I look,' she answered mockingly. 'Old enough to know all about your kind, and to hate them. You're such victims, all of you.' There was venom behind the mockery.

'Be quiet.'

'Certainly. That's what you pay me for, isn't it? Do you want me to scream when I come?'

'Be quiet!' He grabbed her by the wrist, pulled her from the chair. Her small bones moved under her skin, and he knew he was hurting her, but still she seemed to be smiling. Whatever he did, she was still always in control. He held her wrists high above her head, pushed her towards the bed, flung her down with a brutality which both satisfied him and wrenched at his heart. Despite that, she landed gracefully, like a cat; in fact, if he thought about it, he had never seen her do anything without that natural grace; it was one of her obscure ways of taunting him.

'Oh, God . . .' he breathed her name. 'I'm sorry . . . I . . . I love you so much. Please . . .'

The plea died on his lips. She could do as she liked, this child, could annihilate or exhilarate him at a whim; hers was the power of fairytale, that gypsy sensuality which transcends reason. She turned over, her fathomless eyes tunnels of rain, a million miles deep. The light caught the curve of her neck, a perfect collar-bone, the white dune of a breast; her beauty was more than bone-deep, it was eternal, like a beautiful landscape, white as the moon. She opened her arms, and he fell towards her with a long, soundless cry of joy.

She moved underneath him like a dancer, unconcerned by his touch, but pushed onwards by some strange unguessed-at lust of her own. Her lips moved over his face, his shoulder, questing, searching . . . her breath held a wild music he took (God help him!) for passion. Her cool hands found his neck, rested there for a moment like those of a weary child. A rictus seized him, half pleasure and half pain, like biting into a sweet fruit, tastebuds cramped with the sweetness, and he threw his head back . . . He felt her lips on his throat, murmured some term of endearment. He felt her teeth on him, small and sharp. Sharp! He tried to jerk away as he felt the bite, but her hands were there, holding his head firmly in place.

'Ouch! Stop it!' His hands were off her body and his legs thrashed with the violence of his reaction, but still she did not let him go. Close against his flesh he felt her breath as she laughed. Then, with a sudden *crunch*, she bit deeper, and he felt part of his neck (a tendon, maybe?) give way with a dreadful collapsing feeling. Blood rushed out as his head lolled bonelessly; blood soaked the front of his shirt, blood rushed down the side of the girl's face and dripped from the stray damp strands of her hair. He tried to scream, tried to move, but the pain, the movement, the sensation of her cool flower-like body against his, all these were at the end of a dark tunnel of feeling, receding to a pinpoint of light and heat in the icy dark. He tried her name; it burst in a bubble of blood and ran down the side of his shoulder, but he did not feel it. He was alone in the tunnel falling further and further away from that bright point of reality . . . and not unwilling to fall, either; in fact, very glad to escape from the memory, mercifully fading already, of that last *crunch* which tore him open like a peach, and the muffled, wet bubbling sound of the girl's laughter against him.

When, some time later, she had sated her appetite, the girl wiped her face fastidiously on the dead man's handkerchief. She always washed after meals.

Two

It was nearly dark by the time they arrived, and the street-lamps were lit on Gwydir Street, where they cast long orange shadows on the dark-blue pavements. Alice, watching from her upstairs window, saw them coming long before they knocked at her door, and she had time to cast a final glance at her immaculate living-room, to tweak a cushion here, to straighten a picture there, before she let them in. She was nervous as if she were on her first date; she had dressed with more than usual care (a red drop-waisted dress designed to hide her figure and draw attention to her dark hair; a red-and-white silk scarf at the neck and low-heeled black shoes), the colours making a red exclamation-point in the shadows of her living-room. Maybe something inside her wanted Ginny to know she had a rival.

Surely not. Alice shrugged at that idea. She hoped she was not so primitive. But all the same, as the knock sounded at the door she took a moment to straighten her hair in front of the mirror and put up her chin defiantly.

Friends, she thought furiously to herself as she forced herself to walk slowly, unhurriedly, towards the door. That was all. It had to be all. It had been she who decided they would be better off living apart. She had no more hold over him, could not hope to gain any now; didn't want any. So just enjoy it, she thought, as she paused at the door. Enjoy it if you can.

Joe stood at the door, flowers in his hands; white roses wrapped in clear, crinkly cellophane paper. The scent, and the moment, engulfed her.

'Hello Joe,' she said softly, and smiled.

'Long time,' he answered with a grin, and raised his fist to his shoulder in a kind of salute, a secret sign they had shared a long time ago. The moment lingered, then he looked over his shoulder, almost furtively, and the moment fell to the ground and burst like a water-drop as a figure emerged from the shadows, a crescent of fiery hair, an arc of light following the line of a prominent collar-bone, the rest black with shadow.

'Hey, Alice . . .'

His voice was slightly unsteady, like that of a child offering another a peep into a forbidden book, apprehensive and yet excited. The roses crinkled unresponsively in their wrapping.

'Alice . . . this is Ginny.'

The girl stepped into the light.

Alice supposed that she made all the right noises; thanks for the flowers, invitations to come in, to sit down; polite commonplaces. But all the time, she was covertly looking at Ginny, taking in every little detail, every line, every hair etched into her remembrance in sharp little razor-cuts of precision.

Imagination was nothing, she thought bitterly to herself.

Nothing. She had imagined that she would not be a prey to jealousy, that she would not be primitive, and yet she had discovered within herself such depths of jealousy and . . . yes, almost *hatred* that she even frightened herself. She could feel the hairs on the back of her neck rising.

Oh, the girl was pretty. That she had expected. That alone should not have been enough to raise such a black welter of feeling from within her. There was

62

something else, something beyond that, something *archetypal* which she struggled to analyse, without success.

Ginny was slight without being small, slender and supple as a wand, light as a dancer in a wide-skirted, powder-blue dancer's dress which reached almost to her ankles, occasionally brushing the heels of her low-heeled blue pumps. Her hair was rather short, curly, artlessly pushed back from her face in a halo of red gold. She was pale, the rosy glow from Alice's living-room only seeming to enhance the perfect china bloom of her skin; but her eyes were filled with lights and reflections, hallucinatory. There was nothing, no feature there, to explain her beauty; it hardly seemed to be a part of her, it was somehow mediaeval, ethereal, abstract. A man might see her once and be haunted forever by that beauty, long after he had forgotten her face. There had been a picture on Alice's bedroom wall in her student days, an indifferent reproduction of a Rossetti watercolour entitled *The First Madness of Ophelia*; it showed the doomed girl, wreathed in flowers, crowned in flowers, long hair loose, pale features a blur of dark eyes and open mouth as she sang, heedless of her friends' concern, sang her sorrow and her madness, childlike in her self-possession. What had Joe said? That she had had a breakdown? That she had spent time in a mental hospital? Alice could believe it. She had that same look, reproduced in black-and-white on that half-forgotten poster, of darkling, doomed purity. Her beauty was an abyss, an insanity all of its own.

Somehow that beauty, that grace showed beneath its fragility an unshakable confidence, and Alice was reminded of her mother, sad and overweight, of herself, lonely and insecure, talking to her cats and eating biscuits. She could never imagine Ginny losing her poise, her purity. Ginny would never be sullied by life. Her purity was tangible, almost taunting, impregnable. For a moment Alice seemed to see herself through Ginny's eyes, as that cool, appraising stare flicked over her; she saw herself as she knew she must seem before that little island of teenage self-possession. Over-tall, her eyes too small behind those wire frames, features too heavy for a woman, and with a stockiness which would have been appropriate in a boy, but which for her was not. She saw her red dress, shapeless and over-bright, the colour emphasizing the full figure she had hoped to camouflage. She saw her movements, graceless and awkward, as she watched herself making coffee and passing the biscuits. She saw Joe watching her, making no comment, but noticing the weight she had put on in three years, the fine tracery of new lines around her eyes. Alice felt insecurity escalate almost into paranoia, imagined Ginny and Joe casting knowing glances at each other behind her back, imagined their conversations, their comments. And the worst of it was that Joe hadn't changed at all; if he had, if she had been able to detect a hint of grey in his hair, new wrinkles around his mouth, extra flab on his thin arms, she might have felt more reconciled to her own imperfections, but she detected nothing. The same smile, the same endearing squint through the glasses, the same thin-as-a-rake body and slightly stooped shoulders. A half-expected jolt as she realized that even now she felt the same attraction.

Alice spent the rest of the evening in a haze of jumbled emotions; places and faces passed without really registering; a pizza restaurant somewhere in the upper Backs, eating, for once without appetite, with the same dogged concentration she had seen in her mother; a path by the river, a bridge. A crescent moon throwing frosty shadows onto the grass and the river. A weir, looking down into the black night water, watching neon reflections in the scum.

She ate, drank, made conversation, without effort,

without thinking. Joe sparkled; Ginny turning towards him, smiling shyly, watching him, taking her words from him. A late-night film at the arts cinema which Alice did not see. Waiters. Usherettes. A student giving out leaflets. Ginny's eyes reflecting light from the screens. Joe buying chocolate, his eyes bright, talking ... talking ... Joe happy, unsuspecting, his arm around Ginny's shoulders, looking down at her with that intent look that Alice knew to be short-sightedness ... Ginny smiling with that passive, vague serenity, her voice the barest whisper, like a child's, glancing at Joe before she spoke, as if he somehow held the key to her words. Soundless pictures, their lips moving without meaning, their colours as random and exciting as a magic-lantern show. Themselves a part of the play, coloured shadows on a flat screen.

And only Ginny's face through it all, watching her as if through glass, slightly distorted, the bones of her face seeming to change shape; here like the face of a woman looking into a fishbowl, there one eye magnifying suddenly, mouth twisting into curling, sneering shapes. Ginny's face, and the beginnings of obsession.

For a moment, Alice had been so absorbed that she could not remember where she was. Colours rushed in upon her, jumbled sounds filled the soundless world. A face rushed towards her through fathoms of water ... then normality, as if nothing had ever been different, as if the dark carousel she had ridden through all that evening had finally tired of her, thrown her back in disgust upon the flat shore of herself, while the fair continued, on some other dimension, maybe just across the water.

The face was Joe's.

'Thank you,' he said, with a wink and a grin, his hand brushing hers ... oh! so slightly, raising the hairs on her wrist.

'It's been really good to see you again, you know, Alice. Thanks for coming. We should have done this a long time ago, but I expect I was too immature, or too bloody arrogant to suggest it.'

'That's fine,' answered Alice mechanically, her voice overbright. 'I've had a great time.'

'I knew you would.' His voice was warm, his eyes brilliant. 'I'm so glad you and Ginny got to know each other. I knew she'd like you, and I really hoped you'd like her.' He lowered his voice slightly, glancing back at Ginny to make sure she did not hear him. 'I hope you'll be a good friend to Gin too, Alice. She needs someone like you, you know. This evening has really done her a world of good; maybe you don't realize it, because you don't know her very well yet, but I can tell how much she likes you.'

Alice nodded, feeling helpless. Already the violence of her previous emotions seemed to hold the logic of certain dreams, which appear to make sense at the time of dreaming, but afterwards dissolve back into the incomprehensible code of the subconscious from which they are born. She looked back at Ginny, who was sitting in a chair by the fire, and tried to recapture that certainty, that awareness of something malicious, something morally tainted . . . She rubbed her eyes with the back of her hand.

'Do you want a drink before bedtime?' she offered, under control again.

Ginny shrugged, with a vague and sweet smile, and looked at Joe.

'Why not?' he said. 'What have you got?'

'Tea and coffee.'

'Tea? Coffee?' His tone was comically aggrieved. 'That's good enough for a pair of little innocents like you.'

'Cold beers in the fridge. It's the best I can do,' smiled Alice.

'Fine,' he said decisively, and went to the kitchen in

search of the alcohol.

'One for you?' he called to Ginny, but she only shook her head, nervously twisting the flimsy fabric of her dress with long, pale fingers.

Alice was irritated. Perhaps it was the utterly passive, dependent persona Ginny adopted which grated on her nerves. It was the way she looked to Joe for every little thing; it was the modest lowering of her eyelids when she was not looking at him. Somehow Ginny, despite her obvious shyness, made her very uneasy. She tried to overcome it, speaking to Ginny directly for the first time in the evening.

'Do you know Cambridge at all?' she queried, feeling awkward, but determined to elicit some response, even a commonplace.

Ginny looked up, her strange eyes like cracked mirrors. Alice saw herself trapped there in reflection.

'I know . . .' whispered Ginny. 'I used to know it, a long time ago.'

'It never changes much, does it?' continued Alice doggedly.

Ginny shook her head.

'What do you like best? The Backs? The colleges?'

Ginny shook her head again.

'I like the graveyards,' she whispered, almost abstracted. 'And the river.'

Alice muttered something meaningless in reply, already feeling exhausted. Joe, however, did not seem to see anything amiss; but he had been drinking cheerfully and steadily for most of the evening already, and Alice had not expected him to notice the tension. He came back from the kitchen carrying a six-pack of beer and some glasses, but ended up drinking out of the cans, as usual.

'Hey, Al,' he said, between gulps, 'I see you still have old Cat. I'm sure she remembers me. When I went to the fridge she came right up to me and started rubbing my leg with her nose. How's that for memory?

I always liked that cat. Even when she shat in my guitar-case.'

'I think she just remembers there's food in the fridge,' said Alice.

'Oh.' For a minute he was crestfallen, then as a new idea came to him, he brightened again.

'Tomorrow we're playing the Corn Exchange. Big-time stuff. Benefit gig with three more bands. You'll enjoy it. Ginny wants to hear us, too. She's only ever heard us once except in practices, you know, and most of the time there's not much to hear then, except Martin complaining that his vocals don't sound right, and everyone shouting at the drummer because he won't shut up. That's not entertainment, it's just masochism. But put us under the lights and . . . wham! We're like quick-growing kelp. We blossom. Perhaps you two could come together; Gin's a bit nervous of being there on her own.'

Ginny gave a little nod, but made no answer. Alice gave a slightly strained smile.

'I'd love to come. What sort of thing did you tell me you were playing?'

Alice knew that any reference to his precious band was enough to keep Joe talking for the whole evening. She knew that he would be satisfied as long as she smiled and nodded and looked interested; and for the moment, she was too drained by the evening's revelations and cross-currents to attempt any other conversation. Besides, there was Ginny; and her very presence inhibited Alice in some inexplicable way; she felt that the girl bled her very thoughts and substance from her, so that she was lighter than air, lighter than paper. This feeling was so intense that she answered Joe almost at random as he spoke, which earned her, despite his self-absorption, a speculative glance.

'You're very quiet,' he said, laughing. 'Has age mellowed you at last, or am I just boring you witless? You always used to have plenty to say for yourself in the old days.'

Alice flicked a glance at Ginny, but detected no reaction to Joe's careless mention of their earlier intimacy.

'And you always used to say that women talked far too much,' she said, pretending flippancy.

'They do.'

'Do you stand for this sort of thing, Ginny?' said Alice, forcing herself to include the quiet girl in their conversation.

'She doesn't have to,' said Joe, opening another can one-handed, 'she's the most restful female I know.'

'Don't be taken in,' retorted Alice. 'Beneath that charming exterior there's a first-class chauvinist pig.'

Ginny gave a little, secret smile, raising her eyes to Alice's, then dropped them again. She murmured something in a feathery voice, which Alice did not hear; but Joe gave a low laugh. Alice assumed that she had managed to counterfeit enthusiasm well enough to deceive him, anyway.

'I'll have to go now, I'm afraid,' he said, with a quick glance at his watch. 'I'll be here in the morning as soon as I can. I have a practice at ten, and we've got another at about three before the gig, but I'm sure I'll be able to find time to take you both out to lunch.'

Alice smiled automatically, grasping at the moment, understanding at last what this was leading to; soon he would be going, and she would be alone with Ginny.

'Would you like a cup of coffee before you go?' she asked, half in despair, because he was draining the last can of beer, because he had his coat on, because he was half-way to the door, because he was at the door with his hand on the handle . . .

'No . . . no thanks, Alice. I'd really better be going. It's getting late. But thanks . . . yes . . . goodbye.'

'Goodbye,' said Alice forlornly to the door as he stepped out into the night. 'Goodbye . . . Oh, Joe . . .'

But Joe had already gone, the orange of the

streetlight making a strange, garish figure of him as he moved rapidly down the street.

'Goodnight,' said Alice lamely; she couldn't remember what she had wanted to say to him anyway. She turned, and there was Ginny, waiting politely beside the stairs, that little, knowing smile on her face, her eyes in a band of shadow so dark that it might have been a mask. Alice tried to smile back, shook her heavy head, took two steps towards the kitchen.

'Would you like a coffee before you go to bed?' she offered, with an effort; there was no desire in her to offer the girl anything at all, she hated coffee, had the beginnings of a headache, and wanted nothing as much as to lie down in the dark and forget everything, but there was nothing she could confide in this quiet, self-contained girl, and nothing to do but act out the part she had accepted to play. Ginny half turned towards the light, her eyes a sudden carousel of reflections.

'That's very kind,' she said; her voice was soft but clear, with an undertone of mockery, her accent light and untraceable, 'but do you mind if I go upstairs and change before I have it? I'll feel much more comfortable.'

'Of course!' Alice's smile felt better now, more sincere. Maybe it was Joe's absence which did it.

'I'm afraid it's a bit makeshift upstairs, but it was the best I could do at short notice. You can put your clothes in the wardrobe, if you like, and if there's anything you need, just give me a shout.'

'Thank you. I'm sure I'll be fine,' said Ginny, beginning to climb the stairs. 'I'm sure we'll understand each other very well.'

'First on the right, the door's open,' said Alice mechanically. (Now what did she mean by that? she wondered, pondering Ginny's last words. Understand each other? Why should we do that?)

It occurred to her, with a jolt, that the girl was

painfully shy, that that comment might have been a way of asking to be friends, and she felt vaguely ashamed of the extent of her antipathy. It was probably *her* fault that Ginny had been unresponsive; she supposed she had been rude. She should have tried to include the girl and make her talk.

Mentally berating herself for the failure of her good intentions, she determined to give Ginny a chance, to be friends with her, and at once, having made the decision, felt a kind of lightening of the spirit, an abating of her headache, a feeling of release. She put the kettle on, set out two cups, smiled and brought out a tin of biscuits as well. As she began to set the biscuits out on a dish, she even began to hum.

One

Fulbourn Hospital, *November 1977*

I dreamed of her again tonight; why mention it, I wonder, when it happens every night, every night without failing, each time in some new and monstrous clothing, my dreams bloated with her hate and her memories like poison fruit? Why write it, when her face looks out from the page at me, when her cold, delicate hands close on mine as I hold the pen? Oh, Rosemary.

Her presence is like a perfume in the air, her voice, a whistle to the winds. She never leaves me. Last night, at midnight, between the time of saints and the time of witches, she came; I dreamed of her. All in grey, she was, with flowers in her hands and her long red hair loose to the winds, singing to herself as she walked along the riverside where the hemlock was growing tall, and I thought to myself; here is a lady lost, in danger. So I stood up and walked through the graveyard towards her; I stumbled over a gravestone in my haste and she turned and saw me. I don't think she spoke, but, as she turned, I saw that she was holding something in one hand, a little round glass something, like a marble, and she held it out towards me, and smiled. The wind whistled through the little round thing as she held it, a strange, mournful sound, and as I stretched out my hand to receive it, I saw my own face staring out at me, long and distorted in the glass surface, mouth open in an impossibly wide, moaning scream. As I looked, the marble seemed to grow bigger and bigger, until I could see trees and houses through its convex surface, houses and bushes and a road and a railway line winding its way through a wood ... Suddenly, and without any apparent reason, I was afraid. I looked around. Nothing.

Nothing but the rails, the trees, the whistle of the engine far away. I looked up at the sky. And then I understood. She was there, had been there all the time, looking down, her hair drifting outwards around the outside of the globe, her eyes great tunnels of death, bigger than the world. And outside the world, in the strange fisheye she inhabited, there was nothing but darkness. No sky but the blue painted inside of the spinning-top, no sun but her eyes, no moon but the round pink imprints of her thumbs against the glass. And I knew that sometime or other, she would remember the handle, the red wooden handle which turns the world ... and where would I be then? Spinning, spinning, there in the dark forever, at her pleasure, beneath her ever-watchful eyes? My blessed Damozel.

Suddenly, I was jolted from my thoughts by a sound; a slow, deep, groaning and creaking sound, impossibly huge, from the very engines of the earth, as if some ancient underground forge had been opened anew. A scraping music accompanied it, like the world's oldest and most decrepit roundabout. The music's pace quickened, became a fairground tune, loud and brash, laboriously out-of-key as a warped musical-box. The light had changed; shadows lay over most of the land, hiding the trees and bushes from sight, except in a few cases, where a sudden spray of light (green, pink, electric blue) outlined a stump here, a protruding branch there, into lurid, swaying relief. Branches? Why had I thought of branches? As the top began to spin faster, the music to play more

74

rhythmically, I held onto the first solid object I could grasp. A branch? In the semi-darkness, I could feel a hard, rippled surface, a jingle of bells, the harshness of a horsehair mane . . . What could be more natural, on a fairground roundabout than a roundabout horse? I closed my eyes (the roundabout was spinning very quickly now, the horse leaping up and down in a way which sickened me to the stomach), but there was no way I could let go of the only solid object in my world, and I held on with my eyes closed until I began to feel a little better, a little more steady, and I dared to open them a crack.

It was light again, not the brightness and clarity of daylight, but a garish kind of fairground light, vulgar, and yet spectral at the same time. And in the brightness, I could see that I was not the only rider on Rosemary's carousel. There were other horses, red and white and black and blue, bells at their saddles, long manes flying in the wind, glass eyes wild and red nostrils flaring. Robert was there too, knuckles white against the reins, coat flapping behind him like wings. I called his name, hoping that he would hear me against the deafening music . . . and he turned his face towards me. He was dead, poor Robert. His face was dead-white, clown-coloured, and his lips were faintly blue. His eyes were turned upwards to the whites. As I cried out in horror and pity, the roundabout lurched, and his head lolled away from me on its broken neck. Then, I saw that all the horses had a rider; a dead rider. Men, women, some I recognized, some total strangers. Some grinned at me as we rode alongside each other; a masked woman blew me a kiss which smelt of carrion. Others slumped over slit throats and broken backs; one rode backwards, head bent completely round, like a doll's. Then a thought, sluggish and murderous as the swollen Cam, overtook me with a cold and seeping terror, as I rode. I had seen all my roundabout companions save one. One.

A coldness at my back, like a sudden draught. A sudden, gassy reek, like putrid vegetables. A kind of touch, horribly intimate, at my shoulder. Turning was an almost unbearable effort, like walking underwater. Another touch, at my face.

Cold.

I began to struggle, vainly trying to avert the predestined. I believe I thrashed my legs, as if in a pointless attempt to outride my pursuer. I tried to turn again. And this time, I succeeded.

My scream was lost in a redoubled burst of the music; my terror heady, ripe as fermented plums. She was masked, only the mouth and the tip of her nose visible from beneath the velvet, but I knew who it was. Ophelia, ten days after her drowning, the stench of the river still on her, mixed with another stench, darker. The slime of the Cam in her hair, her limbs hunched and misshapen, bloated beneath her white dress. I had once owned a Japanese print, showing the six stages of decomposition of the corpse of a young girl left out on a mountainside; I had found it gruesome, but fascinating, to see how the corpse, in her jewellery, her white burial-robes had changed, had swollen, then shrunk ... fool that I was, I had thought that possessing it meant that I was one of the rare mortals unaffected by the sight of death, that I was serene. Ha!

In the face of death (and I speak as one who has seen it, and often), no one is serene.

'I am a maid at your window ...' she croaked at me, and I screamed again, scrabbling at the flanks of my horse, pushing myself backwards with my fingernails, burning the palms of my hands, leaving shreds of my skin on the polished wood, my sanity leaving me in great, sparkling bursts of light, like fireworks (and for a moment, I could *see* them, brighter than any fairground illuminations) as she began to creep towards me.

'A maid at your window ...' she went on,

76

relentlessly, 'to be your Valentine . . .' Then her hands met around my neck, soft and cold, her mouth opened, sending a great cloud of that dark, graveyard reek towards me, and I fell towards her open mouth, all will gone, all feeling gone, into the tunnel of blackness which was Rosemary, where even screams become meaningless.

Two

'Do you want cream or m—?' Alice broke off in mid-sentence as she turned towards Ginny, who was standing by the door, cool as ever, as if there was nothing untoward. The tea-tray Alice was carrying wobbled, but did not fall.

'Thank you,' said Ginny softly, (and *was* it mockery in her voice, Alice wondered?) 'but I don't think I'll have that coffee after all. It makes me tired, and I'm going out for a while.'

'Oh. . .? Oh yes, of course.'

Alice was so stunned by Ginny's transformation that she was unable to say anything, but her mind raced uselessly on. Was that really Ginny there? She would hardly have recognized her after her abrupt change . . . and it was not only her clothes which had changed, but her whole self, the image she had adopted sloughed off effortlessly to reveal something more savage, closer to the bone. She had taken off the chaste, powder-blue dress and low, cotton shoes which had given her such a medieval look. She had aerosol-sprayed a band of black lacquer across her eyes, from brow-bone to brow-bone, like a mask, and her red hair had been made to stand up, rigid, around her face like quills. She was wearing faded jeans (a long tear positioned high on each leg to reveal white skin), and a T-shirt with the sleeves torn off which sported the picture of a grinning skull and a flowery DEATH logo. Her boots were of purple suede, laced up to mid-thigh, and the spiked heels had left little indentations in the pile of Alice's living-room carpet, little gaps, like airholes for something which might be living under there. She looked even younger than before, vulnerable, somehow, in that lurid adolescent's garb, still wrenchingly, pathetically beautiful, but wiser somehow . . . not a dancer, but. . .?

Her eyes danced, a roller-coaster of troubling, multicoloured lights.

'There's a fair,' she said, brightly. Even the voice had changed, adopting, instead of the whisper of a shy child, the slightly nasal, ungrateful intonations of the adolescent girl.

'Yes?' said Alice.

'On Parker's Piece. It's only eleven. It won't be shutting down till midnight. It won't take me long to get there.'

Her eyes were a band of fractured light behind the spray-paint, glimmering dangerously, and she seemed entirely unconscious of the effect she had created, as self-possessed as a child, and with the strange, only half-innocent arrogance of the very young.

'It's a sudden decision to go, isn't it?' said Alice rather coldly. She was thinking of Joe, his goodbye . . . his certainty that Ginny had no friends in Cambridge. 'When will you be back?'

Ginny shrugged, an oddly graceless, adolescent gesture.

'Not very long. That is . . . I'm meeting some friends . . . don't wait up, will you?'

'I'll leave the door open.'

'Thank you.'

Her hand was on the door-handle. Suddenly, Alice felt an abrupt rushing of turbulent emotion; anger, anxiety and reaction against all the things she had been made to feel during the evening. She reached

80

impulsively for the girl's arm; held it. The skin felt cool and smooth.

'Ginny?'

'Yes, what is it?' The note of mockery was there again, almost . . . almost as if she knew what was in Alice's thoughts better than she did herself.

'Joe . . . Joe loves you, Ginny . . . You like him, don't you?' Ginny faced her for a second, then she ticked her head to one side, like a doll. Behind the grey of her eyes, the fairground lights cavorted.

'Joe? Joe? Joe?' she said in a strange, birdlike voice. 'Who's Joe?'

Then the door opened, and she walked off into the night.

Alice paused at the door for a moment, her emotions a mixture of anger at having been manipulated so effectively, shame at her impulsive reaching-out towards Ginny when it seemed that the last thing she needed was friendship or comfort (to Alice, Ginny was far too self-contained to be the fragile innocent Joe thought her), and an odd feeling of . . . well not *fear*, precisely, but . . . unease.

She could not resist the temptation to peep through the slats of the blinds out into the street. She despised snooping, hated spying, loathed the view through the long parallel slashes in the window, but she looked all the same, not a brief, casual look, such as she might have taken by accident, but a good, long, calculating stare. She felt like the picture of the paranoid man on the front cover of Brand X's 'Unorthodox Behaviour'. What was worse, she knew what she was looking for, and that thought made her *really* uneasy; it was hard to admit, but she was looking for a glimpse of those friends; some shred of proof to justify her feeling that Ginny would be bad for Joe, that she would be somehow *wrong*. She shook her head in irritation, turned away from the window in disgust at herself, but not before she had seen what she expected, what she hoped for. The man was standing beneath a lamp-post, face turned away from the house, but his silhouette was outlined sharply in the bright orange light, and Alice saw him well enough. He was tall, long hair drawn back in a pony-tail, long greatcoat with a turned-up collar, motorcycle boots with chains on the back which winked at Alice from the shadows. As she watched, Alice saw Ginny half run towards him, her steps light as a dancer's despite those preposterous boots, and tuck her hand confidingly under his arm. He half turned towards her, spoke, touched her shoulder with a strangely intimate gesture, laughed. Alice heard the faint echo of Ginny's answering laugh, ringing tinnily in the deserted street. She clenched her teeth angrily. No, she didn't like Joe's Ginny, or her friends either; there was something disturbing about that man in the greatcoat, something more than arrogant about the set of his shoulders, the gaudy winking of the metal on the instep of his boots, the protective way his arm went around Ginny's shoulders, almost hiding her from sight. For an instant, Alice wondered if Ginny would be safe with him.

And then, she turned away from the window, her cheeks flushing, for impossible though she knew it to be, it had seemed to her during that instant that the man had turned, too far away for her to see his face, and had stared at the house. Only for a moment, mind you, and there was no way, thought Alice angrily, no way at all that he could have seen her, let alone know that she was watching him, but all the same . . . she was sure he had *known* she was there, that his eyes had sought her out as she hid behind the blinds . . . that he had seen her and, seeing her, had smiled.

Alice turned onto her left side and tried to blank out her mind. Tried to sleep: Images filled the darkness of her closed eyelids, images, faces, voices, glimpses of

her paintings and unformed ideas for others. A snatch
of music throbbed somewhere on the fringes of sleep,
a rhythm and a lyric:

> One day see a strange little girl look at you
> One day see a strange little girl feeling blue
> She'd run to the town one day
>   leaving home and her country fair
> Just beware when you're there
> Strange little girl . . .

Alice shook her head on the hot pillow, shifted
position again.

Damn.

She flicked on the bedside lamp with abrupt
impatience, reached for a book. Maybe half-an-hour's
reading would do it. Her hand paused on the
paperback's cover, reached out again, paused. Froze.
There it was again, a sound, like whispering. Voices.
Alice sat up in bed, alert to any sound, then relaxed.
It's nothing, she thought. It's just Ginny back from the
fair. For an instant, there was nothing; then the
whispering began again, soft and unpleasantly
intimate, and definitely coming from Ginny's room.

Ginny's friends of that evening?

The thought appalled Alice; the memory of Ginny's
strange and sinister appearance, her dreamlike
conversation, the way she and her unknown friend
had disappeared into the dark without a sound . . .
these things all convinced Alice that there was
something wrong going on, and, knowing that, there
was nothing, absolutely *nothing*, she repeated inwardly, which was going to persuade her to get out of bed
and interfere. Who Ginny invited back was none of her
business. She certainly wasn't going to make a fool of
herself by going to find out. After all, it might even be
Joe. She would make sure Ginny and her belongings
were out of the house by the end of that week, without

fail, and then she would be free to work on her new picture and look after her cats and . . . The voices came again, more than two, maybe three or four. Alice knew she would have recognized Joe's voice if she had heard it.

Almost angrily, she turned her head on the pillow and tried to ignore the whispering. A snatch of music, half imagined:

> One day see a strange little girl look at you
> One day see a strange little girl feeling blue
> Strange little girl . . .

Dammit. Why couldn't she leave it alone? It wasn't any of her business. She wasn't going to interfere.

Her train of thought stopped abruptly as she realized that, despite everything, she had thrown back the covers and had got up. Worse still, she recognized within herself a feeling that she *was* going to interfere, that she was not going to be happy until she had left the safety of her bedroom and had sneaked a look into Ginny's room, just to know, she told herself firmly, just to see . . . if there was anything to see. She pulled on her jeans and a T-shirt, careful of the occasionally creaking boards, padded to the door in her bare feet. Still the stealthy, almost mocking undertone of the voices, at the edge of sound, elusive and tantalizing. A soft *Shhhhhhh* as the door opened over the thick pile of the carpet, then the steps, each one an endless held-breath-long over the landing, muscles aching and the carpet sinking into the soles of her feet like pine-needles as Alice edged her way along the impossible distance of the landing towards Ginny's room. Under Ginny's door, a spray of light. As she came closer, the voices blossomed in the darkness, huge and formless as flowers of smoke. Their sense eluded her, the sounds amplified by the straining of her ears into booming, giddying syllables. Here and there, a word found its way into her comprehension, menacing and full of secret meanings.

A man's voice; 'She . . . when she sleeps . . . the picture . . . know . . . think she . . . the picture . . .'

Another: 'Some quiet place . . .'

Ginny's voice, above the rest and more audible, its vagueness gone. With her friends, Ginny's voice was clear and commanding:

'Be quiet. I don't want to run the risk of him suspecting. It was a mistake . . .' (the voice blurred again as she turned away from the door) '. . . give me time . . . I remember everything now.'

Alice felt her head spinning with the strain of standing there, channels of blackness all around her. A sudden, idiotic desire to laugh seized her, and she chuckled nervously to herself in the shadows.

What did she really expect? The Ku Klux Klan? Black magic? Green men from Mars? Another joyless burst of nervous laughter choked her, and she began to feel ridiculous as well as afraid. She had no desire to be surprised here outside Ginny's room by Ginny and her friends, no desire for a scene, exposed before their scorn. So what if Ginny was entertaining without Joe's knowledge? Most likely all they were doing was smoking joints or something, where they knew they wouldn't be interrupted. It was really no business of hers. Joe could and would look after himself. She did not want to know what was being said in that quiet room, hated the thought of the whispered intimacies behind the door, of herself crouching in its shadow like the shy bride in a Gothic novel, waiting for the beast she had wed. Footsteps on the other side of the door, a voice, clear with proximity, dizzying . . .

'Enough talk . . . too much time wasted . . . waited . . . long time . . . find it . . . do what . . . should have been done . . . ready . . . find it and get rid of it . . . not safe for it to still be there . . . one day someone . . . might know who . . .'

Ginny's voice, crisp and carrying: 'No need to worry. Poor Daniel is already dead and done for. He just doesn't know it yet.'

And then the door opened.

From the crack behind the hinges of the darkened bathroom Alice saw the flowering of light across the stair-carpet, saw the three figures cross the lighted stretch, saw shapes; a wedge of light on an upturned cheekbone, a flare of red and purple from the braiding on someone's coat, a cold spark from the chain on a motorcycle boot ... then the light snapped off abruptly, and their steps were only subtle shiftings in the darkness, their whispering the sound of dust against dust in the spangled dark.

'Mustn't wake her ... door latched ... simple enough ... sleeps like the dead ...' (laughter, light as cobwebs) '... back before light ... child's play ...'

(Warning;) 'Suspects ... remember ... picture ... quickly ... find it and get rid ...'

Down the stairs ... *Shh* ... *Shh* ... *Shh* ... *Shh* ... as the skirts of a long greatcoat brushed the carpet. Alice opened the door of the bathroom a crack wider. There was no light. Somewhere a little beyond the stairwell she detected, or thought she detected, the tiny gleam of a street-lamp through drawn curtains. The door opened wider. Her feet made tiny sounds against the floor, but she took careful steps, avoiding the squeaky board, holding onto the banister to stabilize her own descent into the well. A ripple of sound pushed its way into the thick blackness towards her; she heard the click of the latch. A bar of light extended into the dark house, probed, flickered three times ... withdrew.

Click. Alice was alone in the house again.

Her steps were light; she ran downstairs in the darkness, parted the curtains an inch ... they were already half-way down the street, figures long as shadows, steps even and purposeful. Alice's foot bumped into her shoes as she moved back from the window. Without thinking anything, she slipped them on. The latch almost drew itself.

Click.

The door closed behind Alice and she set off after them into the orange-lit silence.

She kept well hidden; her shoes were soft, her clothes, accidentally chosen, were dark. She knew the streets and kept to the shadows; they were dark and dense, and alleys and archways were plentiful. The night air was still and cold; here and there the pavements twinkled with a light frost; Alice's breath spiralled away behind her . . . her steps were easy and elastic. She crossed the town; deserted streets, the Colleges blank carnival-masks with the occasional winking eye at a late-night student's window . . . she left the town behind. The road grew narrower and darker, the buildings few. They crossed the river, twice, crossed a road, waded through a field of green corn. Alice waited until the others had crossed the field before she began to make her own way across it; the delay left them far ahead of her, but she was virtually certain of where they were going; this was the short road across the fields to Grantchester. She knew this way by day; by night the path was loaded with signs and portents; the sky was bright with hidden moonlight, the clouds huge. In darkness it dwarfed the ground more efficiently than it ever did by day. Alice felt unease, but accepted it, dreamlike, and broke into a half-run to catch up with the three shadows, the ground flying beneath her like a magic carpet. She did not feel tired or impatient, only thrilled with the chase, the hairs on her arms electric with cold and anticipation. The snatch of song still played inside her, matching the rhythm of her padding feet:

> Strange little girl, where are you going?
> Strange little girl, where are you going?
> Do you know where you could be going?

Grantchester crouched at the end of the road, the squat little tower of the church with its stubby spire black against the luminous sky. The three figures were almost upon it. Then, at the gate, they slackened their pace. A voice, clear and almost careless, reached Alice from further down the road. Its message was inaudible, but the speaker was unexcited, unafraid.

There was only a tiny spark of sound, metal against metal, as he leaped up onto the spiked gate, then down to the other side. A second figure followed suit, then the third, with equal ease. A languid word spoken; laughter . . . The figures were at one with the dark; the church swallowed them up. Alice was trembling; no student prank, this, her mind told her frantically, no joke; this they had done before, maybe many times, to be so relaxed. The thought of black magic did not seem so laughable now. But still she followed them, fascinated and appalled, her mind spinning its own mandala of fear and foreboding, until she stood in front of the gate itself. She surveyed the church for a moment, somehow disliking its cold face, its mean little windows. The gate was not too high; not higher than the college gate which Alice used to climb on sly Cambridge nights . . . but it was locked.

She wondered why a churchyard should have to be locked; remembered, or half remembered Joe telling her (on the way back from some nocturnal escapade, her hand in the pocket of his overcoat), his voice warm and humorous.

'Beats me why they lock them. The way I see it, no one wants to get in, and no one's likely to be wanting to get out!'

The memory was a sad ghost in the still cold night, its warmth evaporated into pale, regretful nostalgia. And the joke seemed sinister now; the thought of people trying to escape chilled her. She touched the wooden bars of the gate; rot had bubbled through the thick, flaky surface of the paint, grains of it clinging to

88

her fingers like sand. Beyond the gate was the Darkside, the other side of the looking-glass. She longed for it and its answers, but was afraid to leave the safety of the road; yet, dreamlike, she knew that she would cross over whether she wanted to or not. She pulled herself up, the world shifting perspective abruptly as she did so; the darkness made her feel seventy feet high, hovering above a chasm of blackness bigger than the sky. She tilted, feeling carefully for the warm wood beneath her . . . swung her leg over the top.

Strange, how easily it came back to her. Strange how it did not disturb her any more to grab onto the bars at the other side and jump quietly down into nothing.

She found them under cover of night, and hid behind a family monument to see what they were doing; but the wall of the third churchyard shadowed them, and she could see only jumbled shapes, shadowplay without meaning, hear their voices in broken snatches, hear the sound of metal against stone, of metal against earth . . . of digging.

The red-haired figure was Ginny, she could see that much, could hear her voice, higher and clearer than the others, could occasionally glimpse her dancer's body moving among the graves. Another figure was tall, had long hair in a pony-tail, metal on the instep of his boots. The third was spectrally fair, androgynous; Alice could see no face.

'. . . somewhere close by . . . has to be here . . . had no time . . . anywhere else . . . find it, even if I have to . . . dig him up . . . sure . . . know it . . .'

She waited there for a long time, listening to the sound of the digging, then the sound of wood against metal, metal against metal. Whatever it was, they seemed to have found it; Alice could tell by their voices. More sounds, a tearing of paper, a sound of metal scraping . . . footsteps. Alice could feel them in her teeth. She crouched against the monument, thickly shrouded in shadow, the throbbing of her eardrum echoing in the cold stone, as the footsteps passed and died away. After a while she got up.

Her eyes were accustomed to the darkness, and she could see quite well; the hammering fear had left her for the moment, to be replaced by a strange, transparent calm. She took two steps nearer to the patch of shadow she now knew to be an open grave; one step nearer and stopped. There was a hole in front of her, not deep, but magnified by the strange night-time perspective, and in front of it, the slab of carved stone had been shifted, laid neatly by the side of the grave. A thought struck her; she had been here before. She recognized the corner of the churchyard, the yew-tree and the hawthorn . . . caught sight, as she spun round, of the place she saw earlier, when it was light, the grave with the little gate. (*Something inside me remembers* . . .) The gate was open now, a line of moonlight touching the frame and for a sudden, panic-stricken moment, Alice thought she could see something on the other side, something waiting to get out. Then it moved, pushed, no doubt by a gust of wind, moved and swung back on its hinges with a little sound of rusty metal, as if some tiny, invisible child were swinging on it. Alice could feel no wind, but the gate swung again, more violently, this time, open, shut, open . . . shut . . . open . . . the squeaking voice had three notes, two falling, one rising, like the song of a marsh bird; *Ti-ri-weeee. . . tiriweeeeeee . . .* hallucinating in its clarity. Alice watched it, eyes wide, mouth wide, stomach falling away within her into a great cauldron of panic, the song of the marsh-bird following her, its three sad, limping notes forlorn as snowflakes in a dark well, and throughout, the gate continued its dance, open . . . (*Tiriweeeee . . .*) . . . closed . . . (*Tiriweeeeee . . .*) open . . .

She wondered why she did not scream.

Two

Cambridge, *April 1990*

Alice awoke with a start, the last image of a terrible dream in her mind, the echo of an unuttered cry on her lips, and, for a moment, she wondered where she was. She ached all over; her neck was stiff, her legs curled awkwardly underneath her body, her clothes clammy against her skin.

'Ginny?'

She shook her head to clear it and sat up, speaking aloud, as if to reassure herself that whatever it was, was really over. What on earth had she been doing? Working? It certainly seemed that way; it had happened to her before to fall asleep in her workroom, but never to wake up with no memory at all of how she had got there. She remembered . . . What? A dream? She supposed it must have been, a dream of uncommonly vivid (or was it morbid?) detail. She remembered getting up . . . But there was her painting, propped up on the easel and covered with a piece of muslin so that the dust would not dry on it, where she had, presumably, left it.

So why was it that she had no recollection of any picture, any picture at all? There was nothing but that damned dream in her aching head, nothing but that and a half-dispelled foreboding, spinning its own mandala of death and fear into her mind. She wondered, momentarily and with a now-familiar paranoia, whether Ginny had drugged her. She stood up, shaking the pins and needles out of her stiff legs, fumbled an aspirin out of a brown bottle, swallowed it with a crunch and a grimace, shook out two more.

She remembered the outing with Joe, remembered going to bed . . . remembered . . . was that the dream? She could not seem to remember going to the workroom, could not remember the painting.

The painting!

Surely if she saw it again, it would trigger some memory, some fragment of that lost time; surely. She paused, hand poised over the sheet of muslin; through the thin cloth she could see green, grey, the palette, still smeared with acrylics, a half-filled water-pot containing green water . . . Suddenly, she was not at all sure she wanted to see what was behind the muslin cloth. But the compulsion was too great . . . that, and perhaps she still could not quite believe in that familiar easel, laden with unfamiliar memories, the paint hardly dry . . . She lifted the cloth.

She was aghast. A blaze of chaotic colour met her eyes, colour which merged form and motion, symmetry and abandon in a composition of perfect completeness. It was her work, all right, her style, her thought, and yet the memory eluded her. Her signature in the corner; there. Her pointed calligraphy at the edge of the work, indicating the name of the picture. And what a picture! A river, a water's-edge spiral of grass and wildflowers, roots trailing surrealistically down into the limpid grey water, the willow-tree, seen dizzyingly from above, a half-reflection mirrored shakily in the river; green, a tunnel of green with a white figure at the end of it, a white lady dimly glimpsed in the green and the water . . . Alice drew nearer. The perspective shifted, and she realized that she was looking at the figure from above, from above the surface of the water, while the white lady lay below. The water and the partial reflection from the tree obscured her image; only the face, by some trick of refracted light, was clearly visible; a pale oval, greenish in the shade of the leaves, open eyes and mouth dark beneath the water, red hair darkened to almost-black under the surface, while above the surface it regained its brightness in patches, like floating weed, lurid against the still grey river. The features were clear, still not clear enough for Alice to be sure, and yet, she was sure; they were Ginny's. And the name of the painting was:

Repentance; The Drowning of Ophelia

Alice stared at it for a long time, this troubling thing from the country of dreams; for it was unlike any work she had ever done. The colours were hers – there was paint on her hands, ingrained into her fingernails – the detail was hers, the tricks of the light, the conscious Pre-Raphaelitism of the composition, that figure posed in just the right position, as luminous as an Annunciation. It was the same size as the first picture of the preceding evening, the impression of space and clarity was the same, the details swiftly and surely etched in acrylics over the luminous tints of the inks . . . My God, it must have taken her hours! She had never in her life worked so swiftly. The suspicion of drugs came back, more plausibly this time, frightening yet reassuring. Easier to believe that she had been fed some hallucinogen than to accept the dreams, the blank in her memory . . . the picture itself. Unable to keep away, she looked more closely. Yes, there was something else there, behind the light, something more disturbing still than the fact that Alice did not remember the slightest detail of how or when she had painted it; an impression of . . . she could not quite put a name to it, but it haunted her . . . something in the strange perspective, deceiving the spectator into thinking that it was *she* who was underwater, she who was drowning, the roots of the willow-tree reaching down towards her, the figure of the woman some above-world fancy, split into a million facets of refracted light, face smiling down into the water, hair trailing towards her . . .

Alice pulled away, fascinated. The illusion of movement was immense. Even as she looked, she seemed to feel the pull of the undertow, the circular movement of the composition dragging her down and around . . . Had she really done that? Looking again, the unease changing slowly to awe and delight, she realized that it was the best thing she had ever done, better than the other 'Ophelia' painting, better than *anything*. And Alice, looking into her canvas, seemed to see the vortex of her subconscious spinning further and further downwards, and each level was like a new and undiscovered world, turning its own axis, kaleidoscope-changing in a continuous loop of shadow and counter-shadow, and as she watched, the movement caught her and drew her closer and closer, and without even knowing it, she began to laugh.

Whatever the spell was, the phone broke it, its clear trill startling in the empty house, and Alice jumped nervously, her mind a blank. A sudden, unbidden dream-memory (darkness, a smell of age and earth, figures leaping and dancing around an open grave) returned, shocking in its clarity, then faded as she rose to her feet, stiff and confused. When she reached the phone, however, it had already stopped ringing. Alice looked at her watch. It was already past ten.

Ginny!

Still shaking off the dream-memories of the previous night Alice made her way slowly into the kitchen and put on the kettle. Davy Crockett was sitting on the fridge, and he jumped down as soon as he saw Alice, yowling and winding his long furry body round her legs.

'Just a minute, Dave . . .' murmured Alice. 'Just let me

see if Ginny's awake.'

She ran quietly up the stairs, paused to open the window on the landing, then went to knock softly on Ginny's door.

'Ginny? Are you up?' she called gently.

No answer.

'Ginny?' Louder, this time.

Still no answer. Alice, glancing at the clock on the landing, saw that it was nearly ten-fifteen.

'Ginny, are you awake?' She tried the handle experimentally; the door opened, and Alice peered into the bedroom.

The window was open, the curtains pulled back, allowing the fresh morning air and a faint scent of wallflowers into the pretty room. The bed was made, the pillows plump and cool, the primrose coverlet in place; Alice found herself admiring her guest's neatness. Suddenly, she felt suspicious. She tweaked the coverlet away to examine the sheet . . . it was as she had thought.

The bed was made because it had not been slept in at all. The nightdress on the bedside table had not even been unfolded. She yanked open the wardrobe (studiously ignoring the fact that she hated spying), looked inside. A few dresses hung there, a pullover was neatly folded over two blouses . . . shoes at the bottom. And right at the back, scrunched up in a bundle, she found those torn jeans, the T-shirt, the purple boots Ginny had been wearing spattered with mud. Feeling somehow guilty, as if she had been looking into a forbidden book, Alice pulled the things out. With them came a few other odds and ends; some muddy trainers, a shiny raincoat, a black leather bike jacket, another T-shirt. Some cheap jewellery; a heavy belt with a grinning face for a buckle, earrings in the shape of skulls, an upside-down cross on a chain. The kind of lurid, harmless clothes Alice associated with the bands of Neo-Gothics who prowled the shopping-centre at night, but pushed

95

as far into the back of the wardrobe as they would go, the way a teenage boy hides his dirty books and his half-smoked joints. And underneath the lot, a plastic bag containing two syringes, one almost new, the other so worn that the tip had begun to take on that frayed, feathered look, like an old mapping-pen.

Alice pondered that for a while, mechanically turning one of those syringes over and over in her hands, as if it might provide an answer to Ginny and everything she represented. So that was it, she thought. The syringes explained everything.

So what if Ginny wanted to be a good little girl during the day and rock 'n' roll a little after dark? She wouldn't be the only one. So what if she had a strange-looking boyfriend? This was *Cambridge*, for God's sake, and what was bizarre elsewhere was just about the norm here; no, what she was thinking about was Joe, Joe who was so trusting and so naive. Joe who had no idea that the little girl he had fallen for in such a big way had gone off as soon as he had been out of the house (in the company of someone she seemed to be fairly intimate with, despite her lack of friends . . .) and had stayed out all night. And the dreams? Just dreams, she told herself. Just dreams.

Oh, there didn't seem to be much mystery any more, she thought. There certainly wasn't anything sinister. If Ginny was an addict, that would explain many things; her abrupt change of mood, her thinness and pallor, her lack of appetite and her strange, haunted look. Joe would be able to live with that, wouldn't he? He wouldn't be shocked. After all, he had done plenty of experimenting with illegal substances; it had been easy and relatively safe ten years ago, and in the music scene, the use of soft drugs had been more or less the accepted thing. It all made sense to Alice now, even the meeting with the 'friends' . . . Ginny had gone out because she wanted to find someone to score from, that was all.

The thought reassured Alice in an odd kind of way. That was something she could understand, a weakness in Ginny which was wholly explicable, and which revealed the girl's real insecurity. Alice began to feel herself warming towards the pale, wan wraith, so arrogantly, desperately lovely in her borrowed clothes. She felt she had been insensitive, had seen calculation where there was only uncertainty, had shown coldness and hostility where she should have offered comfort and understanding. And now Ginny had gone. Alice closed the bedroom window and went downstairs. She made some tea, fed the cats, went to the fridge for milk. After a leisurely cup of tea, her mind was made up; she decided to be a friend to Ginny, to help her if possible, to make up for her appalling prejudice and her paranoia. Immersed in her own ideas, Alice had forgotten how young Ginny was. It must be hard to be young in such a world as this, she thought, torn between the arid cross-currents of adolescence and politics and the disapproval of adult society. Ginny, despite her seeming coldness, must be very vulnerable. Putting the anger aside, she stroked the tortoise-shell cat which was sitting beside her on the fridge, poured milk for the others, cut herself some bread and put it under the grill to toast. The cat jumped onto the side of the cooker, meowed and sniffed the toast with interest.

Alice picked the cat up and cuddled her, feeling cat-fur in her nostrils and cat-whiskers in her face. Through the window the sky looked grey; not a day for going out-of-doors, she thought, and she went to the door, picked up the paper which was still lying on the doormat and settled down to read it while the bread toasted. She usually only read the *Cambridge News* for the cinema programme and the plays, and would in normal circumstances not even have noticed the first page, if she had not recognized the picture. Under a picture of a middle-aged man and the headline LECTURER DIES IN RENTED ROOM SEX SCANDAL a photograph caught her eye. At first, she did not realize where she knew the place from; the photograph was dark and rather blurry; the short paragraph contained four spelling-mistakes, and had obviously been a hasty addition, but she did recognize the picture.

That wall, that gate, the side of the church there at the left, the outline of one pointed window along the side of the dark wall ... it was Grantchester church, the photograph taken just alongside the gate which led into the churchyard.

The churchyard!

A fleeting memory crossed her mind again (a girl dancing alongside an open grave ... the sound of digging ... mud ... metal ... wood) then faded. The article was short and simple; the information therein minimal, but disturbing.

GRANTCHESTER VANDALS WRECK CEMETERY

Vandals broke into the grounds of Grantchester churchyard late last night, causing damage to both the church itself, which was disfigured by graffiti, and to some of the graves.

Police are investigating the damage, which is reported to be 'quite extensive', but are not prepared to give details at present.

The Rev. Martin Holmes (45), present Vicar of Grantchester, describes the vandalism as 'a petty and cruel attack on our community', and lays the blame on 'irresponsible student pranksters'. He has denied the allegations of witnesses that the churchyard has been used in the past by practitioners of black magic.

Alice re-read the article, the half-memory growing stronger and stronger. The dream? Had it been a dream? She remembered the sound of metal against wood, metal against stone. She remembered hiding in shadows, crossing the field of green wheat. Remembered mud on her shoes . . . She lifted her head, saw her trainers on the doormat, caked to the laces with graveyard mud . . .

And remembered everything.

One

Dreams, dreams. Sometimes I wonder how much of my life has been dreams, or the dreams of dreams. Maybe I will wake to the teeth of my fantasy in my throat, or maybe I will simply float away on a river of ether like Wynken, Blynken and Nod. My nice young doctor came again today and frowned over my veins. He too, has teeth which bring dreams. I asked him to stop the dreams, but he just smiled. For a minute, I thought he was Rosemary.

Ah yes. Rosemary. Well, we never go far from her, do we? No, that we don't. Still, I've written my story now; I don't flatter myself that she doesn't know about it, but I think I've hit on a way to keep her stymied for a while. Don't you know? Yes, I thought you did. That should Keep Me Safe, don't you think? Because she'll be coming soon, I know that. Coming to bring me back, like Elaine and the others. But I'll not go to her. No. Better the dark. Better the . . .

One more glass of whisky against the dreams.

What did I write last night? I meant to tell you about Robert, and of how he was ensnared, but instead I find that in a whole evening I wrote nothing but my dreams, as if I did not have enough of them already, as if I needed to multiply the madnesses which assail me in every part of my life. I go to Grantchester still, you know; they let me go, because they think it does me good . . . not to see her (I see her every night), but to make sure . . . that she is still there. If she came back, I would know it. I know I would. But she is powerless to hurt, as yet. She is laid. But sometimes I see her, feel her, deep in the dark earth, moving. Maybe she sucks life from her shroud, like the witches of old. But I have faith. Faith is the answer. I tell myself that when she comes to me: I look the other way and pray. I am strong. Strong!

The writings are on my side; all I need is Faith.

Maybe it was Faith which saved me then; I know that I was infatuated by her, bewitched by her every movement. Do not blame me; I was a fool, but she was so lovely! She was a prism, a sunbeam, a dancing bolt of light, chaste as snow. I remember that first and last meal I spent with her; the sunlight like needfire in her hair, motes of light and dust circling her face like an aura. I was shy at first; staring tongue-tied at her over my untouched supper, she eating delicately, cat-like in little, precise bites, her teeth leaving tiny, even indentations in the piece of bread by her plate, the small sounds of her soup-spoon against Mrs Brown's best china plate horribly magnified, like an eye through a lens, in the troubled air. I did not think to speak; I think I stared, foolishly smiling, unaware that she too was watching me from beneath her demure eyelashes, that she was *seeing* everything through the veil of her mockery. Nothing escaped her. Not Robert. Not I.

I'm sure she spoke first; over a dish of fruit, piled high. Apples, peaches, oranges . . . some parts of Cambridge had stayed almost untouched by the rationing; I think Mrs Brown prided herself on the way she supplied her 'young men' with the kind of food they would have found difficult to find even in the best restaurants. I reached for the dish to offer it to Rosemary just as she reached for it herself . . . my hand slipped clumsily and brushed hers. I drew it away hastily, blushing hectically, with a muttered apology. Her hand was cool, like a child's.

'Oh, excuse me, Miss . . .' I stammered.

Rosemary gave me a shy smile of heart-wrenching sweetness.

'You don't even know my name, do you?' she said.

My confusion increased. I mumbled something totally unintelligible.

'It's Rosemary,' she said. 'For remembrance, you know.'

'It's a beautiful name,' I answered foolishly.

'And you?' she insisted. 'I know I can't even begin to thank you for what you did, but at least tell me your name.' Her smile lit up the room again with its brightness.

'Maybe it should be Lancelot,' she said, with a touch of charming mockery. 'Or maybe Galahad.'

I was not an accomplished flirt; in fact, I was uniformally dull and gauche with ladies. Even if I had not been, this one would have left me speechless. I shook my head and tried a smile.

'Gawaine?' she laughed softly.

'No, Holmes. Daniel Holmes.' I wrestled with my shyness again for a moment. 'I'm so glad . . . I mean . . . so happy . . . you're feeling better, Miss . . .'

'Rosemary. Please call me Rosemary.'

'Rosem . . . rose . . .' I gave a nervous laugh.

'And I am feeling better,' she continued, 'Thanks to you, Daniel. How brave you must be, to tackle the complete unknown like that, to leap in the river after me . . . And you don't know me at all, do you? I could be anyone. I could have done anything.'

'I don't care,' I replied, braver now, 'You're the . . . most marvellous adventure I've ever had . . . like a story.

'Her arms across her breast she laid;

103

She was more fair than words can say;
Bare-footed came the beggar-maid
Before the King Cophetua.'

'A poet!' cried Rosemary, clapping her hands.

'No, no,' I blushed, appalled at the vagaries of my tongue. 'That was Tennyson. Not me.'

She smiled, more sadly now, it seemed to me. She turned her face away into the sunlight, a rogue sunbeam lighting up the transparency of one of her irises into a crescent of brightness.

'I can hardly believe it now,' she said softly, 'that I wanted to die, I mean. But it's only a reprieve, you know. One day there will be no Daniel Holmes to save me and make me feel whole again; there will only be the river, waiting its time. Soon, I'll have to leave you, and you'll forget me.'

'Forget you?' I gasped.

'Nothing lasts forever,' said Rosemary. 'I had friends, Daniel. I thought they were good friends. But now, I'm alone, and there is a coldness inside me which can never be melted. You called me the beggar-maid; perhaps I am that, forever on the fringes of things, forever alone.'

'But . . .' I stammered.

'I have a face,' said Rosemary cynically. 'Was that what you were going to say? A beautiful face? I wish I didn't!' She closed her eyes; the tragic mouth thinned, her fists clenched in her lap. I longed to touch her, to comfort her, but I did not dare, so inviolate was her air of tragedy, of innocence. I will never forget what I felt then, that passionate rush of pity and love, that adolescent longing, the hopelessness. I felt the tears spring to my eyes: I make no apologies. She was a superb actress.

'My parents were poor,' she said, a hitch in her lovely voice; 'I don't blame them for that, or for wanting me to use my face to help them . . . they didn't understand. They thought that it would be easy, with my face, to find the kind of husband who could look after me . . . and them . . . lots of nice young men in Cambridge, they said . . . Oh, God!'

'You don't have to tell me,' I said, biting my lips. 'None of it matters . . . Rosemary!'

'I want to tell you,' she insisted. 'I want you to know . . . even if it means you despise me afterwards . . . I want you to try and understand. I found a job in a pub.' She shuddered. 'It was hot, and noisy; sometimes I worked very late, and I was afraid to walk home at night. I lived in a little flat in the town centre; it was too far to go back to my parents' house in Peterborough every day . . . my landlady was suspicious of me . . . jealous, perhaps, of my face. Sometimes, men would follow me home, because of my face . . . but never nice young men. I never let them in!'

She stared at me, her lavender eyes intense and passionate.

'Understand, Daniel, I never did!'

I nodded. You would have believed her too, I swear it.

'Then, one day, I met . . . well . . . even now, I dare not tell you his name. It doesn't matter; it may not even have been his name. He said he was a professor at one of the Colleges. He was handsome, intelligent . . . and, I thought, kind. As soon as he saw me, he said he fell in love with me . . . told me that it was wrong for me to be working in that place . . . said that all he wanted was to look after me. I was suspicious at first; ready to slap his face if he as much as tried to lay hands on me, but he seemed sincere . . . walked home with me that night and did not even ask to come in . . . He broke down my defences with kindness and consideration . . . presents . . . made me give up my job, and led me to think that he wanted to marry me. He never said so, but . . .' Here, she broke off, and passed her hands over her eyes.

'Weeks passed. He was kind and considerate. He held my hand when we walked in the park, he took me

to the theatre. One day he took me to London in his car
. . . but never to his house. I didn't mind. I knew that if
he married me, his family would be shocked . . . a
barmaid! I waited, patiently, blinded by my happiness.
Then, one day, I saw him as I was carrying some
shopping home from the market. I saw him and called
his name in the street. He turned around . . . and I saw
that he had a lady on his arm.'

She stopped, her eyes brimming, and wordlessly,
impulsively, I took her hand.

'I think that I must have understood everything as
soon as I saw his face,' she continued. 'His mouth
went slack, his eyes slid from mine, his hands went to
his collar as if he were sweating. Then he turned away,
without a word, without a . . . Well, as he turned, I
heard the lady say: "Who is that young woman?" And
he said . . . Oh, God, I can still hear it now! "Nobody,
darling."

'Nobody! That's who I am, despite my pretty face.
Nobody good enough to earn the respect of a good
man. The beggar-maid! You couldn't have put it better,
Daniel. My dear Daniel.'

I tried to stop her, to comfort her, but she went on
inexorably.

'No!' she cried, 'I want you to hear the whole. I
suppose I knew then that all hope was gone, but I
simply couldn't bear it to be ended like that. I watched
for him on every street; waited in vain for him to call
and explain everything . . . I think I was still desperate
enough to want to believe any lie, just as long as it
could be like it was before . . . but he never came. I
could not bear to work in the pub again; so I did
sewing work for my landlady . . . earning just enough
to keep myself alive. That woman was glad, I know it.
She knew that something had happened . . . you
cannot begin to believe the scornful words she heaped
upon me . . . hints . . . comments . . . but I was afraid to
leave. I was afraid that no one else would agree to

house a single woman on her own. I drank . . . alone in my room at night . . . I drank gin, like the lowest of sluts. I hated it, but it would appease the loneliness and the despair a little. Then, one day, I saw him again, coming out of the theatre with some friends. I was afraid to speak to him . . . I was shabby . . . maybe I had been drinking, I can't remember. I followed him home. I waited at the door until the friends had left . . . I don't know how long. A long time, I think. Then I knocked.

'He didn't come to the door straightaway; I was beginning to be afraid that he would not come at all . . . then I saw him, through the glass of the door. He opened it . . . looked at me for a moment. His eyes were cold.

' "I don't know you," he said. "Don't come here again." And he closed the door on me. I waited there for a long time, cold . . . despairing, until I saw the dawn beginning to rise. I had been there all night. I never understood why he had changed so much, and not knowing was worse than anything else. When I came back to my flat, my things were waiting for me on the doorstep, neatly packed into a bag and a suitcase. I am sure it must have given her pleasure to do that . . . to handle and gloat over all my poor possessions . . . to write that little note I found pinned to the door. What it said, I don't think I could tell even you, Daniel; though I was innocent, it shamed me to the core, made me dirty. And so, I went to the river, Daniel. And somewhere, there must have been a little pity left in the world, because you came. You came.'

And then, she did cry; long, hitching, tearing sobs which bruised my heart, her face in her hands, like a little girl. I put my arm around her, mumbled sorry, sincere, adolescent words of comfort to her . . . felt that jerk of the heart which I never felt before or since as I held her, that moment of epiphany when she looked up at me and smiled.

No, I could never have blamed Robert, even if he had not been my friend, for taking her from me. Rosemary was the wedge which drove friend from friend, drove the honest man to crime, the good man to murder. In his place, no doubt I would have done the same, and sometimes my blood runs cold to think how easily our roles could have reversed. It could have been me, there in Grantchester churchyard. Maybe it will be yet.

Part Two

The Blessed Damozel

I am to Thee the harlot crowned with poison and gold, my garment many-coloured soiled with shame and smeared with blood ... To Thee am I this woman-thing, nameless because unique, an unimagined pit ... I am to Thee virgin and bride, Thy ring upon my finger ... I sought Thee only, but I fixed fang in all flesh that I found ... I spread fear, I kindled hate, I maddened and slew whom I bit, I burned, I thirsted ...

Aleister Crowley

Part Two

The Blessed Damozel

Aleister Crowley

Two

Cambridge, *April 1990*

The Reverend Holmes was a small, thin, rather insignificant-looking man, the lovely stained-glass window of the nave behind him bleeding all colour from his round and oddly childish features, but the pale eyes behind the magnifying lenses of wire-framed glasses were shrewd and bright with humour. His eyebrows were thick and very dark, giving him an earnest, rather faraway look, and at the moment they were drawn together in a would-be stern frown which managed only to convey bewilderment. His voice was that of a much older man, or a man who is so much involved in his own little circle of events that the comings and goings of the world simply pass him by, and he spoke slowly, with much hesitation, his voice the cultured, gentle, slightly bleating voice of the country priest.

'Ahh ... Well,' he said, shaking his head, 'I can't really say any more about it than ... ahh ... you know. Just a prank, albeit a nasty one ... just one of those student tricks. Though I fail to see any humour at all in the ... ahh ... digging up of graves and the vandalizing of a church ... I'd rather see it as a prank, my dear.'

'But what happened?' insisted Alice, trying to curb her impatience.

'No one knows,' said the Reverend with a shrug.

'Just another of those incidents ... rather nasty, though, and a bit of a shock for me, actually.'

He lowered his voice and turned to her conspiratorially. 'I think it's ... ahh ... a personal *dig* against me, ahh ... no pun intended, you know,' he said.

Alice looked suitably interested, though privately she was beginning to think that she must have been crazy to look up this mild-faced but slightly disturbing little man in the first place. What she thought she remembered had never happened; what she had seen in the paper had been a coincidence, nothing more. She fixed a sympathetic, interested smile on her lips and prepared to manufacture a pressing appointment.

Martin Holmes beckoned her closer.

'One of the graves which were tampered with,' he said darkly, '... I knew it. It was my uncle's.' He paused for a moment to allow that to register. 'We're an old family, Miss ... er?'

'Alice Farrell.'

'Ahh ... yes. An old family, as I was saying; Cambridgeshire born and bred, you might say ... ahh ... though I have not actually lived here very long myself. It could be that ... ahh ... rancour still exists ... old grudges, you know the kind of thing ...'

Alice glanced at her watch. The Reverend Holmes did not notice, but continued his halting, gentle narrative with the air of a man who has found a captive audience.

'I ... ahh ... can't say I was a ... ahh ... *popular* choice as Vicar of this parish. There were ... let us say ... ahh ... factions ... who found me ... unsuitable. There was a bit of an upset in the family long ago ... ahh ... insanity, you know, that sort of thing ... I suppose they remembered it still. Long memories, Cambridgeshire folk ... ahh ... maybe some of the young ones thought it was funny to dig up the grave of my poor Uncle Dan to tease me with it.'

'Oh, was he. . .?' questioned Alice.

112

'Mad as a hatter, poor chap,' said Martin Holmes with a shake of his head. 'Left his wife and holed up in a little house down by Trumpington way ... took to drink ... died in some kind of a home ... hanged himself, so I've been told. Not that I knew him at all ... ahh ... can't remember him too well. Uncle Dan kept himself to himself rather. Remember seeing him once, with my father, when I was a boy ... he tried to give me a shilling, but Father wouldn't let him. Father told me afterwards that he was as mad as a hatter, poor old Dan. Talked endless nonsense about ... ahh ... *devils* ... and ... monsters, at the end. He wanted to be buried in Grantchester churchyard because he wanted to ... ahh ... keep an eye on things. Keep an eye on things!' The Reverend laughed gently, as if at some schoolboy prank of his youth.

'Keep an eye on things!' he repeated to himself, and laughed again.

Alice looked at her watch, taking advantage of the break in the conversation.

'Well ...' she said brightly, 'if there's nothing else ...'

'Nothing else?' said the Reverend vaguely. 'No ... except that they were fooled, of course. Poor old Uncle Dan.'

'Fooled?'

'Well, he's not there, of course,' said the Reverend Holmes simply. 'Whoever dug him up didn't find a thing. There's nothing in that coffin except a box and a few oddments.'

Catching sight of Alice's astonished face (she now had no desire to go away), he turned an apologetic smile towards her.

'I said he was mad as a hatter,' he said.

'Well, where is he?'

The Reverend laughed again, very softly.

'He's here,' he said, 'right here in the church. They ahh ... *cremated* him, you know, then they put him in

113

the east wall, behind a plaque. It was all in his Will, you know, and ... ahh ... my father felt ... ahh ... obliged to carry out his last wishes, even though he was so ... peculiar.' He paused again. 'Funny,' he mused, 'it looks as if he may have been right in hiding away.'

'Why?' (I can't believe I'm hearing all this, thought Alice desperately, can't believe I'm still here *listening* to all this . . .)

'Because that's what he was afraid of all that time,' explained the priest, patiently. 'Being dug up.' He shrugged. 'Kept on spouting a lot of ... ahh ... nonsense about ... being *dug up*, don't you know, and ahh ... used in some kind of ... ahh ... Though why it happened now, after all these years, beats me. Just a coincidence, a nasty coincidence. Poor old fellow.' He turned to Alice again.

'Look there,' he said. 'No, there,' pointing to a dark section of the far wall.

Alice couldn't see anything.

'*There*,' insisted the Reverend. 'Just at the end of my finger. Can you see a little brass plaque?'

Alice moved forwards, squinted, moved forwards again. Yes, she could see it, set into the wall about eight inches above the ground. The plaque was very small, about twelve inches by ten, and it was drab with oxidization. She peered at it to read the inscription, traced the words with her fingers with a growing feeling of unease. It said, in very plain letters, cut deep into the thick metal:

KEEP ME SAFE

That was all. No name, no date, nothing. For a moment, she wondered whether the priest had not invented the whole thing as an excuse to keep her there talking. '*Keep me safe*'? What kind of an inscription was that? She had not even known that it

114

was legal to hide a body in the wall of a church like that. She examined the plaque again, rubbed it with the tip of her finger, not liking the dirt which came off onto her hand.

'That's where he is,' chirped the Reverend Holmes behind her, 'just his ashes, of course, and his papers, ahh . . . and the like. He was a writer, you know, in the . . . ahh . . . old days. Quite famous too, in his way. Had his manuscript buried with him. I always wondered what was in it.'

Alice ignored him. Behind the half-inch or inch of plaque and the three-inch wall behind it, there was a mystery. A story as immediate and as poignant as the one behind that little metal door on which was engraved:

Something inside me remembers and will not forget.

She jerked away from the plaque as if she had been stung. The Reverend Holmes was standing above her, an expression of slight concern on his good-natured face.

'Are you all right?'

That's a question, thought Alice bitterly. What had she been doing? For a moment there, she had been somewhere else, had almost *seen*, almost *known* something of tremendous, dizzying importance . . . Not for the first time in those few strange days, she wondered if she was quite sane. Surely, there had been a man . . . a scent of peanuts and candy-floss and the circus in the air . . . an altered light. And more than that, a strong, an overwhelming compulsion to pull back the plaque, loosen the stones of the church wall . . . to *find*, to *see* . . .

'I'm fine,' she said, with an effort. 'This is . . . very interesting. I really had . . . no idea . . .' The sentences were meaningless in her mouth, but sufficed to give her the courage to ask the question she wanted to ask.

'Tell me . . .' she said, trying to sound unconcerned, 'do you know a girl called Ginny? Virginia Ashley? Red-haired girl . . . slim, very pretty? She has a friend, a dark man with a pony-tail . . . black trenchcoat. Have you seen them near here?'

The Reverend Holmes thought about it for a moment.

'I don't think so,' he said at last. 'Not that that means much, you know . . . my memory isn't what it should be . . . especially . . . ah . . . faces . . . but I might . . . Redhead, did you say? No . . . I can't . . . But I'll certainly look out for her if she's a friend of yours. What was the name again?'

'No, it's all right,' replied Alice hastily. 'It's nothing. Really it is. I just thought you might know her. I really do have to go now,' she added, looking at her watch again. 'Thank you so much for talking to me . . . it's been really . . . Thank you.'

And on that rather incoherent ending, she turned and left the church, almost running through the churchyard, even though most of the mess had by now been cleared up; only a broken gravestone and some scrawlings in red spray-paint on the nearside wall of the church (as she passed, she half noticed the word *BASTARDS* slashed aggressively across an angle of masonry) served to show that anything untoward had happened. The sunlight was bright in the lane outside, the walk across the fields to Cambridge so different from the walk of her dream that Alice began to feel better. No, it could not have happened. Could not be true. Even the trail of footprints across the cornfield (three tracks together and a fourth, winding cautiously round the outside in the shadows) might have been someone else's. Were almost certainly someone else's.

And while Alice made her way along the Backs towards the town, smiling to herself and occasionally whistling a little tune, picking a cornstalk here and there and pointedly not thinking about Grantchester church, a figure walked softly into that same church, came in through the vestry door and hesitated at the entrance to the nave, the light from the stained-glass window throwing multicoloured reflections onto her bright hair. For a moment, she watched the priest standing by the altar in silence, then she came towards him with hardly a sound, her ballet-shoes barely a whisper of leather against the stone as she ran, catlike, to the altar. As she passed it, the sanctuary light went out, but the priest did not notice.

One

Cambridge, *April 1947*
Fulbourn Hospital, *November 1977*

Robert was my friend; my best and only true friend.
He was two years older than I; that made him
twenty-seven, but to me he was so much more mature
and aware that he seemed to move in an entirely
different sphere. He had been in the war (I myself had
been judged unfit for service because of my poor eyes
and flat feet) and had been sent home from Alamein
after taking a volley of shrapnel in his leg; now he
walked with a limp which in my eyes gave him even
greater sophistication. I would have given anything to
be like him, to be handsome and popular, to have
followed him to the war and to have been a hero. He
was everything I admired and wanted to emulate. He
was taller than I was, loose-limbed and naturally at
ease in the slightly overlarge suits and overcoats he
tended to affect, with brown hair falling carelessly over
eyes which were clear and humorous. He was
studying English Literature, the course he had been
obliged to give up at the beginning of the war, and had
already nurtured in me a passion for Keats and
Swinburne. He liked smoking long, foul-smelling
cigarettes, spending hours in crowded coffee-shops,
drinking cup after cup of black coffee and talking
about literature. He was creative; I had read some of
his writings, and they were youthful, incisive,

119

sometimes gently self-mocking. There was never any doubt in my mind then that his work would some day be published; I followed his progress with pride and admiration, but no envy. That came later, with Rosemary.

I would no more have hidden the events of those few days from Robert than forget to breathe; I told him everything in those days, he accepting this proof of my admiration of him as if it were his due, and with the kind of half-contemptuous indulgence he might have shown to a younger brother. I never resented this, feeling privileged that he should choose my company over that of so many others (you see that I was immature in all my relationships), and with him I shared my passions and my enthusiasms and even my dreams.

Now you must remember that Rosemary was the most wonderful and bizarre and tumultuous thing that had ever happened to me. Of course I told him.

I was half delirious with excitement, and anxiety that if I dared to leave the house for an instant she might be gone when I returned, but I found him nevertheless, drinking coffee in his usual place, and hurried to tell him my news. I must have looked a sorry sight; I had not slept that night at all for thinking about Rosemary, my suit was crumpled, my eyes watery and my hair uncombed. Besides that, I had the beginnings of a streaming cold from jumping into the river; my throat was sore and my limbs ached. I told you I was no man of action. He grinned easily at me as I came in, stubbing out his cigarette in the marble ashtray in front of him. He put down the book he was reading (Morris' *News from Nowhere*) and beckoned the waitress to fetch another pot of coffee and a cup.

'Have you read this?' he demanded, waving the book vaguely in my direction. 'Marvellous. Did you know . . .' His brow creased slightly as he took in my crumpled appearance. 'What happened to you?' he

120

queried, with some amusement, 'you look like a mad inventor. Have you been out on the tiles again, or are you simply cultivating a kind of Byronic disarray?'

I swallowed, trying to tame the hair which was falling over my eyes.

'I thought you had to give a class this morning,' continued Robert. 'Aren't you late?' He looked at his watch. 'It's past nine.'

I shook my head, flinging my hat on the table. 'I cancelled it.'

'How very dashing of you,' he said comfortably. 'Go on then, don't keep me in suspense. I suppose whatever it is is something terribly exciting to make you skip classes. You're always so enviably precise.' And he sighed, a kind of self-mocking dramatic sigh you might have expected from Keats or Beardsley. He was laughing at me again, gently making fun of me, but underneath that I could tell that he was really puzzled, perhaps a little worried. Robert's veneer of sophistication was really rather thin, despite appearances; what others often mistook for pretentiousness was in reality nothing but protective coloration. I think retrospectively that he was an insecure man, projected from the hermetic atmosphere of public school and Cambridge into a traumatic, though mercifully brief, period of combat, he had returned to Cambridge to escape from ugliness in whatever way he could; he retreated into the close circle of the Cambridge intellectuals, going to lectures, staying up late to talk about art and poetry in smoky coffee-shops. To him it was all escapism, and while his doting father was willing to encourage and finance his study, Robert was happy to remain the eternal student, gravitating towards ever more intellectual pursuits, shielded from pain and the unwanted complexity of adult relationships. Young as I was then I saw only the carefree, handsome exterior; later, with Rosemary, I saw my friend stripped to the bone, saw the uncertain,

121

crying infant beneath the good-natured posturing, but at the beginning Robert was my strength, my buffer against the unthinking cruelties inflicted on me by the world. He encouraged me in my work, talked to me, tolerated me; my gratitude was such that at that time I would willingly have died for him.

As it happened, our roles were reversed.

My story must have sounded garbled to him; I remember his quizzical smile, his hand coming down soothingly on my shoulder.

'Steady down, old fellow,' he said with a youthful grin. 'I don't know about you, but I'm never at my best first thing in the morning.'

I accepted his offer of coffee, tried to stop my hands from trembling around the china cup, began again. I think I was more coherent then; he listened to me, a faint crease between his brows, the cup held in the palm of one hand, a cigarette in the other, its smoke idling unhindered towards the ceiling. Once or twice he asked a question, nodded; I stumbled forward in my narrative, trying vainly to put words to what I felt, the words cleaving to my tongue as I spoke. When I had stopped speaking, I drank deeply from my cup, blew my nose and waited, watching him over my glasses, half contorted with fear lest he should laugh at me, for he did sometimes hurt me with his mockery, although he never meant to. Maybe he saw the fear in my eyes, because he paused, almost appraisingly, as if deciding whether to treat my story seriously or to take it as a joke. He took a drag at his cigarette, blew the smoke out of the corner of his mouth and frowned.

'Seems like a funny kind of business to me,' he said blandly, pouring himself another cup of coffee. 'I wonder if you're not landing yourself in trouble somehow.'

I shook my head violently. 'Oh, no! If only you'd *seen* her, Robert, you'd know that isn't true. I know how odd it sounds, old man, but . . . oh, confound it!

There's no way I can put it into words . . . but . . . she's a miracle, Robert, a dream come true. It isn't her fault that she was a . . . that she . . . I swear it couldn't be. She's from another age.'

Robert cast me a humorous look.

'She certainly seems to have taken you back to the age of chivalry,' he commented slyly. 'However, you do have a history of being taken for a ride.' (He was referring to an earlier, abortive liaison of mine which had earned me a certain amount of good-tempered mockery from this young man who had never had a moment's difficulty in making himself popular with the ladies.)

'Oh, please be serious!' I pleaded. 'If only you had seen her.'

'I doubt whether it would have made any difference,' he said lazily, 'I think I'm immune to women. They never seem to have any conversation other than themselves and their clothes and other women. I know your experience isn't very vast, but believe me, after you've known a few they all seem to melt into each other and form a kind of broad tapestry of tedium.' His eyes twinkled, and I knew he was making fun of me; that languid tone was not the real Robert, but the man behind the many affectations was an elusive character, and I had not encountered him often.

'Robert!' I was twisted and cramped with tension and embarrassment, for Robert had spoken in a loud voice, and a number of other members of the coffee-shop's clientele had turned to look at us. He grinned at me, a roguish light dancing in his eyes.

'However, I admit to some curiosity,' he added, 'I have not yet encountered the Perfect Woman, and I would very much like to see her.'

I sighed with relief, clapped Robert on the back and managed to spill a cup of coffee in my enthusiasm. I felt like a schoolboy who has just been complimented by a sixth-form hero.

123

'Good man!' I cried. 'We'll see her now. Shall we? You won't be disappointed, Robert. You'll love her, you really will. You'll see. You won't be disappointed.'

As it happened, I was right; he did love her, and he was not disappointed. Cold enough comfort that offers me, even though I could not be expected to know – how could I have known? I am blameless, I know that, but the knowledge does not stop my ultimate guilt, or obliterate the memory of that singing, youthful joy I felt that day, as I happily led my friend across the river to his destruction.

Two

Cambridge, *April 1990*

Well, thought Alice, that line of enquiry had only led to a baffling dead-end. The Reverend Holmes had certainly never seen Ginny or her friends, nor had anything he told Alice seemed to corroborate her strange, prophetic dream. She was still inclined to think that Ginny had gone out with friends to buy or sell drugs (the syringes in the wardrobe certainly pointed to that), and what Alice herself had experienced had simply been an isolated incident of memory-loss caused by exhaustion or the beginnings of some virus. Fair enough. It even sounded convincing. But there was still the mystery of Ginny to solve; still Alice's resolution to befriend the girl and try to give her what help she could; and to do that, she needed to know more about her. Joe? She remembered his chilly response to her earlier questions on the phone, and doubted that he would be of any help. Who then?

Alice pondered the question for a moment, frowning, then her face cleared. Reaching for the directory, she flicked quickly through the medical section, allowing her fingers to come to rest on the letter F.

'Hello? My name is Alice Farrell. I wonder if you could give me a few details on a former patient of yours.'

'Please wait a moment.' The receptionist's voice was cool and competent. 'I'll put you through to the doctor on duty.'

Alice waited for a few minutes, while the hospital's hold system piped would-be soothing music through the earpiece. Then she heard the tone change, and a man's voice, dry and faintly irritable, answered.

'Yes? Doctor Menezies speaking.'

Alice repeated what she had told reception.

'Why the inquiry?' the doctor asked warily. 'Are you professionally interested?'

'Not exactly.'

'Well, in that case, I'm very busy.'

'Just a few details, please. This girl is going to be staying with me for a few days, and I'm a little worried about her mental condition.'

'Then make an appointment for her. All cases are treated as confidential here. I don't discuss my patients.'

'I don't need confidential details,' began Alice, 'I just need to know if a girl called Virginia Ashley was a patient here, and whether she is likely to need special help while—'

'Look,' snapped the doctor. 'There are dozens of doctors in this hospital. I don't know the case at all. Obviously someone else treated her. If you will just wait a moment, I will tell you the name of the colleague who dealt with her case, and you can contact him.'

And he slammed the receiver back onto hold.

Alice waited again. After a much longer time, the receiver was lifted, and she heard the man's voice again, more distant this time, as if the line had suddenly worsened.

'Ms Farrell?'

'Yes?'

'I can only give you details which we would consider available to the general public,' began Doctor Menezies. 'However, anything of a more confidential

126

nature must be authorized by Miss Ashley herself. She was admitted to Fulbourn last Christmas on a short-term basis, suffering severe depression following a suicide attempt.' The doctor sighed. 'She was here as a boarder for nearly a month, then for six months as an outpatient. She made good progress on the medication we prescribed for her, and should be on her way to full recovery. That's all the information I'm prepared to give without the patient's prior consent.'

'Can I talk to the doctor in charge of her case?' asked Alice.

'I'm sorry; that's impossible.'

'Could you give me the name of the doctor?' insisted Alice, swallowing her irritation.

'Look, I'm afraid there is no way you can talk to Doctor Pryce,' he went on. 'My colleague died last week. In fact, the funeral was yesterday.'

'Oh!' Alice was disarmed. 'I'm sorry. I . . . Thank you . . . you've been very helpful.'

So Ginny *had* been a patient at Fulbourn Hospital (whatever had prompted her to believe that Ginny had lied about that?), and she already suspected that the girl had been an addict. Joe had hinted at earlier misfortunes; Alice guessed that these might stem from previous, less loving relationships, leading to an inability to cope with other people. This, coupled with Ginny's extreme youth and the enforced isolation of drug-dependency, could well lead to severe depression, lack of confidence and possible suicidal tendencies. Yes, Alice, as she sat by the phone looking out of the window, began to feel a growing sympathy for Ginny, a desire to know her, to share her problems. After all, if Alice had been eighteen when . . . She remembered her father in hospital the last time she saw him, his yellowed flesh fallen in on his bones, the smell of him, like talcum powder and acetone and stale denture breath. Remembered seeing him and not seeing him; a young newly-wed with a passing resemblance to Cary Grant, a middle-aged man with a shiny bald head like a toffee-apple; making corn-dollies for Alice and showing her how to plant the little broad beanplants in neat rows. Her mother arranging the funeral with dull and applied precision, lining out the plates of sandwiches and sausage rolls and little individually wrapped cheeses. Herself in the months after Joe; the illness which had not really been an illness (like *Rolling Stone*, I just went out of circulation for a while . . .), the loss of momentum which had left her drifting and directionless, out of orbit.

Yes, she knew all about isolation and the inability to cope.

Poor Ginny.

One

Cambridge, *April 1947*
Fulbourn Hospital, *November 1977*

She was gone when we got to the house, and I knew a
dreadful instant of panic, certain then that I would
never see her again, half distracted with the idea that
perhaps she had never been real, that I had imagined
her, and that like the Snow-child, she had simply
dissolved into air and water at the first rays of the sun.
Mrs Brown was out, and I remember my voice, eager
and cracked as a schoolboy's, calling flatly through the
house, every room throwing back the sound of her
absence in my face, every breath a new emptiness. I
must have been more ill than I thought, for my head
raged with fever and my eyes felt like eggs behind the
swimming lenses of my glasses, but none of that
registered. All I could think was, she was gone. She
was gone, and the one person I could trust with my
mystery, my only friend, the only one who could
understand my worship of her was looking at me with
a mischievous expression in his eyes, as if he did not
believe me; to tell the truth, I harldy believed myself.

'Look, there's her bed,' I cried violently, the
crumpled coverlet in my hands. 'The pillow she rested
on . . . There'll be hair on it . . . let me see . . . Look! The
cup she drank from . . . her flowers!'

'Come on, old man,' said Robert, still with that
humorous expression. 'Don't take it so badly. Like as

not she's just stepped out for a walk . . . and even if she hasn't, you know, it won't do to get all in a fuss about it.' He patted my shoulder, perhaps meaning to reassure me, but I flinched away like a startled puppy.

'She was here a minute ago, I swear it! She was—'

'Have a drink, there's a good chap,' he interrupted patiently. 'Sit down, stop moving about . . . that's the ticket.'

He pushed me gently into one of Mrs Brown's soft leather armchairs, pressed a glass of sherry into my hand. My arm jerked violently; some of the sherry spilled. Patiently, he took the glass from me and refilled it. I drank, shuddered (I was not a drinking man in those days), drained the glass and closed my eyes, fever washing over me in a fetid wave, an ache in the pit of my stomach. I have no way of explaining the power Rosemary had managed to gain over me, nor the spinning litany of despair which played in me over and over, like the monotonous whirring of a toy train in a child's spinning-top . . . but there were wheels within wheels spinning for Rosemary that day, and I suppose she knew it. She was gone, she was gone, she was gone, she was gone . . . Fragments of poetry entered my brain like flying glass, images like pieces of a torn canvas, tantalizing . . . the curve of a collar-bone here, the light on her hair, a certain turn of her mouth . . . Memories of her showered me like confetti, fairy-like or sensual. I had had time to fall in love with her, and the love which was in me knew that she had gone from me forever; call it premonition, if you like, but I knew. I tried to get up from my chair . . . slipped . . . the world tilted. Suddenly the air was thick, opaque, my breath spinning into blackness, the tiny sound of the sherry-glass falling onto the carpet a million miles deep beneath the night. I grasped the arm of the chair, missed, heard Robert, his voice muffled by the night, call my name.

'Daniel!' His words were spindly structures rising

towards me out of nothingness. 'Are you all right? Hey, Danny! Stop horsing about, you idiot. Danny!'

A tremor in the earth as I fell.

Spangled darkness all around.

A voice, light as an aspen leaf, crystallizing in ether; 'Is anything wrong?'

A brief glimpse of a figure standing in the doorway, head and shoulders etched in copper.

'Where's Daniel? Who are you?' A voice sharpened by controlled hysteria.

Robert's voice, 'So you're Rosemary.'

Then, in the darkness, a vision of wheels. Turning.

Two

Cambridge, *April 1990*

Joe's band were on the stage setting up; Joe waved and grinned at Alice as she came in, then returned to the business in hand, oddly competent in his chosen element, positioning speakers and amps and coiling cables with speed and economy of movement. Ginny was not yet there.

With a shrug, Alice made her way to the bar and ordered a drink, seating herself at a table by the side of the stage, where she would be able to see and hear everything. Little by little, the room began to fill up with all the variegated and bohemian night-lifers of Cambridge, rubbing together in the semi-erotic closeness of the neon and shadow. Alice stood up and looked around the crowded room; Ginny was still not there.

The first band played, and the crowd settled down to listen, some talking quite softly amongst themselves as they stood at the bar, most of them drifting to the music. Somebody near the back lit a couple of joints, and soon the room was permeated by the scent, thick and heavy as patchouli. Alice ordered another drink as the group left and Joe's band took their place; she even took a stroll around the hall to see if she could find Ginny, but without success. She had just returned to her place by the stage when Ginny appeared; a slight, hesitant figure in a pale dress, and Alice beckoned to

133

her to come and sit with her. The girl acknowledged her gesture with a nod, but made no movement to come across.

The lights dimmed; and the band went into the introduction to a slow, traditional song Alice knew well; it was a favourite of Joe's, 'The Dalesman's Litany'. Joe had come to the front to sing, his bass around his neck, a single spotlight on his face. His voice was stronger than Alice remembered it, the northern accent still in evidence, the tone still charged with emotion, but more mellow. She liked the change.

> 'It's hard when folks can't find their work
> Where they've been bred and born . . .'

She reached the back of the hall, where a few latecomers were standing, holding cans. She scanned the darkness for Ginny. The spotlight was off now, the quiet mood of the music highlighted by soft green and blue filters which lit the faces of the audience with a drowned underwater glow.

> 'When I was young I always thought
> I'd mind my roots and corn . . .'

Ginny was waiting at the other side of the crowd; Alice could see her drowned-girl's face, the livid dress, her hair black in the stage-lights, face impossibly pale, eyes supernaturally huge.

> 'But now I've come to work in towns
> And here's my litany . . .'

For an instant Ginny looked at her; and perhaps it was the light, but it seemed to Alice that her tragic mouth curled in a rictus of such complex malevolence that it transfigured her entirely, illuminating her from within with a ghastly radiance, like radioactivity.

134

'From Hull and Halifax and hell
The good Lord deliver me . . .'

Then the expression was gone, and there was only
Ginny, with her air of blank and almost simple-minded
sweetness as she watched the stage. But whatever
Alice had seen or imagined, it was enough to kill any
desire to be near her; she lingered at the fringes of the
audience, still holding her drink, and was it her
imagination again, or had the atmosphere of the
concert suddenly changed? Had that group of people
standing by the door been there all the time? Had there
been that subtly charged undercurrent of tension and
ugliness trembling at the edges of the hall?

The band had gone into a solo instrumental, the
violin stretching, almost unbearably, through the
registers, groaning and shrieking, a raw tendon on the
edge of exquisite, undisclosed tortures. It was too
much for Alice. She felt stifled, drowning, spread-
eagled in the cross-currents of emotion coming from
the crowd and the stage. Instinctively, she began to
move towards the door, where there was some room
to breathe and stand away from the audience. A few
others must have had the same idea, she observed, for
there was a little group of people watching the stage
from the doorway; a girl with hair almost to her knees,
outlined in neon from the EXIT sign, a youth with dyed
red hair and a bird tattoo on his face, a blonde girl, her
head laid confidingly on the red-haired lad's shoulder
. . . a man in a dark greatcoat, face in shadow.

Alice felt the hairs on her bare arms rise. The stance
was familiar, arrogant and relaxed . . . so were the
lights reflected from the metal tip of a motorcycle boot.

So what? she thought, half angrily, taking another
step towards the door. There were dozens of men who
looked like that. There was no reason to think that it
might be Ginny's friend of the night before. No reason
to remember her dream, to suddenly feel the sting of

sweat under her arms, in her throat's soft hollow. No one looked her way. Another step ... and suddenly their eyes were upon her, and the blonde girl lifted her head from the shoulder of her red-haired companion. No girl, this. It was a young boy, spectrally fair, beautiful, disturbing. The redhead grinned at Alice, showing a gold tooth, beckoned ... and Alice knew, without doubt and with suddden, blinding clarity that she could never go near them, perhaps touch them ... that behind their beauty was something corrupt and terrible. She pulled away, unreasonable panic raising the hairs on her arms, feeling their savage humour reach out to her as she rejoined the crowd, and with the humour, a kind of attraction, a glamour which promised exquisite contradictions in bliss and despair.

She tried to concentrate on the music, but the spell was broken. Only the watchers behind her remained, thrilling the nape of her neck. The spectators around her seemed restless too, like a herd which scents the predator.

She glanced to her left and saw Ginny, closer now, almost by the door. As she watched, the group closed around her, protectively. Ginny lit a cigarette; the sweet smell of cannabis reached Alice across the hall over the hot reek of sweat and lager.

A voice behind her, raised angrily, the sound a raw wound in the dark's throat. A ripple ran through the audience, a shiver, like anticipation. She turned, saw an older man approach the little group of watchers at the door. She could not hear what he was saying, but saw his face, briefly, swollen with anger. He did not look strong, not beautiful with the beauty of these strange savage ones; he was balding, hiding the fact beneath a leather hat, long wispy hair trailing out from the back. To Alice he looked oddly vulnerable, half drowned in the lights and his desperate, questing rage. She heard no words, but saw the tall man smile, speak. Ginny stared, blank, flawless. The man gestured

136

wildly, turned, was engulfed into the crowd. Alice did not see the fight break out, but she saw the repercussions. First, a depression in the rising tide of people; a dimple of bowed heads. It exploded outwards, ripples moving towards the outside. Someone fell. The music faltered but did not stop; a woman screamed, the sound a flight of birds in the dark. A voice from the stage, through the PA its message lost in a squeal of feedback. She looked to the door; they were still there, untouchable, blank, but she could feel the power coming from them, the attraction and the amusement. She moved towards them, irresistibly, the crowd already beginning to push at her back. She saw a man fall in the crowd, shockingly close, saw another strike out, almost aimlessly, at a woman, who stumbled into the wall. The music stopped. Some instrument began to feed back on a high, unbearable frequency.

As if at a signal, the voice of the crowd was raised, ululating in a toneless music of its own. As Alice reached the door someone screamed; 'FIRE!' Someone threw a full glass at the stage. The glass exploded under the lights like fireworks. Someone shoved her hard in the small of the back and she was sent flying uncontrollably towards the dark man at the door. She felt his arms around her, holding her upright against the crowd's undertow. He whispered a word in her ear which in her panic she did not assimilate, something low and intimate against her hair. He smelt of something sweet, almost sugary, like toffee or candy-floss. His hands were cold as stone, his breath cool against her face. For an interminable second, Alice was absurdly, utterly convinced that he was going to kiss her, and that in that moment she would die, but the knowledge was something abstract, nightmarish, her scream someone else's voice heard from under water. She was aware that she was about to pass out and tried to speak, but could not form words. She tilted helplessly into the rushing silence.

It was only a minute later, when she was safely outside, stretched out on the damp grass, looking up into the concerned face of a medic that she remembered what the man had whispered in her ear.

The word was *chosen*.

One

Cambridge, *May 1947*
Fulbourn Hospital, *December 1977*

I was ill with Cam fever for a long time; long enough for Rosemary to do her work, and more, and in my fever I dreamed and cried out in suffering and in joy. For she was there always, haunting and caressing me, singing wild songs, flying through the air, riding the wind. I dreamed of her by the side of a river, flowers in her hands; I dreamed her drowned, hands folded over her pale breast, weeds in her mermaid hair; I dreamed her a witch, riding the storm astride her broom, hair flying, white legs tantalizing in flight, beckoning. For near to a fortnight I was ravaged by fever and by dreams of such potency that they left me gasping for a breath of reality, and while I raved and sweated out my fever I betrayed my friend Robert for the first time, leaving him alone with Rosemary. When I recovered it was too late.

My first inkling of it was when Mrs Brown came to give me my broth. I remembered her doing so at intervals during my illness, but in my mind she became confused with many people, and I had not yet been able to speak lucidly to her. But that day, I was feeling weak but clear-headed, and my first thought was of Rosemary.

'Where is she?' I asked her, between two clumsy

mouthfuls of broth. 'Is she all right? She hasn't been ill, has she?'

'Now, now,' scolded Mrs Brown. 'Plenty of time for that later, my lad.'

'Please!' I begged. 'Is she still here? You didn't send her away?'

'Mr Robert's found her somewhere to live, so don't you fret,' answered Mrs Brown bluntly.

That was the moment when I began to suspect that more had gone on in those two weeks than she wanted to admit. But she would tell me nothing; all she cared about was to see me well again; as for the rest, that could wait until I was better prepared for it.

Robert did not come to see me; I assumed that Mrs Brown had told him that I must not be disturbed, and did not worry, but I missed Rosemary desperately, and I was anxious that she might attract criticism from Robert for her unwitting part in my illness. And so I continued to fret until the day the doctor told me I could leave my bed, and then I dressed hastily, ignoring all protests from Mrs Brown that it was raining, that I was still not well; with my battered hat on my head and a crumpled woollen cravat around my sore throat I went off in search of my friend. He was not in his usual place; not in any of his usual places, and his lodging was shut. I tried all the tea-shops, all the bars; I tried his tutors, who told me that they had not seen him for nearly a fortnight, and at last, I began to suspect that there was something wrong. Not that my suspicions were anywhere near the truth, but as I dragged my weariness and my anxiety through the drizzle and the greyness of the unchanging Cambridge streets I began to feel a sense of foreboding and hopelessness which in my weakened state almost prostrated me. The mirage of Rosemary followed me everywhere; it was she I saw when a girl in a yellow scarf pushed past me through a gateway, she I saw sheltering under a bridge, she the face looking through a streaming window-lattice, she I ran to when I caught a glimpse of her behind the counter of a shop. And then, I really saw her, and the joy which broke upon me was like the sun. Robert was holding his umbrella over her, his arm on hers, looking down at her so that I could see his profile; a smile on his aquiline countenance, dark hair falling over his forehead. Rosemary was wearing a black raincoat several sizes too big for her, the large cuffs turned over and over to reveal her small hands, her hair tucked into the side of the collar so that I could see the white nape of her neck. I called, but the rain snatched away my words. I ran towards the two of them, splashing clumsily through the puddles ... then I stopped. Rosemary turned towards Robert, her hands on the lapels of his coat, uttered a word ... then he kissed her, lightly, with the intimacy of long acquaintance. I froze, then he kissed her again, with passion this time, his arms tight around her, the umbrella falling from his hand.

The world slipped with it.

My unspoken words slipped away like watercolours in the rain, to join the floating debris in the gutters. I wiped my glasses, trying to bring the world back into focus, but the image doubled again, trebled, so that I did not know my tears from the rain. I was close enough to them to see the water-drops fall onto Rosemary's shiny black raincoat. One ... One ... Many. So much to say ... so much already said ... I stood there, my pain within me in a tight ravelled ball, and wondered whether I would ever speak again. Oh, Rosemary ...

And then she turned, her face a fathom deep, her mermaid hair framing it damply, darkly, and looked right at me. I'm sure she did; she looked at me, and for a moment her eyes held me, the colour of rain ... and I read humour there, and a cold, wise contempt, and something else ... something like triumph. Oh, she knew, she knew all right; I would have staked my life

141

on it, she knew I was watching, and she knew all my pitiful thoughts and jealousies, knew all my life, my future and my death, saw them without pity and dismissed them all. She had Robert, and she had me, and knowing that, she turned away with him into the Cambridge rain, taking my innocence with her.

Two

Cambridge, *April 1990*

Alice went home feeling sick and dizzy, the unbearable
tensions of that evening having left her exhausted.
After the crowd had stampeded in the Corn Exchange,
she had found Joe in confrontation with a police officer
who was trying to persuade him to come to the station
to give evidence. At the far side of a little group of
stragglers and police, she could see the garish, almost
menacing figure he made in the bright lights, shaking
his head angrily, with the over-emphasized gestures of
shock or drunkenness, turning away. The policeman
tried to catch him by the arm; Joe shook him off
abruptly. Another policeman, sensing trouble, took a
step towards him, a fairground figure in the revolving
lights of the departing ambulance.

Damn.

Alice knew Joe's relationship with the police of old;
he had a habit of picking quarrels at demonstrations,
and had been taken in on several occasions for
supposedly violent behaviour, although Alice knew
that he had never really meant to cause trouble. She
supposed she would have to intervene before Joe hit
someone, or got hit himself, and she ran out of the
Corn Exchange doorway towards the little knot of
people which had gathered around the cars. A dozen
or so were standing around, though there was no sign
of Ginny's friends.

Joe turned when he heard her voice, his face registering relief.

'Thank God. Is Ginny with you?'

Alice shook her head.

'Shit! Where the hell did she go? Where was she standing?'

'Relax, Joe. She was right at the back of the hall, with some friends. She must have got out right away, and gone off with them. Don't worry.'

'What do you mean?' His anger focused on Alice. 'What friends? She doesn't have any friends.'

'She did tonight,' said Alice, with a glance at the policeman. 'Look . . .' (putting her hand on his arm and hoping she could make him cool off) '. . . she's probably gone home, and I'll find her waiting for me on the doorstep. There's really no reason to worry about Ginny. I'm sure she can look after herself.'

Joe didn't look convinced. His mouth tightened in a stubborn expression she knew of old.

'I'll take you home in the band's van,' he said, then, turning to the policeman, continued. 'So you see, I can't help you. I didn't see anything, anyway. I was on stage. The first I knew of it was when someone started throwing bottles. Sorry. OK?'

'I'll have to ask you to come with me, sir,' answered the policeman (politely enough, though his patience seemed to be wearing thin). 'It won't be for long, but—'

'Dammit, what's with you! I told you . . .' (shaking away the officer's restraining hand) '. . . Get off me!' He took a deep breath and, with an effort, brought himself under control.

'I'll phone you to find out whether Ginny got back,' he told Alice.

Alice gave him a quick smile.

'Fine. And keep your temper, hey?'

'I'm okay.'

She hoped he was.

*

144

The first thing she did when she got home was to make a pot of tea. The cats were imperious, demanding their food, and she opened a tin for them and mixed the fish with bread. There were biscuits in the cupboard, and she opened a packet and ate them, without hunger or pleasure, between swallows of tea until she began to feel the helpless panicky aftermath of the night's events subside. Ginny hadn't been waiting on the doorstep, but then again, Alice hadn't for a minute imagined she would. Very likely she was still with her friends of the other night, the friends Joe didn't know about. (Clothes hidden in the cupboard like murder victims; syringes wrapped in silver paper.) Alice suddenly found that she didn't care. In fact, she thought fiercely as she sipped from her mug, the less she learned about Ginny the better. It was none of her business.

She put down the empty mug, reached out to switch on the gas fire beside her armchair . . . sat up. Just for a second, she imagined a movement out there in the night – a figure shifting into the darkness. She stood up. Nothing. It was probably her own reflection in the window. She reached up to pull down the blind . . . and hesitated. There it was again, that movement, part furtive, part mocking. Inviting her out to investigate. Ginny?

Alice jerked down the blind, inwardly cursing her nervousness. There was nobody there. Even if there had been, it was the height of paranoia to think that someone could be spying on her . . . even more ridiculous to imagine for even one minute that it could be *him*, Ginny's friend with the pony-tail, the one who had steadied her during that mad rush towards the door. No, that would be such a stupid thing to think . . . that . . . that . . .

Very carefully, Alice parted the cane slats of the blind. Nothing there but the street, she thought furiously. No one there at all. Only the street-lamp and the trees. Only . . .

There were two figures standing beside the street-lamp. Alice flinched back towards the kitchen, switching off the light as she did so. Adrenalin flushed her, fear stapled her tongue to her mouth.

No!

Not him. Not him, standing so close she could have seen his face from the window, watching, somehow knowing she was there . . . She would not look again. She would simply go and sit down, listen to some music, ignore whatever was going on outside. He was waiting for some girl, probably. Standing outside Alice's house waiting for a girl.

Not just any girl.

The thought overtook her before she could stop it, flooding her with mingled relief and apprehension. Of course. That was it. He was waiting for Ginny. He knew she was staying there with Alice, and he was waiting for her to come back. Maybe he loved her. That thought steadied Alice for a moment. Slowly, she forced herself to go back to the window in the dark, to part the blinds again, to look. Coldly, she noted what she saw.

It was him again, and this time she could see him clearly. He was still wearing his greatcoat, collar turned up so that a wing of it hid part of his face. Alice could see long hair, tied loosely back and spilling over the collar below a pale, angular face with deep shadows at the eyes and cheekbones. He seemed to be looking straight at her, but she knew now that it was only an optical illusion caused by the shadow play. His companion was the blond boy, and she could see his face clearly. He was thin and bony, with that half-grown graceful angularity peculiar to adolescent boys. Alice took him to be no older than sixteen, and his face, beneath a shock of bleached blond hair, was disturbingly beautiful. Under a black leather bike jacket, Alice glimpsed a white T-shirt with the slogan DEATH OR GLORY printed on it, and was poignantly reminded of Ginny; a few centuries ago, without those cheap adolescent trappings, he might well have posed for Botticelli. He turned to the taller man, said something. The tall man shrugged, without taking his eyes from the window. The boy shivered, looked at the sky, pulled his jacket tighter. Maybe they were cold, thought Alice.

On the tail of that thought came another, at the same time compulsive and terrifying: Why not ask them in? That way she would find out who they were and what their exact relationship to Ginny was. Maybe she would find out what Ginny had to hide . . . maybe find a way to gain her intimacy. She hesitated for a moment, remembering the syringes and the obscure sensation of dread she had felt on first glimpsing them, remembering the concert, and her certainty that they had orchestrated what had happened there. Then she shook off the thought, irritated at her own cowardice, flipped on the light and opened the door. Light flooded out, spilling onto the doorstep and she found that she could hardly see the two figures as they merged into the shadows.

'Excuse me,' she said to the darkness, 'are you waiting for Ginny? I think she'll be back soon; in fact I thought she might have been with you. You're quite welcome to come in here and wait for her, if you like.'

For a moment, there was no answer, and Alice had the peculiar sensation that she was calling down a tunnel, with only the echoes of her own voice to answer her. Then two faces turned towards her from the dark.

'We're friends of Virginia.' It was the tall man; his voice was quiet and cultured, unexpectedly, given his bohemian appearance. As he stepped closer to the light, Alice noticed that he was older than she had first thought; the fine-boned face was lined, giving it a hard look, and the long hair was touched with grey.

'Do come in,' urged Alice. 'Wait for her in the warm.

I'll make you coffee if you like.'

The door was wide, but the stranger made no move to go in. The boy stepped through the gate, lingered at the fringes of the light, but said nothing. There was a silence, rather too long for comfort, and Alice began to feel a little embarrassed. A little frightened. She shook herself mentally. What possible harm could come to her here, in the light? In her own house? Cat poked her head through the door to see what was going on, hissed furiously and fled back in, knocking over a plant-stand as she went.

Alice shrugged and smiled, still feeling uneasy.

'Cats,' she said apologetically. 'Who knows what's going on in their heads?'

The blond boy grinned, exposing slightly uneven teeth.

'Do come in,' said Alice, rather desperately. 'It's getting a bit cold out here.'

At once, as if they had only been waiting to be asked a third time, Ginny's two friends came through the door into Alice's living-room, bringing a cold draught with them.

'I'm Alice,' said Alice conversationally. 'Are you old friends of Ginny's?'

'My name is Java,' said the tall man with a smile. 'My young companion is Rafe. Yes, we're old friends.' His smile caught the blond boy's sharply, intimately.

'Very old friends,' he repeated.

It had been a long time since anyone had offered them anything in good faith, and they glanced at each other from their pale eyes and smiled secret smiles over their coffee-cups. They said little, knowing that the girl was embarrassed, knowing that she had no idea why she had invited them in, scenting her distrust and her fear.

'You're a painter.'

It wasn't a question; there was hardly any change in his tone of voice. His eyes stayed on his hands; one

148

finger in the palm of the other, tracing the lines there.

The girl nodded, seemingly with an effort. She looked around for her cats, but they had vanished with that peculiar ease only cats have, and her hands twisted uselessly in her lap.

'Do you do portraits?'

'No.' She took a swallow of her tea; he could tell it tasted vile to her, but she took another gulp anyway. 'No portraits.'

'All painters do portraits.' Again, that glance at the boy, as if hinting at some intimate joke; his eyes were a strangely cold, pale shade of green, like a cat's, the pupil tiny as a pinprick. He nodded at the two finished paintings of the girl she had tacked to the cork notice-board.

'They're portraits.'

'I finished that the other day. Do you like it? But I didn't use a model; the figure is just made up, you know, just there to complete the mood of the painting.'

'It looks like Virginia.'

Alice looked up, startled. Her gaze bounced away from his like a polar magnet; he could tell she was looking at the painting, all her peace destroyed.

'That's because of the hair,' she said. 'Red. Very dramatic. Good for the colour-scheme. And I kept it anonymous on purpose ... you know ... her face is mostly hidden, so it could be anyone.' She laughed, nervously.

He smiled. 'Not anyone,' he said, fixing her again with his cold green glare. The humour in his smile was lazily contemptuous as he watched her, relishing her: the play of her hands in her lap, belying her efforts at conversation, the turn of her face as she tried not to watch him too closely, the attraction which sent her eyes flicking towards his in spite of herself. Such a mild dark gaze, thought Java, the eyes of a tame rabbit in a cage; but behind the mildness, something closer to himself, something like the promise of destruction. He

149

found himself looking forward to the time when he would know her better.

He knew that she heaved a sigh of relief when they left; had known how she locked the door behind them and drawn the curtains. Sensed her at the window, watching them leave, her thoughts simmering.

'Come on,' he told the boy, who was lingering behind, regret in his beautiful eyes. He knew he would have liked to stay awhile, and he knew why, but there would be others. The boy was unwise and impulsive, always thirsty, uncaring of consequences. Java was older, more conscious of the forces which drove them both, the trails they left, the hunters which followed. He stretched out his long hands, rested one on the nape of the boy's neck, one on his cheek, a shiver of cold sensuality running through them both. The boy reached out to touch him, his lips slightly parted, but Java drew away with a warning gesture.

'Later,' he said softly.

He knew Alice would follow as she had once before, trusted in that half-conscious promise of chaos in her eyes. He waited for her like a lover, with a lover's tenderness. He sensed the moment of her decision, smiled as she left her vantage point at the window, gave a low laugh as she drew the bolt. She was his.

The night was close and hot, street-lamps flinging orange reflections onto the low clouds, and Alice wondered whether it was going to rain. Let it, she decided; she was not going to turn back for that. She kept to the shadows, never moving closer than a hundred yards to the two garish neon-lit figures as they half ran at a slick pace down the narrow streets, casting long arcs of shadow onto the pavements as they moved. They made no sound; Alice was conscious of the scuffling of her tennis-shoes on the pavements, of the sounds of her clothes as she brushed walls and archways, but Rafe and Java were utterly silent, never exchanging a word or slackening the pace of their eerie nightwalk. Almost panting, Alice followed.

The town centre was empty; windows and doorways were dark blind eyes and closed mouths, the occasional lighted window like a defiance to the conquering night. A couple of tramps waited on benches by the side of the market-square, occasionally dipping into a brown paper bag which contained a bottle of cider and watching the night with streaming, incurious eyes. This was their time, the people of the night, when the Colleges had locked their gates and the pubs closed their doors and the security-men patrolled the shopping-precinct to make sure no undesirables were lurking in the shop-fronts. That was when the old men came out of hiding, silent, hunched in their tattered overcoats and fingerless gloves, perpetually cold, even though Alice had long since taken off her pullover and flung it across her shoulders (the sweating heat of the night was more than she could bear, and the thick wool prickled against her damp skin); they met under the bridges and in the shelter of church-buttresses and bus-stops, signalling to each other in their unknown ways and taking over the night secretly, arrogantly, as if to say:

'This is our time, and don't forget it.'

Alice spared them not a glance as she crossed the town centre; but their eyes were on her.

She allowed that compulsive curiosity to drive her; absurd as it was, it would not leave her alone. The foolish circle of her thoughts kept on turning in her mind like an irritating tune (. . . Ginny . . . remembrance . . . Joe . . . words uttered hastily and almost inaudibly behind a closed door . . . the gleam of metal in the near-darkness . . . a dancer's figure pirouetting at the edge of an opened grave . . . one word whispered intimately in her ear as she stood on the brink of unconsciousness); impelled and drawn by

151

some force which was much more than mere curiosity, she was about to set off again, when she became aware of a presence at her elbow and she turned to see who it was. An old tramp, scrubbily bearded and muffled in a dirty pink scarf, a woollen hat on his greyish-white hair, and carrying the inevitable brown paper bag, had hesitantly moved to her side. Both arms were clamped around the precious bag, and he seemed reluctant to speak, but his eyes were feverish with something wild and senile, like hope.

Alice started. For a moment the tramp's eyes fixed her, and she knew, with a strange, hallucinating clarity, that some message of dreadful importance was about to be delivered. Then the moment passed, and with sudden, terrible urgency she turned and fled in pursuit of the two men on the road to Grantchester.

Alice was not certain what she had expected: another visit to St Mary's, perhaps, but Java and Rafe did not stay on the Grantchester road for long. Instead they turned towards the river about a mile before they reached the village, leading Alice down a dark section of street bordered by derelict terraces. There were no street-lamps, and Alice lost the two men from view on several occasions, feeling her way along the slick façades of the houses in almost total obscurity. From time to time she caught sight of Rafe's pale hair or a spark from one of Java's steel-capped boots in front of her, but apart from that she was totally blind. Sweat plastered her hair to her face, dripping in an irregular rhythm from her fringe into her eyes, and there was a tightness in her throat which no amount of swallowing could dispel. A snatch of music began to play, inconsequentially, in her mind:

(Strange little girl, where are you going?
Strange little girl, where are you going?
Str . . .)

*

Suddenly she heard a sound, shockingly near, and froze. She had come much closer than she had intended in the dark, and she was almost on them. A door opened, metal sparked against metal, and the flame of a cigarette lighter blossomed, impossibly bright, in the darkness. Instinctively Alice drew back; Rafe was standing at an open door, one foot on the step, and Java was holding the lighter, a cigarette between his teeth, hands cupped around the flame. A nimbus of light surrounded his head. He looked up as Alice shrank back towards the side of the wall, and although the shadows seemed impenetrable, smiled directly at her.

'Alice,' he said mildly. 'Won't you come in?'

For an instant, Alice's mind was a total blank. She murmured something unintelligible, took a step backwards, hit the kerb with her foot and almost fell. Making a partial recovery, she tried to smile, said something incoherent and implausible about going for a walk and getting lost, half turned to go. Java's quiet voice halted her; she imagined his mesmeric, inhuman gaze drawing her backwards like a fish on a hook.

'You have come such a long way,' he said reasonably. 'Perhaps you would like a drink before you go? Besides, Virginia is here.'

At Ginny's name Alice turned abruptly, her panic dissolving. She had been foolish, certainly, trying to shadow two strangers in the middle of the night, but her sudden terror was irrational. Surely no harm could come to her here, in Cambridge, no more than a mile from the town. Even now, she could see the tips of the College towers, black against the floodlit orange sky. Foolish, and perhaps ridiculous, but surely in no danger. Surely not. Besides, if Ginny was here . . . She shifted her gaze to the door, where Rafe was still standing, a tiny, secret smile touching his lips. If she backed out now, she told herself firmly, swallowing the panic which even now threatened, she might as well give up trying to find out anything else about Ginny or what had happened in Grantchester. She had dared to come this far, and she couldn't back out now.

'Do come in.' For a second time Alice was conscious of an undeniable attraction to him, an almost unbearable awareness of the beauty of the man, of the flawlessness of his angular features, an admiration of the perfect grace with which he stood, that more than sensual poetry of movement indicating that here was a creature entirely self-possessed, content to be himself and prey to none of the anxieties and insecurities of normal people. He radiated a glamour which was almost irresistible. Alice found herself smiling in response, and before she even knew it she was through the door and in the house.

By the cigarette-lighter's hesitant flame Alice found that she had entered a kind of lobby, where a number of stained and yellowed cards still bore the names of former residents. Beyond that a narrow staircase led to the upper floor. Rafe led the way with the light, and Java followed behind in silence. They passed several doors until they reached the correct one; Rafe opened it and went in. A spirit lamp by the window lit the room with a yellowish flare, casting monstrous shadows against the damp-stained walls, and Alice looked round. The room was filthy, with wooden boxes covered in blankets to serve as seats, and the remains of several meals littering the floor. A table stood in the centre of the room, with newspapers to cover it, and a dozen or so empty wine-bottles winking green and white in the lamplight. There was a smell of mould and dust, and a sweet undersmell, like incense. Ginny was sitting on an old sofa in the corner of the room, legs crossed, face turned up towards Alice with a peculiar insolence.

'So it's you,' she said without interest. 'Is Joe with you as well?'

Alice shook her head. 'He was looking for you. After

you went off he was worried.'

Ginny shrugged. 'So you came to find me. How nice. And now you're here? Now what do you want?'

Java's voice from behind her; 'To learn, of course. To know what we do in here.' He laughed lightly, touching the nape of Alice's neck with thrilling, icy fingers. She shivered. Rafe came a step closer, a cross-shaped earring dangling hypnotically . . . the sense of unreality was so overwhelming that Alice even forgot to feel afraid.

'I . . .' She realized that she had no idea what to say; feeling eerily light-headed, she gave a low laugh. A hand came up, with dreamlike slowness, to wipe her damp forehead; for a moment the arc of its motion seemed to fill the world. Java's arm crept round her waist, cold and intimate, and she caught another breath of the sweet circus smell which clung to him. She must be very tired, she thought vaguely; for a second, she was sure her eyes had closed of their own accord. Her head tilted back like a sleepy child's, her eyes beginning to close again . . .

A voice jerked her back to reality.

'Not here!' cried Ginny shrilly. 'Don't you have any sense?'

Alice started, aware for the first time that she had been half asleep in Java's arms, her face almost touching his.

'Soft,' he whispered against her hair, not releasing his grip.

Ginny sprang up from her reclining position on the couch.

'I said not here.'

Alice felt Java's movement of irritation, but his voice was still coaxing, seductive.

'Wait.' In a moment he had released Alice; still disorientated, she allowed herself to be propelled towards the little door at her back. Before she knew it she had been pushed through, the door shut after her.

Voices drifted towards her through the wood.

Whatever glamour had possessed her in the other room left her abruptly as soon as she was alone. A fear which was not only a fear of the dark came crashing down upon her like a giant wave. She tried the door, but it had been locked. She considered shouting to the others, but felt her tongue cleave to the roof of her mouth at the very thought of those three soft strangers. Claustrophobia overwhelmed her momentarily and she flailed out at the encroaching dark; then, forcing herself to be methodical, she began to feel along the walls to gauge the size and shape of the room.

It was barely larger than a cupboard; maybe six by eight feet, that was all, and she guessed from the tiles along one side that it had once been a bathroom. All fittings were now gone, however, and the only furniture was a stool or small table by the door. In the half-minute in which she had been in the room her eyes had had time to accustom themselves partially to the darkness, and she could just distinguish a thin silver scratch of light around the door-frame, etching a narrow line of brightness onto the tiles. And below that she imagined she could see a patch of shadow which was darker than the rest – something like a hole in the wall.

In a second she was on her hands and knees, exploring the hole; the bath had been ripped out of the wall, which itself was only plasterboard, and the wall was broken right the way to the other side. If only she could get her head and shoulders through . . . she thought she might. If the hole was only a little bit wider . . . On impulse she picked up the stool and jabbed at the rotten plaster. Something gave with a crumbling sound, and the air was suddenly filled with mouldering dust. She jabbed again. A voice from the other side of the door:

'Alice?'

Another voice, unintelligible but commanding. Alice needed only that. Head first she dived for the hole and pushed her way through the damp plasterboard, eyes watering, sweating face caked with dust. She grabbed a piece of rubble and used it to clear away the debris before her as she emerged into blackness. She took two reckless steps and half fell down the stairs; grabbing hold of the banister, she used it to guide her as she limped, at an agonizingly slow pace, down the stairs and into the street. Once she heard voices quite close behind her, bolted in panic, and almost fell, but somehow she reached the ground floor in spite of her panic, and within a minute was racing down the Grantchester road, mouth paper-dry, her heart a double bass-drum in her throat, her shadow a capering demon at her tail. She did not slacken her pace, her feet skimming the pavements as she was carried on a hot wave of adrenalin through the town and back to her own safe, warm house, slamming the door behind her. Only then did she allow herself the luxury of exhaustion; and later, as she sat in front of the fire trying to analyse what had happened she felt that slow, certain terror come upon her again, not the primitive terror she had felt in the dark of the derelict house, or the superstitious fear of the beautiful strangers who were Ginny's friends, but something far older and heavier. Her cheeks burned as if with the imprint of Java's touch, and as she looked at herself in the bathroom mirror she noticed that she was flushed and feverish-looking, with a strangeness in her eyes. She splashed cold water on her burning cheeks, then undressed and showered quickly, scrubbing her body with a kind of fervent anger which temporarily blocked the fear. But even as she scrubbed and splashed she remained conscious of that persistent feeling, a strange, unfocused *desire* . . . But for what? She did not know.

One

Cambridge, *April 1948*
Fulbourn Hospital, *December 1977*

Dreams again; more dreams. She walks them like a general walking a battlefield of her own making, the screams of the dying a hymn to her glory and her pride. Sometimes I try to write, sometimes I just drink gin and sit in the light. My books tell me many things, but never how to combat her, how to destroy her and her satellites. I am alone, as I was from the beginning. My walls are lined with books and pictures; her face stares out from every one, her names are written everywhere. I know her now; know her for what she is and has been for centuries: the Beast, the Nightwalker, the Scarlet Woman of poor Crowley's deluded worship ... Her face looks out from Grimm's fairy tales, from Dante, from Shakespeare and the Apocrypha ... from all countries and times when she has walked and fed, been feared and loved. I pray for deliverance, but hear only the howling of the pit below me, my words dead Latin in my withered mouth, the crucifix turning to blood on my lips. God is not home today. He walks with Rosemary.

It was a long time before I saw her again, after I came across them that time in the rain. Robert avoided me, as I avoided him, ashamed maybe of his betrayal, but more likely too much ensnared by Rosemary to care about old friends. I plunged back into my work; I began writing *The Blessed Damozel*, little knowing the truth of what I wrote, and time passed. Summer came and went in a blink, wet and cheerless, and I huddled in my cold room, cut-off gloves on my numb hands, and worked and read while Mrs Brown alternately fussed and worried, and rumours and insecurities chased catspaws of gritty wind outside. I visited galleries, libraries, the Ashmolean Museum in Oxford where so many of Rossetti's lovely pencil-drawings are exhibited, the Fitzwilliam Museum in Cambridge where his 'Girl in a Lattice' and his 'Mary Magdalen at the Door of Simon the Pharisee' and Millais' 'Bridesmaid' all lie hidden in basement archives. Rosemary's face blurred into wistful regret, fused with the beauty of other dead Pre-Raphaelite women, and though I did not forget her (who would?), there were times when I wondered whether she had not been a dream, and I made up for my longing with hours of unceasing work. I wrote hundreds of pages on technique, learning how the Pre-Raphaelites created their luminous effects by painting only with pure colours on a wet white background, on how Rossetti used red and green lead for flesh tones, knowing that he used impermanent colours which would fade and be lost with time, but not caring, as if the creation of beauty alone interested him. Perhaps he too was afraid of immortality. I studied their models, those strange tragic enchantresses; Lizzie Siddall and Jane Morris and Maria Zambaco, until I knew every aspect of their faces and histories. They were artists in their own right, most of them, fascinating and untouchable, serene and troubling. They peopled my fantasies, walking my dreams with Rosemary, the most Pre-Raphaelite of them all. I explored their influences, the poets they loved, Mallory and Tennyson and Keats. I re-read Grimm's fairy tales, Greek and Roman mythology, explored the dark side of the fantasy-world from which they came, discovered the works of Jung,

160

adapting all that I read to my newly emerging theories. I lost touch with most of my friends, cancelled many of my classes, made myself a virtual recluse in my lodging, saw the first version of *The Blessed Damozel* almost finished with midwinter ... worked on. I earned extra money by writing articles for the University art publications, things more of fiction than fact; lurid, self-indulgent works which now had little to do with technique and everything to do with a kind of Gothic craving for the sensations which my austere and scholarly life denied me. I interspersed my descriptions and essays with fairy-stories which grew ever blacker and stranger as the year bled into the next, and I kept writing, with a fevered and hungry lyricism, through all those Rosemary months which led up to her death in August and Robert's in the winter of '48. I existed in limbo until the spring, and although time had for the most part ceased to have any great meaning for me, it must have been something like a year after I first pulled Rosemary from the river that I found myself there again, early in the morning, on my way to my favourite small gallery at Kettle's Yard, my overcoat tightly drawn across my shoulders, my nose red and watery with the cold I had dragged with me almost constantly since the winter, eyes streaming behind lenses which seemed to have become even thicker and heavier as time passed. A stray thought escaped my memory, insubstantial as the steam which puffed from my nostrils; a girl in white, pale face, dark eyes, dark open mouth ... and for a moment, I almost thought I saw her, just a little further down the river, saw the curve of a bare arm, took a clump of weed to be the tangle of her hair ... I blinked and wiped the lenses of my glasses with a clumsy one-handed movement.

There *was* something there, caught in the rubbish at the head of the weir; a bundle of rags, perhaps, or a floating log ... The similarity to that day in April threw the hallucination into sharp, surreal perspective, and I actually *saw* the limp body with eyesight far too sharp to be my own, saw a drifting arm, the line of a neck lolling gently into the dark water . . .

It was too much; I had to see.

I jumped down onto the river-bank (there were punts moored there, but no one had been using them that disastrous spring), gingerly squelched my shoes into the muddy tow-path, slipped, regained my balance, hobbled a hundred yards down the path on the sides of my shoes, long grass brushing the hem of my overcoat and leaving swollen droplets, like insects' eggs, on the wool. The weir was livid, bloated to overwhelming size, deafening; and the stink from it was palpable; it was the smell of slime and mud, salt and decay and all the rubbish of summer dragged beneath the water by the undertow to dark and muddy oblivion. And as I squinted at the pale bundle caught in the rushing greenish flow, I saw her; no mistaking the shape of the arm, the movement of the hair, the clothes . . .

'Rosemary?' I whispered.

But it was not Rosemary. The woman I had found by Magdalene Bridge was old; the hair was greying, wispy, the arm which had caught my attention by its whiteness was short and sturdy, even in death, the trunk stiff and twice as thick as Rosemary's slender figure. That the woman was dead could not be doubted; the exposed flesh was like lime, greenish-white and bloodless, the clothes half torn from the body, allowing a glimpse of a leg and some dirty underwear. I felt a sudden ache of pity for the poor woman, pitilessly exposed by death in all the harsh light of an April morning; pity, not horror. In a way, I was glad I found her; that one stab of pity I felt for her then was the only caring thought given to her in her strange and loveless passing. Later, with the police, came the horror and the disgust, but then I could almost have imagined her as Ophelia, trapped by the weeds in her muddy dignity, face still and pale, turned downwards to fathom the depths of the secret Cam. And there my imaginings ceased abruptly. For a sudden, perverse twitch of the living water loosened the weeds which held her, and the body rolled bonelessly over like a tired old whore, and I saw her.

Only for an instant; the moment after, I was on my knees in the long wet grass, coughing and retching, slime drooling from my mouth, my glasses slipping from a face which was suddenly, despite the chill, slick with sweat. I told you I was no hero; I vomited until my throat was pinprick-tight, the violence of my retching enough to black both my eyes as efficiently as a punch from a boxer, and all the while my skin was hot and prickly with panic and my hands were shaking with terror . . . not that she would rise after me and touch me, poor woman (though the time would come when I was ready to believe in such things), but that the thing which had fed upon her might.

I never saw her face.

That, at least, will never be there to haunt my dreams; for that I am grateful. But as for the rest of her pitiful violated body . . . the thought of it, so long ago, blots out the horror of a war in the space of a memory. There was . . . no blood. Only ropes of coiled intestine like swollen blue sausages. That and bone and a dreadful black-lined hole which had been her chest cavity, and was mostly empty. Oh yes, something had fed.

I wiped my mouth gingerly on a handful of the coarse, gritty grass of the river-bank, and stood up, legs weak and head spinning. I shouted out first:

'Help!' or 'Police!' or something like that; began to stumble and slide my way back along the muddy bank towards the bridge. There was a man standing on the bridge, looking my way; a tall man, slightly hunched, collar turned up against the damp. He did not walk away, but seemed to wait for me, his very presence a comfort to my shock and fear. Tears of gratitude filled my eyes; I reached out towards him.

'Thank God!' I cried fervently. 'There's a body there by the weir . . . Police . . . please . . . stay with me . . .' I stumbled towards him, one knee printed with mud as I fell, tears in my eyes. Through their mist, the man seemed vaguely familiar. For an instant, I felt his eyes meet mine, though the expression on his face was still unclear. A tiny sound escaped his lips, a white hand twitched and withdrew into the pocket of his coat . . . then, with a single movement, he turned away and ran, in long, jerky strides, away from me, away from the bridge, and disappeared through a gateway out of my sight.

I must have cried out loud, because, just then, a group of students rounded the corner, laughing and talking, and in an instant I was surrounded by friendly, sympathetic faces, hands touching mine, arms around my shoulders.

Their cries of: 'Make room!' and 'Give him air, you chaps . . .' surrounded me. 'Poor fellow, looks to be in a bad way . . . All right now, old man . . . just a minute . . . get your breath back . . . that's right . . . drop of brandy'll do you good . . . had a bad shock . . . that's the ticket!'

I tried to smile, to breathe normally, to tell my story, to stop the dreadful palsy in my arms and legs. Slowly, the tilted world righted itself. One of the boys ran to the police station, bringing back with him two solid-looking constables and an ambulance. I refused to get into the ambulance with the body (even though I was assured that it would be covered with sheets), but accepted a drink of brandy from the flask of one of the ambulance-men. I began to feel better. I told my story three times, once to the students who had helped me, once to the policemen, once again to the hard-faced young inspector with a surprisingly gentle voice who interviewed me at the station and gave me a cup of tea. I did not mind telling the story; every time I did seemed to remove it a little further into the realm of fiction. Over the teacup, looking into the grey eyes of Inspector Turner and comforted by the sympathy in his voice, I felt almost a hero. I had been in the war, yes, but now it was over.

'What made you think there might have been a body there, Mr Holmes?' asked Turner softly. 'The two men I sent out tell me there was nothing to be seen from the bridge, and . . . you tell me yourself that your eyesight is not good.'

'I know,' I replied. 'I can't explain it.' I told him some of the events of the previous spring, about Rosemary and how I had pulled her out of the river, and he nodded, as if he understood.

'I see,' he said. 'And did you recognise the deceased?' I shuddered, but this time it was a controlled reaction, and my tea did not spill.

'I didn't see her face,' I said in a low voice. 'When she . . . turned over . . . I was sick.'

Turner smiled narrowly.

'Don't be ashamed of that, Mr Holmes,' he said briskly. 'I've seen more corpses than you have, and this one is enough to make any man wish he hadn't had any breakfast.' He paused and closed his little book.

'That's it for now, you'll be glad to know,' he said. 'Are you going to be all right to go home now, Mr Holmes?'

'I think so, thank you, Inspector.' I smiled, hesitated, fumbled with the buttons on my coat for a moment, then asked the question he had known I would ask all along.

'Are you treating this case as a . . . I mean . . . do you think it's murder?'

The Inspector sighed and appeared to contemplate my question deeply.

'I don't know,' he said. 'Do you?' and for that moment, I felt as if he were asking me a serious question, as an equal, as if he thought I really might be able to tell him something.

'Well ... maybe a marauding animal ...' I suggested, feeling foolish.

The Inspector cocked an eyebrow.

'Maybe,' he said mildly.

'What sort of *person* would do that to someone?' I asked, helplessly.

Turner shook his head and sprang his last question.

'Are you sure you've told me everything you saw?' he asked, and his grey eyes were cold in the middle of his smile.

'Of course ... at least ... I think so,' I stammered. 'Why? I'm not suspect, am I?'

'No.' The Inspector's denial was offhand, almost disinterested. 'There can be no suspect until there has been a murder, and that will be for the pathologist to decide.'

'Oh.' The syllable sounded lame, and I immediately began to *feel* suspect, the guilt spilling unbidden into my mind like dirty dishwater. 'I see.'

I looked at Turner's smile, and a secret chill crept up from my feet and raised the prickly hairs on my thighs. I am not good at lies, and I think the Inspector knew that I had not told him everything, but this thing was too much, too secret for me to hand it to him just yet. Besides, I hardly believed it myself, and I had to know before I acted, before I decided what to do.

Because, you see, the man I had seen on the bridge, the man I had called out to, and who had run away with the abrupt graceless movements of total panic, the man whose eyes had touched mine in a second of horror and understanding ... I had known him.

It was Robert.

One

Cambridge, *May 1948*
Fulbourn Hospital, *Christmas Day, 1977*

What I had seen of my friend Robert plagued my mind for some time before I gained enough courage to do what I did; I remembered his grey face and the way he had looked at me before he ran away – not the look of a sane man – and I was afraid. When I eventually went in search of him, it was as much for my own peace of mind as it was out of concern for Robert, for I had brushed with horrible death, and I was certain that my old friend had somehow the key to the secret, whatever it was.

The *Cambridge News* had published an article on what they called the 'Body in the Weir' case, describing how I had found the woman, 'as yet unnamed' but presumed to be 'a missing person'. Apparently the pathologist's enquiry had been inconclusive over the cause of death, but had uncovered the fact that the injuries I had seen on the body, which the newspapers had euphemistically termed 'a massive internal insult' had been inflicted after death. No one knew at time of printing whether it had been murder or not. Except, perhaps, Robert.

It took me some time to locate him, for since we had lost touch with each other, he had moved from his lodging and had left no forwarding address. I contacted his College, but his tutors were as bewildered as I; they had not seen him or spoken to him regularly for weeks. At last, after another three days of fruitless inquiry, I was directed to an unwholesome cellar-bar at the end of Mill Road, where, my informant told me, the drink was cheap, 'If you're not particular about the company', and there I found Robert, alone at a table with a bottle of wine. The change which had been wrought in him even in those few days was horrific. His hair was unkempt and had grown too long, and he had not shaved. He was wearing no tie, and his suit looked crumpled, as if it had been slept in, maybe more than once. His eyes were red-rimmed, like a drunkard's, his face drawn, his cheekbones too prominent in his sunken face. He gave me one brief, incurious glance and poured himself another glass of wine, propped up on his elbows on the greasy table like an old man.

I sat down beside him, saying nothing, but my mind boiled over with questions. He drank again, the smell of the cheap red wine overpowering in that small, close place, but even then, not managing entirely to camouflage the under-smells of sweat and dirt of the cellar.

After a while, he spoke.

'What d'you want?' His voice was only slightly slurred by alcohol, but his tone was expressionless.

'Oh, Robert . . .' I think my voice was unsteady; I felt close to tears at seeing him like this, in this place. 'What are you doing to yourself? Why didn't you come to see me if you had any trouble? Why hide away in this awful place like . . .' My voice failed me, and I laid a hand on his arm, more to steady myself than to comfort him. Robert had always been my touchstone in times of trouble, he had always been stable, carefree, happy. What could have changed him so much?

The answer leapt unbidden to my mind . . . in fact, it had never been very far from my thoughts . . . anyway.

'Rosemary . . .' I whispered. 'Is it something to do with Rosemary?'

The reaction was immediate.

168

'No!' he snapped. 'Nothing. Nothing! Leave her out of it. It's me. My business. Leave me alone.' His voice was the harsh, bitter, self-pitying whine of the habitual drunkard. The urbane, facetious and affected Robert I had known had coarsened, his nerves stripped raw, and with the terrible underlying current of weakness, of helplessness one can sometimes see in drug addicts or mental patients, that sense of abyss. For a moment I was disorientated, everything I had thought solid and permanent in my world dissolving around me.

'But I'm your friend, Robert . . .' I protested. 'Your best friend . . . if you're ill . . . need help, I can always—'

'*I don't need help!*' His retort was so loud that the coarse woman behind the bar glanced his way, wondering, perhaps, whether he was going to cause trouble. Robert saw her reaction and lowered his voice, but his eyes were still overbright and hostile, and there was venom in his voice.

'I don't need help,' he repeated. 'I'm very happy with Rosemary. In fact, I've asked her to marry me.' He paused. 'And she said she would,' he added, as if to dispel any doubt I might have as to the authenticity of his story.

'Oh,' I said in a small voice. 'Marry you? Congratulations . . . old man . . . I . . . really . . . When?' His announcement had taken the wind out of my sails to such an extent that I could hardly string two words together without stammering.

Robert saw my confusion and made an obvious effort to speak normally again.

'Rosemary thinks . . . in the autumn. That will give us plenty of time.' He tried to smile; the result would have been a good approximation if the eyes had not been as blank as plates. 'I don't know what bee you've got in your bonnet about me, old man, but there's really no need, as you can see. I would have called, of course, but I've been very busy, you know, with

Rosemary and the preparations for the wedding and so . . . family to contact, you know . . . not much time . . .'

'You look . . . well . . . ill,' I said, lamely.

'A few too many late nights,' said Robert shortly. 'A little attack of *Weltschmerz*. You caught me on a bad day, what else can I tell you? Rosemary was busy tonight; I went out a-roving on my own and ended up on the edge of Lethe.' His tone was deliberately flippant; the fact that he was trying hard to deceive me frightened me even more than when he had snapped at me. I looked at my friend and saw a total stranger, bright psychopathic eyes behind the carnival-mask of the light-hearted dilettante I had once thought him. A sudden pain in my heart as I realized that I had never known him at all.

'I saw you on the bridge, Robert. You ran away, but I recognized you all the same.'

'What bridge?'

Briefly, I told my story, beginning with my finding of the body, then how I had seen him and called for help. His reaction was frankly incredulous, touched with the old half-good-natured contempt of the old days.

'It wasn't me, Dan,' he said. 'You're really off on the wrong track here.'

'I'm certain it was! You were wearing the same coat . . . you looked at me, for heaven's sake!'

For the first time that evening, my friend looked me straight in the eye, and put his hand on my arm.

'Look, old man,' he said, not unreasonably. 'If it had been me, and you had called me for help, do you really think I would have run away?' I shook my head helplessly. 'What's more,' he went on, 'you say yourself that you'd had a shock. And I know what bad eyes you've got. You were feeling rocky, you saw a man in a coat like mine, shouted to him . . . your imagination did the rest. No wonder the poor devil ran away.' He tried the smile again; this time, I was almost convinced.

'And as for being ill,' he said, 'you don't look so good

170

yourself. Too much worry, old chap. Now take yourself home and get some rest, and stop fretting. I'll call round one of these days, and we'll go out and have a drink. Just like the old days. Right?'

I nodded dumbly.

'Just like the old days. See you later, Dan. Push off, that's a good chap, and come to see me when I'm more sociable.' And at that he turned to pour himself another drink, leaving me feeling isolated and rejected. Helplessly, I went up the cellar stairs and out into the fresh air, furiously thinking to myself. There was something wrong, I *knew* there was something wrong, and none of his arguments could change that, but why did I think he had lied to me? Why would he have *needed* to lie to me?

Rosemary. Everything came back to Rosemary. She was the root of it; she was the one who had changed him and taken him from me. Maybe she could give me an answer; maybe she could explain. I halted at the top of Mill Road, the germ of an idea forming in my mind.

Then I went back to the cellar.

A few words with the female behind the bar were enough to obtain what I needed to know; she remembered Rosemary well, though not by name, of course; she had seen her with Robert often enough, yes, and she knew where she lived, described a row of shabby apartments outside the town and overlooking the river. I looked at my watch; it was just past ten o'clock. Maybe, if I was lucky, I would catch her before she went to bed.

I quickened my pace, trying to tell myself that it was only the unaccustomed exercise which made my heart beat faster, and it was only twenty past ten when I came to the row of apartments, a long terrace which had once been lodgings for one of the Colleges, and was now privately owned. The building was mostly dark, but here and there a light shone, tinted red or blue or purple with the colour of the curtains, and at the base of each staircase there was a lighted porch for the letter-boxes bearing the name of each resident.

I tried six staircases before I found the plaque which said ASHLEY 2; then I made my way up the stairs to apartment 2. I knocked, but no one answered. I knocked again, straining my ears for a sound, but no one came, and there was no light under the door. Rosemary was out. I looked at my watch and frowned; it was twenty-five to eleven already; rather late for Rosemary to be out on her own. But maybe she was not on her own. I thought about that for a while. Had she found another waitressing job, or a job behind a bar?

Had she found another man?

I wondered if I had not hit the nail on the head then; the fact that Rosemary was in love with someone else might possibly account for Robert's despondent, almost aggressive mood of this evening; it would explain why Robert had been less than eager to see me: maybe he thought I still harboured some resentment against him for having taken Rosemary from me – it would explain . . . I resolutely pushed the episode at the bridge from my mind; that had been explained already. I went down the stairs again, intrigued, but with a certain satisfaction that I had solved the mystery. Poor Robert. No wonder he had snapped my head off when I asked him about Rosemary. No wonder . . . The first time he had ever taken a real interest in a woman . . . had even gone as far as to propose marriage to her . . . not that I hadn't suspected something of the kind before this, in view of her disloyalty towards myself. I was pondering this as I happened to halt at the window of the first landing, and a movement from outside caught my eye. There was no reason for me to believe that it was Rosemary; and yet, with an obscure certainty, I knew. Maybe there was something about the way she moved, the way she held her head, flowerlike above the dark coat;

though how I could have been sure, how I could still have been so poignantly aware, even after all this time, of her every gesture, even half glimpsed through a first-floor window, I cannot say. Maybe it was simply that Rosemary, once seen, however briefly, was not so easily forgotten.

I wasted no time in trying to distinguish her features through the blurry glass; instead I ran as fast as I could down the staircase, steadying myself with my hands as I crashed against the wall on the landing and again, in the porch. I tore out of the front door and into the night, her name on my lips, my face flushed, my cry wasted on the cold air. She was gone.

I ran down the road after her, searched every side-street, every porch, every archway. I ran back on my tracks and tried the back of the building, the alley where the dustbins were kept in neat rows; nothing. Rosemary had vanished.

Cursing, I even went back to the dingy cellar in which I had met Robert, but by now it was closing down, and Robert was gone too.

I went back to Rosemary's apartment then, and I waited for her to come home; I waited for a long time, but she never came.

From that night, when I waited outside Rosemary's door, I felt outcast from my life and from the lives of ordinary people. It was then that I began to dream again; dreams of Rosemary, overpowering in their imagery, and the more I dreamed, the more my dreams became reality and my life spun meaninglessly away around me, like water down a drain. I dreamed of her every night in longing and a transfixed kind of fear . . . she was the witch of my secret desires, my Blessed Damozel, her hair the blood-red veil through which I beheld my dreams. I was sick with renewed longing for her, sick with guilt and worry for my friend Robert. I forgot to eat, forgot to work, spent my days in idle and morbid contemplation of my bewitchment. I sat in coffee-shops, hoping for a glimpse of her, as if seeing her again would solve everything, while around me the summer blossomed, and Cambridge grew heavy and restless with the coming of it. There must have been something in the air of the place even then, for the papers were full of reports of crimes, thefts and assaults, and the continuation of the police investigation on the 'Body in the Weir' case (now being treated as murder and coupled with warnings and exhortations to the public to stay away from the river, or any isolated place at night), but I hardly noticed them, moving through life as I did without a ripple. Twice I caught sight of her, once from afar, alone, and once with Robert. They stopped when I greeted them; Rosemary looked pale and ill, her face robbed of all colour in the strong sunlight, but she was still beautiful, her deep lavender eyes fathomless in her angular face, her bright hair tied strictly back beneath a dark-green scarf. Robert, to my astonishment, looked rested and well, with no sign of the haunted, hunted look I had noticed in him before, and he responded to my cautious inquiry with good-temper and a friendliness which reminded me strongly of our earlier friendship and of the old days, before Rosemary. She, however, said little; she had been unwell recently and had had to stay in bed; nothing but a touch of influenza, Robert assured me, but he knew that she was not yet in the best of health; she was delicate, she was too thin, and she needed rest. Robert was expansive, almost possessive, with me; he talked incessantly while Rosemary said virtually nothing and I mouthed platitudes. I had never felt as remote from him as I did then; he was a minor character in the chequered background of my existence, bled dry of individuality beside the complex and lovely thing which was Rosemary. His facility for talk, which I had once admired, was revealed to me to be the light, pretentious banter of the dilettante; I saw no real intelligence behind his brittle charm, felt ashamed that once I had almost worshipped this man with the unquestioning awe of a high school freshman. What I felt then was the first step in Rosemary's domination of me; I began for the first time to envy my friend.

I watched the pair of them go with mixed feelings; but uppermost in my mind was the fact that they were to be married in August, and that if I was to act, I had better act quickly. You see, I had wrestled with my conscience for long enough; I was infatuated, and maybe I fancied that Rosemary was not as happy as she might have been with Robert. Clutching at straws, I imagined her forced into an unwelcome marriage with a man I had seen to be disturbed and unstable; I fancied her falling ill with worry, pining, maybe, for the man who had saved her from the river, and who now seemed too busy to pay any attention to her; I conveniently forgot about the day when I had seen her in the rain with Robert ... behaved, in fact, like the moonstruck young fool I was. The truth was too simple to be obvious to me; it had been a novelty for me to play the part of the hero; it was a feeling I wanted to experience again.

And so one night, maybe two weeks later – it must have been near the end of May – I went back there, to the place where she lived, and since then I have lived in hell, reality passing me by in a bright, remote flow, myself a shadow among shadows. I see monsters everywhere and know that they are real, for she has made a monster of me too, in allowing me to know what should have remained unknown, and she mocks me, as well she might, knowing that for all my knowledge I am helpless. No one will believe me, no one will touch me. She remains inviolate.

I sought her out of my own accord, at dark of night and after having imbibed more courage than was good for me, hoping, perhaps, to find her alone. I had built her up so high in my fancy that I believed that on a

175

single word from me she would abandon Robert and come to me unquestioning, her wan face bright with hope and admiration for her knight-errant; I believed it so desperately that as I came to her door, my face slick with sweat, my glasses slipping down my nose and my heart fluttering like a bird's with something other than the steep climb up the stairs, her absence hit me like a blow. The door was locked, all the lights out. I hammered on the door; no answer.

My disappointment was too much for me to bear; I sank down on the dark landing beside her door, the useless adrenalin and the alcohol ebbing from my system like blood. I could not have moved if I had tried, and I knew that if I left the place, I would never have the courage to come there again. Some part of me must have known that it was all folly, that I had betrayed my friend and made myself ridiculous, but I refused to admit it then, and I waited, curled up against the door-jamb like a leper, my eyes closed, my heart a bubble of blood in my throat. As I waited, despite the discomfort of my position on the floor, I must have gone to sleep.

It was dark, as I said, and I waited for a long time between sleep and wakefulness. Once I was aware, in the haze of my drowsiness, of someone passing me by, stealthily; once I heard clear voices from another world come to me from the stairwell. I do not know how long I waited. The dark pressed upon me like the lid to my seething emotions, I smelt dust and floor-polish and turpentine, and maybe I dreamed. Sometimes, I still hope I dreamed.

In my dream I awoke to darkness; even the lamp at the bottom of the stairwell had been put out, and the night was cold. I shifted on the wooden floor, pulled my coat further around my shoulders and tried to think. Maybe I already regretted my impulsive decision to come in search of Rosemary; maybe I was afraid of whatever it was which had brought me to her door; in either case, the white-heat of my ardour had cooled, and cautiously, I considered going home.

Shaking the stiffness from my cramped limbs, I stood up, automatically brushing back the skirts of my coat (I was more fastidious in those days than I am now), and a bitter, burning disappointment crept over me like the first blush of plague. I was a fool. I had failed in everything; as a friend, as a scholar, as a lover. Since I had pulled Rosemary from the river, everything I had ever cared about had fallen apart; and what had I done? I had fallen apart too, slowly, like an old scarecrow, and crawled here to die in front of her door, in front of her ridicule. What on earth had I hoped to achieve? Spleen filled me; suddenly my anger changed direction, and Rosemary was its target, Rosemary with her lovely face and her strange ways, Rosemary who had been gone all night, Rosemary who was going to marry another man, Rosemary who had brought me here, somehow, and in a blaze of irrational anger, I turned towards the door and threw myself at it with all my strength. Well, I am not a very strong man; I was too thin for my height, pale with the indoor pallor of the book-learned town-man, and short of sight and of breath, so I can only surmise that the reason the door opened then was that it had been unlocked while I slept. Whatever the reason, it burst open on its hinges and I catapulted into the room, off-balance, coming to land against an armchair at the far side of the chamber. My glasses fell off as I stumbled, and it took me half a minute or so to find them again in the unfamiliar place, so that it was some time before I was in a fit state to look around.

The room was dimly lit by a lamp draped with a green silk scarf, and there were a number of simple items of furniture neatly positioned around the small room; two chairs with embroidered cushions, a dressing-table, on which rested bottles and boxes and toiletries, a bed, pictures on the walls, a fur rug on the floor. There was a strange smell in the air, too sweet, like incense, which made my head spin. I remember this now, but at the time, very little registered in my mind but the two men sitting by the door, one on a chair, the other slumped on the floor, both looking at me with an amused, but savage intensity.

My first reaction was horror; I had come to the wrong room. I backed away in desperate embarrassment, mumbling some excuse;

'Excuse ... thought ... wrong room ... late ... sorry ... thought a friend lived ... excuse me ...' but before I reached the door, which was still standing open behind me, another thought struck me, so forcibly that I stopped again and stared at the strange tableau upon which I had just entered.

Firstly, the young man on the floor was ill. Not just ill, but frighteningly so, his face livid even for that greenish light, his eyes and mouth gaping holes in his face. What was more, he looked hurt; a thin dark trickle of blood embroidered the side of his mouth, disappearing down the side of his throat and into the collar of his shirt. As I stared at him, I realized that he was just a boy, still in his teens, his hair ragged and as fair as flax, and from the exhausted way in which he was lying on the ground, he looked to me to be close to unconsciousness. The other man was older, maybe between forty and fifty; black hair allowed to grow long, a dark, heavy coat, features which were at the same time sharp and disturbingly feminine. He too was pale, almost sick-looking with the consumptive look of one who has exhausted himself with debauchery, and although I judged him to be considerably older than myself, he exhaled something much younger than I had ever been, some primal radiance which transfigured him. As I watched, he covered the boy over, protectively, with his arm, and watched me without a word.

Maybe it was this gesture which led me to believe

178

that he had hit the boy; maybe I took it for defensiveness – you must remember that I was still as close to being drunk as I ever got, and in those days it took considerably less alcohol to do that than it does today – but I took a step forwards.

'What's going on?' I asked. 'Who are you?'

'Friends,' said the dark man softly.

'Whose friends?' I demanded, my voice a little too shrill.

'Well, Rosemary's, of course,' he replied with quiet amusement. 'Sweet Rosemary.' He paused for a moment. 'And you, of course,' he added, 'are Daniel Holmes.'

I was rather taken-aback at that.

'How do you know me?'

'We know all Rosemary's friends,' said the dark man with a slow, strange smile. 'Don't we, Rafe?' And he smiled down at the flax-haired boy, reaching down to brush his face with one long white finger. The boy did not answer, but turned slightly towards me, and I caught a glimpse of long lashes shadowing a high cheekbone; he too looked oddly androgynous, and in that position he reminded me suddenly, sharply of Rosemary. I wondered for a moment if he could be her brother. I took another step towards them.

'What are you doing here?' I asked. 'Who are you? And where's Rosemary?'

'Rosemary? . . . She'll be here soon. We're friends.' He gave a short laugh, as if what he had said amused him. 'Friends,' he repeated.

It may be difficult for you, in your different time and with your different morals, to understand fully the sense of outrage I felt then, hearing his casual words. Sometimes I find it difficult myself to remember what it was like to be young and principled.

'Rosemary is going to be married in August,' I said coldly. 'I don't think that she should be entertaining *friends* in her rooms at this time of night.

179

Does she know you're here?' The dark man shrugged as if it was not important. I glanced again at the figure collapsed on the floor.

'Is that boy sick? Is he hurt?'

'No.'

His insolent tone nettled me.

'He looks sick,' I retorted, 'and he's bleeding. If you don't tell me what's going on now, I'll report you to the police. That boy should be at home in bed. And you . . . you shouldn't be here in Rosemary's room without her knowledge!'

His tone was flat, almost bored. 'Rafe's all right. He's been drinking, and he's not used to the stuff yet.' Idly, with a long, pale index finger, he wiped the trickle of blood from Rafe's cheek, then, without taking his green eyes from mine, licked the blood from his hand. The gesture was somehow more explicit than any pornography, and I felt myself flushing angrily.

'A boy that age shouldn't be drinking at all anyway!' I cried, partly to hide my sense of unease, and I stepped closer to the boy he called Rafe.

'Look, boy, look at me. Wake up. Where do you live? I can take you home, if you like. Are you all right?' I cast a smouldering glance in the direction of the dark man, only to see that he was smiling again.

Rafe said nothing, but gave a faint moan, and turned his head away petulantly, like a sick child.

'Where do you live?' I took hold of his shoulder; it felt very cold beneath his thin shirt. Another thought struck me.

'What were you taking?' I questioned urgently. 'What was it? What were you drinking?'

It seemed to me that the boy's breathing was shallow; that his face was too pale, his skin too cold.

'For God's sake, what was it?' I almost screamed. 'Can't you see he's dying?'

But before the other man could say anything to answer or to refute my question, the half-open door

180

swung open, and in she came, the Blessed Damozel, her glorious hair loose over her shoulders, slim as a switch in a long dress of black muslin which swirled around her ankles like smoke. She ignored me totally, and turned to the dark man.

'Java, who let him in? I told you . . . no one to be let in, especially not Daniel. Why did you let him come?'

The man said something unidentifiable. Rosemary shook her damp curls impatiently.

'Can't you think of anything else?'

'. . . No! . . .'

'*No!*' Then she turned towards me again.

'Poor Daniel,' she said, and, believe me, her smile was everything a man could dream of, loving and tender and sweet as an angel's.

'Poor, stupid Daniel.'

And before I could say another word, she had opened the bathroom door behind me and pushed me in. I was taken off-balance; my glasses slipped, I reached to steady myself, shouted uselessly as I saw her slam the door in my face, fumbled for the door-handle, found the door jammed from the outside, slipped again, dropped my glasses on the floor (I heard them rattle against the tiles), fumbled for the light-switch, and with one thing and another adding to my own panic and confusion, it was a full two minutes before I found the light and realized exactly what it was that was in the room with me.

It was in the bath. It was naked, what was left of it, and the white enamel was smeared darkly with its drying blood, fingerprints and handprints and long formless Rorschach-stains where it had been pulled to and fro in the bath-tub, as if by the greedy hands of children fighting over some treat. It was entirely dismembered; the limbs separated from the trunk like the hams of a slaughtered pig, repulsive as is the pig in its whiteness, its bloodiness, its headless anonymity . . . for the corpse was headless, the severed neck

181

black and white with blood and bone. And the ewer beside the sink was filled to the brim with a dark and sticky liquid which had already begun to form a natural lid of a darker crimson over its sluggish, reeking contents, though when I dared to touch the side of the ewer the enamel was still warm . . . And I realized the source of the blood I had seen around the mouth of the boy called Rafe, and I understood which grisly wine he had drunk. Panic bloomed in me, monstrous and surreal; I tried to scream, tried to think . . . fell . . . spinning . . . turning . . . away from the light . . . into nothing.

Part Three

Death and the Maiden

O pale and heavy-lidded woman, why is your cheek
Pale as the dead, and what are your eyes afraid of
    lest they speak?
And the woman answered me: I am pale as the dead
For the dead have loved me, and I dream of the dead.

                        Arthur Symons

One

Cambridge, *May 1948*
Fulbourn Hospital, *January 1978*

Maybe I dreamed it all: on the dark days when I no longer know man from beast I sometimes wonder whether I dreamed it all. I seek my answers at the bottom of my whisky glass, but too many are the days when I look there for comfort and see nothing but the beast grinning at me from under the surface with death in his eyes. I cannot complain overmuch; they are good to me here, a least, as good as I can expect from these people who cannot see the demon in their midst. Kind nurses in clean white uniforms come and go; some spare a moment of their time for the poor old drunkard in Room Nine, and last Tuesday one of them – no more than a child, on her way to a meeting with her young man, no doubt, brought me a gardenia from her hair and put it in a glass at the side of my bed. You can't imagine how precious that gardenia was to me, how soft and fresh and scented, like a breath of sanity in the dark and stinking circle of my world. For a whole evening I was filled with a new hope, a certainty that I was not alone, that if I managed to wait out the dawn, with the new light I might at last glimpse God ... but when the night came, and the shadows crawled from out of the corners of my room to squat around my bed like hungry demons, I broke and reached for my bottle again to find sleep in its bitter quenching, and, as I slept, I dreamed again. And again.

I awoke from a drugged, animal sleep with the reek of the circus in my nostrils, and I quivered like a beast scenting the slaughterhouse, jerking up onto my elbows on the cold ground and shivering with an icy sweat. I felt as if I had been buried alive.

For a moment, I could remember nothing, then as the memory of what I had seen returned, I gave a cry and scrabbled to my knees in the dark. I was blind; I could feel stones and hard earth beneath my hands, could feel beads of graveyard sweat on my face, my clothes, could smell dirt and blood and the over-powering chemical-smell of cheap whisky. I had no idea where I was.

No longer in Rosemary's apartment, that was sure, I thought to myself, then, on the tail of that thought; had I ever been in Rosemary's apartment? Had I dreamed? I had been drinking; had I simply passed out in some side street and stayed unconscious there for hours? My head spun suddenly; I put my hands on the ground in front of me to steady myself, and pinpricks of light danced at my fingertips like angels. I waited for an instant for the world to stabilize, then I began to crawl. I was not in a side street, that was for certain; my rapidly clearing vision could by now discern a dim pattern of light and shade on the uneven ground, and what I took to be the light of a street-lamp was shining through a crack in the darkness somewhere to my right. It looked as if I was in some kind of building. A shack, I thought as I crawled, or a derelict farmhouse; maybe an animal-shelter. I had probably staggered there in my drunken stupor to shelter from the cold, and had collapsed there out of sight. I must have been very drunk; only that could explain the dreadful clarity of my nightmares, the horrors which had arisen from the pit of my subconscious to plague my rational mind. I touched the wall at my left, hoping to pull myself to my feet, but the stone was sweaty and loathsome to touch, and I shrank away as if from dead flesh. The light was nearer now, and by its pale and glassy glow I could see the outline of a doorway, a pile of stones or rubble on one side, a slick, moist wall at the entrance. Beyond the doorway I could just see a gate of some kind ... spiked metal railings with an ornamental cast-iron design ... and with a sick jolt which brought the remnant of the sour whisky I had ingested churning up the narrow channel of my throat in a bilious flood, I realized where this place was, realized, as I then thought, the source of my nightmares.

It was a crypt.

As soon as this realization came to me, I was able to see a dozen hitherto unnoticed details; the light of the church window outside, the rows of plaques in the damp wall where the coffins had been slotted like drawers, the mouldering remains of a wreath hanging on the railings like a trophy. Maybe I gave a little moan. It was not so much the fact of finding myself here which frightened me than the fear of insanity. Why had I come to this place? Why had my subconscious formulated such bizarre and intricate fantasies about Rosemary and her friends? Was I still so shocked by my discovery of the body in the river that I must needs subject myself to still more of the same? I stumbled towards the entrance of the crypt, quite sober now, though my stomach roiled painfully, fell over a stone, half fell to one knee, put out my hands to steady myself, slipped ...

My hands met something soft and wet, cold as mud, but as I looked down I saw that it was not mud. No mud could have that oily, slightly rainbow gleam, that horrible, yielding, elastic softness, that gelid pallor ... And as I looked down, still, unable to scream or to look away or even to move, entombed forever in the hellish timelessness of that moment, I understood that if this was reality, then I had not dreamed, had not been drunk, had not been at the mercy of my own subconsciousness, but of something deadlier by far. Maybe I had known already; maybe I had fled the truth with all the fervency of the logic-worshipper I was.

But now, with the truth twelve inches from my face, I could hardly deny it. For it was the body I had seen in Rosemary's bathroom, dismembered, bloody, headless, and I was kneeling above it like a lecher, embracing it with both hands, my arms buried up to the elbows in the meat of its shattered ribcage, like a washerwoman over her tub.

Two

Curiosity, and something more, had impelled her to go to Ginny's room again. It was nearly three in the morning; the girl had not yet returned, and Alice, in spite of her fatigue, could not bear the thought of sleep. After her shower Alice had put on a robe and tried to read a few pages of a novel, then, throwing the book down she had doodled for a while in her sketch pad, then had made a sandwich, but had put it down after a couple of bites. What was wrong with her? She pushed the bedroom door tentatively, as if Ginny might have magically come back there, and flipped the light on. The bed was still untouched, the room as neat and impersonal as if it had never been inhabited. Alice went straight to the wardrobe and opened it, throwing Ginny's clothes onto the bed with a kind of fury. Damn you, she thought wildly. There was a secret there, she knew it, and she also knew she had to find it, find it or choke on her terrified, suppressed rage. Discarded clothes flew around her as she searched; a couple of syringes and some ampoules were scrutinized for a moment then tossed aside. Nothing. Alice almost wept in frustration. She was *sure* there was something to be found, certain with the irrational, compulsive knowledge of dreams. As she began to replace the clothes where she had found them, folding jumpers and hanging up dresses, her eye caught the squarish

189

outline of Ginny's suitcase half hidden under the bed. She pounced on it, pulling it out and snapping it open with a cry of triumph. Inside the case, roughly wrapped in old newspapers, was a box.

It was about the size of a fair-sized church Bible, and it was of some kind of hard wood, bound with metal. There was a handle with which to carry it, and though the wood was scratched from being dragged out of the hole in which it had been placed, it was still easy to read the inscription on the lid:

D.L. HOLMES
1922–1978
KEEP ME SAFE

It took Alice a few moments to remember where she had seen that inscription, but when it came the realization was like a redoubling of her submerged terror. The trap closed upon her.

The lock was secure; it was the wood which finally gave way, the metal coming loosely away from the body of the box with a sound like tearing cardboard as she prised it open. For a moment, Alice paused.

What was a box, if not an opening into the unknown, a doorway into a world of secrets? Alice was quite sure that she had had enough secrets for the moment, enough of doors. What she really wanted was to be able to forget all the events of the past few days, to lie comfortably in bed and go to sleep, with all the secrets back where they belonged.

Unopened.

But it was too late; she had already taken the box into the workroom where she could not be disturbed. She had broken the lock; even if she did not look inside, Ginny would know Alice had spied on her. She had declared war; she knew it. She could not go back.

She flipped back the lid, looked for the first time into the box, and fell headfirst into Looking-Glass Land.

190

Her first reaction was amazement; her first, incoherent thought; 'My God! It's a Rossetti!' Trembling, she reached into the box, drew out the picture – the pictures. Delight flooded her, as she spread the pictures out over the floor of her workroom, eyes flitting from one to the others as if she were unsure which one to study first.

They were beautiful, but they were not Rossettis.

There were maybe twenty of them, watercolours, pen-and-inks, chalk studies, all under twenty by fifteen inches square, edges ragged as if they had been carelessly trimmed with a paper-knife, the thick, creamy paper yellowed with age. They were old, old and lovely, all studies of women, no, of one woman. Head-and-shoulders portraits, full-length portraits in different poses, nudes, elegantly draped over a couch, lushly mediaeval in glowing blue velvet, delicately pencilled, leaning against a wall holding a musical instrument, studies of eyes, lips, hair. . . eyes closed, toying with a strand of hair, head thrown back, head angled forwards. . . It was some time before Alice was even able to look at them properly, even longer before her mind began to work normally again. Her next rational thought was; 'The old devil. He had no right to immure these in Grantchester chapel. They're master-pieces. They must be worth a fortune.' She picked up a picture at random; a delicate pastel in shades of brown and red. Her first reaction had not been so stupid; it did look like a Rossetti, although looking at it more closely, she could see that it lacked the over-emphasized lips of a Rossetti. It showed the head and shoulders of a young woman, head bent at a strange and slightly menacing angle, as if looking back at someone. The hair was luxuriant, painstakingly textured in differing shades of red, and pushed to one side so as to expose a rounded and perfect expanse of bare shoulder. It was dated 1869, and monogrammed in precise, interwoven letters: W.H.C.

The monogram meant nothing to Alice, though the style and the date did; she flipped the drawing over, but apart from a rough sketch on the other side of the picture, could see no more clues there. She reached for another drawing, a pencil, touched with brown ink around the eyes and lips. Again, the monogram. Again, a date, this time 1868. The pictures were a puzzle to Alice. First, they looked genuine; they were clearly finished works of the first order, Pre-Raphaelite in origin, though not signed with the initials of any Victorian painter she knew of. There was some Rossetti there, some Burne-Jones, some Waterhouse, and yet the pictures were none of these; there was a strength in the lines of those compositions, a power in the features beside which Rossetti's pale and wilting damsels and Burne-Jones' angelic but weak-featured ladies of legend seemed slightly ridiculous. These pictures were something different. From sheet after sheet of the thick yellow paper, her eyes stared out at Alice, taunting, aloof, enticing, and faintly familiar, in the way that all really classic works of art can appear . . .

Familiar.

Alice was jolted out of her reverie by a thought which was as ludicrous as it was terrifying; of *course* that face was familiar! She had drawn it herself, that same face, the wide eyes, the lips which were a curving mockery of their own childlike sensuality. . . She reached for her file of artwork, fumbled for the string which closed it. . . tugged. Papers spilled out, faces which were all the same face, hallucinatingly similar, images laid upon images like reflections along a hall of mirrors, a hall which reflected not only images, but time. She looked at the pictures for a long while, her gaze moving from her own portraits to the ones marked W.H.C., and back, searching vainly for logic. And though there was no logic to be found there, the facts still stared out at her from the pages which a dead man had thought important enough to hide forever in a church wall, and her growing certainty was a little like hysteria, a little like insanity.

For the pictures of Ginny and those of an unknown Victorian model, no doubt long since buried, looked very like twins.

One

Cambridge, *July 1948*
Fulbourn Hospital, *January 1978*

How long I knelt there in the dust, myself and the
corpse in an embrace as intimate and unholy as ever
was shared between monster and prey, I cannot tell
you. The last of the whisky had faded like mist into the
cold pre-dawn, leaving a crypt-like emptiness in me
where for a timeless time my sanity flickered, tiny and
helpless as a child's nightlight, assailed by monstrous
shadows which capered and spun like the turning of
dark machinery. Maybe I wept; after all, I had the
right. I could not move; I was at the end of all
movement, all hope; I had seen what no man should
ever see, and, mockingly, scornfully, they had let me
live, knowing that I could be no danger to them;
knowing that they had made a monster and a fugitive
out of me, they had let me live. Maybe it pleased them
to. It would have been very easy for me, at that
moment, to crawl back into the crypt, like a snail into
its shell, into the comforting dark, and hide; my
despair was more than I could stomach, and the
darkness beckoned, alluringly deathlike, womblike,
promising oblivion. I was so close to accepting what it
offered . . . I stood, my arms gloved in blood almost to
the shoulders, stumbled, began to turn away from the
light. . .

Then I remembered Robert.

The thought was like a shower of cold water. I gasped, clapped my hands to my mouth, felt cold blood smear across my lips. In all my fear and betrayal and self-pity, I had forgotten my friend, Robert, my friend whom I had gone in search of . . . Robert who was going to marry Rosemary.

Rosemary. The name alone brought me out in a cold sweat. Everything was centred around Rosemary, my Blessed Damozel, my pale lady of death. Even then, I did not begin fully to understand what she was; there were no words, no thoughts in my world for that. Already, as I began to slide out of my catatonia, I had begun to rationalize, to think in terms of *crime*, of police (I hastily put out of mind that thin trickle of blood at the side of the fair-haired boy's mouth), for I liked to think of myself as a rational man; I could *believe* in murder. The rest I chose to ignore. So I closed my eyes to the truth again and began to sift the evidence for what was acceptable to me. She was a murderess. Her friends had probably committed the actual deed, but the fact that the body had been in her apartment proved that she was as guilty as they were. Maybe they were all three of them insane . . . only an insane man could bring himself to drink blood . . . if Rafe had been drinking blood. I chose to believe my frenzied imagination had created that. They had been panic-stricken when I had walked in on them; they had been afraid to kill me, and instead had dumped me in the churchyard, with the body, hoping, perhaps, that I would be discovered unconscious and reeking of alcohol, the next morning, and accused of the crime. It made sense.

By this time, my panic had grown cold; my mind had begun to function again, and coolly I surveyed my situation. It would not do to be caught. No one, on seeing me, could fail to suspect me of the murder; I was up to my armpits in blood; there was blood on my face, my knees where I had knelt on the bloody floor,

196

my clothes were torn and filthy, and I suspected there was a wild light in my eyes, born, perhaps, of having seen too much of that which should never be seen with the eyes of sanity and reason.

I stepped over the body and made my way to the gate of the crypt; I had wasted too much valuable time, and I could see the beginnings of a pale grey dawn on the eastern horizon. The rest of the sky was dark; I judged it to be about four o'clock in the morning, but even that was too late for me to pass unseen in the streets of Cambridge. It would take only one person ... a milkman, perhaps, on his way to work, to see me, and I would be lost. I ran my hands through my hair, pushed my glasses up the bridge of my nose, tried to clean the smeared lenses with a hand I had wiped on my trouser-leg, and carefully, with newfound stealth, I made my way out of the churchyard and down towards the Grantchester road. I followed a line parallel to the road, keeping low in the fields, dodging behind trees, occasionally crawling on my stomach through thin vegetation to avoid being seen. Only once did I see someone, and even then they were so far away that I could not make out whether they were men or women, walking slowly in a group of three or four down the road, but although I knew I had not been spotted, terror nailed me to the ground, my tongue cleaving like paper to the roof of my mouth, and I cowered in the ditch for a full ten minutes before I gained enough courage to go on. It took me almost an hour to reach my house, and by that time a red dawn was blazing, the mullioned windows reflecting blood as the sun came up. Spurred by panic, I ran for the door, grasped for the keys in my pocket, fumbled the key into the lock. One endless moment of terror as the key jammed, then the door was open, and I hauled myself in, as a drowning man hauls himself aboard a lifeboat. Two, four, six, eight stairs, and I was in my room, gasping for breath, the air thick as blood in my lungs, panic still tearing, mindlessly, at my throat.

For a nightmare instant I caught sight of my reflection in the mirror and I almost screamed, then, coming closer, I recognized myself behind the deathmask of blood and ivory, my hair on end, blood smearing the lenses of my glasses, a long scratch across my forehead, puffy, broken bruises on my neck. Only my eyes were sane, very bright behind my thick lenses. Looking into my own eyes in the dark, lead-marked mirror, I knew I was no monster.

Methodically, I stripped off all my clothes and put them in the fireplace. With paper and wood, I lit the fire, and as I burned every scrap of evidence that I had ever been in that crypt, I washed very carefully, using Mrs Brown's antiquated bathtub, a pitcher and cold water, washing my glasses too, so that not a smear or speck of blood remained. Then I washed the tub and the pitcher, stirred the ashes of the fire with the poker, dressed in fresh clothes, and with a damp cloth painstakingly wiped the door-knob, the banisters, the inside and outside door-handles and the keys, before deciding that I had done all I could, and that none of Rosemary's grim work could be traced back to me.

A glance at the hall clock told me that it was now a quarter to six in the morning; I could hear sounds from the kitchen, where Mrs Brown was making breakfast for herself (she always was an early riser, although I never tended to get up much before nine), and I crept upstairs again before she could come out and speak to me. After everything I had been through, I felt drained and exhausted, and all I wanted to do was lie down, sleep, and try to forget. I locked my door, undressed, fastened my curtains so that no light could enter and trouble my sleep, then, with a long sigh of total exhaustion, I crawled between the cool lavender-scented sheets into oblivion.

A tapping on my door awoke me, and I sat up in bed, my eyes crusted and sore, my head aching. The tapping continued.

198

'Are you all right?' It was Mrs Brown. 'Don't you want any breakfast?'

'What time is it?' I asked, both hands on my head as if to still its ache. My eyes felt gravelly and hot.

'Near ten. Would you like a cup of tea?'

I shook my head.

'No. I... I don't feel very well. I need some sleep. Let... me... let me sleep, Mrs Brown. Don't wake me up. I...'

Clucking noises from behind the door. 'Come back too late last night, did we? Well, if you do want a bite to eat later, just give me a call, won't you?'

'Thank you, Mrs Brown.'

'I'll just be in the kitchen for a little while, just call.'

'Thanks.'

I heard her footsteps recede, and I crawled under the covers again, thankful of the darkness. The sheets were no longer cool and fresh, but clung saltily to my sweating body. I rolled over, trying to find a cool spot, instinctively shielding my face from the glow of the window. I wished the curtains were darker, for their deep crimson allowed the sunlight to cast a coloured nimbus of light around the window, which hurt my tired and sensitive eyes. My throat too felt swollen and sore, my face puffy. I pulled the covers over my face as far as they would go, and in the cryptlike, uneasy darkness, I slept again. And this time, as I slept, I dreamed.

I was in the crypt again; damp, clinging darkness all around me, the smell of grave-earth in my nostrils and grave-sweat at my fingertips, and I was hungry. My hunger was a coiling sickness at the pit of my cavernous stomach, a spinning delirium in the echoing chambers of my brain, worse than panic, more demanding than the sexual urge, more overwhelming than drug-withdrawal. My eardrums boomed with it, my tongue was dry with it; I was weak. I turned towards the light at the end of the chamber and winced away, though the thin filaments of daylight which showed there were weak indeed. Hunger drove me on. I left the cool, comforting darkness, put one hand on the gate, stopped. Beside one of the graves knelt a figure, a young girl, her back turned to me, a shawl wrapped round her thin shoulders. Tendrils of light hair had escaped the confines of the headscarf to flutter around her face.

The hunger hit me like a sledgehammer; I staggered. My lips were dry; despite myself, I licked them. The palms of my hands were slick; I rubbed them on my trousers and came a little closer. The girl was praying; she did not turn as I came to stand behind her, did not move as I reached out my hand, almost close enough to touch her face. Her warmth was palpable; the thin ribbon of the exposed nape of her neck between the shawl and the headscarf was pale, almost translucent; I could see the delicate tracery of her veins beneath the skin, living deltas in an alien landscape. I reached for her; spun her round, imagined her head thrown back, eyes wide, mouth open ready to scream. . . and saw none of those things.

She was smiling, arms open to receive me, lavender eyes huge in a pale, delicate face, beautiful eyes in which I read a hunger akin to my own. It was Rosemary.

I hesitated, knowing in my dream no fear, only hunger. I had caught her by the wrist; I allowed my gaze to travel down her bare arm, down the sensual river of her veins.

'Daniel.' Her voice was breathy, erotic. My own caught in mid-breath as I looked at her. Never, never, had I seen anyone as beautiful. She smiled again, lifted a small hand to press it against my cheek.

'What's happening to me?' I spoke almost to myself, but my eyes were lost deep in hers.

'Love me,' she whispered. Her hand was warm on my mouth. I caught a sudden, exhilarating scent from her skin; lavender and sweetness, and warm, quick blood.

'My God!' I cried out incoherently, her wrist against my mouth. My arms were around her, her hair in my face, her thin bones so light against my embrace, the pounding of her blood against my lips . . .

'Love me.' With a sudden wrench, I twisted her hand towards my mouth; her skin was smooth, salty beneath my tongue. I bit deeply into the flesh; it was sweetly, sickeningly yielding, like the skin of a fruit, then the blood came, clean and salt. I gagged on it in my eagerness, fumbled against the wound, licked abjectly. Blood trickled down the side of my mouth, awakening a memory . . . though of what, I could not quite remember. The sides of the incision had a faintly metallic taste, were slightly uneven, and I pushed my tongue between them to feel the pulse of the rushing blood, my breath ragged and laboured in an excess of delight and greed. I remember the taste of her, my God! The pattern of every line and vein on that wrist . . . could I have dreamed it? Am I insane? The blood was power, was life. . . I lapped it deliriously, fearfully, aware that at any moment she might choose to withdraw her favours and leave me to hunger and hopelessness again.

And as I fed, I looked up into her pure, fathomless eyes.

And the stars in her hair were seven.

Restlessly I dreamed and whimpered for hours beween my damp and fevered sheets, and she walked my dreams in glory. It seems strange, now that I live my life in the midst of such dreams, to remember how new and how terrifying it was to me then, to enter the rank and fleshy crypt of my subconscious. I was racked with lust and horror; my limbs were water, my head a bead of blood which pulsed, heartlike, with migraine. I don't remember Mrs Brown knocking on my door again, though I expect she must have heard me cry out in my sleep, and twice I was just able to drag myself to the sink in time to retch a bitter darkish slime into the white porcelain basin . . . at that time, I took it for bile. The scratches on my face hurt wretchedly; touching them with the numbed tips of my fingers, I realized that they had become great raised welts, reaching from my forehead, across one cheek and right down my neck to the collar-bone, though I had been protected to some extent by my shirt. There were marks like needle-tracks on the inner part of my wrists, half explaining my disorientation and my nightmares. They must have drugged me. My throat was swollen, and I wondered whether one of Rosemary's cronies had tried to strangle me, but I was too weak and too feverish to examine the damage any further.

It was near dark when I awoke completely; I looked at my watch, and was astounded to see that it was half past seven. Never in my life, even after all-night parties, had I slept away a whole day, and I flung back the sheets and stood up, feeling more refreshed, but still rather sick and light-headed. I put on my dressing-gown and went to the bathroom, where I switched on the light, washed my face, took two aspirin, and looked at myself critically in the mirror.

I could not have said that I looked well; I was pale, and my eyes were bloodshot and bright with fever. I am not the kind of man who looks at all attractive when he is unshaven; I simply looked dirty, and the scratch down my face was an ugly weal, beaded with pus. The bruises on my throat were visible now as finger-prints; four roundish points, each with a crescent of broken skin where the nail had penetrated the flesh, and on the other side of the throat, below the jugular vein, a broader, less defined bruise where the thumb had been. A little way above that was an incision I had not previously noticed, a crescent-shaped wound, some three inches long, slightly raised. I frowned at myself in the mirror. That was not the mark of finger-nails, nor had it been accidental. It had been deliberately placed. But why? And how? By the size and shape of the mark, the slight irregularity of the incision, it almost looked like the mark of . . . I shook my aching head irritably. I had had too many nightmares. What possible reason would anyone have . . .? And yet, they did look very like the marks of teeth. Angry with myself and my fancies, I deliberately turned away. Those scratches would have to be disinfected, otherwise I would have more than bad dreams to worry about. I found a bottle of iodine, and, standing in front of the mirror, dabbed at my face and neck until all the cuts and scratches were covered. That was better. Now for something to eat, for I still felt weak and dizzy, and I realized that I had eaten nothing since the previous morning. I went to my room to change, and stopped as I noticed a screw of paper tacked to my door. I had been in such a hurry that I had not seen it before, and I took it (correctly, as it happened) to be a note from Mrs Brown.

Dear Mr Daniel,
    I have had to Pop out for a While to Visit my Sister, I will be Back this Evening. I am Sorry you are not Yourself today. Should you be Wanting a Bite to eat I have left a Pot of Tea on the Hob and a Nice Piece of Cod in the Oven for your Supper. And help Yourself to Anything in the Larder.

    Yours Sincerely,
    V. Brown

I smiled. That meant I had the house to myself for the evening, and I was glad of it; I would have no awkward questions to answer, for Mrs Brown was as protective as she was good-hearted, and I sometimes found her affection rather overpowering. I did not bother to dress, knowing that I was alone in the house, and I made my way down to the kitchen. There was food left for me in the oven, as promised, and tea on the hob, and I settled myself down at the kitchen table to eat. I had hardly eaten more than a mouthful, however, before the sickness came upon me again; my head swam, my stomach roiled, and I pushed the plate away unfinished. I drank two glasses of water in rapid succession, fighting off nausea, and remained for a few moments in front of the fire, shivering with fever. The events of the previous night had taken more from me than I had suspected. I reached my trembling hands towards the comforting fire, and began for the first time since the beginning of my nightmare to review the situation logically. I prided myself on being a logical man, a man of learning, and my natural pragmatism had begun, with the help of a bath and a long sleep, to return to me. This I must emphasize; I was not neurotic, nor am I yet; all conclusions I have since reached are based on my own experiences and research. Even then, dragging myself from a vortex of horrors, I began to view the situation objectively.

My first thought was a profound gratitude at being alive at all. I had obviously witnessed something which incriminated Rosemary and her band of murderers to the hilt; they had tried to be rid of me, and in some way had bungled it. Perhaps they had intended me to be accused of the crime; perhaps after having tried to throttle and drug me, they had abandoned me for dead. It was clearly a police matter, as much for my own sake as for Robert's (I refused to believe that he had in any way been involved in the affair, and it struck me suddenly that he was in almost as much danger from Rosemary and her friends as I was), and I racked my brains for the best way to handle the situation.

By now, the murderers would have disposed of the evidence; the body, I knew, was hidden in the churchyard, and would no doubt be found sooner or later. Rosemary, in her apartment, would be unassailable. Rafe and Java ... they were my only chance of being believed, and I had no idea of who they were or where to find them. I myself ... well, there was no doubt that even as a police informant I might be suspect; I had already been strategically placed to discover one corpse, and the circumstances in which I had found myself this time might easily be seen to be suspect. I shrank from placing myself in a situation where it would be Rosemary's word against my own ... where would it end?

My head had begun to ache again with the effort of concentrating. I knew that this was by no means the first violent death to hit Cambridge in the past few months. Could Rosemary somehow be implicated in the death of the woman in the weir? Or was my evidence circumstantial, and Rosemary innocent?

I wanted to believe it. Remembering her face, the sweetness of her features, the innocence which shone through her eyes, I wanted it, for I loved her, have maybe never ceased to love her, and I wanted to believe it with all my heart. My brain began to formulate wild and attractive hypotheses. She was innocent; a pawn of Java and Rafe, somehow in their power. They had hypnotized her. They had drugged her too. They were somehow blackmailing her. From my earlier suspicion and horror of her, my delusions led me to believe that she was the persecuted one, that she needed my help, that my fearsome nightmares were only the product of jealousy and the trauma of what I had seen the previous night. I told you, Rosemary made children of all of us.

Contact the police? I dared not, as much for fear of incriminating Rosemary as myself; could I expect them to fail to suspect her? The newspapers had by now revealed that Scotland Yard had been called in to investigate the 'Body in the Weir' case; I expected to be

205

contacted for questioning again at any time. The last thing I wanted was to draw the attention of the investigators towards myself, or towards Rosemary. I saw that I would have to act on my own, and that as quickly as possible. I went back to my room, dressed in a plain, dark suit, a light overcoat and my hat, returned to the kitchen, and lingered over the drawer of knives. Finally I chose a small carving-knife, sharp, but small enough to hide in my sleeve, and set off out, feeling slightly ridiculous, but excited too. I suppose that for a man of action, to set out into the night with murder on his mind and a lady for the rescuing would have been no great thing; but I was no man of action.

My watch told me it was close on eight o'clock; the day had been hot, and had given way to a sultry, cloudy evening. I was still shivering, however, and glad of my overcoat, though most of the people I encountered were more lightly dressed than I was. My step was purposeful, my left arm slightly stiff from the pressure of the knife against my elbow; I knew where I was going. Where? To her apartment, of course, but in stealth, this time, forewarned and careful. I had walked about half the way to the town centre when the first cramps hit me; one moment they were sudden but bearable, like a stitch in my side, the next they had me doubled up beside the road, almost on my knees, cold sweat running down my face, my jaw locked in agony. The road was not a busy one; no one came to help me. I sank to my knees by the roadside, hardly even able to breathe, to wait it out. A breath, drawn out an eternity-long, acid in my belly, my lungs . . . another breath. The pain ebbed, ceased. Carefully, I stood up, afraid to move too quickly lest the pain came on again. I straightened, took several deep breaths.

Satisfied that the cramps, whatever had caused them, were indeed over, I began to walk again, with more care, down the deserted road. I had hardly gone more than a hundred yards, however, when the cramps hit me once more, flooring me immediately this time, paralysing. The world spun around me like a carnival ride, my consciousness reduced to a flight of moths in the bright darkness; I retched agonizingly, spat blackness onto the road. Maybe I cried out; maybe I imagined it. My glasses slipped onto the grass, I fumbled for them, touched only grass, tried to stand, slipped, fell to my side. I think I suspected I was having a heart attack, and with both hands clasped to my chest I managed to crawl onto the road, where a street-lamp threw uncertain fragments of light in an ellipse around me. Then, I fainted.

When I regained consciousness (not, I believe, more than a few minutes after) the pain was gone, and the street was still deserted. I stood up carefully, felt no hint of a cramp, straightened up to my full height. I brushed my clothes, feeling rather foolish now that my malaise was over. I was inclined to disbelieve the whole thing and put it down to my lack of food, or perhaps the after-effects of whatever poison they had injected into me, for now I felt quite recovered, indeed, I had the beginnings of a healthy appetite. I found my glasses, wiped them and put them on, immediately feeling better. I brushed my hat, replaced it on my head and set off on my way again, feeling distinctly hungry now, and wondering whether I should not stop somewhere on the way to Rosemary's apartment for a bite to eat. It would not do for me to pass out while I was there. A group of students, strangers to me, passed me as I joined the main road into Cambridge; I caught the sound of laughter as they went by, a merry call of:

'Good evening!'

Maybe they had surprised me; I started as I heard the voice and my steps wavered again. I was suddenly, acutely conscious of the cold, of the sickness in the pit of my stomach. I felt dizzy once more, raised my hand to touch the brim of my hat in greeting, and paused in mid-gesture, my smile faltering on my lips. The hunger was suddenly very acute. They passed me, still chattering; only one young fellow looked at me askance as he went by, wondering, perhaps, if I were drunk. He was the closest to me of the group; the lamplight reflecting from his broad, ruddy face as he loomed out at me from the darkness. For an instant, my sense of perspective was distorted; his young face seemed to rush towards mine like something grotesque seen through a fishbowl, and I backed away; his vapid blue eyes, his broad laughing mouth, the beads of sweat in the enlarged pores of his shaven cheeks horribly magnified in my mind's eye. The sudden heat of him was overwhelming; I could *smell* him, ripe and fetid as a parcel of meat in the hot night, the scent of his hair-cream only an accompaniment to the primal throb of his young blood. Before I knew it, I had reached out a hand to touch him . . . but the party was gone, laughing and unconscious into the night, and I was left to stand beneath the lamp-post, shaking and appalled at my thoughts. Surely, I had not been thinking . . .? I cursed under my breath and went on my way. My experiences of the past twenty-four hours were giving me delusions. I walked on, and the hunger stalked me, whetted, as I resumed the hunt.

Two

Alice painted swiftly, precisely, thinking over the facts as she had read them in Daniel Holmes' journal.

The facts. They loomed overhead like apocalyptic birds, spiralling out of a dim, uncomprehended past with their message of destruction. It was tempting to go beyond the facts, to imagine all kinds of rare and disturbing things, but Alice frowned at her canvas, her deft fingers handling airbrush and paintbrush and masking gum and thinner as her mind went over and over what she had read in compelling, primal rhythms of thought.

She painted absently, unconsciously, her hands moving deftly and quickly, her mind elsewhere. She supposed that she had planned what she was going to do; had made preliminary sketches, had mixed paints and wiped brushes, but hours later as she looked at the canvas, she saw it with the eyes of a stranger. It was not that she had not looked at it before, but as she had been working on it, she had only ever seen details; a hand here, a patch of vegetation, a square of sky; she had seen only effects of pigment and form. Now she saw a work of art, utterly individual, compelling her to *look* at it, intricate in detail, but stark in meaning. She took a step backwards, looked calmly at the canvas for a long time, and listened to the deceptive beating of her heart as everything swung slowly into place with the inevitability of a pendulum.

A riverside scene again; perhaps even the same

place; Alice recognized the little twist in the riverbank, the overhanging vegetation, the pale reflections of the trees in the dark water. Again, everything was rendered in painstaking detail, somehow clearer than reality, cleaner in shape and with its own lambency. Two figures stood in the foreground, one facing Alice on the far side of the river-bank, though with his face turned down towards the water, the other seen in profile, standing up to his knees in the river, trousers rolled up to reveal thin, pallid legs, comically foreshortened by the refraction of the light from the river's surface.

Both were young men, dressed rather formally in suits with broad lapels; the one with the glasses, facing Alice, was wearing a hat. Alice could not quite read their expressions, but there was something in the way both of them were standing, something *strained*, as if by curiosity, but at the same time holding back from the object which floated between them in the river. Alice squinted to see it, then as she realized what she had painted, she gave an involuntary grimace of distaste. God! What on earth had possessed her?

The canvas was small; the figure should have been mercifully indistinct, but was not. On the contrary, as she approached it, it seemed to move sharply into focus, so that she saw it in far more detail than she would have liked. It was partly submerged; she could distinguish its pallid bulk just below the surface, resting bonelessly on the greenish water; could imagine the lazy movement of the ripples around it. But she could see its face, turned towards her, saw it and recognized it, despite the discoloration and the bloating, recognized the mass of red hair which pooled around it, and as she peered closer, Alice thought (no, she knew) she saw the expression on that ruined face, the eyes piggy with swelling, the mouth open to reveal a black hole framed with yellow and carnivorous teeth . . . the expression was triumph, morbidly out-of-place on the face of that corpse, no, not even triumph; it was *rapture*.

Alice was mesmerized; it seemed that the closer she looked, the more detail she saw; imagined every twig, every blade of grass to contain infinities of divergences, though whether this delusion came from the picture or her own subconscious, she never knew. Maybe the picture was her way of dealing with ideas her rational mind was at first incapable of accepting; while her conscious mind struggled to make sense of what she had read in Daniel's papers, her subconscious was sifting the information and drawing (literally, it seemed) its own conclusions.

Alice had somehow believed it all along.

In some ways, it was a relief to accept this; believe in the irrational, she thought inconsequentially, and anything becomes possible; even in Looking-Glass Land there were rules, if you only knew where to look. She studied the picture further, paying especial attention to the two figures standing by the water; it seemed to her that at least one of them, the one with the hat, should be familiar. There was something about the way he was standing, the slight stoop of his shoulders, the light reflecting from the lenses of his glasses . . .

Joe.

Joe and . . . Daniel?

Joe and Daniel.

And as the last important piece of the strange puzzle slammed into place like a door onto the world of reason, Alice picked up her paintbrush one last time, and added the name of the picture to the bottom of the canvas, without thinking, knowing that the act was as inevitable as all the other acts which had led up to this one moment.

Poor Daniel, she thought, and wrote, in neat precise capitals:

Retribution; The Chosen of Ophelia

One

Cambridge, *July 1948*
Fulbourn Hospital, *February 1978*

I walked in nightmare along that road, the hunger at my heels all the time. The cool, pragmatic brain of which I was so unjustly proud was filled with unaccustomed turmoil; the tantalizing, dizzying scent of blood was in my nostrils, and though I fought my growing certainties with all the bigotry of logic, I weakened in the face of that hunger, weakened as any normal man would.

I told you she made monsters of us, didn't I? Maybe you thought I was being metaphorical. Rosemary made a monster of me the first moment I saw her; made me into a child in the body of a man, made me into a betrayer of my friend, a betrayer of myself, but there was more. I knew it by instinct.

I have always thought of myself as a Christian; I did not lie or steal, and if I had lustful thoughts I hid them very well; my sins were the little sins of a man very like other men; my thoughts never touched either despair or the sublime. Suddenly, in the space of a night and a day, everything was different. I would never be like other men again, and the knowledge was like damnation inside me. How can I convey to you the depths of my horror then, the first time I looked at myself and saw the beast under the skin? Later, when I had looked upon such things too often to be broken, I was able to view what happened dispassionately, almost scientifically, but there were many mirrors and icons to be broken before then, many forbidden pages to be turned. So I walked, and I hungered, and I kept my face in shadow so that the passers-by could not recognize the murder in my eyes.

Murder.

The word meant nothing to me as I walked blindly through the streets, my hands in my pockets to hide their trembling. It was a pit, spiralling downwards into never-never-never, huge as destiny. Just a word, superimposed like a photographic negative over everything I saw, bigger than God. Believe me, I fought it as long as I could, but it was insidious, twisting and turning in my mind, hallucinating, casting kaleidoscope images into the painful grid of my reason. For seconds at a time I was apart from reality, spinning, the hunger riding the convolvulus of my brain like a child on a fairground helter-skelter; several times I ducked into side-streets or shady archways and retched, pain digging sharp fingers under my ribs. And all that I endured, ultimately, for nothing. Strange, that I should still feel pride at not giving in immediately. Grant me that much humanity, at least, that I did not give in at once.

I never made it to Rosemary's apartment – I did not expect to – though I did get as far as the river. The streets were not as crowded as I had feared, and though groups of students congregated outside the public-houses, I was not obliged to touch them or go too near. I was glad of that; the very smell of them made my head spin. A couple of policemen passed me; I was conscious of a wary glance flicked in my direction. Suddenly paranoid, I quickened my step, imagining that they had seen something of my altered condition. My hands were shaking. As I came to Magdalene Bridge (and the irony of the place was not lost to me even then), I suffered a particularly violent attack which left me breathless and trembling, and I managed to climb down onto the banking, and from there, under the bridge itself, where it was dark and cool, and, I thought, I would be able to rest without being seen and questioned.

I settled myself on a narrow ledge in the dark shadow of the bridge, and took a few deep breaths. The air was cold and sweaty, the underside of the bridge green and soft with mould, but at least I felt safer there. Someone passed over the bridge above my head; I felt the heat of their footsteps, imagined I saw it, like a torch shining through thick cloth, a faint glimmer on the water, closed my eyes. Only a few moments, I deluded myself, just a few minutes' rest, and I would be myself again. All I needed was the coolness of the water to calm my fever, the moist silence of stone to still what was raging inside me. I waited.

'Daniel.'

My eyes snapped open, my hands raised automatically to steady my glasses. For a moment I thought the voice came from the water, and I felt a stab of superstitious dread; it was her, the dead lady, her ribcage torn open like a sack of laundry and her eyes staring accusingly at me. Maybe there was worse; maybe the wreckage of her face would show a wide, desperate smile, and her arms would be open to receive me . . .

'Danny.'

I turned so suddenly that I nearly fell off the ledge.

'I'm so glad I found you, Danny.'

It was Rafe.

For a moment, the essential meaning of his presence eluded me and I simply stared at him. He was crouching on the ledge, barely two or three feet away from me, and a ray of light, freakishly reflected from the water, fell onto his face. I had thought him beautiful before when I had seen him in Rosemary's apartment; beautiful in a disturbing way; now he was spectral, ethereally fair, his pale eyes at the same time innocent and corrupt. I was beyond fear; my terror of what I had already begun to discover within myself was enough to eclipse any fear a normal man might have had at being alone with a vicious murderer.

'My God,' I whispered, 'what have you done to me? What did you give me?'

Rafe smiled, the smile of an engaging schoolboy caught performing a not-too-serious prank.

'Don't worry, Danny,' he said lightly. 'Everybody's like that at first; I was too. You'll get over it soon enough.'

'Over what?' I began to raise my voice. 'What have I become?' I reached over and grabbed him by the front of his coat; shook him. Rafe just smiled.

'Soon you'll be one of us,' he said softly. 'That's what you wanted, isn't it? To be one of us?'

I shook my head, dumbly.

'Yes you did,' chided Rafe. 'Isn't that what everybody wants? To belong to someone? You belong to us now; you don't like it at first, because you are not used to the idea yet, but you will. You'll live for ever, Danny. You'll be more than a man; and Danny, the things you'll *know*! Everybody wants that, believe me.'

'What did you give me?' I gasped.

'You know,' said Rafe.

The fact that I did know, and more than I wanted, made me see red. I pulled the boy towards me and hit him twice across the mouth, as hard as I could.

'You bastard! I don't know *any*thing! All I know is that you're murderers, all of you . . . God help me, and you're poisoning me. You're poisoning me and I feel . . . I want . . .' My voice soared above its normal register, shrill with panic; hearing myself so badly out of control frightened me even more, and I loosened my grip on the boy, pushed him away.

'I don't know anything.'

There was a thin trickle of blood running out of the left side of Rafe's mouth; still smiling, he wiped the blood with the ball of his thumb, then, very delicately, he licked it away. Deliberately, he passed the tip of his tongue over his lips; the gesture was, in a man, obscene beyond words.

'You know.'

I slumped against the side of the bridge, feeling more than defeated. His pale eyes pinned me to the stone like a moth under glass; his smile was more than I could bear. I began to weep quietly into my hands, the tears falling through my fingers like lost worlds. I wanted to die.

Rafe watched me for a long time, then he stood up. His head was ringed with light from the reflections on the water; he looked like an angel. I was panic-stricken at the thought that he was about to go away, and I clutched, convulsively, at the skirt of his coat.

'Don't leave me.'

'Then come with me,' he said, 'if you dare.'

'Stay with me. Help me.'

Rafe nodded.

'That's why I'm here. That's why they sent me.'

'Who sent you?'

'The others. Rosemary. You belong to all of us now, Danny. You have nothing to be afraid of now, I promise you. From now on, you will be feared, as we are feared. You're one of us.'

'But what are you?' I asked, still clutching at him like a lost child.

Rafe flung up his head in a wonderful gesture of pride and defiance; my heart was filled with admiration for him then, admiration and love for the savage freedom of that gesture. For an instant, I wanted nothing more than to be like that, free and beautiful and cruel with the terrible inhuman cruelty of youth, unchained from the shackles of the sordid world. I wanted to be a law unto myself; yes, I wanted to belong to him and to his kind forever, to run with them, feed with them . . . to be forever blessed.

God forgive me, I wanted that.

He smiled at me, and I basked in reflected glory.

'We're the Masters, Danny,' he said softly. 'The chosen ones. The lords of creation. The natural predators. Forever.'

I shuddered with a cold joy; half-understood images danced before my eyes. I was a child again, impressionable and eager as a child, waiting on the brink of the longest and most exhilarating fairground ride of my life; I could smell popcorn and candy-floss and the dull, hot under-smell of the animal-house.

'Oh, yes,' I murmured, hardly even aware that I had spoken.

'Oh, yes.'

One

Cambridge, July 1948
Fulbourn Hospital, *March 1978*

Black night had fallen, and I ran with the night. In the shadows we ran, Rafe and I, and as we went through the town, following secret channels through which he led me, the others joined us silently, Java and Rosemary and others whose names I knew without having to ask them: Elaine with her long matted hair and huge eyes; Anton, seven years old, his hand tucked trustingly into hers in a parody of real childhood; Zach with red hair like Rosemary's and a bird tattoo on his face; *my* people, I thought with a whirling pride, *my* people, and, God help me, I loved them that night, loved the feel and the scent of them and the throb of the hunger which was our friend and only ally. Most of all I loved Rosemary, loved the ripple of her hair on her shoulders, the turn of her head, the whiteness of her bare legs beneath the black raincoat ... I walked in dreams, the apotheosis of all dreams, and, forgive me, I felt ecstasy, I felt *joy*, and the dreams will never rest in me again, though she is gone, and the joy buried in the slow earth of Grantchester church-yard, never to blossom again.

Try to understand; I was born a lonely child among adults with their own problems to live with; I grew into a lonely man. My life was sterile; I immersed myself in study in order to compensate for the lack of order in my life; I surrounded myself with the lush art of the Pre-Raphaelites to satisfy my need for sensuality.

What child has never craved the company of others, the wild thrill of the pack, the dare-devilry and the feeling of running forever, away from the adult world and the confines of society into something purely primitive, darker than prehistory? And I was such a child. I saw myself as we ran; the lonely boy with glasses; constantly left out and jeered at, the out-of-breath boy in the race, the clever boy desperately seeking in books the reasons for his lack of love. Try to understand me when I say I am sorry, but believe me (for the time for dishonesty, even with myself, is past) when I say that despite everything, I felt joy. I believe I would have felt it even without the substance Rafe had injected into my arm before we set off; no drugs could entirely explain the euphoria, the fulfilment I experienced. The train inside the bubble of my spinning-top had broken free at last, and I rode it in one glorious night of wild exhilaration, bearing down upon my destiny with cries of triumph.

I no longer questioned anything; the sparkling glamour of the night was enough for me, and I followed the pack down alleys, under dark archways, across bridges and back across the river until we came to the poorer part of town; once or twice a passer-by caught sight of us; we answered his stares with cat-calls and whoops. Java was carrying a knife; light from the street-lamps slickered off its blade like mercury, but I was not afraid; the hunger was like the most powerful of drugs in my system, a strong, compelling music in the soundbox of my skull. Tribal rhythms drove me on. How long we travelled I do not know; I suspect it was not long, but it might have been forever. Like Peter Pan, I felt as if I were walking on magic dust, effortlessly; and I know the others felt the same. Elaine was singing softly, her voice a thin lost warble in the shadows. Only Rosemary was untouched; utterly serene, she led the way towards the place she had chosen, and the hunger pushed us from behind like a strong wind.

It was a place I knew slightly; a run-down public-house with a reputation for cheap drink and illicit hours. Even then, I thought that the place must surely be closing, for it seemed deserted, and the light from the dusty, narrow windows was yellow and drab. But the others looked so sure of themselves that I followed, afraid to hesitate, fumbling in my pockets for money. Even then, you see, I had not really understood; maybe I still suspected that I might be dreaming; whatever the reason, I fumbled for money in my pockets, as if I were planning nothing more serious than an evening out drinking with my friends. It might have been ridiculous if it had not been so horrible.

Rosemary led the way in; the door was open, and I found myself standing in a grimy and poorly lit tap-room, where two people, a man and a woman, were clearing glasses and bottles from the bar. There was sawdust on the floor of the room, a pall of greasy smoke in the air; mingled under-smells of mould, wine and vomit.

The man was wiping the bar with a damp cloth; he did not even look up when we came in.

'We're shut,' he said brusquely. 'Eve!' (This was addressed to the woman.) 'Lock that door before anyone else turns up.' The woman he had addressed as Eve stood up from mopping the floor, a cigarette hanging from her mouth. I had a moment to notice that she was young, and might even have been pretty in different circumstances; as it was, she looked sullen and drab, a dirty cloth tying back hair of a cheap, metallic blonde.

'You heard,' she said, without removing the cigarette. 'We're shut. Sorry.'

221

There was a short silence; I saw Java glance at Rafe, saw Anton take a step forwards, pulling away from Elaine.

The young woman stared at him.

'An' what's more, that kid ought to be home in bed,' she said. 'Don't you know what time it is?'

I shifted uneasily, remembering, perhaps, my own words, rather too similar for comfort, when I had spoken to Rafe and Java a short twenty-four hours previously.

No one moved for a moment or two, then Rosemary stepped forwards.

'We won't be very long,' she said quietly.

Eve ignored her. 'I'm locking up,' she announced, moving towards the door.

Java stepped to one side to bar her way.

'What're you doing?' she demanded, an edge of fear lending animation to the flat voice.

Java ignored her.

'Tony!' This time the edge of fear was unmistakable, and the man who was mopping the bar looked up for the first time. His eyes met Java's.

What happened then I could never quite recall; the unreality of it all washed over me like a breaker, tipping the world sideways, and when it stabilized a few moments later it was over. I think that it was then that Java drew out his knife; no, the knife *sprang* from the palm of his hand like an animal, and with one pure liquid movement it touched the woman's throat. A touch was all it took; she gave a cry of surprise, (I'm sure it was surprise), then the blood flowered down the front of her blouse; she clutched at the wound, eyes getting rounder and rounder; the blood sprayed. Java had never ceased to look into the eyes of the man at the bar. I don't remember who went for the man first; I think it might have been Zach and Elaine. Anton was groping for the body of the woman; blood sprayed his face, and I saw the look of *hunger* there, the bright

222

gleam of greed in his eyes, older and more corrupt than any child's eyes have a right to be, but the hunger was on me then, terrifying and totally uncontrollable, and before I knew what I was doing, I had pushed the child out of the way and was feeding myself. Bright, arterial blood starred the lenses of my glasses; the world swam in shades of red around me. I fed messily, without any other thought than appeasing the blood-god within me, fed without tasting, biting at the flesh of the woman's throat, feeling her shudder beneath me. Anton whimpered like a puppy, trying to push past me again, clawing at the body with his thin little hands; somehow we both fed. As I rolled over, drugged and sated, I saw the man at the bar – at least, what they had left of him. They had ripped him apart, from belly to throat. Elaine had found the till and was stuffing coins and banknotes into her pockets. Java had found the bottles of oil for the stove and was beginning to splash the floor and furniture with it. Rosemary was cleaning the blood from Rafe's face with her tongue, a mist of tiny droplets sprayed across her eyes like a mask. She looked up and smiled at me.

'The chosen ones, Danny,' she said. 'That's what we are. And I chose you. Remember that, and be loyal to me. Be mine.' She smiled at me through the blood-smeared negatives of my glasses, and the hurt, helpless love for her welled up in me again for just one moment before reality flooded me like acid, dissolving my dreams and my joy.

Love and horror; both sides of Rosemary. The Blessed Damozel and the Lilith. The coin spun; the wheel turned on an axle of blood and bone; the Prince awoke, blood drying on his glasses.

I began to scream.

Two

Cambridge, *April 1990*

Alice managed to get to sleep at about six that morning. Ginny knocked on the door at half past five and went straight to her room without a word; Alice let her go with a guilty quickening of the heart as she thought of the box she had stolen and followed her up. Her vision was scrambled from too long trying to decipher Daniel Holmes' crabbed, neurotic handwriting, and her head felt terribly heavy. Perhaps after a couple of hours' sleep she might be able to see things in a better perspective. Perhaps she might wake up and find that all the events of that night had been a dream.

She awoke at seven o'clock, pulled on her robe and tiptoed down to her workroom. For a long time she looked calmly at the box and the picture she had painted. She knew that it was a false calm, but she welcomed it all the same, allowing her perception of the situation to shift again, like sand, into a new pattern.

It was real. She had not dreamed it; she was not crazy. In a way she could find it in her to feel a sick relief, although the realization only served to open the gateway to a different type of abyss. There was a choice, she told herself firmly; a choice between herself and Ginny. Either she was crazy, and Ginny was vindicated, or Ginny was guilty, though of what Alice was not yet certain.

It was light, and a thin grey dawn was filtering between the blinds as Alice went back to her room and dressed, wondering how best to deal with the situation. As she began to regain her calm, she realized that the only answers she was likely to receive would be from Ginny herself, and she began to try to make sense of the situation.

Her reaction against Ginny was unreasonable, she told herself firmly. Triggered by jealousy, it had escalated into a full-scale paranoid delusion in which Alice had begun to suspect the girl to be the focus of all kinds of sinister activities. The truth was probably more prosaic, she said dryly to herself. Ginny was an addict, or at least a user of hard drugs. She didn't need the co-operation of Fulbourn Hospital to guess that part of Ginny's mental illness might have been due to an addiction, or its indirect consequences. As such, Ginny was doubly vulnerable to all kinds of undesirable influences, such as the two individuals Alice had encountered the previous night. She was too passive a character to play the leading role Alice had mistakenly attributed to her; more likely she was a victim. She and her friends had somehow known of the diary and the pictures hidden in the wall of the church; they had planned to steal them (the pictures were unique and probably worth a small fortune), and had panicked when they realized Alice suspected them of something. Their treatment of Alice had been an effort to frighten her; they would never have really hurt her. But in the dark of that derelict house she had lost her nerve, that was all.

Now that she felt that she had made some sense of the situation, she was feeling very much more in control of her feelings. She would have to confront Ginny, she decided; maybe Ginny would admit everything as soon as Alice told her what she already knew. Perhaps Ginny needed help.

She looked at her watch; twenty past seven. Joe

would be coming round soon, she imagined. She would have to talk to Ginny before he arrived.

'Tea, Ginny?' That was better. Her voice was steady now, her smile confident.

Ginny was sitting by the fire, still barefoot, but wearing jeans and a dark-coloured jumper which high-lighted her bright hair. She shook her head, with the reluctance which characterized so many of her movements.

'You look ill.' The little voice was colourless, and it must have been a remnant of her earlier paranoia which led Alice to believe that there were fairground lights cavorting behind those broken-glass eyes.

'I didn't get much sleep.' Alice's tone was carefully casual. 'I was too busy thinking about last night. Maybe you could give me some kind of explanation?'

Ginny looked at her.

'You can tell me, Ginny,' continued Alice lightly. 'I know more about it than you think. I know you're in trouble, and I don't think you know how to handle it.'

Ginny just looked at her silently, giving no indication she even understood.

'Rafe and Java,' said Alice, coming closer. 'Do they live in that old house? Is it theirs?'

Ginny shrugged.

'Don't you know?'

She shook her head.

'But they are your friends.'

'Sometimes.' Ginny had begun to rock gently in her chair, her eyes distant, like those of an autistic child. Alice took her hand.

'Ginny. Look at me.' The lavender-grey eyes fixed on hers, sweet and empty, as if the soul behind them were simply a blank, with no more life in it than a beautiful mirror.

'I found the syringes in your cupboard. I saw you go out with Java. Is he selling dope? And what else is he doing? At the church . . . what was he doing there?'

Ginny stared blankly.

'You have to tell me, Ginny. You have to tell Joe. He'll help you, you know, whatever you're involved with. All you have to do is tell him. Will you?'

But Ginny had withdrawn again, this time completely, her eyes blank and dilated in her thin face.

'Ginny. You have to tell someone. You have to get help before you become too involved. If it was only drugs they were involved with it might be OK to keep quiet, but I was there in Grantchester that night. I saw you digging in the churchyard. And what about the box in your suitcase? I know where that came from. It was in the wall of the church, marked with a brass plaque. Why did they take it, Ginny? What are they doing it all for?'

Ginny smiled, with the blank, heartbreaking sweetness of a brain-damaged infant, and her voice was a shifting of dust.

'I'll tell you everything,' she promised. 'Just wait till Joe gets here.'

Half an hour later, when Joe knocked on the door, Ginny was still there, looking into the fire and rocking gently to herself, like a cursed princess in a fairy-tale.

One

I suppose they think I'm safe here; safe from myself
and my delusions. I have a nurse to bring me a
soothing drink of camomile when I go to sleep; I much
prefer whisky, but they tell me it excites me. On sunny
days I am allowed to go for a walk around the grounds,
but I prefer to stay in the library and read. Sometimes
my doctor comes to keep me company; I beat him at
chess. I like him, inasmuch as I like anyone here, and I
talk to him, though I am certain he does not believe
me. My proof, the books and the pictures, mean
nothing to him. His concern is with my mind, though I
tell him that only my soul is worth saving now. A
young man, Doctor Pryce, young and strong and filled
with health and laughter, the way I remember Robert
in the years before Rosemary.

He tries to help. He even brings me books, all the
ones I ask for; he shakes his head and grins and says;
'They'd have my neck for this if they knew I was
encouraging you,' but he brings them; Frazer and
Crowley and Ahikar, even the writers of fiction,
Lovecraft and Poe and the modern ones, whose names
I forget, book-titles emblazoned in red foil on cheap
black paperback covers; all those whom I thought
might have met Rosemary in one or another of her
guises, kindred spirits who might somehow give me a
clue as to how to escape her . . . though I never find
what I am looking for. He sits quietly with me as I

229

search feverishly; sometimes I read him passages from works in Latin and French and German; I do not read Romanian, which is a pity, as many of the texts I need are not publicly available in translation. I send money to the local university, so that impoverished and unquestioning students can do the work for me, but it is a slow and impatient business. The young man nods and seems to listen; sometimes I find myself wanting to warn him; all your knowledge, I want to tell him, is nothing in the face of her knowledge, her hunger. If she were to look at you, just once, you would become what I became, with all your intellect and your certainties. She knows, by God! Knows and remembers. Remembers and waits.

My research is fruitless, I know; there is no way to stop her. I tried once; maybe she was careless. It took her thirty years to return; by now she is reborn. Maybe by the time you read these pages, she will be full-grown. All I know is that I will be dead; maybe by my own hands, maybe by hers. She will never allow me to interfere again.

The young man is intensely logical; he tries to use my research to prove me wrong. How can she be a vampire, he says, when the medieval accounts of vampirism in Romania do not correspond in the least with what you believe you know of her?

No factual or folkloric source describes a creature such as you have described.

No name fits her, I tell him; in the same way, all names do. All I know is that she is old, as old as the corruption from which she came, though at the same time monstrously young, and pure. More so than any human has the right to be. She is power, I tell the young man; he nods and smiles at me behind his hands. She is something which transcends legend, as God transcends childish superstitions of loaves and fishes. I suppose that Jung would have called her an evil anima; you see, I can speak in your language too, I can use your arguments better than you yourself, but that cannot exorcise the demoness which rides my dreams, revealing my innermost fears, my lusts and fetishes. The image of blood which transcends all my visions of her sickens and excites me, as I suppose you would say my conception of my own sexuality appalls me.

I am a man who prides himself on intellect and rational thinking; inconceivable, that there should be such elemental forces beyond my conscious thought; repressed, they only grow, like mould in a crypt, bursting out at last, unbridled, into a positive orgy of self-recriminatory, sadistic fantasy. The part of myself I cannot accept takes on a different identity ... half lusting, half terrified, I call the entity Rosemary. I imagine that it is she who is responsible for the darkness I have uncovered within myself. I make it into a werewolf fantasy, of murder and feeding by night, of blood, mystic river of the subconscious; Rosemary the vampire, irresistible and lethal ... I substitute the kiss she gives me for an act of aggression, a bite (is not every sexual act an act of aggression, and am I not inherently afraid of women?) which makes me into an imitation of herself. Part of me wants it, to be wanted, loved, aggressed, the other part fears it, disassociates itself once more, and distorts the very natural desire for a beautiful woman into something perverse, monstrous, even to the point of deluding myself into believing that I was guilty of the most bestial of atrocities.

You see, I tell him, I speak your language. A guilt-complex involving my basic fear of women, perhaps a latent homosexual tendency based on same, and emerging on the event of the tragic death of my best friend ... and here we have all the classic elements of a neurosis.

He smiles doubtfully; he has heard me speak in this fashion before; the first time, he was elated; could it be that at last I was showing some proof of recovery? He

231

has heard me speak; he is puzzled at the apparent coherency of my arguments, my apparent sanity in all areas except one.

She is not a neurosis.

She is neither vampire nor werewolf nor neurosis, but a real entity. Fragments of her walk the pages of books, but her reality is something more real even than that; she is an infection of the soul, no human being, but something older and more archetypal than the most familiar of Jung's figures. I call her the Blessed Damozel.

They took me home, you know, after that night at the bar; it would never have done to leave me to my own devices. The police would have found me half an hour later, still screaming as the café burned; as it was, they found nobody, and the others half dragged me, almost catatonic with the shock of what we had done, to Rosemary's hideout. It was a disused warehouse, half burnt to the ground in a fire several years previously, and damp, but it was an excellent place to hide. She took me in hand; I remember her hands around my neck, her breath on my cheek as she held the beaker of hot whisky to my lips; I gagged, drank, spluttered, but managed to keep down the drink.

'Don't worry,' she told me, her hair hanging down towards me, almost touching my face. 'The worst is nearly over. You'll feel ill for a while, you'll have a fever and bright light will hurt your eyes, but it will be over in a week or two. Drink some more.'

I swallowed convulsively; my tastebuds cramped. I struggled to raise myself to my elbows and looked round. Rafe and Java were sitting together in a corner, their backs turned to me, somehow secretive. I could hear the intimate sibilances of their conversation, light as cobwebs on the still air. Zach was asleep already, hunched beneath a pile of sacking and blankets, his face turned at an odd and somehow touchingly youthful angle into his folded arms.

232

Elaine was nursing Anton, rocking him to her thin body and singing a little meaningless song.

'Be still,' admonished Rosemary. 'Everything will be all right.'

But I could not be still.

'What happened? Did I . . . I must have been . . .? Did we . . . What happened?'

'We are the chosen ones,' said Rosemary softly. 'We do what we have to do. You're with us now; we chose you. Don't worry; you'll get used to it in the end; all the others did.'

With a lunge and a wrench which pulled every muscle in my aching back, I sat bolt upright. I was caught between an unhealthy laughter and a pinnacle of mounting hysteria.

'What do you mean?' I shrilled. 'You're telling me I'm a kind of . . . *vampire*? Like Dracula? I'm a creature of the night? I drink blood? I'll have to live in a coffin all day and burst into flames if I go into the sunlight?' I thrashed at the beaker of whisky and knocked it out of her hand. For a moment the liquid was an amber necklace strung out across the dusty room. I made a grab for her, meaning to shake her; maybe I shouted something. I saw Java make a sudden movement in the corner, caught the veriest flick of a glance from his cold eyes, and knew he was ready to intervene if I showed any sign of offering violence to Rosemary. The poisoned laughter welled up in me again.

'Vampires!' I hooted.

Rosemary looked at me with a cold, sad calm.

'No one mentioned that name but yourself,' she chided gently. 'There are no vampires. But we are different, as you are different now. We have certain . . . privileges. And we must feed. You know we must.'

I shook my head.

'No! I don't want . . . I mean . . . I wish . . . don't want to live forever . . . don't want to be chosen . . .'

'Neither did Moses,' said Rosemary. 'You'll get used

to it, I told you. We're different from other people, Danny; we've got power. The rest of them are like cattle to us. Do you ask cattle whether they want to be eaten? In the Bible it says that God gave us dominion over all the other beasts of the field; and Danny, *they* are the beasts of the field. When you get used to this idea, you'll realize what a chance we've given you . . . no, not to live forever, even I can't do that, though I've lived longer than you could ever imagine, but to live more, and experience more, learn more than any other man you know. I've given you life.'

'You've made a monster out of me,' I said bitterly.

Rosemary looked angry. 'You're still a little man, Danny,' she said with contempt. 'You haven't understood a word of what I have been saying. There are no monsters. I have given you more than you ever dreamed of, powers . . . and with power come new appetites. No, I have not changed you into a vampire; your appetites come from *you*, not me. You see, Danny, your subconscious knows what you need a lot better than you do. And it compensates, allowing you to transfer the commonplace, but very normal, feelings of guilt you are experiencing onto me.'

She smiled. 'You will adjust soon enough,' she said reassuringly. 'Soon you will wonder why on earth you had to make such a fuss about it all. But it is normal, and after all, you are still very much a normal man. Later, I will begin to teach you.'

Well, I suppose you have seen her pictures; you know how lovely she was, and maybe you can begin to understand how easily I was subjugated. But it was not simply her beauty; as she told me, she had *power*; it radiated out from her like the points of a star, and it was pure. To me, bloodstained and half-drunk and crushed beneath the dictates of religion and morality, she looked like a thing out of legend, and the cup she offered me was *freedom*, no less, freedom from everything, from my lonely life, from the law, from my

God and my conscience and the consequences of my actions. From then onwards, I would be free to take whatever I wanted from life, and there would be no one to stop me. Suddenly I wanted that freedom so badly that I was overwhelmed with panic that she might mysteriously withdraw her offer, and I reached out for her like a beggar.

'Teach me now,' I said.

What Rosemary taught me that day, on a pile of old sacks and blankets in a dusty, disused warehouse with the sunlight strung out like skeins of silk across the broken rafters, I try not to remember. Enough to say that she was sweet and soft, her hair smelt of lavender and I loved her with a desperate frenzy of which I would never have imagined myself capable. It was true then, that my altered state brought new appetites, and I sated them fully in the endlessness of Rosemary until there was nothing of me left. They had all loved her; that I knew instinctively; Zach and Rafe and Java and Elaine and Anton (seven years old, going on fifty), and that somehow made it all the more liberating and marvellous. Rosemary was the vial of eternal life; we had drunk deep of her, all of us, and she had given us grace.

Maybe you find me ridiculous, maybe blasphemous, as you read these lines; try to understand. I am not writing this for my own glory, or even to salvage my conscience, but to warn you. I am inventing nothing; I write only what I felt. This is Rosemary; this she can be again.

It is proof of the depth of the enchantment she laid on me that it was only as I was ready to leave (Rosemary having pointed out that it would be unwise to stay away from home for long enough for Mrs Brown to call the police on my account), combing my disordered hair and washing in a tub of rainwater, that I remembered Robert. I froze, the sensation of epiphany falling from me in one sudden instant of shock.

'My God!'

Rosemary turned to look at me; she was sitting on a pile of rubbish at the doorway, all fire and ivory in the sunlight.

'Danny?' Her smile was questioning, but disinterested for all that.

'Where does Robert fit into this?' The coldness grew; I began to recognize it as guilt. 'Does he know . . . I mean . . . is he . . .?'

Rosemary arched her back, stretched, and rested her head on an outcrop of masonry.

'Be realistic, Danny.' Her voice was faintly contemptuous.

'You mean he doesn't know?' I gaped for a moment. 'But he's going to marry you,' I said weakly.

She laughed.

'Poor Danny. No, he isn't chosen,' she said. 'I know it's hard for you, because you still haven't outgrown your quaint notions of loyalty, but you must, you know. Someone who is chosen must put aside all loyalties to the cattle; they are misplaced loyalties, unworthy of you. I have my own uses for Robert, but he has no part in our plans.'

'But . . . I mean . . .' I stammered.

'When you are truly one of us, I will tell you why I need Robert,' said Rosemary, still with her serene smile. 'Until then, Danny, know your true loyalties, and be satisfied with them.' I wanted to say more, but there was a stiffness in her posture and a crease between her eyes which belied the lightness of her tone; I had displeased her, I knew, by mentioning my friend, and by then, I was too much her creature to risk doing so again. I took my leave of her, without arranging another time to meet ('You'll know when I need you,' she had told me, and I had to be satisfied with that), and with my hat pulled hard over my eyes and my coat buttoned to the neck, I began the long walk home over the fields.

Two

Joe was wearing the same clothes he had worn for the concert the previous night, and he looked crumpled and tired, his mouth drawn down and his eyes narrowed and swollen. As Alice opened the door he was lighting a cigarette, hands cupped round the lighter flame to protect it from the wind.

'How's Ginny?' Alice felt a sting of irritation that he should make his indifference to her so obvious.

'She's fine,' she said. 'She's—'

'Where is she?'

'In the living-room. Look, Joe,' she caught hold of his arm as he began to open the living-room door, 'stop here a minute. I want to talk to you about Ginny.'

'Can't it wait?' he said, an edge to his voice. 'I've not slept, and I'm not up to talking much yet. You know what I'm like in the mornings.'

'I'm worried about her.'

'Why? I thought you said she was OK.'

'It depends what you mean,' said Alice. 'Do you know she takes drugs? I found some syringes in her cupboard.'

Joe stiffened slightly, and nodded. 'I knew she did,' he answered. 'She was taken off them in Fulbourn. So what?'

'I think she's still taking them,' said Alice, ignoring the hostility in his gaze. 'Last night I . . . she didn't come back till about five. The night before she—'

'Don't try to engage my enthusiasm. Just tell me what you're getting at.' He took a drag from his cigarette, ignoring her disapproving look. She forced herself to sound calm and reasonable.

'I think Ginny's in with the wrong crowd,' she said. 'Two friends of hers came by here last night, asking for her, and they were . . . they weren't nice people,' she finished lamely. 'They frightened me. I went out and followed them to an old house near Grantchester, a kind of squat. They were at the concert too, and Ginny was with them all the time.'

Joe frowned, his eyes as blank as Ginny's. 'You've been very active on Ginny's behalf,' he said neutrally.

'Well, that isn't all . . .'

'I'd better talk to Ginny, hadn't I?' he said, and pushed past Alice into the front room. She followed.

Ginny was standing by the window looking out into the street, but she turned when she heard Joe come in. Her face lit up like a child's in one of the abrupt changes Alice had seen in her, and she ran up to him and threw her arms around his neck.

'Good to see you again, Gin. You're not too tired?' His voice had softened for Ginny, Alice noticed, but there was still a hard line between his eyes, as if the sunlight hurt him.

Ginny shook her head. 'Did they keep you long last night?' she asked.

Joe shrugged. 'Too long. The thing is that the bloke they picked up and took off in the ambulance decided to snuff it on the way to the hospital. They don't know who he was yet, and no one seems to have seen what happened to him. There was too much confusion, people fighting and trying to get through the door, people thinking there was a fire and freaking out. By the time the police got there most of the people who could have witnessed something were gone, and the guy bled to death before anyone got organized. So what they did was to grab the nearest bass guitarist and say, "hey man, you were there, you must have seen something." You didn't get close enough to spot what happened, did you, Gin?'

Ginny shook her head. Alice, remembering the group of Ginny's friends at the door, frowned, and in spite of herself, spoke up. 'Maybe your friends saw something,' she suggested.

Ginny looked blank. 'What friends?' she queried.

'Rafe and Java, and the others who were there last night,' continued Alice patiently. 'You were standing with them at the back of the room.'

Ginny shook her head, a slightly puzzled expression on her face. 'I didn't know anyone at the concert except you and Joe,' she said mildly. 'I don't have any other friends.'

'But they came to see you last night,' insisted Alice. 'I saw you at the house. Come off it, Ginny, don't be silly. You have to tell us about it sometime. You said that when Joe got here . . .'

Joe was beginning to look angry, and Alice remembered the expression on his face from the early days of their friendship, that white, strained look of helplessness and rage. His fists were clenched. She continued nevertheless.

'Rafe and Java came looking for you, you know, but you never came. I followed them and saw you in the house. You can't have come back before about five, because—'

'I didn't go anywhere last night,' said Ginny, turning to Joe in dismay. 'I went to bed.'

'You didn't come back from the concert! I waited for you, but you never came. Then your friends turned up looking for you; the same ones I saw you with at the concert. They said they were called Rafe and Java. Don't lie to us, there isn't any point. We just want to know . . .'

But Joe had stepped forwards, all the softness gone from his face. He looked pale.

'Look, Alice,' he said levelly. 'I don't know what you're trying to lay on Ginny, but right now I can do without all this bloody hassle. What the hell does it matter if some friends of Gin's were at the gig? What business is it of yours anyway?' He turned to Ginny apologetically. 'Don't mind her, Gin. She has an odd sense of humour sometimes.' He looked at Alice, his eyes strange and wary, almost challenging her to say any more.

'What do you mean?' Alice began to feel angry, and tried to swallow the feeling. The last thing she wanted was a row wih Joe. 'It matters that for some reason of her own Ginny won't tell us where she's been going at night.'

'Don't start that. You want to talk, we'll talk about it later.' Joe was wearing his stubborn look, the 'you can talk and talk but I'm not listening' look Alice knew of old. For a moment he looked very like Ginny.

'We have to talk about it now,' insisted Alice, trying hard to keep her temper. 'There's no good time to start on something like this. I'm sorry if you're tired, but—'

'Just *leave* it, Alice!'

'Give me a minute, Joe, just one minute to tell you what I know, then we can leave it alone. Just let me—'

'Fuck it, you *want* a quarrel, do you? That's where you're heading. You'd really like that, would you?' The Northern accent had intensified as he raised his voice.

'Sorry,' said Alice, feeling sick. 'I thought you'd have the decency to listen to what I have to say before getting abusive. I told you, there were these two men waiting outside the house. They told me they were waiting for Ginny. I recognized one of them, the one who said his name was Java, from last night, when Ginny went out to the fair. So I asked them in.'

'Fuck it!' His voice cracked, like an adolescent's.

'Great.' Alice was almost past the point of no return now, her rage rising like warm blood. 'I ask for one minute, just one, and you can't even grant me that.

240

Don't you see that you're being made a fool of? Don't let her lie to you! I tell you, those friends of hers came here and threatened me, and she didn't come back till this morning. It's true, I can prove it. I can take you to the house. Tell him!' She turned to Ginny. 'Tell him I'm telling the truth! You can tell me. I already know far more than you think, anyway.'

Tears had come to Ginny's eyes, and she turned away, hiding her face. Alice grabbed her by the arm, pulling her round.

'Stop it!' Joe's intervention was as rapid as her own. 'Let her alone! I said, get your fucking hands off her!' His hand was lifted, as if to strike Alice; the high frequency of his emotion palpable. He was shaking, his eyes almost closed, then he gave a cry of helpless rage and hit the wall with all his strength, knocking plaster from a patch the size of a beer-mat.

With a sick feeling, Alice realized that only a tremendous effort of will had prevented him from actually hitting *her*. The thought was so ugly, so uncharacteristic, that she stepped back from Ginny, tears of reaction starting in her eyes. The thought that he might have the satisfaction of seeing her cry dried them up at the source.

'Oh, that's very mature,' she said in a silky, spiteful voice. 'Very masculine. If you find you can't cope with the truth, demolish a wall. I hope you feel better now.'

Joe was cradling his hurt hand, sobered by pain. 'I think I've cracked my knuckles.'

'Good.'

His voice was quiet again now, the shuttered look back behind his eyes. Alice had never felt such a cold rush of hatred from him, or anyone, ever before.

'What a cheap trick,' he sneered. 'What a cheap fucking trick to turn me against her. Just because you spied on her and found out that she'd taken dope you thought you'd try a bit of a smear-campaign. Did you really think I'd believe anything you had to say about

Gin? You spiteful bitch. You haven't changed, have you? Going on and on, never letting up about anything. I was well rid of you.' And he took Ginny's hand and turned towards the door.

Alice made a little noise of contempt and dismay. 'Ha! That's right. Stick your head in the sand, you poor idiot. Haven't you twigged yet? Don't you think it's obvious? There's only one reason she would want to lie to you.' She turned to Ginny. 'They're pushers, aren't they? Pushers, thieves or worse. Go on, say it. It won't make any difference to Joe, he'll stand by you whatever. But don't make it look as if I'm lying. You know I'm not.'

Silence. Ginny's eyes were brimming with unshed tears, brilliant as sunlight.

'Ginny, please!'

Joe looked grim. 'If you say another word . . .'

'Joe . . .' Alice tried to put her hand on his arm to calm him; he shook it away with a violent, uncontrolled gesture.

'Get the fuck off me!'

'Just listen, Joe!'

But Joe had clapped his hands to his ears to avoid hearing any more. Alice was speechless with amazement at the utter childishness of the gesture, and opened her mouth to make some comment, but was interrupted by Ginny.

'It's all right, Joe,' she said softly, tugging at his sleeve so that he turned back to face her, the white rage draining from his face. 'I'm sure it was a mistake. Maybe someone from the past that I'm trying to forget. Maybe someone . . . I'm sure Alice didn't mean to be rude.'

Rude? For a moment, Alice was completely disorientated. For a moment, she even began to believe she had been in the wrong. Alice saw red.

'Rude?'

Her eyes glinted dangerously.

'You were ready enough the other night, to ring me up and talk me into putting her up for you. You were ready enough to be friends.' A wave of bitterness rose in her, stifling, and she raised her hands to her face as if to revoke it.

'Old friends, we were,' she repeated, feeling suddenly very tired. A part of her remembered that the two visitors had used those very same words.

Joe looked shamefaced, the anger submerging a little, but still there, somehow.

'Look, Alice . . .' He tried to smile. 'I think we're all a bit freaked out today. I haven't slept at all, and we've all been through quite a lot, and we both overreacted, right? So there were two blokes here; that doesn't mean Ginny invited them. There were a lot of weird people in her life before she met me.'

(Before she . . . oh God! thought Alice.)

Joe looked rueful. 'You know . . .'

'Don't be afraid to say it,' said Ginny softly, grasping his arm as if to steady herself. 'I want Alice to know. I need her to. She has to know all about me before she can trust me and be my friend.'

Her eyes flicked to Alice's face for an instant; Alice caught the neon flash of a carnival wheel turning.

'There were all kinds,' she said, still looking at Joe. 'Pimps, addicts, prostitutes . . . some of them unhappy, most of them half-crazy.' She shivered. 'Crazy enough for a crazy girl like me.'

He tried to speak but she stilled him with a gesture, something which Alice, in all those years, had never managed to do.

'Sometimes they come back, though,' she said, very quietly. 'The ones that still remember me.'

And as she looked directly into Alice's eyes then, and the word 'Remember' echoed in the spaces between them, Alice was seized by the peculiar feeling that she was being given a message, a very important message which she could not understand, and the understanding of which might change the world.

Alice waited for a long time after Ginny and Joe left the house, then she went into her workroom where she had left Daniel Holmes' manuscript. She put the papers carefully back into the box, hid the box in a cupboard in her workroom, and went back into her living-room to think.

Yes, she decided, some part of her wanted to believe Daniel Holmes. Maybe the scene with Joe had finally decided her; or maybe the feelings which had assailed her since that first evening with Ginny, the dizziness, the odd, imagined scents she had associated with her; sugar, peanuts, the lower, more intimate reek of animals . . . Daniel had mentioned those too. The suspicion, the hatred Alice had felt for Ginny, the alien sense of dread. Rafe and Java, perfectly described. Ginny's face on paintings over a hundred years old. Ginny's face in the Corn Exchange hall; the way she had looked at the man in the leather hat. The Reverend Holmes, Daniel's nephew, in the church. Doctor Pryce, Daniel's doctor, Ginny's doctor, dead in Fulbourn. Ginny's denials in front of Joe. Yes, she thought she might be beginning to believe him.

'Hello? Fulbourn Hospital. Can I help you?'

'I'd like to speak to Doctor Menezies, please.'

'Just hang on a moment, I'll see if he's here.'

Again, the soothing music, as Alice was put on hold. Tapping her fingers irritably on the side of the receiver, she waited, all the while keeping her eyes on the box in which she had filed all Daniel Holmes' writings.

'Hello. Menezies speaking.'

'Good morning. It's Alice Farrell; maybe you remember speaking to me the other day. I . . .'

'Yes, I remember.'

Alice hesitated. 'I'd like to arrange for us to meet . . . I have a . . . problem I'd like to discuss.'

'I see. Perhaps you'd like to give me some idea of the nature of your problem before we meet?'

'No.' Alice shook her head. 'I'd rather not discuss this on the phone . . . I wouldn't know where to start. I'd . . . rather make an appointment.'

'As you wish.' The voice was cool, almost disinterested.

'Today? This morning?'

'I have a slot at half past twelve.'

'Fine.' Alice was relieved. 'That'll be fine.'

'Right. Well, if that's all . . .'

'Wait.' Alice took a deep breath, marshalling her energy. 'Who did you say was the doctor who died recently? Doctor Pryce?' A long silence from the other end of the phone.

'Hello?'

Menezies's voice, sharp and maybe wary. 'If you're from the Press, you're wasting your time. I don't give interviews.'

'I'm not from the Press. I just want some help,' said Alice firmly. 'Why? Is there any problem? Is it something to do with Doctor Pryce?'

Another long pause. Then his voice, cool and remote. 'I think that maybe we do need to talk, you and I. I really think we do.'

One

Cambridge, *July 1948*
Fulbourn Hospital, *March 1978*

I could not remain in my apartment any longer, for fear that Mrs Brown, who knew me too well, might comment too publicly on my changed appearance and manner, and so as soon as I arrived home I locked myself in my room and began to plan my escape. First, I bathed thoroughly and burned my bloodstained shirt; an expensive habit, no doubt, but I had had to learn cunning, and though my brain was wracked by wheels within wheels, my new-developed sense of self-preservation took over and planned, coldly, my new life with all the precision of a man born to the ways of Cain.

By now I was beginning to feel light-headed again; remember, I had hardly slept, hardly eaten, except for what I will not mention, and I had seen more in twenty-four hours than I ever imagined in all of Heaven and Hell; and the knowledge I acquired on the way was written across my face. Looking at myself in my old mirror, I saw a half-stranger, unshaven and hollow-cheeked, eyes brimming with the light of power, frightening and ... yes, oddly beautiful. I smiled at myself, noting a hitherto undiscovered sensuality about my mouth, a savage carelessness which had not been there before. I remembered Rafe, and how like an angel he had appeared to me under the bridge, and I straightened my back with a fearful pride; I was chosen. I turned away from the mirror, went to the cupboard, found the bottle of whisky and a mug. I poured myself a good two inches of undiluted whisky, drank it in one draught, like medicine, and set about my packing.

There was not very much of this; a trunk of clothes and books was everything I needed to take, but my problem was really to make good my departure without having to meet Mrs Brown; I was afraid that if my kind, motherly landlady confronted me with my bizarre behaviour I might weaken; fortunately for me, she was out, and I contrived easily enough to have a cab remove my belongings to another part of town in her absence. I left a note for her, of course, as well as two five-pound notes in an envelope in thanks for everything she had done for me (I lived frugally for the most part, hardly using up half of my generous study allowance, and I was only too happy to still my conscience to a certain extent by leaving ten pounds for her, for she really had been more than a mother to me); and by the late afternoon I was already settled in my new apartment by the Cam, a suite of three rooms on the top floor of a three-storey house. There were three other lodgers there besides myself, as the surly landlord vouchsafed. Having set eyes on the man I guessed, rightly, that as long as my rent was on time, and I did not disturb the peace, any strange habits of mine would pass unnoticed. I settled down on my bed and slept.

My rest was poor; I was troubled by dreams and memories worse than dreams, and though my eyelids were heavy with lack of sleep, it hurt to close my eyes, as if the memories which resided behind them had turned to broken glass beneath the flesh. In my moments of wakefulness my eyes were sore and crusted, and when, in the early evening, I rose and turned on the light, the brightness of it was more than

I could bear, and I had to sit in near-darkness for almost half an hour before the streaming and stinging abated.

By this time, I was hungry, and knowing that there would be nothing available for me to eat at that hour, (the landlord had informed me that only breakfast was provided – 'An' only between seven and half eight, mind?' – other meals I was expected to take outside, or to contrive for myself in the little kitchenette on the second floor), I prepared to go out.

Having dressed with care, and shaved, I made my way to a small restaurant I knew on King's Parade. I chose it particularly because my friends rarely frequented it. I ordered drinks, followed by a rare steak and mushrooms, and sat back in a comfortable chair and looked around. Despite the bland normality of the place, I had an odd sensation of dislocation, of unreality, as if the little restaurant were simply a theatrical set, with sinister engineers working behind the scenes; I imagined wheels turning behind closed doors, the familiar sounds and smells and sights of the Cambridge evening outside a cover for the cryptic machinery of another, darker world. I sipped my drink quietly, waited for the world to return to focus, but the sensation intensified . . . not an altogether unpleasant sensation, and yet it disturbed me. Two people passed the window – a young man and a girl, faces pallid in the greenish light of the street-lamps. I saw them for a moment only, but their image remained fixed in my mind for several moments after they had passed; the young man turned towards the girl, animated, she fixing her gaze demurely on the ground. For an instant, I seemed to see, with this newly acquired vision, the bone and muscle beneath their skin, the movement of the machinery of their bodies, occult and silent capsules of sinew and blood.

The thought chilled me; suddenly I was appalled at my own morbid imaginings. I told you I had never been fanciful; these thoughts seemed not to be my own, but those of someone else, some incubus with a macabre and facetious sense of humour. I turned my thoughts to the arrival of my steak, red and steaming in a pool of rich juices; the waiter set the plate down in front of me, smiled in the mechanical way waiters do, and left me to my meal. I set to eating with a hearty appetite, inhaling the rich subtleties of the meat as I cut and swallowed without even chewing, feeling the power return to my weakened body and my traumatized mind. That was all I needed, I thought to myself in satisfaction, just a good meal to set me to rights again. Rosemary and the others seemed very far away now, very unreal; inconceivable, that I had seen so much, suffered and experienced more than a normal man may in a whole life ... I even began to doubt the happenings of that night; suspecting that the powerful hallucinogen administered to me by Rafe might have been responsible for those bloody, joyful visions.

The world sideslipped again with a lurch. I looked down at my plate, at the meat, the blood ... and suddenly the sight of that blood sickened me. I remembered that other blood, so fragrant and lavish, how it had pulsed, how it had sprayed wantonly, generously ... the acidic, metallic taste of the open wound. Human flesh was whiter than beef, I thought inconsequentially, but still there was a kindred among cattle. I was chosen.

Strange, that my horror should not be of the crimes I had committed; maybe they were too much for my scrambled mind to understand. The fact that I had fed on the murdered body of a woman before she was cold seemed unreal, distant; I felt only the vague dislocated guilt I might have felt on remembering a perversely sexual dream. No, what frightened me more than I can say, what still frightens me, was the fact that such things exist, behind the still façade of humdrum life.

There was a whole world of scurrying, roiling life behind the scenes, once glimpsed, never forgotten, and I was a part of it now, inescapably caught in its busy machinery. I felt as if, in the middle of an exciting, joyful ride on the big wheel of a fairground, I had happened to look downwards, and had seen the exposed organs of the mechanism which bore me, or as if I had seen the painted sky peeled back to reveal God, like a giant puppet-master, surrounded by the wheels and pulleys which keep the stars in place, grinning down at the Earth and holding the sun in place like a sleeping yo-yo.

I pushed my plate away, unable to eat any more. My heightened awareness taunted me with new and horrific sensations; I felt the warmth of the meat on my plate calling to the warmth of my belly where, even now, the unseen machinery was converting what I had eaten into faeces; I felt, for a loathsome instant, the boiling of bacteria in my intestines, the death of millions of cells in my brain even as I thought, and I saw myself, as if through a grotesquely magnifying lens, one moment infinitely large, the atoms of my body rushing away through space at the speed of light to the vast dark forges at entropy's end, the next, infinitely tiny, endlessly dying, a mote on a mote in darkness, helpless and lost, infinitely far from God.

I reeled, disorientated, and in that moment everything returned to normal once more; the restaurant, the dim light of the candle in front of me, the fragrance of the meat, the red wine in the glass. A moment of limbo, and I could hardly even remember my previous unease, as I cut into my steak once more and ate with satisfyingly primitive joy. I was chosen.

I ordered fruit and cake and more wine, then coffee and brandy to finish. I asked the waiter for a paper, and read the *Evening Post* for a quarter of an hour or so, noticing with some satisfaction that the body in the crypt had not yet been discovered. Even the 'Body in

251

the Weir' case had been relegated to third-page status, with no new developments except that Scotland Yard were still at work investigating the cause of death. I scanned the rest of the paper for news of the previous night's activities in the tavern, and eventually located the report, half-a-dozen lines on the fourth page entitled BLAZE KILLS TWO. Obviously the fire the others had lit to cover their traces had fooled the police, at least temporarily. Feeling very much more master of myself, I paid my bill, oddly pleased at my unusual extravagance, took my coat and hat, and began to walk back to my new rooms, taking the path along the river, enjoying the carelessness of the moment, the quiet sounds of the Cam and the darkness of the path. I was not at all tired, though by now it was late, and I was not usually given to late nights, and I think that as I opened the door of my room I might have been planning to do some of my research while I waited for sleep, but as soon as I stepped through the doorway, all thoughts of books fled my mind. Even as I reached for the light, the voice stopped me, a voice shockingly feeble and hoarse, but still uncannily familiar.

'No, Danny. Don't put the light on . . . it's me.'

I squinted in the darkness, took off my glasses to see more clearly, made out a pale, unformed shape to my left.

'Robert?'

No answer, but a kind of creaking, choking sigh.

'Robert, are you all right?'

That ghastly sound again, accompanied by a scraping, shuffling sound from the direction of the bed. I was unused to the room; in addition, I had drunk far more than I was accustomed to; I struck a table in the gloom as I tried to move towards my friend, lost my balance and almost fell over a fold in the carpet.

'How did you find me? Are you in trouble?'

'Dannyyy . . .'

I reached him at last; from what I could feel, he was half lying on the bed, fully clothed. He reached for my hand, clasped it with feverish strength; he was very cold. A faint medicinal smell clung to his clothes, mingled with a much stronger reek of whisky. I put my arms around him and held him like a child, all the while wondering desperately what Rosemary had told him. That this was somehow her doing, I did not doubt; only she could have reduced him to this state. Robert was a light-hearted, practical man with a firm hold on reality and on himself; but I had long since realized that he was not strong. One glimpse of what I had been allowed to see in those past twenty-four hours would have been enough to annihilate him; somehow, I had adapted, and for the first time in all our acquaintance, our roles were reversed. He clung to me, his breath jerking painfully from his body, and I rocked him like a child, desperately thinking of some way to calm and reassure him. Whatever happened, I told myself, he must not know the truth; he must not learn about Rosemary, though whether I wished to protect him or her, I did not yet know.

'Come on, old man . . . that's better.' I rocked him until the rigidity left his body, whispered inanities while all the time I planned and calculated my approach.

'Had a bit to drink, eh? That's better . . . Hold on . . . I'll make us a pot of coffee.' I stood up without difficulty (my eyes had by now acclimatized to the darkness), went to the sink, lit a small lamp there. I ran some water into the kettle, opened the door again to go to the kitchenette.

'Don't go!' Robert's voice was high and trembling with barely suppressed panic.

'It's all right, old chap, I'll be back in a tick,' I said cheerfully. 'I'll bring us a pot of coffee, you'll see, that'll make you feel better.'

When I returned I found him slightly more under

control. He was sitting in one of my armchairs, his back to the light. His hat was lying on the floor beside him. He looked as if he had been crying; even in that dim light his face looked blotchy and flushed, oddly childlike, and his hands, clasped on his lap, showed a tendency to clench and unclench with small convulsive movements as he spoke.

'Thanks, old chap,' he said, with an effort at cheerfulness, 'good of you to salvage the wreck. I'll be all right now.' A tremor in his voice as he spoke the last syllable belied this, but I ignored it, and turned to light the fire, which had gone out in my absence. In the piling of coal and paper, the striking of matches, the fanning of the flames with the bellows, and the final deft poker-work which set the flames crackling merrily, Robert had time to collect himself still more, and when I turned to him again he was sitting upright in his chair, and his face, though drawn and rather pale, was almost back to normal again. I poured coffee for both of us, knowing that this sequence of normal, everyday gestures; lighting the fire, spooning out sugar and passing milk, was reassuring my friend better than any words I could have spoken.

'Now then,' I said lightly, when I had judged that the coffee and the warm fire had begun to take effect, 'why don't you tell me what's on your mind?' I smiled, and passed a tin of biscuits. 'Help yourself.'

Robert shook his head. 'Thanks.' He took another sip of the strong coffee (he drank it black, with a lot of sugar), then set the cup down. 'I'm sorry, Dan,' he said, still shakily, though I was glad to hear that high note of panic gone from his voice, 'I've behaved like the world's worst brute to you about the whole of this business ... I don't deserve your friendship ... especially as you've been so good to me all this time. I'm sorry.'

'Nonsense,' I said bracingly, 'it's not like you to be maudlin.'

'You're a good friend, Dan. I'm—'

'None of that,' I interrupted hastily. 'What's up?'

'Right.' He nodded, began to speak, paused. 'I don't know where to begin,' he said helplessly, 'or whether you'll believe me when I've told you. It all sounds completely mad.'

'You'd be surprised at what I can believe,' I told him grimly. 'I'm listening.'

'Right,' he said again, and as the fire died down again, between sips of the hot, fragrant coffee, I heard Robert's story, in snatches, punctuated by little incoherent asides, but as I was beginning to know the whole story better than I had ever wanted to, I understood his narrative only too well. I listened in silence, for the most part, only prompting when my friend became too tongue-tied to express himself correctly, and it was then, listening to that tragic little story, that I reached a decision which was to influence all my later actions, and may still cost me my life. Chosen or not, I had a loyalty to my friend, and I would keep faith with him. I would protect him, even from her. Even from Rosemary. Though at that moment, I still had no idea of where that decision would lead me, and into what fateful realms I would have to travel before I could call my soul my own again.

From that very first moment, Rosemary had bewitched him. Robert was very much a 'man's man'; with his public-school, army and University background he had had little contact with women, and revealed himself to be surprisingly innocent, an ideally susceptible candidate for Rosemary's special kind of seduction. He had never been in love before, nor had he ever thought he was the type, but he realized immediately that Rosemary was the woman he would love forever, and though he was torn at the thought of stealing her from me (for he knew how much I had been dazzled by her), he hoped that I would not bear him too much of a grudge. In her taunting way, she had led him to believe that she could love him, and there had followed a few weeks of idyllic happiness – seeing Rosemary, protecting Rosemary, living for Rosemary. He had forgotten everything else, working at the university with growing reluctance, ceasing to write, neglecting his friends. I guessed how cleverly she had contrived to isolate him from the world, to make him totally dependent on her; that was how she worked, eliminating everything which might interfere with her total domination of his life, setting herself up as his witch and his icon. Her mystery tantalized him; sometimes she failed to arrive at their meetings, and when he demanded an explanation for this, she would simply look at him from her bruise-coloured eyes and say, 'There are things in my life that you will never imagine or know, my love.'

Sometimes, as their intimacy deepened, he began to glimpse new facets of her. On certain days she would not leave her rooms, refusing to see even him, and occasionally, when he came to see her regardless and would not go away until he had seen her, her face was unaccountably pale and drawn, as if she had not slept, and her movements were sluggish, almost drunken. She never gave any reason for her strange behaviour or her mysterious illnesses, but looked at him with those steady, tragic eyes, and told him that he would never understand her.

He tried getting angry; but her essence slipped away from him like smoke. His new-found jealousy threatened her, but she flitted ghostlike through his grasp, retreating into herself like a flower. Her frailty was a net of steel mesh over him; his thoughts of violence and his harsh words filled him with repentance and self-loathing. He hugged his love for her to his heart like a bleeding wound, made promises and broke them immediately, was tormented by jealousy and the fear of losing her. When he glimpsed her one evening in the company of two men, his jealousy knew no bounds; he challenged her to deny that she had a lover; she ordered him out of her house. For a whole week, he was wracked by guilt and shame at what he had told her; he tried to find her, but was told by her landlady that she had moved away.

Robert began to feel afraid; he became convinced that Rosemary had committed suicide in her despair at his rejection; he began to haunt the river, he drank far more than he ought, both in public-houses and at home, drank desperately and without enjoyment, advertised in the papers for information concerning her . . . without success. Six weeks had passed already, and Robert was in a state of near-breakdown. He was afraid to come and see me in case I blamed him for his treatment of Rosemary; such was his sense of guilt that when he saw me on the bridge, and later, when I found him in the tavern, he was unable to tell me anything. He slept little, ate less, and was willing to do anything to ensure her return.

She knew it, of course.

He found her late one night in a cheap drinking-house, looking ill and dazed. Her glorious hair was loose and tangled, her face thinner and paler than ever. Her dress was grey, enhancing her frailty and her wraithlike appearance, her head thrown back against the greasy, peeling wallpaper and her eyes closed. Robert felt his heart turn to water, and for a moment he was paralysed, scarcely able to believe that he had found her at last. His next reaction was panic; she looked so ill, so wretched. He took her back to his rooms; she was unresponsive, almost catatonic, as if she had suffered a terrible shock, or taken an overdose of some hallucinogen. She was barely able even to walk, and he half carried her up the stairs, laid her on the bed, and forced hot coffee between her white lips until she seemed to recover a little.

I always knew Rosemary was a marvellous actress;

her story was superb, and Robert, susceptible as he was, believed it absolutely. She told him that she was a drug addict; that she had been one for several years, since, in fact, she had left home at the age of sixteen. It was this, and not her affair with the married man, that had driven her to attempt suicide, and though she had tried many times to rid herself of this pernicious and frightening habit, she had always failed, either due to a lack of willpower on her part, or, more likely, a lack of friendly support. Her few friends were all in the same situation; they had derived, in the past, a little comfort in being together, but it was a dangerous comfort, which sapped the willpower even more, and which made outcasts of all of them.

She had begun to take drugs under the influence of her first landlady and her husband who had given her pills to combat her sleepless nights, then she had progressed to stronger doses, and had finally discovered that she could no longer manage without them. The landlord and landlady, who had at first provided the drugs free of charge, began to demand larger and larger sums of money for their services, until Rosemary was giving them all the money she earned. She began to take on other work, to make more money. At first she was selective, taking sewing and knitting jobs or helping in public-houses, then less selective, accepting cleaning and scrubbing jobs in disreputable bars. She was noticed, of course; it was impossible for a girl of Rosemary's looks not to be noticed, and, several times, she was solicited. She rebuffed these offers with proper disgust, but the two people who had once been her protectors began to pressurize her into being 'agreeable' to various guests who frequented the house, uncouth types for the most part, who drank heavily and played cards for money late into the night. Rosemary found out that her landlord and his wife were running a private gambling-parlour under cover of their boarding-house, and her presence at their parties was considered an asset and a lure. From that point to accepting to offer her favours for money, there was a terrifyingly small step, which Rosemary, nevertheless, quite properly shrank from taking, and the poor child was reduced to a state of almost perpetual wretchedness and nervous prostration, harried from all sides, and never with enough money to make ends meet. On the scene then appeared the married man of whom she had previously spoken, giving her, for the first time in her life, hope that she might once and for all escape the fate which seemed to threaten her, and when even this hope was denied her, she saw no other solution than the river to end all persecution forever. Enter the god from the machine; myself, who at the eleventh hour saved her life and gave her the hope of a better world, and then, in the person of Robert himself, the unhoped-for, ever-dreamed-of spectre of true love, at which she clutched like the drowning infant she was. But fear had chilled her idyll for her before it even began; she was tormented by fear that if Robert ever found out what she had been, he would leave her, as the other had left her; she tried to combat her addiction in solitude, afraid to ask for Robert's support, and, predictably, she had failed. She had sought out her ex-friends in secret, and paid them to procure supplies for her, and when she had been caught out in their company by Robert, she had not known what to say to convince him of her innocence. Terrified that, if told the truth, Robert's love might turn to disgust, Rosemary gathered her pride and told him to leave her house, hoping that he would come back and promise to trust her, but he left, in his rage and jealousy, and Rosemary, believing him to be lost to her forever, succumbed to despair, and returned to the only source of comfort she had ever known. She sold the jewellery which Robert had given her, grieving bitterly for every trinket, but unable to help herself, each day which passed a new link in the chain which drew her closer to the abyss. The friends, all people of ill-repute, pimps and prostitutes and other addicts and the like, became all the more necessary to her in her isolation; she became involved in strange dealings, hinted that members of her circle might have turned to crime to finance and protect each other and, though not directly involved, seemed afraid of the police, afraid that she might be accused of being in league with criminals. It was at this point that I encountered them again, Rosemary looking ill and drained, and Robert in fine fettle, their roles seemingly reversed, but this state of affairs had not lasted for long. Rosemary had become less careful with Robert; knowing that whatever she did he could no longer make any move to challenge her, she began to show the underlying cruelty of her nature. She introduced him to Rafe and Java and Zach, insisting that as her friends they should always be welcome in his house. Sometimes they openly spent the night at her rooms. At this point I don't suppose Rosemary could have known whether Robert was infatuated enough to accept this, but I don't think it mattered to her. Perhaps the cruelty of it alone was enough to afford her the entertainment she craved. Robert was unable to deal with the situation. He tried on several occasions to leave her, but never managed; her personality changed by the hour, childlike and innocent one moment, corrupt and perverse the next. He, poor wretch, attributed this to the drugs she was taking. But even he could not help feeling suspicious of the large amounts of money Rosemary was spending; he himself had been giving her a small allowance from his own savings and his study grant, neither of which were particularly vast, but it soon became obvious that she was receiving large amounts of money from elsewhere. She had already hinted that her friends were involved in some kind of crime, and Robert became convinced that she was aware of it. And the night he had finally come in search of me, drunk and panic-stricken, he had seen something . . . at this point his story became so garbled that I could only conjecture as to what he had actually seen, but he mentioned blood on Rosemary's clothes, lots of blood, he kept saying. Even then he refused to admit that he believed Rosemary to be implicated; she was innocent, he maintained, a victim of circumstances. He knew it.

Oh, yes, she had told him a fine story. I knew Rosemary's stories of old, had been fooled by them once before, and I knew what an actress she was. I knew her, you see; not as my poor friend believed he knew her, not as Robert believed in her tales of persecuted innocence, the doomed virgin crying out for love in the cold world . . . Rosemary was no virgin; she was corrupt, steeped in darkness and in the terrible glamour of the underworld. You see, I loved her too, loved the darkness and the danger of her, loved her hate and her destruction and her promises of death. I was insane with love of her; and maybe it was that love which saved me. I loved her then, and loved no woman after her, but it was then, despite all of that, that I knew I would kill her.

Poor Robert, to be so much in love, and never to have seen her face. All he ever saw were the stars in her hair; he never felt the heat of her or tasted blood against her lips, he never knew her, the dread of her, had never taken the fruit from her hand. He never loved her enough to know that the only solution was indeed to kill her, to bury her deep under stone where her glory would be forever trapped, unseen and unguessed-at.

As I listened to him I grieved for his folly, but there was something in me which laughed too, scorned his futile sentiments, something which felt greater, stronger than a man has any right to be; after all, I was chosen, and he was . . . cattle. I pitied him, but with no tenderness. Rosemary had bled me dry of tenderness. What happened in my mind as I listened to Robert spill his tale, I do not know. I wish it had been love which prompted me; I wish it had been loyalty. I do not think it was either. If it had been Robert in that bar, where I had fed not twenty-four hours earlier, if it had been his blood spraying, I do not think it would have made any difference to the greed with which I fed; the chosen have no loyalties. There was a great coldness in me, a thinking coldness; I was not afraid. I knew then that I would not be like Robert, would not be the deluded fool feeding from her hand on what carrion she chose. She had opened chasms all around me, had dazed me with her many-faced brightness, but somehow, I, the bumbling fool, the fugitive, hiding behind the lenses of my glasses, had shown another face too. Do not mistake me, I never acted out of remorse or loyalty. I accepted the gift she had given me – the appetites. I am still not certain why I acted; maybe it is that each man kills the thing he loves . . . and I did love her. The truth is, I wanted power. To be free of her, so that I could taste the cup she had offered me.

So that *I* could be Rosemary.

262

One

Cambridge, *July, 1948*
Fulbourn Hospital, *March 1978*

I left him sleeping; curled up in the middle of my
crumpled eiderdown, face pressed childishly against
his hands, he looked self-possessed as an animal. My
poor friend. I watched over his sleep for a while, not
ungently, but with my new contempt, and at about
half past three, as the night ticked away into a darkly
virgin dawning, I went out, locking the door behind
me. The night was still, the silence filled with
hallucinations. My breath was a bright genie coming
from my mouth and hovering nimbus-like around my
head. I walked the deserted streets like a lord (*my
territory*, I found myself thinking, and I smiled),
relishing the cold, the darkness. As I left the town,
automatically veering towards Grantchester, in the
absence of street-lamps I glimpsed the dawn hitherto
only guessed-at, a thin line of pale phosphorescence at
the edges of the horizon, as if the lid of the sky had
slipped a little to reveal the seething crowds of angels.
I sniggered, childishly, at the thought, and drew closer
to Grantchester. (Not long now, I thought, then
wondered what I had been thinking about.)

A black cat crossed my path, eyes twin mirrors for a
second in the glint of the fading moonlight. It paused,
one paw raised, delicately, its thin shadow motionless
on the road, an absurd symbol of death and

misfortune, then I saw its jaws open in a soundless flexing of mew or hiss, I could not tell, and it was off into the bushes like a spray of black water. My stomach grinned, and I realized that I was hungry again. Oh, not with the desperate, stabbing sickness of that first time, but with a clenched anticipation which began at the root of my groin and spread, with a quick burst of warmth like a shot of whisky, to my stomach. Appetites, she had said.

I cursed myself for having waited so long. I should have left at midnight, when the bars closed; I might have found a drunk on a bench, alone, a waitress coming home from work ... my mind recoiled from the thought, but my stomach kept on grinning as I quickened my step. Suddenly, I needed Rosemary (*appetites*); I needed the touch of her cool lips against my head, I wanted her absence of passion, her obscene purity. I wondered that not half an hour earlier I had actually considered killing her ... and for what? I could have no loyalties, no jealousies; I sneered at myself and my prosaic values; she belonged to all of us, we belonged to each other. She was the host; we ate of her and drank of her and tasted her from a million vessels, but she could never belong to any one of us. From my earlier state of elation I was plunged into a sudden pit of blackness. My hunger was no longer pleasant; my grinning stomach twisted acidly and cramped; one, twice. My erection felt knotted, cancerous. Tears of abject repentance clouded my eyes; I had betrayed her in my thoughts, and she had turned away from me. I felt like Judas.

Later I began to recognize this frame of mind, and I took measures to avoid it, but at that time I really had very little knowledge of what had happened to me, and I became very frightened. I suppose that users of certain kinds of drug must have experienced this kind of reversal, but until I met Rosemary I had really been very sheltered, and I had not been prepared in any way for the hurricane of conflicting passions into which she had swept me.

I began to whimper, helplessly, from exhaustion and self-loathing. The world doubled, trebled, and ran down my face. My stomach sobbed and cramped; I tried to steady myself, lurched, almost fell. My hat fell off, and seeing it there on the ground I began to weep in earnest, with the tearing sobs of a young child, in whom the sorrow transcends all reasoning.

It was then that I felt a touch at my elbow, and my nostrils caught a sudden, half-pleasant odour of weeds and damp. Someone whispered my name, and I turned, with a joyful terror. It was Elaine, one of my companions of the previous night, the waiflike, wan girl with the child.

For an instant, my disappointment was so great that I could not speak; I merely swallowed my tears and pushed my glasses back into place. After a while, I put my hat back on.

'Don't be afraid,' said Elaine softly, 'I've been looking for you.'

'Why?' I intended my voice to sound bitter.

'I knew you'd be like this.'

'Like what?'

'We call it "the little death",' she explained quietly; she had the gentlest voice I had ever heard. 'You get used to it after a while.'

'I don't understand,' I said sullenly.

'I don't expect you do,' said Elaine, 'but you will. You have to eat, you know,' she added, reluctantly, as if afraid to touch on a taboo subject. She gave the word 'eat' a bizarre inflexion which made me shudder; it was as if she had said: 'You have to die'.

I looked up, my face sticky with tears, and noticed her for the first time. She was not especially beautiful, and when Rosemary had been there, I had not spared her a glance. My first impression had been one of long, tangled hair like that of a storybook witch, and giant, dark eyes in a smudgy, triangular face. Looking at her again, I saw that she did have a kind of passive beauty, not the tragic, lambent delicacy of Rosemary, but something buried deep in the bones of her face like a ruined cathedral, despoiled and burnt-out, and yet with the vestiges of grace outlined there still. Starved, I thought; she looks starved.

'How old are you?' I asked suddenly.

She laughed, softly, without joy. In the shadows, her face was paper-white, and seemed to hover, disembodied, above the collar of the ragged black coat she wore. She looked terribly young.

'Seventeen?' I hazarded. 'Twenty?'

Elaine turned her face away with a tiny sound, and I realized she was crying.

'How old are you?' I cried, realizing as I did that my meaning was different from the first time I asked.

'I don't know.'

'Who are you?' Suddenly my need to *know* was very urgent. 'Where do you come from?'

She stared at me, passively, as if she did not understand my question, or as if the whole concept was ludicrous. Then she said: 'No one. Nowhere,' quite as if it did not matter.

'You have to eat,' she repeated; it was the uppermost thought in her mind, and from the pocket of the coat which dwarfed her, she drew out a package, wrapped in cellophane paper. It was warm and loathsome to touch; I almost dropped it, until I realized that the heat had come from Elaine's body. I dropped the package into my pocket without a word; I felt my pocket exhale with its weight, like a lung. I nodded.

'Thanks.'

I paused, a world of unformulated questions on my tongue, and found I could not speak. Elaine looked at me, seemed to consider something, then smiled, painfully like a frightened child.

'You don't understand, do you?' she said.

I shook my head.

'But you love her. We all love her.' She looked unhappy, as if repeating a truth in which she had long since ceased to believe.

'I love her.' It was nearly true.

'I was a model. People painted me. At first I used to work in a milliner's shop, you know, serving customers . . . I helped to make the hats, too; I used to be good at that . . . then some men came one day, and they saw me. They said a lot of things I didn't understand . . . about my face. They said I was a stunner. They paid me really well, just to sit, with a book or a harp, while they painted me. I was sixteen. Then I met Rosemary . . . but she wasn't called Rosemary then, she was called Maria. But that wasn't her real name either.'

'When?' I felt as if I were on the verge of making a discovery; the feeling came and went; Elaine ignored me.

'She was a model too . . . they all tried to paint her, but no one managed; she was the most beautiful thing I ever saw. She was engaged to be married to a young man; another painter, William. I liked him. She was seeing a married man too. She called him Ned. He was crazy about her as well, but he wouldn't leave his wife. She didn't care about either of them, really; she would create scenes . . . you can't imagine . . . threaten this and that . . . suicide . . . but inside she was just playing games. She told me . . . made friends with me . . . taught me.'

'She chose you.' I was beginning to understand more than I dared.

'The young man . . . William,' Elaine looked at me pleadingly, 'he went mad. He burned all his paintings. He went for her with a knife.'

'Yes?'

'He killed himself.'

'Why?'

She ignored me. 'He killed her first.'

I stared at her. 'You must be wrong,' I stammered.

'No, he killed her all right,' insisted Elaine, 'but she came back. She always comes back.' There was a bleak despair in her dirty face.

'Dear girl, it isn't possible,' I snapped irritably, with the vestiges of my old, academic rationalization. Elaine turned away, and I knew that she was crying again.

'Elaine . . .' My attempt to comfort her was clumsy; my hand reached for her arm, missed, and brushed the nape of her neck with embarrassing intimacy.

'Excuse me,' I mumbled, withdrawing my hand as if it had been burnt. She did not look at me; her face was buried in the long rags of her hair. Despair emanated from her like a darkness. I was helpless in the face of it; she was like a damned soul, and the tiny keening sounds which came from her mouth were bleak as winter wind.

'Elaine.' I turned her, forcibly, to face me; pushed back her hair. Streaked wih dirt and tears, her thin face looked unmistakably erotic, and I began to see the beauty there, which had caused men to call her a 'stunner'. I opened up my arms and held her; light and thin as a child, she was, huddled up in that man's coat, and the new appetites which Rosemary had awakened in me stirred greedily. I almost expected her to draw away from me; she was such a child, but as I unbuttoned her coat, drawing my own around her body so that she should not be cold, then her dress, leaving her standing in only a torn and dirty shift, she melted towards me with a sigh and a sob. Her white skin was smooth as ivory, and her limbs were like ice, but there was warmth there too, warmth upon which I gorged myself, there on the road, heedless of who might see us. She remained passive throughout our lovemaking, childlike, without passion, but I sensed her despair abate very slightly, and when I had

268

finished, my face flushed and sweating, despite the cold, she leaned towards me and kissed me, very gently, on the cheek.

'I was beautiful once,' she said irrelevantly.

'You're beautiful now.' I said it because she wanted me to say it, but she ignored me.

'Please.' She said it with such intensity that I gaped at her, startled and uneasy. 'Help me.'

'How?' I began to stroke her tangled hair, but she pushed me away with the irritability of a child who does not want to be petted.

'Kill her.'

I stared.

'Kill her. I can't bear it . . . every night the same . . . do it while you still can . . . you never knew her . . . oh God! It's been such a long time . . . I was glad he killed her . . . I thought I'd be free . . . but she came back. She found me again. Since then . . . she knew I betrayed her . . . it amuses her to . . . oh God!' Her voice broke, and I felt the wave of despair flood from her again, as if it had never been gone. 'So long . . . and she won't let me die . . . so long with nothing but blackness and blood and death. She won't let it end . . . oh, kill her, kill her . . . please . . . please . . .'

I shrugged, once more in control. Kill Rosemary? The thought hovered on the brink of imagination for an instant, and was pushed away again. My meeting with Elaine, as well as the presence of the parcel of food in my pocket, had restored my feeling of power, my ambition. I might yet kill her, I thought, indeed I might . . . but not for Elaine. She would be mine then, as she was Rosemary's now, I said to myself; she and the others with her. Not now; but maybe. Maybe soon.

I looked down at her, but she was crying again, her face hidden in her hair. Without a second glance, I turned and walked away down the road to Cambridge, my shadow, faint in the greenish dawn, spindling before me. Even as I reached the turn of the road, a hundred yards away, I thought I could still hear her voice, whispering; 'Kill her . . . please . . .' but by then I was beyond compassion. My hand crept to check that the package in my pocket was still there; it was, and despite the cellophane wrapping I thought I caught the ripe and dizzying scent of meat. I quickened my pace, instinctively. I didn't want to be on the road when the sun came up.

One

Cambridge, *July 1948*
Fulbourn Hospital, *April 1978*

When I returned, Robert was still asleep, sprawled across my bed with the touching helplessness of deep exhaustion. Behind his pale, almost transparent eyelids, the dark blur of his eyes moved restlessly from side to side, and his nostrils flared with the anxious sensitivity of a nervous animal. I latched the door behind me, feeling light-headed from hunger and lack of sleep, and made myself comfortable in the armchair, keeping my eyes on Robert. Elaine's package was still warm in my pocket, its shape moulded like dough into the palm of my hand, and I drew it out, feeling suddenly queasy with hunger, and opened it. What flesh it was, I do not know; some dark, anonymous cut of meat with a thread of fat running through it at one side, beaded blood clinging to the cellophane wrapping. It was easier the second time; the meat was rich and high, its texture at the same time compulsive and slightly repellent; unfamiliar. I ate quickly, with nervous, guilty bites, like an overweight housewife eating biscuits, watching Robert all the time, ready to stuff the remains of my food into my pocket if he should appear to be on the verge of awakening. A few times, he twitched, catlike, his eyes moved, but did not open, and I finished the meat, cleaned the cellophane wrapping with my fingers, and licked them like a greedy child. My friend was still sleeping, his intense face strangely tranquil, milky, in the new light. Patiently, I waited for him to wake, refreshed and strengthened by the food, and once again perfectly certain of what I was going to do, as I watched and waited, my thoughts turned again, compellingly, to Rosemary.

What Robert had seen the night before, whatever it was that had distressed him so much that it had sent him running to me to be comforted like a child in the night, he had not been able to tell me, except in broken, breathless phrases. He thought he had seen Rosemary having some kind of an attack, he had said, had thought he had seen her *change* somehow, had glimpsed, or thought he glimpsed blood. I had heard enough to guess, however, that whatever it was, he still had no inkling of the truth; his rapid recovery, his deep sleep, his return to sanity all suggested to me that whatever he suspected, he could have no proof, no certainties which might endanger either Rosemary or any of the rest of us; but I could not let him go without knowing that for sure. Strange, the ease with which I slipped into my new role; strange, how easy it was for *us* to become *them*. As I looked at my sleeping friend, I felt nothing of friendship; I saw an alien, noted with critical interest the turn of a weak mouth, the fall of dark hair, every detail highlighted, focused, magnified; blue grain of dirt under the fingernails, coarse grain of unshaven face, fine, oily grain of the eyelids, behind which the trapped soul turned and twisted . . . I looked at a stranger from a different race at that moment, our shared memories, our tender friendship reduced to meaningless interchangings. I looked into the face of the stranger who had been my best and only friend, and all I saw was Rosemary.

What had he seen?

'Dan. . .?' The voice rose, waveringly; my eyes caught the gleam of his in the pale shadows, the dark

272

hole of his mouth opening plaintively, like a doll's, to call my name.

'Dan.'

'I'm here.' Tenderness, misplaced, absurdly overwhelming, flooded me again, and I reached for his hand across the bedclothes. 'It's all right, old man. I'm here.' Colours flitted psychedelically across my mind, emotions spun and blurred. I recognized the euphoria of the night before, blood spraying firework arcs across my heightened consciousness. Emotions roiled sickeningly, conflictingly, in my brain, and I stumbled, half falling across the bed where Robert was already sitting up, rubbing his eyes, his face grey in the morning light which even now filtered through the curtains. It occurred to me at that moment, and not for the first time, that I might be losing my mind, but as I began to form the thought, I returned to normal with a suddenness which left me trembling with withdrawal.

'I'm here,' I repeated, my smile falling into place with the ease of long practice. I felt so *normal* at that moment, that I could hardly believe that the tide of feelings which had assailed me not five seconds ago could have been real. *Little death,* I thought suddenly to myself, then, unpleasantly, on the tail of that thought: I'll have to eat again soon. I turned to draw the curtains; Robert was talking to me, his voice a blur of unstructured vowels until I turned to listen to him; the voice fell into place with shocking precision.

' . . . said last night, old man,' he was saying. 'But it must have been a bit of a shock to you!' He laughed, the sound barely forced. 'Don't know what came over me. I hope you weren't too worried.'

'Why . . . dear chap,' I mumbled.

'Have to face up to it,' he continued. 'Wasn't quite sober. All the upset about Rosemary, you know . . . wasn't myself. Can't begin to say how sorry I am.'

I listened with half an ear as Robert sought to justify himself; contempt and relief filled me at once. No, I

273

would not have to do anything to help him; the fool was already on the way to thinking that he had invented whatever it was that he had seen. It helped for him to have been drunk, of course; no, there was nothing for either me or Rosemary to worry about.

' . . . out of my mind . . .' I heard what he said in snatches, caught up in my own thoughts, more intense than his, ' . . . failed her once . . . not again . . . look after her . . . responsible . . . be married soon . . . happy . . . no need for anyone else . . . forget this little . . . trust . . . keep her safe . . . hope she's all right . . . coming here . . . mistake . . . glad you . . . friends again . . . was a jealous fool . . . blamed her . . . you . . . never knew how good . . . drink too much, old man . . . not good for the . . . think all sorts of . . . stupid, dangerous . . . lose her . . . damn fool . . . don't deserve her.'

I nodded when it seemed expected of me, hardly able to mask my contempt. I was relieved that he suspected nothing, of course, but at the same time I felt a keen disappointment for my friend. To think that Robert, whom I had always thought of as being shrewd and critical, could have been face to face with that terrible wild glamour and not seen it; that he could have held it in his arms, all palpitating with love and hate, and not seen beyond the frail pale envelope of flesh into the unspeakable rushing thing which possessed it. I looked at his earnest face and was hardly able to prevent myself from laughing. He was eager, wild-eyed with eagerness to believe his own fiction; his relief when he realized that he had not told me anything irrevocable the previous night was pathetic. By turns, he blustered, laughed, gazed at me soulfully and told me how lucky he was. Maybe he was, at that; after all, *he* was the one who was going to marry Rosemary.

He even managed to convince himself that he had been drunk the night before; better to believe that than to be forced into believing that the world is a wheel

274

within a wheel, and that a beloved red-haired girl may be at the axis of a hundred worlds of ecstasy and despair. After coffee, whisky, and more of his desperate conversation, I managed to persuade him to leave; by this time I was feeling very tired; bright motes danced behind my eyes, and besides, I had my own truths to confront, alone, in the privacy of my room. I was supportive, comforting, sympathetic, and between my comfort, my sympathy and my support, I managed to manoeuvre him to the door at last, to open it, and with a final smile and pat on the back, to propel him through it. I closed it with a sigh of relief; took a few deep breaths, my back against the door-frame, closed my eyes. The world sideslipped, not unpleasantly, moved on. I opened my eyes again, righted myself, moved to my armchair, sat down. I stuck my hands in my pockets (I was still wearing my thick overcoat; it was cold, and I had not bothered to light the fire); my fingers encountered the rolled-up cellophane package in which Elaine had wrapped her present. For a second, I was reminded of my schooldays, of the neat little packets of sandwiches with which my mother always crammed my pockets; ham, cheese, pickle and onion, and sometimes a great thick slice of plum cake, to be opened and eaten with great care, under the lid of a school-desk, in the dim yellow light of the winter schoolroom . . . the memory was so unexpected and so incongruous that I gave a shocked snort of mirth, clapping my hand to my mouth with a rapid, guilty gesture, then the laughter bubbled forth again, uncontrollably, cramping my stomach and my jaw, so that I half moaned and went off into another high, gassy wail of laughter, striking my palms against the side of the wall in a vain attempt to stop the hysteria.

Suddenly, someone knocked on the door.

I stopped, all traces of my laughter dissolving as if it had never been. Silence. Not a sound. Only the psychic echoes of my last carefree memory wailing, like unhappy ghosts, in the empty chamber of my thoughts.

'Who's there?' I called, trying to keep my voice from shaking. If it was Robert again, frightening me like that, I promised, I would give him a piece of my mind. But why should a knock on the door frighten me? I wondered, and hastily pushed the thought away.

'Who's there?' No answer. Only that eerie silence.

'That you, Rob?'

Nothing. The silence was more terrifying than any sound you could imagine; a rushing, cold silence like death. I almost lost my nerve; imagined myself opening the door into another world, imagined opening the door to monsters . . . imagined breaking down there and then, beginning to scream, unable to stop, to scream and scream until I was found later, still screaming, on my side of the door, with no one on the other side. But *I'm* on the side of the monsters now, my brain cried; *nothing* on the other side of the door can hurt me! Still my mind spun, breathless, out-of-control; craven. With an incoherent cry, I yanked open the door, braced myself to look on horrors. For a split second, I actually *saw* them; the shambling Freudian beasts of my imaginings; a monster's monsters. Then the shapes coalesced into one shape; neither small nor tall, a neat and felt-hatted shape, features sharp and hard, cynical blue-grey eyes like broken glass.

It was Inspector Turner.

Two

Cambridge, *April 1990*

Doctor Menezies was older than Alice had expected; a big, fat man of about fifty, with thick, bushy black hair and a full beard, who wore his blue pin-striped suit with reluctance and unease, as if he would have been more at home in a lumberjack shirt and jeans. His voice seemed less sharp than it had sounded on the phone, and Alice noticed that he moved his legs with difficulty, as if the joints were painful. Sharp, colourless eyes caught her glance as she preceded him into the office, and he smiled.

'Polio,' he explained shortly, manoeuvring himself into an armchair by the window. 'Do take a seat.'

He gestured towards a couple of chairs by the side of a desk; Alice sat down. Her eyes flicked over the room, liking it. Green plants in front of a wide, sunny window, a Thai sculpture on a stand, some Indian abstract prints.

'Nice room,' she said, pausing to marshal her thoughts and fidgeting nervously with the handle of her raffia bag.

'I don't know how much sense all this is going to make,' she said at last.

'Take your time,' said Menezies blandly, turning a paperweight over in his large sunburned hand.

His colourless eyes gave nothing away; his body language carefully studied to give the impression of quiet interest. He asked no questions, simply allowing Alice to talk, and when she finally stopped, he waited for a long time before he said anything in reply. When he spoke, it was to ask a question.

'Have you been to the police?'

Alice shook her head. 'I didn't think they'd believe me,' she said. 'Besides, I don't have proof of anything. It all sounds crazy.' She shrugged. 'But somehow it seems to make sense. That's why I wanted to find out about Ginny. I just wanted to . . . I needed some kind of an explanation.'

Menezies watched her, inscrutably, for a moment, then his eyes hardened and left hers.

'I'm sorry, Ms Farrell,' he said abruptly. 'I can't deal with your problem. However, I'd be happy to recommend a colleague who . . .'

'Why?' Alice was completely thrown. 'I . . . I want *you* to help. Why can't you?'

He shook his head. 'I don't feel qualified,' he said in a clipped, professional tone. 'I'm too much involved already. I'm sorry, but I don't want to have anything to do with this.'

'What do you mean?' Alice was dismayed. 'How can you say that? At least give me a chance. Read the manuscript. Daniel's manuscript. I tell you, it all makes sense. Read it!'

Menezies gave a long sigh and ran his hands through his thick hair. He looked tired, drained somehow, his eyes shuttered.

'Ms Farrell,' he said wearily. 'I don't have to read his manuscript.'

Alice opened her mouth to say something.

'Please don't interrupt,' he said irritably. 'I don't have to read it because I already know what's in it.'

Alice looked at him questioningly, but he continued in his new, weary voice, as if every word was a little too heavy for him to enunciate.

'I used to share a room with Jeff Pryce,' he began, 'back in the days when we were young doctors and didn't have very much money. We were still training; we were each assigned an "incurable" at the hospital to write part of our thesis on. Jeff got Daniel Holmes.'

He swallowed, almost painfully. 'For three years he worked with Holmes, night and day. It began as professional interest, and developed into a real friendship. He used to think, eat, sleep, breathe Holmes. He used to go to libraries all around the country to try and find the books Holmes was always asking for. In a way, I think he loved that old chap. I met him a few times, but most of the time Jeff and I discussed him. He was a casebook schizophrenic, intelligent, erudite, and Jeff always claimed he was non-violent, despite his fixation with violence. He was a chronic alcoholic and he was taking a lot of heavy medication, but it never seemed to do much good. Jeff and he used to talk psychology together, and he would show Jeff the chapters of his book. In turn, Jeff showed me.'

He laughed softly, as if reminiscing.

'God, the arguments we used to have about Daniel Holmes! I used to twit Jeff all the time about how much effort he wasted on the man; I wrote the whole of my thesis on the basis of a few preliminary visits to my "incurable", but Jeff . . . there was no stopping him. I think he would have gone on seeing Daniel Holmes forever, if he'd lived. What was worse, I'm not sure Holmes hadn't convinced him, in some odd way, that what he believed was true.'

Absently, Menezies traced the lines on one worn palm.

'He'd been talking about dying long before his suicide,' he continued, 'making arrangements and the like. He seemed to think that the people he was afraid of were getting closer, that they wouldn't let him live much longer. I took that for a typical paranoid delusion, and if Jeff had had any sense, he would have too, and taken steps to protect Holmes from himself. But by that time Jeff was nearly as bad as he was. Out of bloody-mindedness he wouldn't give the case to anyone else, so it was too late before anyone got an inkling of the old boy's deterioration. Then one day Holmes cracked and hanged himself, and the whole thing came out. It nearly ended Jeff's career.'

For the first time since he had begun to speak, Menezies looked at Alice and smiled. 'For years after, Jeff Pryce was a man consumed by guilt,' he told her. 'He blamed himself for Holmes' suicide, kept saying that he should have looked after him better. I think the reason for his being such a good doctor was something to do with the fact that he never forgot about Daniel Holmes, and spent his life trying to make up for that first, youthful mistake.'

'But I don't understand,' said Alice, 'if you already know about Daniel, why can't you help me? You're probably the only person who might be able to . . .'

'No,' Menezies shook his head. 'Because that isn't the end of the story.' He pulled at his tie to loosen it, and went on. 'Because when you phoned me about Virginia Ashley the other day, and I said I didn't know her, I lied.'

Alice glanced sharply at him.

'Ginny was Jeff's patient,' said Menezies, 'I told you the truth about that. She was admitted for a few months only. She had been taking drugs, amphetamines mostly, but some hallucinogens too, things like belladonna and muscarine. She was in a state of emaciation, she was addicted to the amphetamines, and she had had experiences while under the influence of hallucinogenic toxins which she could no longer distinguish from reality. Jeff and I had been good friends for a long time; he used to tell me about the most interesting of his cases; nothing unprofessional, you understand, but enough for me to see that he was really quite excited about this girl. I never saw her, but he used to tell me how pretty she was, how innocent. I think he was quite taken by her. Then one day he came to my house to see me, and he was white and shaking. I thought he was going to have a stroke. I tried to calm him down, but I really couldn't get much sense out of him, except that he'd seen something or someone who had disturbed him. I gathered that it was something to do with Ginny, or some friends of Ginny's, but on top of that he was also ranting about Daniel Holmes and some things he had read in his manuscript. It didn't help that he was more than a little drunk when he came to see me.' Menezies shrugged.

'I did the only thing I could at the time,' he carried on, 'I gave him a Valium and put him to bed. The next day when I tried to talk to him, he wouldn't tell me anything, and pretended he didn't remember. That night he took an overdose.'

Alice stared at Menezies for a moment.

'He saw Rafe and Java,' she said, somehow knowing it to be true.

'I don't know what he saw,' said Menezies. 'But maybe now you see why I won't help you.'

He shook his head slowly. 'I'm sorry. That damned manuscript.'

'Look,' said Alice desperately. 'Don't you see? No one else *can* help me! You're the only one who will believe me. You knew Daniel, you knew Doctor Pryce. You have to help me. If Daniel is right, then Ginny *is* Rosemary.'

'I don't want to know.' His voice was flat. 'I'm a doctor. I do my job, and I'm good at it. But I do know my limitations, and this is where my involvement ends. I'm not interested in finding out any more about this case, and I wouldn't be any good to you if I was.'

'But she killed Daniel,' pleaded Alice. 'And probably Jeff Pryce too. Who knows what else she might do?'

'I don't know!' His calm was gone, and his voice was strained, almost cracked. 'I don't want to know!'

'If she went to the trouble of finding Jeff Pryce,' carried on Alice pitilessly, 'how do you know you won't be next?'

Menezies nodded, a thin smile on his lips, as if he had expected her words. He hesitated for a long time. Then: 'I won't promise anything.'

'You'll think about it?' Alice was overjoyed.

'I said I won't promise anything,' he repeated. 'Just leave the manuscript with me. I'd like to read it all the way through. But don't expect anything more; any help I can give you will be for my own interest, and nothing to do with my personal practice. OK?'

Alice nodded.

'OK.' She drew the manuscript out of her bag, took it out of the box she had carried it in. 'I'll ring you up tomorrow. Is that all right?'

He nodded.

'Don't get your hopes up too high,' he warned. 'You'll probably find that there's nothing I can do to help you.' For a moment, he hesitated, then, deciding abruptly, he reached up to a shelf above his desk where a number of old books were stacked.

'You might as well have this, Ms Farrell. I'm sure you'll find it interesting.' Alice looked at the spine of the book, and smiled. It was Daniel's book, *The Blessed Damozel, a Study of Pre-Raphaelite Archetypes*. Glancing at it briefly, she saw that it had no illustrations except for the black-and-white reproduction on the cover; (a rough-looking sketch by Burne-Jones of his own Blessed Damozel, Maria Zambaco) but she held it tightly, her eyes bright, impelled by the sense of *rightness* she felt at having it. Impulsively, she opened it at random. She recognized Daniel's style immediately, and, in doing so, felt a warmth, almost like reading a letter from a distant friend. Somehow his insanity did not seem so shocking now that she shared it, and she read the page avidly, taking in every word and reference, feeling somehow proud that she and she only could understand what the writer had been speaking of. There was Rosemary in every paragraph, every description. The whole thing was a kind of exorcism of Rosemary, as had been her three Ophelia pictures. The whole thing seemed like an extension of the diary; like the diary, it might have been written for her alone.

'Thank you,' she said. 'Thank you so much. I knew I was right to come to you for help.'

Menezies gave a twisted smile. 'I'll take the manuscript. Nothing more. No promises,' he warned. And though Alice smiled and nodded agreement as he stood up, carefully placing the manuscript into a big Post Office envelope, and though she kept her features carefully indifferent while she shook hands with him and left his office, she still felt a tiny lifting of tension within her ribcage, as if a small bird imprisoned there had just begun to sing.

One

Cambridge, *July 1948*
Fulbourn Hospital, *April 1978*

I cannot believe that he did not see the guilt written so
clearly on my face; it seemed to me that for an endless
moment we stood there, speechless, in the little circle
of the knowledge we shared. My head spun with
delirium as his cold eyes held me, appraisingly, and
his thin, cruel smile cut into me like a scalpel. Then I
recognized my paranoia for what it was and slipped
into my role with a slick ease which delighted and
terrified me. There. I was committed. I had declared
war against the light.

'Inspector Turner!' I said, with a little laugh, as if to
deprecate my own forgetfulness. 'Do forgive me; I
really wasn't expecting you. For a moment I even
found myself forgetting your name.'

The Inspector neither acquiesced nor denied
anything; he simply fixed his piercing grey gaze on me
and raised his hat with meticulous politeness. I
recognized the technique; he wanted me to speak too
much, thereby giving something away. I smiled;
incredible, how easily it all came to me.

'Do come in,' I offered. 'I've just made some coffee;
would you like a cup?'

'I wouldn't refuse one,' answered Turner, with one
of his grave half-smiles. I opened the door, showed
him in. I noticed his eyes flick over the room, taking in

the unmade bed, the cold grate, the neat, ascetic rows of books on the shelves by the fireside. I indicated the armchair.

'Please take a seat,' I said casually. 'The coffee won't be long, in fact,' I added, as if on an afterthought, 'I'm rather glad you've come to see me.'

He gave me a mildly questioning look.

'I've been wanting to thank you for your support last time we met,' I said, pleased with the mixture of openness and slight embarrassment in my voice.

'I wasn't myself, you know,' I admitted. 'I'd had a bad shock, as well as having just recovered from a severe cold at the time, and I'll always appreciate the way you put me at ease.' I wondered if I were overdoing the act; turned, rinsed him a coffee-cup in the sink, and began to fiddle with the coffee-pot, waiting for him to state his business. He did not. I poured, set the cup on a saucer, offered the biscuit-tin, watched him help himself to two iced rings. He dipped them, methodically, in his coffee, with the same serious watchfulness, and I began to wonder whether my earlier awe of him had not been the product of my imagination. Then I realized that the biscuit-dipping was an act; he was watching me from beneath his eyelashes, waiting to see if I would break.

'Anything I can do to help?' I said. 'Have you found anything new out about that poor woman?' (*For all you know or care, you might have been eating a part of the poor woman for breakfast*, remarked a sour voice inside me, and the thought was so ludicrously ironic that a bubble of laughter rose in my throat, and I was forced to look away to hide my grin.)

'No,' said Turner.

'Then there's been another murder?' I said, boldly – it wouldn't do for me to seem too obtuse.

'What makes you think that?' he said sharp as a scalpel, though to all intents and purposes, he was still engrossed in the milky surface of his coffee.

I made my voice a trifle louder, cultivated a hint of the boorish dogmatism of the layman.

'Well, it stands to reason, doesn't it? If a man can commit a crime and get away scot-free, then he's likely to start again at some time, isn't he? Especially . . .' I lowered my voice again, 'well . . . he must be a lunatic.' The tone, I liked to think, was just right for the role of ordinary citizen repelled but fascinated in the face of insanity. I allowed a moment to pass.

'Are you on his track?' I inquired, with feigned interest.

He shrugged. 'It isn't as easy as people think, being a policeman,' he said, drinking his coffee. 'In fact, there's no reason for anyone to think that the two deaths are even related.'

'So there *has* been another death?' I queried.

The inspector nodded.

'Two,' he said neutrally. 'A waitress and a bartender in a public-house late the night before last.'

I frowned.

'Wasn't that the inn which burned down?' I asked, looking puzzled. 'I read about it in the paper. A place called The Swan.'

Turner nodded mildly. 'That's right,' he agreed. 'But the pathologist's report seems to suggest that the two victims hadn't been killed in the blaze, as we first thought. The bodies weren't very badly charred, you know,' he added pensively. 'It takes quite a big fire to destroy bodies.'

'Ah,' I said lamely. Curse the man, he seemed to enjoy my embarrassment. 'So did the criminal try to hide his tracks by setting the place on fire?' I poured another cup of coffee, glad to be able to shift my attention from his cold, ironic eyes. 'It's amazing what modern science can discover, isn't it?'

'Certainly.'

'Do you think it's the same man?' I kept my voice eager, interested, though inside I was reeling with the panic of utter certainty; *he knows, my God! He knows*.

'I don't think anything.' His tone was final; he did not intend to be distracted. 'I'm not in charge of the case; Scotland Yard are better equipped to deal with that. It's just that ... well, I do like to keep a professional interest in these things.'

'Ah.' His face was unreadable, but I thought I was beginning to understand a little. Turner had struck me from the beginning as being a forceful, dogged character. He had questioned me himself instead of asking someone else. His manner was understated, efficient. And this had been his case, the body in the weir had been 'his' body; quite natural, in fact, that he might feel some resentment at the way his case had been taken in hand, publicly and flamboyantly, by the Yard. Suddenly he spoke again, changing the subject abruptly.

'I see you've changed your lodgings,' he said. 'Was there any especial reason for that change? Your landlady tells me it was very sudden. You left without even saying goodbye.'

'Ah, yes.' I stumbled over the words, hesitating. 'There was a reason for that.'

Turner waited patiently.

'I ... have begun to be ... er ... intimate ... with a young lady,' I began. I did not need to feign embarrassment; my unease was real enough. I simply hoped that the Inspector would mistake my blush for one of modesty. 'There are reasons, which I am sure you would not like me to go into ...' I continued, 'for which the young lady and I—'

'Of course,' interrupted the Inspector smoothly. 'Please don't feel that I am prying into your private life. Everything you say will remain confidential, naturally.'

I smiled and nodded.

'I wonder,' he went on in the same smooth tone, 'whether you could recall whether you were in the

288

company of this young lady the night before last, Mr Holmes?'

He saw my change of expression. 'A purely routine question, I assure you,' he told me.

I frowned hard, as if I were trying to remember.

'No, I was on my own that night, and I really didn't do very much, I'm afraid, Inspector,' I said. 'I went for a walk around the town, as I usually do on a fine evening, then I worked on my thesis.' I caught his questioning glance. 'I'm writing a book,' I clarified.

'Fiction?'

'Oh, no.' I shook my head, laughing. 'Another stuffy academic tome, I'm afraid. A study in Pre-Raphaelite archetypes. It's a bit of a hobby-horse of mine.'

Turner nodded as if he understood.

'And the Swan Inn? Have you ever been there?'

I shook my head. 'I don't go out very much, Inspector,' I explained. 'And when I do, I tend to go to restaurants or the theatre, not to inns. I don't have a good head for alcohol.'

I saw his quick glance at the open whisky bottle on the bedstand, and cursed myself for being too talkative. 'For a friend,' I explained quickly.

The Inspector lingered for another few minutes, endless minutes spinning off into blackness like evil seeds, then he left, raising his hat to me with a polite 'thank-you for your time, Mr Holmes', and as soon as he was safely behind that door again, I gave myself up to the outpouring of my tension. With a cry of rage, I flung myself onto the bed, biting at the pillows and the coverlet in helpless fury and despair. I was certain that he knew; how, I could not tell, for I was equally certain that he had no proof.

When I had expended the main part of my anger, I began to think rationally again, and to consider what danger he might present to me. He was a policeman; he was trained to detect guilt; but I was inclined to think that the advantage was nevertheless on my side.

The truth was so incredible that it would take him longer than a lifetime to discover it; and now that I suspected that he was watching me, I could prepare myself. But what if he had me followed? I wondered. I had to go out to eat. What if he had me followed?

The immediacy of my mind's reply stunned me for a moment; unhesitatingly, it flung back, not a thought, but an image of such stark intensity that it over-whelmed me momentarily, loaded as it was with sense-impressions and a startling sense of *yearning* . . . it was the image of myself striking, leaping as an animal leaps, my knife held facing upwards, a flicker of straight, cold light in the shadows. I imagined myself striking, blood spraying across my face in a mystic arc, precious as the fount of life; saw the man beneath me fall, drowning under beauty, disbelieving, mouth open like a black hole above a larger, gaping mouth . . . felt the joy . . . joy. I felt the day's meal clench once inside me like a fist, pounding at the lining of my stomach, and I retched, dry, sharp bursts of nausea which turned into a recurrence of my hacking cough.

Not yet, my mind whimpered desperately, as I clutched my stomach, doubled up on my bed, but the knowledge, untouched by remorse or nausea, stayed with me all the same. *Thought made flesh* I thought to myself, with the hysterical cackle of laughter, and though a part of me still whimpered and wept, it was that thought, the knowledge that if I had to I would kill him, yes, and feed on his corpse, that followed me, relentlessly, into the unconsciousness of sleep, and the cryptic convolutions of my labyrinthine dreams.

Two

Alice could no more have passed a fair by than she could have ignored a packet of biscuits in her food-cupboard. It was not that she particularly liked fairs; rather, she liked the *idea* of them, the memories of childhood that they re-created, better than the reality. Popcorn stands, coconut shies, candy floss, pink and sugar-sticky nests for wasps and bees (memories of a much younger Alice; 'Here, take this, it's nice,' with candy-floss in her hair, in her eyes, everywhere, watching the fat wasps from the corner of her eye in mute terror, afraid even to speak in case one of them managed to fly into her mouth), tall men with loud voices and cold travelling eyes ('Wanna try the hoopla, girlie? Wanna win a gol'fish?), the roundabouts and the big wheels and the hot dogs and the litter and the smells; wagons with gilt doorways and exotic secret signs. (Gipsy Rosina; Crystal Balls, Tarot Cards, Palms; All Fortunes Known!!) Pushing and shoving, wise-eyed gipsy children jostling for pockets in the crowd ... doughnuts ... spending all her pocket-money on the shooting range only to win a single yellow balloon which burst on the way home ... the high reek of animals in tiny cages ... flying high on the big wheel ... catching the pompom on the roundabout and winning a free ride ... walking through the fair late at night with Joe ... Joe winning a coconut on the

291

stand ... laughing. Joe eating pizza from a greasy paper plate ... watching the stars both electric and real ... A maelstrom of conflicting memories, like confetti, showered her from every side. For a moment, she pretended to consider the worn, faded sign; gilt and red; FAIR! BIGGEST IN THE SOUTH! ANIMALS! BIG RIDES!! ALL THE FUN OF THE FAIR!!! Remembered, reached for the money in her pocket (her hand closed automatically round her purse, in memory of childhood warnings and lost pocket-money) and walked in.

Voices, music, voices, noises; beginning-of-summer British at play. And in the background, the lovely spires and turrets of the Colleges, incongruous and timeless above the roiling crowd. Alice smiled, tucked her shopping-bag under one arm and began to move towards a toffee-apple stall, bought the biggest, stickiest-looking apple she could see, and moved away, taking her fragile little circle of tranquillity with her. Aimlessly, happily, she wandered through the field, occasionally pausing to watch the roundabout with its thin, wild-eyed horses rushing past, the people at the stalls (a father of three trying to win a teddy bear at the shooting-range; 'Go on Dad!'; a wide-eyed schoolboy staring enviously at the Hoopla, twenty-pound notes taped enticingly onto wooden blocks; the caption RING IT RICH; a tall, thin boy of sixteen at the dart-board, grinning, lifting a giant pink rabbit into the arms of a laughing girl).

A man pushed past her, one hand stuck in the pocket of his coat, the other holding a can of Strongbow; he was almost close enough to Alice for his swatch of dyed black hair to brush her face. For an instant, he seemed fleetingly familiar, and she strained to see his face, but he disappeared into the Amusements arcade before she could know for sure. She bit into her apple again; it was a good one, tart and pink inside, the deep-red toffee still slightly warm from the steaming vat of sugar on the stand, outer shell just beginning to go hard. She wondered why toffee-apples always turned out to be so difficult to eat; too wide to bite into, too sticky to get a firm hold onto, she had to take tiny, tiny bites, delicately working at the outer shell with the tip of her tongue. She was engrossed. A man with tattoos on his face was selling rides on the roundabout; for a moment Alice was tempted, but decided against it; fairground rides are only fun when you're not alone, she thought (doggedly shaking the memory of another Alice, hand-in-hand with another Joe, endlessly neck-to-neck in an interminable roundabout race between two horses, dappled grey and pink with cornsilk manes, while the roundabout played 'Camptown Races' and the world spun to a different tempo) . . . and moved on.

He was standing by the main gate, unmistakable this time, stranger in the sunlight than he ever was at night. Even the crowds of students (dyed red hair, string vests, leather trousers, slogans) seemed to skirt him, so that he stood alone in a little pocket of isolation. Despite the warmth of the day, he was wearing his coat buttoned and turned up at the collar, and beneath it, at his ankles, she caught the gleam of sunlight on the chains of his motorcycle boots. Impossible to know whether he had seen her; surrounded by people as she was, there was no cause to be stricken with panic, or to clutch furtively at the fabric of her dress, but she was, and she did.

He seemed to be waiting.

She turned abruptly, mingling with the crowd again, thin sweat prickling at her armpits and temples. Suddenly, her eyes were everywhere, testing, measuring the crowd with a new insight . . . 'If Java is there, then maybe Rafe is too,' she thought, and on the tail of that, 'if Rafe is there . . . maybe the others . . . Elaine, Zach, Anton . . .' maybe other ones she had not yet seen. Perhaps their faces were watching her in the crowd, unguessed-at. Perhaps they already knew of her visit to Fulbourn. Perhaps they were waiting for her.

She quickened her pace, swallowing panic. The smells of the fairground were much stronger now, dizzying; the crowd parted to allow her to pass, and she felt singled out, too noticeable in her yellow and white dress. She began to jog towards the far end of the field, where the caravans and the animals were, where she could slip out unseen, in safety. A face snapped up out of the mill of people to look at her; a man with red hair tied back, black crosses dangling from his ears. Alice met his eyes for a moment . . . saw the bird tattoo on his face. He flashed an insolent, disturbing grin at her, blurred again into the crowd. A woman brushed by her with a touch as light and cold as snow; she started, looked around, but the woman was gone. From the corner of her eye, she glimpsed a thin figure standing beside a hot-dog stand, flaxen hair shocking in the bright sunlight . . . she wheeled round, convinced that this time, she knew it . . . she saw a girl, eyes hidden under a spray-mask of black makeup, bleached hair puffed out from her head like tattered flower-petals. Not Rafe, she thought, almost delirious with relief. Not this time. She ran in slow motion to the end of the field, slipped in between two caravans, washing hanging from a guy-rope between them, looked for the way out. A goat, tethered to a railing, interrupted its grazing for a moment to fix her with a long, glassy stare. She skirted round a sleeping dog, muzzle in its paws, and rounded the caravan.

'Hello, Alice.' It was the girl from the hot-dog stand; for a moment, Alice felt no panic. Then, as she took in the face, the features behind the makeup, the hair coarsely sprayed white showing traces of red still at the roots, she froze. Stupidly, she stood there, her eyes wide, her hands dangling absurdly, the only motion in a world of stillness. Her mind moved in slow motion, repeating idiotically to itself; 'Ginny. Rosemary. Ginny.'

Ginny took a step forwards.

As if released from a catapult, Alice bolted, no more able to stand her ground than to face a charging rhino. She dodged in between the caravans, heedless now of the dog, which looked up and started a loud, aggressive barking. She was a long way from the crowd of holidaymakers now, isolated at the end of the field, the panic a sick flower in her lungs. Her feet were flat and heavy on the baked ground; the world juddered and jolted as she ran. There was a man coming towards her; red hair and earrings, a bird tattooed on one cheekbone.

For an instant she contemplated calling for help ... then he smiled, the sunlight snickering off his gold tooth. He pulled something from his pocket, some-thing which flicked the sunlight into Alice's eyes in a long trembling ribbon of polished steel. With a whimpering gasp, she changed course abruptly and dashed off across the field towards the people.

Behind her, Ginny made a tiny sign to Zach and Rafe, and the three of them fanned out, walking calmly and purposefully towards the other end of the field. Beneath the sprayed mask Ginny was smiling, and in her hand she carried a fat Post Office envelope.

Two

Cambridge, *April 1990*

Joe quickened his step, eyes flicking restlessly to the left, to the right, to the left into the sidestreets as he moved. His pace was elastic, half running, half walking, the motion of his head as it turned relaxed, almost mechanical. His hands were deep in the pockets of his greatcoat, his shoulders slightly hunched, with the selfconsciousness of the man who thinks himself to be too tall. He might have been an eccentric poet, on his way to some wild mysterious rendezvous, some crazed bespectacled inventor racing to build the atom bomb. His thoughts were jangled with fatigue, razor-edged with the beginnings of worry for the red-haired girl.

Absently, he pushed back his hair from his eyes; in the bright sunlight he had begun to feel uncomfortably warm; already a thin film of sweat slicked his forehead, pricked his underarms, belying the apparent lack of tension of his long body as he pushed himself forward. For an instant, he stopped in mid-stride, thinking he saw her, then moved on. He saw her in a dozen places after that; in the turn of a face, the swing of a summer dress, a fall of hair over a bent head, heard her in the intonation of a burst of voices from an archway . . . but when he turned, Ginny was never there. It was past two now; she should have been home. She should have left a message. She . . . He slowed his pace fractionally, trying to analyse the sense of urgency which had motivated him. The nagging feeling (where is she? Should've been back, where is. . .?) underpinned the rest of his thoughts like a pedal point in a complex rock song. A sudden, unbidden, unwelcome memory returned to his mind; Alice talking . . . telling him how Ginny had gone out that night after he had left . . . telling him how two men had come looking for her. . . two men who were her friends. A vision of Ginny sitting in some JCR, some public lavatory, maybe a bus shelter or a bandstand in the park, Ginny flanked by two men with pale faces and hungry eyes . . . Ginny talking, her head averted . . . Ginny smiling . . . nodding . . . Ginny shooting a long needle into her thin arm while the friends looked on, almost smiling, and the world fragmented into a myriad lights and surfaces.

He began to run, checking every little passageway, every shop window, every arch, railing, gate with a hot, prickling urgency. His blood was the deepest of bass signatures in his throat, the sunlight a thin wire of pain driving between his eyes. His head throbbed with the possibilities, a vortex of wild and fearful imaginings. She should never have gone without telling him, he repeated laboriously to himself as he ran, each footstep a juddering that shook his bones to the marrow. The world was full of crap, he thought, enough bloodsuckers and coldhearts and profit-merchants to kill someone like Ginny; how she had managed to get this far without going under he didn't know, especially after what she had told him the other night, strangely childlike, strangely untouched, sitting in his armchair, hugging her knees. She had told him everything, the drugs, the dirt, the men . . . with a little smile and a wistful, half-alien clarity in her eyes. By all rights the bloodsuckers should have got her.

Strange little girl . . . but she was a strange little girl with guts enough not to let the bastards grind her down, he thought with pride. She had gone right to the edge and had come back all on her own, and that made her stronger than he was in some odd way; stronger and braver.

The world receded back into a false calmness; his steps began to slow. He pushed his glasses back into place, feeling somehow dazed, and tried to think beyond the circular pattern of his thoughts. (Why didn't she tell me? Maybe she's in trouble. Dammit, that wasn't getting him anywhere.)

Cursing the sunlight which wormed its way mercilessly into his aching head, Joe continued his search of the streets of Cambridge. Dreamlike figures milled around him, fast and throbbing with the anonymity of corpuscles. The primitive rhythm of the crowd intensified the throbbing of his headache; the distant music of the fairground tunnelled into the cortex of his brain. Strange certainties chased each other, like playful dragons. Ginny in danger . . . Ginny shooting subtle poisons into her system . . . Ginny hunted by the men Alice had seen; and if Alice had seen them, then Ginny had lied . . . and if she had lied . . . Ginny ginny ginny ginnyginnyginny.

After a while, as he repeated it to himself, even her name began to lose its identity, like a record played too carelessly and too often. The fairground music was louder now, tinny echoes amplified to huge, jangling unmelodies like sirens. He was beginning to encounter the fair-time crowds now; families, children with balloons, kids with radios, fathers carrying oversized coloured teddy bears, beautiful adolescent girls eating lollipops with the sly beginnings of knowledge in their lowered eyes. Joe didn't like fairs much. There was always something sinister about them, about the people who came and went, carrying the promise of returned childhood under those faded canvases, under the lights of that well-oiled and hidden machinery. Once, when he was a child, his father had taken him to the fair; like all little boys, he had loved it, had eaten candy-floss and baked potatoes, ridden on the roundabout, bought a balloon from an old gipsy woman with a scarf round her head and the warmest, most twinkling eyes he had ever seen . . . and right at the end, when his father had suggested that maybe they might get going home now (night had begun to fall, and the fair had taken on a new kind of magic, all lights and the smell of roasting chestnuts), he had insisted on having one last ride on the roundabout.

'OK, Joey.' Joey's Dad had always been the most tolerant of fathers; half a child himself, he had had just as good a time as Joey himself that day, and he sat Joey comfortably down on the jewelled saddle of the big fairground horse and turned away to look at the Arcade.

'Hi-yo, Silver!' he whispered, deep in an intimate fantasy of flight and adventure. 'I'm the Lone Ranger.' Liking the sound of the phrase, he repeated it. 'I'm the Lone Ranger!' As if in agreement, the roundabout began to move (being six, Joey momentarily felt the ripple of Silver's muscles beneath the hard pink hide; the horse bucked, and Joey/Lone Ranger fought bravely to keep on. 'Hi-yo, Silver, Awayyy!' he cried, and the roundabout speeded up, the horses spinning and bucking, black horses and white horses and exotic red and blue and yellow horses, their manes flying, their glass eyes wild and frenzied. Joey was ecstatic. He felt as if all eyes were turned towards him, the brave boy on the wild horse. He gripped the jingling reins with fierce joy, faces blurring around him with the speed of the ride. Suddenly, a face swam up towards him out of the half-gloom; neon-lit and almost ghostly in the changed light, he recognized the balloon-woman, earrings glinting exotically in a million refracted undersea colours.

'Heyyy!' shouted Joey, recognizing a friend, but the roundabout had moved on, spinning like a sun. I'll call to her when I get round the other side, thought Joey, grinning in anticipation, holding his breath for the biggest shout he could give, loosing his left hand from the reins to wave . . . but when he reached the other side, the shout died in his throat, the grin from his face; the sight of the balloon-woman etched into his memory long after the roundabout moved away, long after it had stopped. She was standing at the edge of a little group of people, a family, perhaps, though there might have been two families, a round, balding, red-faced man, a younger man with a beard, two women, one with a baby, and some other children. The one who fixed Joey's eye was a little boy, maybe his age or maybe a little older, a round, sturdy little boy wearing dungarees and holding a blue balloon in one hand and a half-finished candy-floss in the other. His eyes were round and very serious. Joey liked to think that the boy had been watching *him*, the brave boy on horseback, and had made sure he looked especially big and reckless every time he passed him. There was a purse sticking out of the little boy's pocket, at the back, the kind of purse you don't miss in a hurry, yellow and with a picture of Donald Duck on the front . . . but this time Joey passed them, the purse was missing. He knew it was missing because he had seen it, for just one instant, in the hand of the cheerful old balloon-woman, before she noticed him noticing and stuffed it into her pocket. And that was why little Joey rode for the rest of his roundabout-trip without shouting, without jigging on the horse and shaking its mane, without doing anything but going over and over what he had just seen with that terrible sense of loss and betrayal. It was as if he had seen Father Christmas, his jolly mask pulled aside to reveal a white and hungry face, blood around his mouth, shoving severed limbs into his sack of toys like broken dolls. In a way, Joey knew that in that moment part of his childhood was over. He got off the roundabout as stiff and straight

301

as a little soldier, suddenly desperate to leave, to leave forever and never come back, neverneverneve . . . but she was waiting for him, witchlike without her mask, and Joey was smitten with terror that she might touch him, that she might *curse* him like those princes who were turned into swans, and he began to run towards the Arcade where Daddy was . . . but not before the Witch had caught hold of his shoulder with a brown old hand like a claw, not before he had looked into her eyes and she had whispered, with all the venom and the ancient rage of those travelling peoples:

'You never saw nothin', you little *Giorgio* prick, no? Never saw *nothin'*!'

And Joey had nodded mutely, going white, backing away like a cornered cat, trying not to cry, because if he did, he was certain that this witch-woman would kill him, kill him and kill him and kill him and here was Daddy, Daddy coming out of the Arcade, calling in his loud and cheerful voice, and in that moment Joey wrenched himself free from the old Witch's claw and ran, ran towards the light. He dreamed of her later, but he never told his Daddy what had happened, though he never quite understood why he did not tell.

And it was on the tail of that half-submerged memory that the thought struck him – no, not the thought, the *knowledge*. Of course! That was where he should look for Ginny. If Ginny was in trouble, it would come from the fair. He did not know why, but the knowledge was real enough, startling as a cattle-prod.

She was there.

He quickened his step.

Two

Cambridge, *April 1990*

Alice realized soon enough that there was nowhere to
go; behind her, Rafe and Zach and Ginny, and at the
exit, Java waited, with that air of steady confidence.
Sounds pounded her eardrums; the sirens of the rides
and the arcades, the scattered cries of children, the
wails of frightened babies; but for all she heard, she
might as well have been alone with them in the middle
of the field, trapped in her little circle of knowledge,
her mind a prickling blank of deaf panic, repeating
(ginnyginnyginnyginnyginny) to itself like a broken
toy. The envelope in Ginny's hand had paralysed her
ability to think; her mind raced in circles, fragments of
thoughts chasing each other around her brain in
delirious playful frenzy. Doctor Menezies . . . he had
had the manuscript. Ginny. The Post Office envelope
filling the world, bearing down upon her like the
Juggernaut. Then she was running, really running, an
odd, fiercely isolated figure in the bright dress, holding
her shoes in her right hand as she sprinted barefoot
across the field like a child involved in some very
earnest game of chase. As she reached the main part of
the holidaymaking crowd, she glanced briefly over her
shoulder, in the typical glance of the hunted thing
which needs to know, even if it means capture or
despair, how far away the pursuers are, and she
caught Ginny's cool, ironic gaze across the heads of
the others, the innocents, the eaters of hotdogs and

winners of teddy bears, and Alice knew instinctively that she was *not* safe, that the crowd could afford no more protection to her than would a herd of cattle. The only realities were here, between the cold lavender eyes of the nightwalker-thing (all vestiges of the human stripped from her face, unmasked for an instant in Alice's vision in all her subtle and ancient hatred) and the knowledge in Alice's own eyes, the knowledge which enabled her to *see* what no one else could see, the thing of blood behind the lovely, innocent face.

Maybe that was what stopped her. Maybe it was that look, that sick innocence above the black spray-mask, maybe the triumph and contempt in the cold gaze . . . she held it, scintillating, like a mythical bridge of ice, held the gaze and returned it, with all the hate and fire which she was capable of conveying.

She could see that Ginny understood her; the irony faltered for a moment (what's here a challenge?) and she ran her tongue over her lips.

Alice (know you now you bitch better be careful) half turned towards her and smiled, showing her teeth. Suddenly, as if her anger had cleansed her of fear and cleared her mind, she felt cool, controlled. From the corner of her eye she saw someone (watch it rafe or zach be careful) moving towards her, and instead of moving back, she took two steps forward (that the way you want it? better be sure i'll be ready and there'll be noise oh yes bitch won't come quiet), smiling all the time.

She felt rather than saw the figure falter and stop, grinned inwardly, and kept coming. Someone in the crowd looked at her oddly, but Alice didn't care any more, somehow Alice had scored some kind of a victory, and the knowledge (so you can be surprised so you don't know everything) was like light in her veins, was the essence of something pure and violent, and her blood was a Mozart mass in her eardrums, and the laughter was good laughter. Somewhere between here and there they had locked in combat, she and Ginny. No more fear, she thought. They understood each other too well for that. Round one began.

Alice (too many people bitch bitch bitch i can walk out whenever i like) turned and began to walk towards the exit, making sure to replace her shoes.

(don't forget i know who you are i know you now i read the diary so you're too late bitch) The others hung back on the periphery of her vision, but made no attempt to come any nearer.

Ginny's cold lavender gaze froze the back of her head (so what do you think you can do no one will believe you daniel died insane i killed him and the others and i'll kill you too you interfering little), and Alice glanced back, almost casually (for a second, actually saw that lovely ice bridge between them), and kept on walking (maybe and maybe you're full of bullshit rosemary); the exit was twenty yards away.

(yes but maybe i'll just kill joe instead)

(oh you bitch)

(he'll never believe you and maybe i've made him like daniel like robert or maybe i'll just drive him insane) The thought, shivering with malice, struck her like a jet of cold water, so that she faltered, almost losing her poise.

(come quiet and we might come to some mutual arrangement) coaxed the other mind, (maybe we'll leave you alone if you leave us alone maybe we'll give you joe back), and for a long moment, she almost did what it asked, almost turned and came back (oh you), but at the last second she drew back (not so easy fooled oh you bitch), and was out of the gate, out of the gate and into the safe and open street, with the echoes of the fair, and the mind-echoes of that compelling, spiteful voice wailing (i'll i will i'll see you both i will) in the empty air behind her. After a while she began to shake.

Two

Cambridge, *April 1990*

There. A movement, a certain tilt of the head, swing of
the shoulders . . . it must be her. Joe craned his neck
above the milling crowd of people, oblivious to stares
and irritation.

'Ginny!'

The figure turned, and it was not Ginny; deep
disappointment sleeted through him, and for an
instant he wondered, angrily, how on earth he could
have mistaken that girl for Ginny. Then it *was* Ginny
again, Ginny almost grotesquely changed, but Ginny
nevertheless, and, calling her name, thrusting with his
elbows, he began to bludgeon his way through the
mass of bodies.

'Ginny! Wait!'

The girl turned vaguely to face him, standing alone
by the side of a shooting-stand, pale face, pale hair,
pale hands, looking desperately frail and thin in her
black clothes, ghostly against the glare of the lights and
the machines, eyes dark and fathomlessly hungry
beneath the makeup. So hungry. As he reached for her
she shrank a little, and he smelled the acetone scent of
the white spray in her hair above a sharper, smoky
smell like burnt paper.

'You came.' This toneless, her voice white and cold,
unreachable.

Questions died in his throat; he held her close. It

was not the time for questions; only for loving, with the sick, pained loving he felt for her, however ill she was, however freaked-out. He was conscious of an almost unbearable sensation of longing, which he tried to analyse and failed.

'Hey, Gin,' he said gently. 'What're you doing out here? Come home with me.' He forced a little laugh. 'You certainly got me going for a while back there, with your disappearing act. I thought you'd walked out on me for good.' He smiled too broadly, looking for needle-tracks and trying not to make it too obvious.

Ginny stared at him blankly, and for a moment she reminded him uncannily of late photographs of Karen Carpenter just before her death from anorexia; wide-eyed and drawn and feverish. For a few seconds his mind blanked out, then practicality re-asserted itself. First of all he had to get her home, make her lie down. She'd probably be OK, she didn't look like someone who'd OD'd and there weren't any needle-marks on her arms that he could see, which reassured him a little. But she did look ill, and he'd had enough experience to know what some pushers cut their dope with; it wasn't called 'shit' for nothing.

'What're you on?' he whispered urgently, putting his arm round her shoulders.

Ginny looked at him, hesitating. Her mouth worked. 'H . . .'

'Have you got any more?' She'd have to ditch it, of course, he told himself; the last thing he wanted was another barney with the police. He kept his voice quiet and patient.

'Have you?'

Ginny shook her head. Good. That was something. Now all he had to do was to take her home and to hope that she hadn't been taking strychnine or arsenic or washing powder or anything else in her China White. Christ, what a mess. And where had she got the money? The last he knew of it she had been broke, just

308

eligible for the lowest of social security payments, certainly not enough for all this heavy shit. He swore softly under his breath as he took Ginny by the shoulders and led her, like a blind child, out of the gates and into the safety of the street.

If he'd had any sense he'd have ditched her as soon as he found out about all this, he told himself sourly. He had enough hassle looking after himself without taking on a screwed-up junkie girlfriend. He'd seen enough of them when he was on the road with the band to know that the bad trips and the cold turkey and the overdoses weren't all you got, no; sometimes you hit the jackpot and you got the collapsed veins, the brain damage and the nasty diseases from dirty needles. Oh yes. That was why he'd never really bothered with much more than the odd bag of grass from time to time – it was cheap, safe and didn't show up on breathalyser tests. Joe didn't mess with junkies; it was a rule for happy living.

But this was Ginny.

Fairground noise faded behind them, their steps real once more against the cobbles of the alley. She followed him passively, head bent slightly at a childish angle which wrenched at his heart, one hand tucked confidingly into his, the other clutching a fold of his coat. His heart did a quirky little off-beat at the sight of her profile, so pure and apocalyptic, her eyes darkened to indigo, the mask of paint leaving her flesh oddly vulnerable, touching. He remembered her in his rooms, her warmth, her sweet untutored tenderness, the promise her cool child's flesh gave to his, her innocence. He ached with his love for her, with the exquisite anguish her frailty induced in him, grieved and rejoiced at her thinness, her air of forlorn abstraction.

Joe had never thought of himself as being much of a romantic at heart, but at that moment, he knew that he would have done anything for her, he would have died for her, like a folk-song hero, her name on his bloody lips. The violence of his longing almost stunned him; lost in thoughts of bittersweet sacrifice, he remained silent almost until they reached the flat. Then, as she paused in front of the door:

'Gin. You've been telling me the truth, haven't you? There's nothing you haven't told me, is there?'

She centred her dark gaze upon him, almost aimlessly, shook her head. The man trapped in reflection behind those vast mirrors raised his hands in a gesture of helplessness, in pleading or benediction.

'You've got to trust me. I love you. I can help you if you let me. You're too smart to be into what you're into, Gin; you've got to ditch it before you find yourself on the fast train to Fuckup City. OK?'

Ginny smiled, almost imperceptibly, nodded.

'Right. Come on in, then.'

Again, the almost imperceptible nod.

'So why do a runner on me like that? Who'd you go running to?'

Inaudible response, a fluttering of breath, like paper. Joe took her hands again, trying not to crush them in his hot grasp.

'I can't hear.'

'Frightened . . .' It was hardly more than a whisper, her lips two white petals on her breath. 'Fri . . . frightened you'd . . . think . . . you'd be angry. After what Alice told you . . . You'd go away . . .'

'No bloody chance.' It was almost beyond him to refrain from grasping her there and then, crushing her to him . . . fear stayed him. She was too small, too slender. He wondered if he would ever dare to seize her in passion.

'No way. I'm here for the duration, Gin. The big one. You and me against the whole fucking world if needs be. Forget Alice, forget all that crap. We don't need her.' The words came rushing out, all the words he had never found for Alice, words he had dreamed,

310

whispered, imagined in the night, words unspoken, hidden away, words terrible and words of comforting, never to be remembered or duplicated, but filled with the awesome poetry of despair and passion. Never had Joe spoken words like that before; but now, somehow, he was a magician, and the veils across Ginny's eyes were separating, the despair lifting into something approaching hope. And in his wonder and the joy of that breakthrough, Joe was still subtly conscious that at some point in that outburst, the details of which were already misting over in his rapturous thoughts, he had made a promise, only half realized, less than half remembered. There would be no regrets, that he knew. Whatever he had pledged, was hers now. Only looking into Ginny's eyes, he knew that. But as he put his arms around her and gently led her into the flat, he was still able to wonder what it was he had promised her.

Two

Cambridge, *April 1990*

There was no time for euphoria, she knew that. She had not escaped, but had won for herself instead a kind of reprieve. No time to glory in that, she thought, but yes, time, a little, to prepare herself for the attack which was certain to come. Glancing through the window at the street, she picked up the phone, dialled the Fulbourn number, let it ring.

(hurry hurry hurry)

(why the hell won't they answer?)

(hurry hurry hurryhurry)

The phone kept ringing; then a voice through the earpiece; 'You have been put through to a queuing system. Please hold the line.' Soothing music once again.

Alice swallowed her impatience; she began to drum her fingers in a quickening tempo on the receiver.

Why the hell wouldn't they answer?

After a long time, the music stopped, and the voice of a harried receptionist answered; 'Fulbourn hospital. Can I help you?'

'Yes, I'd like to speak to Doctor Menezies, please. It's very important.'

'I'm sorry, the doctor isn't available at the moment. Who is this please?'

'I'm Alice Farrell. I saw the doctor this morning. I have something very urgent to tell him. Please, when

313

will he be back?'

'I can pass you to another doctor, Mrs Farrell,' continued the receptionist.

'Please!' Alice felt her throat tighten. 'I need to speak with Doctor Menezies immediately!'

'I'm afraid that isn't possible,' was the reply. 'The doctor is ill. Doctor Lowrey is dealing with all his cases for the moment.'

'But he was fine when I saw him this morning!' exclaimed Alice.

'There was an accident, just after lunch. I'm sorry, Mrs Farrell, I can't help you.'

'What kind of accident?'

'I really—'

'What kind of an accident?' Alice heard her voice rise out of its normal register, out of control. 'Please!'

The receptionist hesitated.

'The doctor was hit by a car as he left the hospital to go home, Mrs Farrell. A hit-and-run. The police are looking into it. That's—'

'I see.' Alice felt sick, a heaviness under her ribs like wet concrete. 'I'm sorry. I . . . Goodbye.'

She was alone again, her sensation of victory dissipated as if it had never been. For a moment, panic bloomed in her skull, her ears rushing tunnels of blood, then coldness, a dead cold of the spirit as she faced the truth which had stalked her since she first set eyes on Ginny.

There was no escape. The air of timelessness which Alice loved so much had made Cambridge a prison, a stronghold for the nightwalkers; a nomad town where nearly two-thirds of the population come and go at intervals of four years apiece, a town of rented rooms and stolen intimacies. They walked the same cobbled streets, stood in the same archways, heard the same hymns from the chapels over the river from decade to decade, their faces mingling with those of their prey in the stream of memory.

314

They passed unnoticed as they lingered on the fringes of the ever-replenished river of humankind, choosing their victims carefully; here a tramp, to be found in a pool of blood and wine, there a tourist travelling alone, elsewhere a student with needle-tracks on his arms and a reputation for dangerous living. Cambridge has a high suicide-rate; statisticians tend to blame this partly on the stress-levels among the students, which are abnormally high. Drug-users, too, abound among the young and imaginative. Easy to find reasons; so easy to ignore the evidence. A scribbled suicide-note, fingered with blood, on a bedside table in a rented room. The account of what a hysterical girl might have seen, on a night when she was drunk or doped. Someone's stubborn insistence that something, half glimpsed or half remembered, was wrong.

How they must have laughed to see it, how they must have revelled in their youth and their power! How like angels they must have felt! How many dreams must they have haunted during their strange time? How many chosen men were there still out there who carried Rosemary in their hearts and memories? Oh yes, they must have laughed, these strangers, as they slipped invisibly through the Cambridge crowds, touching flesh in a million erotic, predatory ways, scenting flesh and the thrill of the trapped blood.

Alice shivered, almost glimpsing for an instant the fatal glamour. Then she stood up deliberately, shaking her clouded head. No more, she told herself fiercely. Time had run out.

(august, die she must)

A spasm racked her at the thought, but the voice within her was compelling, somehow alien, with a clarity which was beyond questioning.

(die she must)

She wondered whether she would be sick. The panic was almost unbearable now, with a momentum of its own, like spinning, like vertigo, like the biggest roller-coaster in the world with grinning Death at the controls and nothing but spangled black horror all around.

(why me oh shit why does it have to be)

(die she must)

(perhaps i'm wrong maybe it's not me they want maybe they'll leave me alone)

(die she must)

'Oh shit,' said Alice, and began reluctantly, with those voodoo drums of panic still hammering inside her skull, to plan her attack.

One

Cambridge, *August 1948*
Fulbourn Hospital, *April 1978*

Rosemary had been right; I was ill for the next few days, and the light hurt my eyes, but in time, even that symptom faded. I lay low in the warehouse, never alone; sometimes it was Rafe who stayed with me, sometimes Elaine, sometimes Zach. I ran a low fever for close to two weeks, eating little, but drinking quarts of water and beef-tea and lemonade, for it seemed to me that I would never quench my thirst. I saw Rosemary only briefly, and then, never alone; she would appear for a few minutes to check on my progress, maybe hand me a drink or a morsel of food (which I ate to please her, nothing more), or show me the newspapers to keep up with Scotland Yard's manhunt. It seemed that the 'Body in the Weir' case had been shelved for the time being, to be replaced by the 'Swan Inn' case, an unrelated case of murder and arson, thought by the Yard to be a cover for burglary. Two bodies had been found, too badly charred to be recognizable, but dental records showed them to be those of the publican and his wife. 'A man is being questioned by the police' blared the newspaper in self-satisfied tones, a pronouncement which afforded my companions a never-ending source of amusement. Rosemary would read these accounts to me in childish glee, then she would be on her way again with a smile and a swirl of her skirts, and I would be left to clutch at my hidden rebellion in secret and grind my teeth in helpless love and hate. She looked radiant on those visits; her face rosy and vivid, her hair like sunset clouds, billowing, or modestly confined at the nape of her neck or beneath a little hat. She wore dresses of flowered crepe and silk chiffon and white linen with rose borders, every time I saw her something different, exotic almost to indecency in that austere post-war decade, dancing through life like a fever dream. She radiated power in those visits, power and purity. The very touch of her cool fingers on my neck was enough to keep me sweating in rage and desire for hours; unstable as I was, I am always amazed that I never blurted my secret revolt, stupidly, in one of my moments of fever; perhaps I did, and my wardens never thought anything of it. I suppose that in that respect, we of those warehouse days and red nights were all brothers.

It was on one of these occasions, as I was nearing recovery, that she told me she was married. I was sitting by a window, looking onto the bare land at the back of the building. I had been reading a book, but had laid it aside when she came in, pulling back the blanket which covered my wasted legs to stand up to greet her. Java was waiting at the door, watching, his shoulder against the door-jamb. She was lovely that day, her hair all windblown against a dress of drab green, her eyes sparkling with youth and life. She looked so young that for a moment I was confused, wondered whether I could have imagined the thing of blood and poison under the pale thin flesh.

'Danny, congratulate me!' Her voice was high, breathless from the wind, her hands stretched out towards me impulsively.

'I'm married!'

I hesitated for a long moment, aware, in the preternatural stillness, of a pulse just below my left ear, ticking away my time, my blood's time.

'Who?' My tongue felt swollen, the roof of my mouth, the ribs of a whale. For a moment, I thought I might pass out, so pervasive the illusion.

Rosemary frowned playfully.

'Oh, Danny, you are a scream. It's Robert, of course. Who else?'

Robert. I had hardly even thought of him for all the strange time I had been here, Robert of my earliest loyalty, Robert, betrayed more than I could bear to think. It was not that the news came as any surprise; no, I had already in my heart given him up as lost the day he came to me with his story of Rosemary, but now that it was a certainty, the sensation of loss and guilt (yes, and maybe jealousy too), came upon me with such heaviness that I was forced physically to slump back onto my chair to avoid collapse.

'Why, Danny.' Her voice was petulant now, her lips pouting charmingly. 'You're cross.'

I found my voice, not without an effort, forced a smile. 'Of course not. I'm very happy. I'm just . . . not well yet.'

'Poor Daniel.' She leaned forwards, her hands cupping my face. A faint scent of lavender reached me from her skin, like a memory. 'Better?'

I nodded, not trusting words.

'Robert . . .' I faltered. 'Is he . . . will he be . . . I mean?'

She laughed, enchantingly. 'Oh, Danny,' she exclaimed. 'You're so sweet. Is *that* why you looked so cross? You thought he'd be one of us? Oh no. I never mix business with pleasure.' She kissed me lightly on the cheek. Her kiss was like a tiny sting, barbed. '*We*'re pleasure,' she explained. 'He's just . . . well . . . he's nothing. Just . . . protection.'

'I don't understand.' I did, really; I just wanted to hear her admit it in words.

She sighed.

'Robert *loves* me,' she said, with counterfeit impatience (in reality, like all vain things, she was delighted to talk about her own affairs). 'He loves me now to the point of unreason. He's a man; he thinks himself strong, protective. I have given him something to protect. He thinks me frail, unstable; it's what he wants to think. It makes him happy; it makes him feel strong. Not every man gets the chance to die for what he loves, Danny; in some strange way, he's one of the lucky ones. These cattle, they don't understand power the way we do; but they do understand sacrifice. They're all so good at that. Your Robert would never be strong enough to face the reality and the blood; I have given him the dream.'

Something must have shown on my face; she smiled, touched my hand with the briefest, chastest of kisses.

'Don't mourn, Danny. He's happy.'

'Why?' It was almost a wail; my shaky self-control gone, I felt like a child again. With unsteady hands, I reached for the murderess and wailed; 'Why?'

Rosemary sat down on the arm of my chair, bent down to me like a young infant teacher coaching a backward, but endearing pupil.

'No one said it was going to be easy, Dan,' she said firmly. 'Being chosen isn't easy. We stand out in crowds. The cattle smell us, envy us our knowledge and our beauty. Even you are beautiful now, Dan; you gain power and beauty every time you feed. People look at you and guess at some savage dream; they guess their own death, and they love it, the way they dream their sacrifices in the night. They are natural prey. Some day you'll be like me, burning and forever. But meanwhile, we have to go unnoticed. We have to have a protector. Someone to lie for us, to shield us, to die for us if he has to. Do you think that the hunt for us will die down? The police are stupid, but some day one of them will get too close. They are slow and dogged;

eventually some accident will lead them unwittingly to our door. We have to feed; we can travel, we can hide, but one day they will catch up with us, they will give us to their laws. And when that time comes, when the search comes too close, we need to give them a sacrifice. Not one of us, but someone to take our place.'

'Like Robert.' I hadn't understood after all.

'He's the ideal choice, Dan. He provides impeccable cover for me, for the others, even you . . .'

'Me?'

'Of course. When he's caught, you can come out of hiding. What better reason for you to disappear than if you think your best friend is a murderer? You didn't want to betray him, so you ran away. At the very worst, all they can charge you with is shielding a suspect, and you know as well as I do that they wouldn't put you in prison for that. And after that? Well, you can find your own protectress then, your Roberta, if you wish. Just let your killer instinct take over.'

I thought that over for a few moments, though not, I am afraid to admit, with the horror I should have felt. I had done too much by then to show a normal human response, and I had betrayed my friend too many times already to feel squeamish about doing it again. Be content in knowing that I made the right choice, though for the wrong reasons. I think it very likely you too might have done the same thing. But at that time I really considered what she gave me; that enticing poison draught. I wanted it. I needed it with all the longing of my killer instincts, a longing older than prehistory. I reached for her, clasped her like a dream in my arms; I felt chiffon, air, smelt the perfume of lavender from her alien flesh, but her substance eluded me as it always did, and it was so gently that I hardly felt it that she pulled away from me.

'Later,' she said softly. When you're whole again. Ask me again.'

'One kiss,' I mumbled.

Rosemary smiled.

'Flesh,' she said, with a smile. 'You're still so human, Danny. You still care too much for the trivia of loving, touching. Later, you'll understand, later, when you're with us for ever, that blood is power. Blood.'

'I love you,' I said (it was almost true).

'Then love me,' she answered, holding out her wrist, its intricacies like deltas under her blue skin.

I did as she said, power flooding my mouth, running down my chin, drowning the pale fountains of my veins in the secret music of its flowing. Great thoughts filled my inspired brain, thoughts which I never quite remembered later, but which flowered there in the darkness as I fed upon her and she upon me (though in ways more subtle and more final than those of the blood), thoughts of creation and infinities, each unfurling in the red darkness like hearts in flower, longings and ecstasies undreamed-of, pleasures of the blood more monstrous and sublime than were ever any pleasure of the flesh. For an instant I was void, a wailing infant in the eternal absence of myself, then I was creator, galaxies in my mind's eye, then annihilator, blood at my fingertips, blood in my voice, blood filling my giant footprints as I walked. Afterwards, I could never recapture that fleeting moment of absolute power, but, God forgive me, I lusted after it evermore, though all I can remember with any clarity now is the taste, so like the taste of tears.

One

Cambridge, *August 1948*
Fulbourn Hospital, *May 1978*

Summer grew hot; the Cambridge crowds came that
year after all, and during all that month and the next
we endured the muggy, waspy heat as best we could.

We came out at night; not that the days could hurt
us; another of your foolish superstitions, that, but
because it was our time. The warehouse was cool, airy
and dry, like a hospital ward, and we were
comfortable. I say; 'we'. Zach and Elaine, with the little
boy Anton, shared my exile, maybe, I thought at the
time, to keep an eye on me. Rosemary lived with
Robert in a house close by, in Grantchester. Where
Rafe and Java lived, I never knew. I suspected that
they kept close to Rosemary, to guard her, but could
not know for sure. The days passed uneasily, but with
a kind of harmony, like the long, almost endless
summer holidays of my childhood, but the nights were
sharp-focused, full of the glamour and ecstasy of the
chase, intensified all the more by the police presence in
the town which was constant, but as discreet as could
be managed. We were careful, however, choosing our
victims carefully among the vagrant population,
singling out a tramp, a tourist travelling alone,
someone who would not be missed until much later. I
did not see Inspector Turner again, nor did I read his
name in the papers; the Scotland Yard investigation

was headed by a Superintendent Lamb, who, as far as we could guess, seemed to be wasting his time and resources in dragging the Cam for more bodies. The investigation had veered away from us almost entirely.

Rosemary had money, stolen in part from earlier victims, some of it given to her by her previous benefactor, and sometimes we bought wine and cigarettes from the late-night off-licence and drank and smoked in our borrowed lodging like dilettante students discussing art and poetry. I saw her every night; she came late, after midnight, and I often wondered to myself how she managed to come so regularly, despite Robert; I should not have wondered. Maybe she drugged him; even if she did not, he was enough under her spell to let her do anything she wanted, even that, without a word.

I kept on the fringes of events; believe me or not, I killed no one, but I did feed, ravenously, euphorically. I rode the carnival-wheel all that time, half controlled, in nights beyond dreaming or description. We drank whisky and wine mingled with blood. We fed from each other. We loved one another in ways which transcended the purely physical, though my appetites called for that kind of loving too. And still, behind the curtain of that past glamour, there was the hidden canker of my hate, the culmination of my love and my hunger. At present, it seems that my descriptive powers are forsaking me; I can hardly even visualize the glory of that time, as if the memory of what happened after that has cast a darkness over the images there. I remember happiness, without knowing what form it took, remember the words, power, joy, rapture, without being able to visualize even the simplest memory.

At times such as these, I can almost delude myself into thinking that she is really dead; it takes a great effort of will to continue my story at times such as these, for the lure of sanity is ever-present here. My young doctor pulls sour faces every time I tell him I have been writing; he thinks that the writing itself is perpetuating my delusions, thinks that as an academic, I have been too much involved in reading my truths from books, and seek to make my fabrication true by writing it. Others disagree, seeing my work as an effort from my subconscious to exorcize the sickness within my psyche.

I tell this to my young friend to cheer him up; he really does seem very depressed about my case nowadays, even when I let him beat me at chess. I tell him it isn't good for him to become emotionally involved with his patients. He smiles, sadly, knowing that my seeming rationality is no indication of any improvement in my condition; sometimes I hint to him, in the words of my namesake, that when he has eliminated the impossible, what remains, however improbable, must be the truth . . . that what he fears might be true, that I might really be sane, instead of almost-sane. Sometimes, when I say these things to him, he looks so wretched, feeling, perhaps, that he has failed me, I grin and fabricate some patently insane thing to say, simply to justify his beliefs. He seems so insecure, so fragile; these people should be protected. On bad days, I invent some new paranoia for him to interpret, and he rewards me with his smiles, and maybe a game or two of chess. He tries to feed my interest in psychology by telling me about some other cases in the hospital; the girl next door is a schizophrenic, sixteen years old and wracked with personality disorders; he feels confident that she will make a full recovery, however, as she responds well to treatment. Responds well to him, more likely, I tell him; such a pleasant young man. I want to tell him to be careful . . . Rosemary was just another such young innocent. Suddenly I feel very uneasy about that girl. I want to tell him to keep well away from her, but I have teased him too much today for him to believe me. He humours me, but does not listen.

Time, time. I must try to remember how short time is; but the pills they give me stretch time into a mystic spiral, so that days melt into days, wasted. I was telling you about the summer, the August before I killed her. Most of all, I have to tell you how I killed her, so that you too can do the same, when your time comes. And you must not be as weak as I; when the time comes, you must kill the thing you love, as I did not.

As a thinking, rational man, I never thought I would turn to the trappings of Christianity, with its rituals and its dark superstitions, but as in this hospital I perused volume after volume of close-written Latin script, penned by monks and scholars in cells by candle-light, I began to see that however mistaken they might have been in their understanding, the priesthood were the only ones to have remotely begun to grasp the truth which I was seeking; I see it dimly, and my heart responds to those long-dead men as it does not to any of the other writers I study; I imagine them in their circle of candle-light keeping the dark at bay; armed only with faith and a pen, charging posterity to keep the faith against the monster. I envy them their faith. I envy them their God and wince at the emptiness inside me when I try to visualize Him . . . God is dead inside me, and the thing which had kept my ghostly brethren sane in their secret fight, the sword of their faith in all good, in the God of love and anger, is nothing but a broken straw in my trembling hands. I close my eyes and try to see the Light, but all I see is the ineffable image of the red-haired girl, mocking me with her strength and her power; my heart weakens at the thought of her, and my brain reels . . . After almost a lifetime of searching I have reached the point at which I am most wise; knowing this I write the extent of my wisdom; that despite all my learning I know nothing.

Much dangerous nonsense has been written around the bleak truth; superstitions about garlic and running water and coffins filled with earth, the twisting of truth into the cruel propaganda of the Church . . . but in amongst those things lie some deep-buried realities; I encounter them rarely, like real jewels in a pile of trumpery rubbish; from time to time I meet with Rosemary in the books I find; her face leaps out at me from a book on Pre-Raphaelite painters; the face of an artist called Maria, cheaply reproduced in black-and-white, but Rosemary all the same. For a moment I think I am hallucinating . . . but a week, maybe a month later I meet her again, this time in a book of poetry . . . there is no picture this time, but everything in me screams out that the dead poet who has written that book was under the spell of a nightwalker . . . only that sick glamour and hungry lyricism could have penned such verses. I move on and see her face everywhere, staring out at me from poems and fairy-stories and legends. But I know enough now, at last; and will you dare to use my knowledge when the moment comes? Would I ever dare?

They can be killed. I know this; I did it. They can be killed, and the action is as simple and dreadful as the taking of any life. Any hand can do the deed, any mind formulate the desire. But this is not enough; their strange life can be taken, but not kept. It re-emerges like some deadly transparent thing of the sea, beckoned by the rays of the moon. They are not immortal, though their kind has lived almost forever, their essence kept in a thousand vessels of tissue and flesh.

Their seed is everywhere, dormant, like the poison tree under the orchard, their roots quartering the earth and spreading like maggots into the minds of men. The evil seed may lie sleeping for a hundred years, in a tower, a drawer, a garden, before it wakes, shaking the snow of winter from its pale face and looking up into the spring sunlight, child of a hundred years, a hundred dreams. The ancient priesthood knew how to stamp out the seed of the night; they burnt it and buried it in stone and lime, but still it lived, in memories, in tales, in song. Every child who has longed to be Cinderella or the Wolf Boy, every young man who has dreamed of raising a dead princess with his kiss has sown the night's seed, Proserpine's underworld seed which grows the blood-red fruit. We blighted our Eden with longing for it, and now the knowledge is with us forever, the knowledge and the desire, more effective a curse than any damnation. We should have killed our children before we let them sow the seed of that dark and lovely dream.

Desire.

It takes a certain kind of desire to access the rottenness beyond the grave, but all it needs is for one person to remain to desire the nightwalker's return in their heart, willing or unwilling, and she will come.

One person.

To be Rosemary; what a dream of terrible, impossible sweetness. To burn bright as Rosemary, who doth teach the torches ... to wield that terrible beauty for myself. What would I give for that? What have I already given?

August ... die she must. September, I remember. If only I did. But my mind wanders so. She had control over my mind that summer, as surely as she possessed my body. It was a sweet possession, feeding me, feeding from me. Intimate. I didn't think about Robert at all; Rosemary was ours ... mine.

How long it might have gone on, I do not know. I was comfortable in the warehouse; Elaine washed my clothes and brought me food (I needed normal food as well as that other, too much of which made me dizzy and nauseous); she even gave comfort to my other appetites when Rosemary was not available. Her only wish was to die, and there were many things in those days that I did not understand, one of those being how Rosemary could keep Elaine alive against her will. I had come to accept that all my companions, except, perhaps, Rafe, had died once before; Elaine had (or at least, believed she had) been dead for about fifty years, Java more than that. Zach had died in France during the first war, but remembered little about it. That, or he was unwilling to speak of it. Anton had been killed by Elaine; from what I could understand, his presence gave Rosemary some kind of a hold on her. Perhaps he was her brother; I could never make her tell me. Perhaps, who knows? he was her son.

All Elaine could tell me was that Rosemary had called them all back, though she knew nothing of the technique she had used. I supposed (wrongly, I see now) that she had used some kind of necromancy; I had already steeped myself in dubious magic and ritual, and fancied I knew something about the subject; God help me, perhaps I had some notion of trying it for myself some day. I never had the chance to try, but it happened that I did see it in action, quite unexpectedly, late that August. The day Elaine finally achieved her heart's desire.

One

Cambridge, *August 1948*
Fulbourn Hospital, *5 May, 1978*

Do not think that Inspector Turner had given up the search for the Cambridge murderer so easily; he had not. I was not accused, but one tentacle of the search had begun to move in my direction; or so Rosemary told me, with a kind of savage glee. I never had the opportunity to find out whether she was telling the truth.

Maybe in our hunting we had become complacent; maybe Turner had been observing us in his careful way for some time, and we had not been aware of it. Maybe he had had Robert watched, and Rosemary had led him to us unawares. Whatever the reason, we were in the warehouse, all of us, one night, drinking and playing cards, when I was suddenly conscious of an unaccountable sense of unease. Maybe there was a stronger psychic link between Turner and myself than I knew at the time.

It was perhaps two o'clock in the morning; we had had to wait longer than usual for Rosemary, and we had hunted among the destitutes of Cambridge for our prey, wary of the lighted late-night bars and the occasional lights in the windows of the colleges. Passers-by were infrequent after the police scare; people were wary of going out late, and we were all the more noticeable for the lack of other folk in the town, but it was always possible to find a tramp or vagrant lurking around the river or passed out in the doorway of a shop. We had even acquired a taste for such victims, as the alcohol in their veins gave the blood an extra tartness.

We were glutted and somnolent, drinking wine brought by Java and Zach and smoking, and the room in which I slept was already littered with the empty bottles. I often drank during those red nights; I think it helped me to disassociate myself from whatever monstrosities were being perpetrated, and to taste the thrill of the hunt, of running with the others without mind or conscience, for its own sake. The light was dim, coming as it did from a couple of candles stuck into empty wine bottles; the windows were covered with sacking. No one could have stumbled upon us by accident.

At first, I attributed the sensation of being watched to paranoia; I drank another glass of wine to still my nerves, but that did not allay my fears. In fact, the wine only seemed to attune my new sensitivity even more.

At last, I could not bear it. I turned to Rosemary.

'Are you sure no one followed us here?' I asked.

She looked at me oddly. 'Poor Daniel,' she said lightly. 'Still so timid? Do you think I care if anyone follows? There are plenty of us to deal with anyone if they did.'

In some ways, she was very innocent.

'I think there's someone outside,' I said. 'Watching the warehouse.'

Zach made a gesture of dismissal; he had been out to fetch the wine at about midnight, and had seen nothing.

No one seemed to want to take my suspicions very seriously, except Elaine, who looked up timidly, her eyes huge in her shadowy face.

'I think Daniel is right,' she said. 'I've been feeling uneasy too, for a few days now. I think the police have been watching us. I've heard odd sounds. I've seen people in the street.'

Rosemary looked questioningly at the others; they shook their heads.

Zach shrugged.

'Send the kid out to see,' he said. 'No one will suspect a kid.'

Everyone agreed, except, strangely, Elaine.

'I'll go too,' she said, with unaccustomed decision. 'It isn't fair he should be sent out on his own.'

'Afraid the bogeyman'll get him?' cackled Zach spitefully. 'What is he, scared of the dark?' He made a face, lifting his arms and waggling his fingers like a storybook witch. But Elaine, in some ways, was as untouchable as Rosemary herself. A soft movement of material from the dark shapeless coat she was wearing, a scuffling of feet, and she and Anton were already gone. I followed them, at a distance, still uneasy, but feeling slightly unsteady because of all the wine I had drunk. I heard the tiny sounds of their footsteps on the cement floor. I was just beginning to believe that I had imagined everything when I suddenly heard a sound, a cry, then the world began to spin, to spiral, and I with it.

Elaine screamed, and I heard her footsteps and Anton's, suddenly much louder, running through the building. Instinctively, I hid in the shadows, making no noise. A light flashed on close by me, and three figures ran past. I heard a voice, shouting; 'Stop! Police! Stop!'

Three shadows rushed past me, dwarfing me, monstrous against the white wall. Sounds behind me, from the room I had just left; I guessed it to be the others, finding their own way out of the building, scuffling, shoving, pushing away from the light. I knew that Zach and Java had a considerable armoury of weapons (stolen or otherwise acquired during the war) hidden in the building. I was inclined to believe that the police might be in for a nasty surprise.

There was a large window in the passage, which was

loosely boarded up. Thinking quickly in my panic, I yanked the boarding away and looked out. The drop was not high; I measured it in my mind, then pulled myself through the uneven gap, looking around for more police. I saw no one; the moonlight was veiled, shadowy. I ran out across the yard and into the bushes and long grass at the back. I lay on my stomach in the undergrowth, the smell of growing grass and cool earth in my nostrils. I waited there, certain that someone had seen me, sure I would be discovered. Across the flat ground, I could hear voices raised, shouting in anger or urgency, I was not certain. Two shots were fired in rapid succession. I pressed my face against the ground. When I happened to look up a few seconds later, I saw three shadows; I guessed them to be Rafe, Java and Rosemary, moving at speed across the yard. In a moment, they were out of the gate and out of sight down the road. I dared to raise myself higher, and as I did Elaine came running silently round the angle of the building, the tail of her greatcoat flapping stiffly out behind her. I could hear her breath, sharp in the quiet night air. She was crying, repeating something to herself which I could not hear. As she reached the path to the gate, I saw her clearly, in the faint moonlight, and realized that not all was well. She was limping, holding her dark coat around her as if for protection. In her hand, I could see that she carried a knife, a long straight blade which flicked the light back at me like a mirror. I think she saw me, as I crouched in the shadows, but she did not betray me by as much as a glance or a call. Instead, she turned to face the men who were following her, with a high-pitched cry of challenge or despair.

One of the officers called to her;

'Here! You! Stay where you are! Drop the knife!'

Elaine drew back a little, holding the weapon in front of her. She knew how to use it; had done so often enough already. The officer began to move towards her, while the other two fanned out to take her from either side.

'It's no good,' he coaxed. 'Put down the knife. Come here.'

Elaine only took one more step back, away from me. For some reason, I felt that she was trying to lure the men away from me, and I shrank back into the dark.

The man was not more than a dozen feet away from her now; as he spoke, he had been edging gradually closer, one hand in his pocket. Now, he lunged at Elaine. One hand brushed her coat, but Elaine was too quick for him. The light arced from the knife she was carrying for a split instant, a wheel of light, then the man was on his knees, his hands to his stomach. His expression was one of stupid surprise as his belly released its contents, then he began to scream, and I cheered Elaine inwardly from where I was hiding. But almost as soon as it happened, the second officer fired his gun, twice in rapid succession, and she fell.

Now it was my turn to stare in stupid surprise; I kept expecting her to get up again, to fight, but she did not. I saw her foot drumming against the ground for a minute or so, then even that movement was still.

The two other officers approached – I recognized Turner, without any real astonishment – still wary. One of them went to his fallen companion, who was still, noisily, alive, his screams great bulges of sound in the stillness. I despised him; he sounded like a dying animal. Turner went to Elaine, touched her with the toe of his shoe, turned her over. I saw her face for a moment, still and very white, lips parted to show bared teeth. Then I heard his voice, quiet and with a quaver in it which belied his apparent calm.

'It's a woman,' he said, reaching into the greatcoat to feel her heart. 'She's dead,' then, with sudden viciousness; 'Shit!'

He hesitated for a moment, then regained some of his momentum. Addressing the other officer, who was trying to move his injured companion into the car, he snapped; 'Don't waste time. Call an ambulance. Hurry!' He was obviously shaken; even though gun regulations in those days were rather more lax than now, perhaps it was the first time he had ever shot someone in the line of duty, and the man's coat Elaine had been wearing had probably deceived the officers as to her size and the danger she might present. I almost sympathized with him, although the shock of Elaine's death had hit me hard. You see, I had really thought that we were immortal.

For maybe ten minutes, as I watched the ambulance arrive, the sound of its bell shockingly strident in the quiet night, I waited for Elaine to come back to life. For that time I was half convinced that she would. It was only when she was loaded onto the stretcher on a polythene sheet that I began to think that there would be no resurrection. Even as the ambulance set off at full speed, its bell ringing, I felt an absurd stab of hope; surely there would be no need for the bell to be rung unless she were still alive? Cursing my stupidity, I realized that I was forgetting the injured officer.

She was dead, all right; but for the most part their words were nothing to me but a twist of bizarre sibilances, half heard on the edge of sleep; for even in the midst of my danger and discomfort, I had drunk enough and seen enough that night to drift into a kind of half-sleep, so that the forms of the two men were nebulous, elastic, like shadows, and their voices had the ringing, distant tones of sounds heard under a dentist's gas.

'I really thought he was here this time,' said Turner in his quiet, intense way. 'I smelt him, damn it. We should have brought more men. Damn the yard, I warned them there was something going on here. What's the good of bringing in three hundred men to investigate if they're going to waste their time fooling about the river? They don't know this town.' For a

336

moment, he brooded. 'Who the hell was she?' he said
fiercely. 'She's a completely unknown quantity. Was
she with him?' The other shrugged.

'Maybe we're on the wrong track altogether,' he
suggested. 'Maybe Holmes isn't our man.'

Turner shook his head. 'He's our man,' he insisted.
'And he was here. I *know* he was.'

'But the woman?' questioned the other. 'And what
about those others? I'm sure I saw at least two more of
them, but in all the upset they must have got clean
away. Where do they fit in?'

'I don't know.' Turner paused. 'But if we find who
the dead woman is, then we'll find Holmes. I'm sure of
it.'

'It would have been better to take her alive,'
muttered the other officer, morosely.

'Don't you think I don't know that?' snapped
Turner. Their voices drifted for a moment out of my
hearing, became a jumble of harmonics in the taut air.
Remotely, I considered my situation, still anaesthe-
tised by wine, blood and shock. For a moment, I
wondered how they would react if I just stepped out of
hiding and said hello. The thought of their slack,
shocked faces amused me, and I almost giggled. Then
the humour of the thought shifted, became something
poignant; suddenly I *wanted* to be able to step out, into
their light, with my thumbs up like a child ending a
game. I wanted to see their faces, to touch them, to run
to them to be comforted. It was more than just a desire
for self-destruction; I choose to see what I felt then as
the essential humanity in me in revolt, the thing which
through everything I have undergone has never quite
abandoned me. I stood up.

'Inspector.' His expression was almost hilarious. I
found myself smiling, an absurdly wide, boyish grin.
Turner brought out his pistol and pointed it at me.

'Put your hands up, Holmes,' he said, 'I want you to
put your hands on your head and turn round. On the

count of three. One. Two. Three.'

I shrugged and did as he asked.

'There isn't any need to be so careful,' I said mildly. 'I haven't got a gun.'

He ignored that, and I sensed rather than saw him bring out his card from his breast pocket. He read my rights quickly, without expression, like a little boy reciting Grace before his birthday dinner.

'Take off your coat.'

I did so, watching as he searched the pockets by feel, still looking at me from the eye of his gun. He threw the coat back to me, keeping out of range of my hands.

'Put it on.'

'You needn't have worried,' I said, trying to reassure him. 'I wasn't going to hurt you.' That was true enough; what I had felt as I hid in the yard of the warehouse, that kind of love, invaded me again. I wanted to touch him, to make him real in my mind. I felt like an alien. I wanted to talk to him, to hear his voice. I wanted his wife, his children, his memories, his secrets, his bad habits. I wanted the cigarettes he smoked, the food he ate, the dreams he dreamed.

'You can turn round now,' he told me as his companion moved towards me to fasten the handcuffs around my wrists. To my dull mind, the situation was unreal, and I an observer, watching with a kind of detached interest, like a man who knows himself to be dreaming.

'Thank you.' As I turned I saw his face with great clarity, like a memory. Thin light sketched his features in graveyard grey, highlighting the outline of the gun in his hand. I know nothing about guns; I couldn't even begin to guess if it was loaded. I suppose it was.

'You killed Elaine,' I told him as we walked towards the Wolsley. 'That was her name. Elaine.' I couldn't see his face, but I thought he swallowed hard, as if he were eating something tough.

'Who was she, Holmes? Your lady friend?'

338

'No.'

'Where does she fit into all this, then?'

'She was a victim,' I told him. 'A victim, like me.'

Suddenly, I realized how tired I was. Like a dreamer awakening from a nightmare feeling more tired than when he had slipped into sleep, I felt exhausted, drained of everything. Perhaps it was the fact that Rosemary was beyond my grasp, possibly forever, perhaps it was remembering Elaine's foot drumming, as she died.

At that instant I gave it all up, the glamour, the promise of eternity, the power and the beauty. It hurt to give it up, but the giving was a deliverance. My anguish was radiant.

'I'll tell you everything, Inspector,' I promised impulsively. 'Everything.'

Two

Cambridge, *April 1990*

He had left Ginny asleep on the sofa, and as he opened
the door quietly to let himself out, he glanced back and
saw her curled up, her face tucked into the crook of her
elbow. A sensation of utter protectiveness overwhelmed him, a feeling which sat comfortably under
his breastbone. Joe, who was normally as jumpy and
ill-at-ease as an adolescent, whose life was a constant
roller-coaster of highs and lows, had experienced only
a very few moments of true stability. Asked to define
his life, the word 'comfortable' wouldn't even have
had a mention. And yet now it seemed to him that all
his insecurities had been bled away, that some
miraculous transfusion had taken place so that
suddenly he felt in control of everything, his bitterness
and anxieties drained from his body. He went down
into the street, the new sense of well-being inside him,
compelling as a powerful rock beat. He was smiling.

Two girls in jeans and T-shirts looked at him
strangely, almost drawing away, despite the hour and
the bright sunlight . . . one of them, trying later to
explain why the memory of the man remained with
her even though Cambridge was full of strange people,
could only vaguely remember why.

'His eyes were haunted,' she said at ten o'clock in
the Union Bar that evening, voice charmingly slurred
after five gin-and-tonics. In a novel, she might have

341

been able to say; *'His eyes were like a doorway into another world.'* But in real life she simply got drunk, went to bed with a young man from another college who she didn't even like, and woke up the next day with a depressive hangover and a vague sense of something lost, something like eternity.

Joe went on his way without even noticing her, riding the jingling carousel of his thoughts. He was singing softly to himself, and absently he rubbed his knuckles, noticing as he looked down that the back of his left hand was dark with bruising.

It was Alice's fault. Experimentally he flexed the hand, feeling the knucklebones move like ballbearings under the swollen skin. Damn, it hurt. He wondered whether he had broken any bones. It was his left hand, the one he needed most when he was playing. If Alice had made him bust his left hand . . . Come to think of it, he hadn't seen the bitch show much sympathy. In fact, he wasn't at all sure she hadn't been glad. Well, he'd get that straight when he saw her too. He'd promised Ginny he'd square things with Alice, and he would. Anyway it was time he got a few things straight with Alice. Time to meet the chef. He *told* her to lay off Ginny. She'd done enough damage as it was. He might as well square it with her now while he was feeling so fucking pissed off. He quickened his step.

Alice picked up the knife, testing its weight. It was a long carving-knife from her kitchen, wooden-handled and singing with sharpness. It made Alice feel almost faint even at the thought of using it on a person, but by now the worst of the sickness and the shaking had dissipated, to be replaced by a troubling, but merciful sense of unreality, as if true logic had been replaced by the strange surrealist logic of dreams. Just follow, thought Alice to herself. The knife knew where it was going far better than she did. Like the point of a compass it showed the way, implacably, back to the house in Grantchester.

Alice swallowed with difficulty, wondering if she dared eat anything, but even at the thought she felt herself gag in nausea (go ahead if you want to throw up alice) and turned towards the door. There could be no more delaying it, she knew. She had to be in Grantchester before night, when the nightwalkers came.

She had taken two steps towards the door, was taking a third, when someone knocked.

(oh shit who's that)

The knock came again, impatiently.

(never mind never mind just ignore it they'll go away when you don't answer)

A scraping at the letter-box—

(someone's trying to look in)

—but the flap was sealed from the inside.

Alice waited for a breath-held eternity of moments, listening to the sounds from outside.

'Dammit, she's out.' He kicked angrily at the door, twice, but only managed to hurt his foot. He looked at his watch; almost six. Ginny would be waiting for him at home, counting on him; he didn't want her to be alone in the house when night fell. She was so afraid of the dark.

But it rankled, it really did, to let Alice win, to go home to Ginny without having done what he promised. Maybe if he . . . He looked round, saw no one in the street except an old man with a dog. Nonchalantly, he turned, walked fifty yards or so down the street, then turned into the alley which led round the back of the houses.

(damn the bitch i bet she's in there bet she won't answer)

Alice's garden was quite large, long and overgrown with weeds and trees allowed to run wild. It was easy enough to cut across the neighbour's garden into hers, easier still to make his way through the tangle of

343

bushes and flowers until he reached her back porch. Joe looked over his shoulder again, and idly tried the back door. It was locked, but he had expected that. He looked at the lock, decided that it was too strong to force. But there was a window. Forcing himself to be calm, he picked up a stone from the path, a heavy piece of soft sandstone, with an edge. He lifted it to shoulder-height, then tapped it – a tap was all it needed – against the corner of the glass. The window cracked. Gently, so as not to cut himself, he pushed the glass, pressed it until a corner of it loosened. Then he worked at the loose part with his fingernails until it came out of the frame altogether. He laid the piece of glass on the path beside him, began to work on another piece. It came easily this time, and bit by bit he soon managed to free the whole of the pane. One pane was all he needed; it was enough for him to be able to push his arm through the door and unlatch it.

Strange how easy it is to commit the irreversible. Such a small step – the difference between opening a door and keeping it safely closed – and Joe was in another world. His eyes were full of lights and reflections, his heart hammering a quick riff on the frets of his ribs as he looked around. The house was cool and deserted, but something (yes something joey-lad you got that one right) told him that (the bitch) Alice was still there (hiding), maybe asleep. Slyly he opened the living-room door and padded inside. Nothing.

Wait (not quite): a tiny sound from the stairs, the squeaky board. He grinned and turned to the stairway, quietly.

'Alice?' he called softly, gently, the riff quickening under his breastbone into a (eat ya heart out jacko) tight little series of jumps and arpeggios.

'Alice? Time to meet the chef.'

344

One

Cambridge, *August 1948*
Fulbourn Hospital, *May 1978*

In 1948 the police station in Cambridge was much
smaller than it is today; there was one officer on duty
that night, and he blinked stupidly as he saw the
Inspector and I come in. I suppose that he had heard
all about the excitement earlier that night; there was a
morgue too, annexed to that little station, and maybe
he had seen them bring in Elaine from the ambulance.
I imagined her lying, somewhere behind one of those
doors, her hair spread out like a mermaid's on the
white enamel. With my new, all-encompassing
affection for humans and their world, I smiled at the
duty officer.

'Don't be worried,' I said. 'I'm not going to hurt
you.'

'Be quiet,' snapped Turner, then, addressing the
other man; 'Have you contacted the Yard yet?'

The officer nodded. 'Yes, sir. Someone'll be here in
about an hour.'

'Good,' said Turner. 'Hold the fort for a while. I'm
going to take a statement from the suspect.'

For a lazy instant, I wondered what he meant, then I
realized that the suspect was me. The thought made
me laugh, the sound unexpectedly bright in the turgid
atmosphere of the station. I laughed again. It felt good.

'This way, please,' said Turner, directing me to the

far end of the police-station. I was absurdly pleased by his polite tone; everything about him pleased me then. I turned and smiled.

'In here,' he said, in his neutral voice. He was near enough for me to see his eyes, cold and grey as nails hammered into his face.

A little square room, tiled in white, as I had imagined the morgue, with a little table, two chairs and a latrine bucket in the corner. A strong smell of disinfectant hung in the air, reminding me, comically, of the boys' toilets in the junior school I had attended as a child.

'Sit down.'

I chose the chair next to the wall, took off my coat and sat on it. Turner sat on the table, looking down at me, his eyes unreadable. The PC who had been with him when he came in had joined us, and was sitting opposite, pen poised over a little pad of paper to write down what I said.

We waited like that, in silence, for a long time. After a few minutes, I recognized Turner's technique of allowing the criminal to incriminate himself and, despite myself, I grinned. I *wanted* to incriminate myself, wanted to rejoin society, even at its lowest level; I had no desire to escape. I felt almost light-headed; there were no more choices to be made, no more decisions, nothing. It had all been done, though, decided for me. Nothing left but my future, my destiny. I felt like the young novice just about to take her vows.

'So, what do you want to know?' I said at last.

'Why you did it,' replied Turner, quietly. 'All those people? The vagrant woman in the weir. Those people in the pub. And what about the body we found in Grantchester churchyard, all cut up into pieces? Was that you too?'

I shook my head.

'Not exactly.' I paused, still absurdly delighted by his face, his sanity, the shaving-cut on his chin, the

346

smell of his after-shave. 'I didn't kill anyone, but I was there when it happened. It was the others. Rosemary.'

Turner nodded, although I could not tell by anything he said or any movement he made whether he believed me or not.

'Rosemary?'

I told him.

I told him everything I knew or had conjectured about her, exposed her utterly. I betrayed them all. I cleansed myself of them. Inspector Turner showed no sign of reaction at all; he simply listened politely, nodding from time to time as if I were simply corroborating something he already knew. When I had finished, he stood up, and I looked at him expectantly.

'Are you going to arrest them?' I asked.

'I'm going to get some coffee,' he said mildly. 'I think it's going to be a long night. Maybe by the time I get back, you'll have thought up a better story than that. I can wait. I like stories.'

And at that he and his companion left the room, shutting the door behind them.

I waited, knowing that he would come back soon. After a while, thinking about the coffee, and while I still had some privacy, I went and used the latrine bucket.

I must have dozed for half an hour or so, when I was awoken by the sound of footsteps. Someone was walking down the passage, their feet making a light pattering sound on the tiles. I remember thinking what a light tread the Inspector had. The footsteps stopped outside the door of the cell; I heard someone fumbling with keys, pulling the latch. I looked idly towards the door as it opened, then froze, the greeting I had intended for Turner dying on my lips.

It was Elaine.

She was barefoot, her toes blue with cold against the tiles, and she was wearing a kind of hospital robe, stiff white linen, tied at the sides with white ribbons. Her face was even paler than usual. There was blood at the side of her mouth, as if she had fed too greedily, and blood had trickled down the inside of her leg, leaving a broad track of dark-red going up from her ankle out of sight into the robe. Her hair was like seaweed, her eyes brimming. With a shock, I realized that what she was wearing was not a hospital robe at all.

My system must have shielded me against the shock somewhat; it is one thing to believe, academically, in eternal life, and another entirely to watch a dead woman come back from the dead. I gaped, my head reeling; thinking; another ride on Rosemary's ghost train.

Elaine beckoned, wordlessly, and until the same happens (God save you) to you, you will never understand the compulsion of that gesture, its not-to-be-disobeyed power. In a similar way does the statue of the dead commander beckon Don Juan to his last meal. There was no refusing her. I stood up, feeling faint, though by then I was used to horrors, and followed her, without a word, into the corridor. The door leading to the morgue was half open, and as I passed, I glanced in. It was how I had imagined it; the tiles white in a crude electric light, half-a-dozen bare slabs for the bodies; the tiny sound of running water, trickling down the gutters by the sides of the room. I followed her into the front of the station, rubbing my eyes. Great dark flowers blossomed behind my eyelids.

The station was a butcher's shop. Two men lay face-down on the floor in pools of tacky blood; someone, in his struggles, had struck the wall as he fell, stricken, and had left the prints of his hands and his body against the white paint, like grisly negatives. A third was slumped across the desk, his head twisted at an unnatural angle; Anton was sitting on the desk beside him, using a scalpel to cut pieces from his face, as absorbed as a child doing a jigsaw. Stunned as I was, I managed to see all the bodies well enough to realize that none of them was Turner. Somehow, the thought gave me an obscure satisfaction; but I said nothing.

They were all there; Rafe and Java standing on either side of Rosemary; I noticed that Rafe's face was bloody, and so was his hair, as if it had dipped in blood as he fed. Zach was standing at the door, keeping watch. Rosemary was at the window, looking out into the night; she turned as I came in, and her lovely face was suffused with triumph.

'Are you still afraid, Danny?' she said. 'Look . . .' and she made a sweeping, ballet-like gesture to indicate the carnage around her. Her eyes were limpid, pitiless; so must Helen have looked upon the wreckage of Troy. 'Is there a limit to what we, the chosen, can do?'

'You raised Elaine.' It was all I could say.

'Of course,' she said dismissively. 'I look after my own.' I heard a sob from behind me, as Elaine's breath caught in her throat.

'But Elaine is a romantic at heart,' said Rosemary, with bright contempt. 'She imagines the peace of sleeping underground. She wants the unsullied purity of death. The innocence of the grave.' She laughed. 'You make your choice, and so do I,' she said tartly. 'And the chosen stay chosen. Forever.'

'But how?' I sounded foolish, a child seeking to comprehend miracles.

She shrugged, with a certain contempt, but I could tell that, as usual, she was happy to tell me.

'It's childishly simple,' she said. 'Even Christ did it, when he said to Lazarus, "Come forth." All you have to do is to call, and the chosen will come. Desire invokes, Danny, and we are the children of desire.'

I didn't understand what she meant at the time at all; I was numb with the aftermath of despair, and this new revelation broke upon me like a great wave, stunning me. It was not a thing my intellect could comprehend, and my emotions were so overloaded that day that there could be no more room in me for intuitive acceptance. I accepted what she told me with the blind, unprotesting apathy of a suffering animal who has never known anything else.

But now, after years of thought, now that passion and terror are both dead in me, I think I understand what she meant. Too late to help myself, but not too late for you to do what I failed to see. She was the child of my desire, certainly; my dream-lady, my Blessed Damozel, the bride and the sorceress of my innermost fantasy. She took the shape of my dreams, as she has always done in all of her aspects, and I loved and hated her as I love and hate myself. Too late, now, for excuses; I know what I know, and should have known then. Rosemary was the noose I made for my own neck; in killing her, I only served to strengthen my desire . . . and desire, as she said, invokes. I thought that after Robert's death I would be safe from her; I thought myself strong enough to withstand her call, but here, at the end of everything, I know better. I was the one who wished her back. I think I recalled her, as she raised Elaine, as she knew I would. In remembering, I recalled her; what is 'remember', except another word for the same thing?

Two

Cambridge, *April 1990*

'Joe?' For a moment she felt utter relief, the adrenalin ebbing from her system in a great slipstream of prickling air. It was only Joe.

(but the door was locked how did he get in?)

She stopped half-way to the stairs –

(hadn't there been the sound of breaking glass and)

– hands unconsciously going back to the handle of the knife –

(oh god it's them he's with them it's not joe at all)

– then moving away.

'Dammit, Joe, you gave me a shock, creeping about like that. What were you playing at?' That was better. There was no reason to freak out just because Joe came in by the (locked?) back door. And if she could imagine even for a minute that Joe meant to do her any harm . . . the sudden memory of Joe's face earlier that day as he turned towards her with that blank and meaningless rage, the sound his fist had made as he crunched his knuckles against the wall . . . and the back door *had* been locked, she knew that, remembered checking the garden before she drew the bolt.

'Come down a minute, Al,' his voice was eerily normal. 'I want to talk to you.'

'Just a minute.' She looked around, the tempo of her panic accelerating, for a means of escape. Somehow she *knew* that the man down there wasn't quite Joe, the

351

way that when she had painted the Ophelia pictures she hadn't quite been Alice; if she went down there to meet him she didn't know what she'd see. Perhaps nothing. But perhaps he would be waiting with blank psychotic eyes and that alien, submerged rage, the hunger of the nightwalker. Alice felt her hands begin to tremble again, stilled them with an angry gesture. The panic was forced deeper, became a dull, controlled ache in the pit of her stomach.

'I was having a shower,' she called brightly, 'I heard you knock. Just sit down, and I'll be there in a min.'

'Take your time.' To her new sensitivity, his voice was a shade too bright, sinister as a grinning clown. She saw him, suddenly, in her mind's eye, standing at the fairground gate like a garish sentinel, a toffee-apple in one hand, his brown hair sprayed red, and with a band of shadow over his eyes . . .

Urgently, she scanned the top floor. The windows were too high to jump from without risking broken limbs; if Alice had been maybe two stone lighter she might have risked it, but as it was she saw herself hitting the lawn with a crunch of broken bones, easy prey to anyone who might be waiting for her there. She would have to use the stairs, she decided; she would have to talk her way past him. She checked the weight of the knife, wrapped in a piece of cloth and pushed awkwardly up her sleeve, and went downstairs.

He was waiting, sitting in Alice's armchair idling with a paperweight, a fist-sized knuckle of white marble shaped like a surrealist cat. A swatch of hair had fallen over his eyes, hiding his expression, but he looked up when he heard Alice's footsteps on the staircase. She looked sick, he thought as he took in her pale face, her thin lips, then the alien rhythm took over again, compellingly, forcing the alien thoughts into his mind. Joe didn't try to combat them; to tell the truth it was a good kind of feeling, a natural high, so to speak, like the buzz you get from a really good jam session with a band you know well. He let the rhythm direct him.

Alice looked at his upturned face, still expecting to see the face of the nightwalker behind his round, academic glasses. For a moment the lenses flashed light from the window into her eyes, then he grinned, a peculiarly Joe-like expression, at the same time endearing and rueful.

'Joe,' she began in a shaky voice, 'I'm in trouble. I . . . I can't tell you what it's all about, but I need you to promise me something very important.'

Joe shrugged. 'That depends on—'

'No!' insisted Alice. 'You have to promise. You have to keep away from Ginny tonight. Make some excuse. Say you're ill. Just keep away from her, just for tonight. Please.'

Joe frowned, suddenly flooded with alien thoughts. He remembered that he had wanted to talk to Alice about Ginny, but didn't quite remember what he wanted to say.

'Why, Al?' His voice was vague, with the aggrieved tone of a confused child. 'What's your big thing about Ginny? Why is she . . .'

Alice sighed and went down the last two steps to stand beside Joe. 'I wish there was a simple way to tell you all this,' she said wearily. 'There's so much I can't prove, and so much that sounds completely crazy, even now. I can't expect you to believe all of that. But I do know that Ginny's friends, and maybe Ginny as well, are involved in something . . . very frightening. I do know that at least one man is dead, and that they had something to do with it. They . . .'

Joe looked grim. 'I'm still listening, Al,' he said in a quiet voice. 'Go on.' And Alice, encouraged by the fact that Joe had not lost his temper or refused to hear her story, began to tell him everything, even more than she had intended to say. She told him about the paintings,

353

the dream which wasn't a dream, Daniel's diary.

'At first I thought it must all be a coincidence,' she said, finding the pace of her narrative now, 'I thought I was going crazy, twisting events to suit my fantasy about Ginny. I *was* jealous of her, you know, that's what made me think that what I was finding out couldn't be true, but there are just too many things all pointing to the same conclusion. I have to find out her involvement in this.'

Joe looked at her in silence for a moment, then he nodded.

'I see.' His expression was blank for a moment (what shall i do now?), then he let his shoulders sag and took his glasses off to wipe them. He didn't look at Alice as he spoke, and his voice was slightly muffled, as if he were talking with his mouth full.

'I've been a bastard, haven't I, Al?' he said in a subdued tone. 'I blew up at you this morning, dammit, I even made a hole in your wall, I behaved like a complete prat, and the stupid thing is, I already knew you were right about those two blokes. I'd seen them before, and I saw them again today with Ginny. I knew they were selling dope to her as well, and she was taking it. Shit, you can't know somebody like that and not . . .' He pushed his hair out of his eyes. 'Oh Al, I just hoped that it wasn't true, I hoped I could stop it being true by bawling you out and not listening. I just couldn't take the idea that I was being taken for a ride again.' He paused. 'I'm sorry, Al.' He made an angry little gesture and rubbed his eyes with the back of his hand.

'Poor Joe.' Quite spontaneously, Alice sat on the arm of the chair and put her arms round him, smelling tobacco from his coat and the clean smell of his hair. Nostalgia overwhelmed her.

Quietly Joe shifted the white marble paperweight to his right hand. The rhythm grew stronger inside him, underpinning his fluttering heartbeat. A fierce, tumbling joy invaded his system, a certainty of the rightness of his joyful rage. A voice, sounding a little like that of (ginny?) Grace Jones singing 'Slave to the Rhythm' began to sing beneath his breastbone, a sweeping, certain melody like a hymn.

(slave to the rhythm . . . sla-aave to the rhythm . . . slave to the)

She saw the movement of his right hand, and some remnant of her earlier suspicion must have escaped, because she twisted, instinctively, to the side, and the paperweight smashed into her shoulder with paralysing force. Joe was taken off-balance as the momentum of his attack pitched him out of the chair, half falling to his knees, and Alice had the time to leap back, to try and get something in between them. Her mind gibbered uselessly at her (oh god they got him they got him after all) as she turned to run (use the knife i can't it's joe), but Joe was already standing, the paperweight back in his hand, a dreadful grin on his face, and closing in.

(can't get away sorry al)

(you're not joe you're)

(too right i'm)

Suddenly he sprang, raking at Alice's face with the hand which held the paperweight. She jumped back, at the same time kicking out at him with her right foot to keep him at a distance. She wobbled, almost lost her balance, and in the time it took for her to regain it he was on her, grabbing her by the hair and lifting the paperweight to smash her face. Alice ducked and twisted furiously in his grasp, feeling her hair coming out at the roots. She kicked again, reaching his shins squarely this time, taking him by surprise. He loosened his grip from her hair for long enough for her to duck forwards, dropping a third kick from behind his shins into the back of his knees, reaping his legs from under him and sending him falling backwards, hitting his head on the angle of the table-leg. It was a

355

messy blow, some of its effect lost because he had managed to transfer his hold onto the front of her sweat-shirt, and she half fell on top of him, crushing his ribs. She hit him in the face as she came down, more by luck than intention, then she had scrambled to her feet and was at the door, unlatching it with trembling fingers. She was half-way down the street, running like the wind, when (i'm sorry joe didn't want to i'm sorry i'm . . .) she heard (his thoughts) his voice, Joe's voice now, bemused and hurt.

(alice what happened did i fall did i what happened)

(oh no joe not falling for that one i'm out of here)

(alice come back i was only joking it wasn't me i didn't mean to hurt you it wasn't . . .)

'Alice! Come back! Alice!'

Drifted consonants and broken vowels on a whistling black wind of speed and salt. Eyes stinging as the wind rushes her down the streets and alleys of Cambridge towards Grantchester. And maybe it is Alice's imagination, but as she makes her way across the river to Rosemary's house it seems to her that with every step she takes, that fairground reek grows stronger; smoke and sweat and roasting peanuts, burnt sugar and petrol fumes and animals.

Part Four

Beata Virginia

The composition is harmonious, the colours muted and blurred, shapes half drowned under layers of light. Her hands are folded, her eyes closed. Only her profile is well defined; eyelids heavy, tragic, half-smiling lips drawn back to reveal the most perfect, the least carnivorous teeth . . . the props around her, the white poppy, the red dove, the symbolic figures and the sundial seem the random peoplings of a morbid and childish sentimentalist. But the woman! . . .

The passive curve of her spine, the studied pose of her hands in the simple homespun of her dress, the simplicity of her loosened hair, bright as a stained-glass window in the evening light . . . all are belied by that smile, more knowing than Mona Lisa's, the veiled half-guessed-at gaze beneath her long eyelashes . . . She knows something, this woman, something we, the public can only dream of, some secret more dreadful than death, more glorious than ecstasy, yet somehow combining them both. In death, Beatrice is at her most alluring; lips parted for the kiss of the chosen one, she promises . . . what? Eternity? Immortality? Damnation? Death?

From *The Blessed Damozel*, Daniel Holmes

The door is old, hanging slantwise in its broken frame like a smile on the face of a witch, waiting and enjoying the waiting, despite rain and wind and woodworm, scarred and chiselled by a thousand trivial incidents, each scar a moment in a life cut short. It waits, half open like a watchful green eye, for someone to pass this way, someone young, someone brave. And when this someone comes, as they always do, the cynical green eye seems to wink invitingly, promising something not quite specified, like love, or glory, something like that. But be careful; magic doors are meant to be opened, but sometimes they lie.

The Prince does not pause for a moment, being a man of action rather than intuition. He has no interest in old doors, only in the secrets which lie behind them, and no strange and morbid fantasies flicker through his mind, only an unassailable sense of pride, and a certainty of somehow being chosen. A careless shove sends the old door crashing into the undergrowth as its rusty hinges leave the frame, revealing a green stain finger-deep in the rotting wood. But our Prince is no believer in omens and it is with a clear, interested gaze that he steps into the frame as if into his own portrait, and, sword at the ready, looks into the accursed garden. Not that there is very much to see; for the doorway and, as far as he knows, the entire garden is a mass of tight-woven and tangled greenery in which rose embraces briar, and nightshade and fern and hollyhock and sunflower and hemlock and blackberry in a tapestry of mystic, disturbing couplings. The Prince can see only the top of the keep through this undergrowth, itself hung with trailing vines, about half a mile away. And the greenery whispers to itself, half musically, a song of hunger and patience.

Yes, it is good that our Prince is a man of little imagination, for at the sight of that monumental task ahead of him a lesser man might have allowed his mind to wander along forbidden lines. Not he.

He is chosen.

For a hundred years she has waited for him, enchanted, cobwebs closing softly around her, red hair spilling onto the pillow, the coverlet, creeping onto the floor, pale eyelids jealous guardians of her sweet, sixteen-year-old's dreams, waiting for his kiss to deliver her. The Prince smiles, strangely tender for one of so few imaginings, steps out of his frame into the garden, and begins to wreak havoc. Giant sunflowers fall beneath his tread, hawthorn and lemongrass and bluebell and veronica loose their jealous perfumes beneath his clumsy boots, but the Prince cares little for flowers; he reaps fields of basil and valerian and thyme with the bright edge of his sword, and as he works, face ruddy and open as any farm-boy's, he begins to sing.

But in the depths of the keep, an ancient curse unwinds its lazy coils and begins to stir. The sleeping Princess senses it and smiles in her sleep as it creeps from its dark hiding-place, up narrow stairways towards her chamber. It is dark, silent, patient and hungry. And it too waits, ever-patient, knowing that what it awaits will come, lured by the shining bait like so many others who were brave and handsome, and like so many yet to come who are clear-eyed and fearless, bright and transient as waves on the ocean. Let them come, it thinks, and within its faceless, joyless, endless waiting, it smiles.

The Prince has reached the keep; leaving the trail Prince-deep in the greenery behind him, he has reached the door.

The Princess moves, a long, pale hand clutches the

coverlet; a coil of bright hair is disturbed and falls across the dusty floor.

The Prince pushes the door of the keep and enters; softly he begins to make his way up the narrow, green stairs to where his lady awaits him.

The door opens.

The Prince, tall, clear-eyed and rosy-cheeked, stands in the doorway. He looks down into the gloom and sees a bed wreathed in cobwebs, on which lies a girl, pale and lovely on the yellowing coverlet. Her hair cascades to the floor, prismic in the sunlight, and her face is in shadow, vulnerable in sleep. This is the enchantment, thinks the Prince; this the promise. He takes three steps forwards and clasps her in his arms. For an instant he finds himself looking into a pair of eyes as grey as lavender, and then he steps back, brave though he is, for suddenly her aspect has begun to change, to take the form of something darker, hungrier. He stumbles, this young Prince, stumbles and turns to run towards the door, and as he does the Princess – what remains of her – catches hold of him by the wrist, and gently but with hideous firmness forces him to look into her eyes.

'One kiss,' she says and ignoring the Prince's struggling, his pleas and his cries, she begins to feed her eternal, unappeasable hunger. A moment later the Princess is sleeping again, sleeping peacefully her endless accursed sleep, and the green eye of the secret door is half closed again, watching the garden with a cynical smile. And still she sleeps, and she waits, enjoying the waiting, despite wind and rain and heroes with their clumsy boots, among lavender and harebell and elderflower, for thus are the dreams and waitings of sleeping virgins, and thus end their promises of love and glory.

Sometimes they lie.

From *The Blessed Damozel*, Daniel Holmes

One

Cambridge, *August, 1948*
Fulbourn Hospital, *May 1978*

She found another, temporary place for us to hide; in the apartment she had used before she married Robert. It was quite large, with two bedrooms, a bathroom, a little kitchen and a living-room, and she said that she had kept paying the rent for it because it was a good place for her to stay when she didn't want to be seen by him.

Not that poor Robert ever asked any questions; when she went out she told him she was going to see a friend, almost challenging him to make something of it, but he accepted what she said without a word.

Rosemary left us in the flat, gave one of the spare keys to me, and the other to Zach, and went home. It had been a long night, and she meant to go and get a shower, and sleep. For myself, sleep was beyond me. I tried for an hour or so to persuade Elaine to talk, but she would do nothing but cry, curled up on the sofa with her face hidden, childishly, in her hands. I abandoned the hope of ever getting a clear account of what had happened from her, so I indulged in a solitary game of chess (left hand against right), drank most of a bottle of red wine Zach had left me, and tried unsuccessfully to analyse the events of that night.

Perhaps even then, I had some hope of proving to myself that there was a logical explanation for what had happened; Elaine had not been dead, merely stunned. Inspector Turner had missed her heartbeat as he felt in the thick coat she had been wearing. It must seem strange to you that I tried to disbelieve it, I the man who had witnessed so many dark miracles that by now I must have been immune to them. But I was not. Perhaps even then, I hoped to awaken from the nightmare, to prove to the ever-optimistic doubter within me that there was an explanation for all of the past few months. I was insane. I was ill, perhaps terminally so; maybe I had a brain tumour which gave me delusions. Somehow, the thought of death did not alarm me as once it might have done. It was the thought of life, yes, of *that* kind of life, which made me shudder. The thing which convinced me of the reality of what I had seen was its very simplicity. If I had had to invent a resurrection my mind would have formulated something complicated; there would have been rituals, invocations, magic, science, anything but the bleak mysterious simplicity of this monstrous act. If there had been something there for me to analyse I would have felt secure; I could have believed in Mary Shelley's Frankenstein monster, brought to life by science, I could believe in secret amulets and magical potions, in words of power and holy signs, but not in this. My mind rebelled, even against Rosemary.

Despairing at last of either sleep or quietude, I decided to go for a short walk, thinking that the cold night air might clear my aching head and calm my thoughts. Even the knowledge that by now the carnage at the police station must have been discovered did not deter me; I found that I really did not care whether I was arrested or not. I took my coat and hat, opened the door to the apartment and locked it again behind me. I saw no one as I went down the stairs and into the street; although the dawn was beginning to show, threadlike, on the horizon, it was still too early for any idle passers-by to be abroad. I was about to cross the street, making my way to the river, when a small movement caught my eye, from the alcove at the side of the building, where the dustbins were kept. My heart jumped, but I told myself that it could only be a dog, nosing for scraps among the rubbish.

'Hey, dog!' I hissed. 'Dog!'

The movement came again, a kind of fitful scrabbling among the bins, too big to be a dog. I took three steps forwards, blinking into the darkness through the smeared lenses of my glasses. The figure pressed itself further into the shadows, as if it were trying to sink into the brick wall of the alcove, It was a man.

'Hey, you,' I called softly. 'Who are you? Come out.'

The man did not reply, but I caught a little sound from his lips, a kind of wordless plea.

'Come out!' I stepped forwards again, overcome by curiosity, and saw him lift grimy hands towards me in supplication.

'No . . .' His voice was little more than a whisper. 'Leave me alone.' There was something in the voice I recognized, and I squinted at the man with a new interest.

'Who are you?'

The face looked towards me, a slack, pale disc of flesh above the crumpled suit, the tie pulled away from the collar, the hat pushed back from the top of the head to reveal lank, damp hair. For a minute I blinked, unable to put a name to the familiar face, then I understood, recoiling, even though the man was in no condition to do me any harm. For what I recognized was another face of Inspector Turner.

'Turner!' I breathed in amazement, and I saw him cringe away from me again with a little whimper. The man's icy poise was broken forever, his face a mass of tics and twitches, as if his very flesh were host to a hundred contradictions pulling their own ways and transcending logic. He was evidently in deep shock.

'I won't hurt you,' I said quietly, stretching out a hand

to touch him. He pulled away with a little cry of loathing, but I followed him into the dark and stinking alcove, overcome with pity and a kind of tenderness. I had known I was strong; but not how strong. What he had seen had destroyed Turner, the ice-cold man of reasoning, had made him a monster such as myself. I felt a sudden kinship with that human, with his weakness which justified my own.

'I won't hurt you,' I repeated, pulling the little flask I always carried out of my coat pocket. I shook it, guessed it to be about half-full.

'Here, drink this,' I said, 'it's whisky.' A grimy hand knocked against mine, sending the whisky-flask slithering onto the greasy cobbles. But I picked it up, forced it against his mouth. Some of it went in. I heard him swallow, noisily, like a dog, and then I heard the sound of him sobbing.

'I followed you,' he said, almost inaudibly, between sobs. 'I didn't know ... where else to go.' He was silent for a minute; I used his own technique on him, waiting for him to say more.

'Holmes, I saw ...' he began, the rest was inaudible. 'I saw ...'

'What did you see?' I insisted.

'I was in the lavatory ... saw ... someone at the door ... Higgins answered ... a girl. Looked to be in a bad way ... he asked her in ... Oh God!'

'Keep going,' I said gently. 'You saw Rosemary.'

'Rosemary ... Rosemary ... I never thought ...'

'Yes,' I said encouragingly. 'What else did you see?'

'She came in ...' he said in his peculiar whispering voice. 'And those ... came in behind her. She caught hold of Higgins and he ... I never thought ... they killed everyone, and drank the ... and drank the ...' He whimpered again, a pitiful sound, like dying.

'What else did you see?' I hated to torture him, but I had preoccupations of my own; I had to know.

'I saw ... she went to the morgue ... and I heard

366

her, say; "Elaine". Just . . . that . . . and the dead girl just . . . got up . . . and walked . . . If I hadn't been in the—'

'Is that all she said?' I asked sharply. 'Just her name? Nothing else?' I could hardly believe it had been so easy. As an academic, I suppose I expected my miracles to be complicated; and yet, thus had Christ raised Lazarus. 'Come forth,' he had said. I still think that some miracles should never be performed.

'Turner.' I tried to make my voice commanding. 'I want you to listen. I need to talk to you.'

He looked at me, his eyes wide. 'I didn't believe you,' he said in his new, trailing voice. 'I thought you were lying, or mad. I was so sure of everything. And now I'm so tired.' His voice hitched. 'Tired,' he repeated dully.

'Listen.' I tried to keep my patience. 'I know a place. It's safe. I'm going to take you there. I want to talk to you.' I lowered my tone. 'I need your help.'

He turned his aimless gaze towards me.

'Help?' he questioned mildly, vaguely, like a child on the edges of sleep.

'That's right,' I said. 'It's safe where we're going. You can sleep there.' I hesitated, thinking, perhaps, that in his condition, he was in no state to help anyone. Yet, I thought, if he was mad he might still be of some use. I had no use for sanity on my side; what I needed was madness.

'You're going to help me,' I told him. I put my arms around his shoulders and half lifted him to his feet. He clung to me, wavered, but held himself upright.

'Help?' he asked weakly, but now with some lucidity. 'How can I help you?'

I smiled at him, almost lovingly, manoeuvred him out of the alley and across the street, my arm around his shoulders all the time. 'You're going to help me to do something very dangerous and important.' I smiled again, reassuringly, with a return of that inexplicable feeling of affection and tenderness, and hugged his shoulders.

'We're going to kill Rosemary.'

I looked after Turner for five days, in the first of a deserted row of houses just outside Grantchester. He was shocked and terrified at first, but began to recover, in some way, as time passed. I developed a kind of friendship with him over those few days, spending as long as I could with him every day, especially while the others were sleeping. I brought him food and a change of clothes, books. I played chess with him and brought him bottles of wine. Most of all, I talked to him, told him my story, my despair and my rapture. He listened to me as if his life depended on it, his eyes wide, like a demented child's. I told him what I planned to do, no longer for my own sake, but to salvage the little humanity left in me. He examined the levels of the monstrous in himself, and he wept in my arms. He had moments of sanity interspersed with long periods of mania, reminding me forcibly of myself in those first dark days of the hunger. When the little death came upon me, I went out and hunted on my own, or I went to Elaine for scraps of the night's hunt, but I did not run with the others again. For one, I was too afraid of discovery by the police, who had now launched a national inquiry into what they called 'The Cambridge Police Station Tragedy'. Hundreds of extra police had been sent for from London, and policemen patrolled the night from ten o'clock onwards, questioning any passer-by. A semi-official curfew had been established, although Lamb of the Yard had proclaimed that the killings had probably been the work of a lunatic, long since fled. So while the police chased rumours and false trails through the town Turner and I talked, feverishly, like two lunatics ourselves. I went over my findings and my theories, sharing every thought with him.

Rosemary permeated all our conversations, Rosemary in all her incarnations, Rosemary at her most beguiling and her most deadly. I shared her with him like a lover; her body, her hair, the sweetness of her and the poison. With him, I exorcized her, invoked her, murdered her a thousand times in thought and intention. And yet, despite all of that, my mind rebelled at the act itself, cringed and shrank at the very consummation of its greatest desire. That, I think, was one of the sweetest charms of Rosemary; her fragility, her air of tragedy ... the logical progression from loving her to killing her, keeping her inviolate, even from myself. For five days we contemplated murder with the fascinated, instinctive sadism of insane children.

It was August.

Two

She was not certain what she would have done if anyone had been in the house; but there was not, as she had known there would not be; it was boarded up and deserted, as were the houses around, and call it empathy or what you will, but she knew, with that brave, bright certainty which was like a blade of light in her mind, that this was where she would find them. This was where the creatures met.

Looking up for the first time in daylight, she saw that the roof had partially collapsed, the slates stripped off to reveal the blackened beams of the eaves, like bones. All but the very highest windows were broken, half shielded from the rain by pieces of chip-board, but at one glass-fanged window the rags of a scorched curtain still remained, flapping in the wind like a black flag. Cautiously, she came closer, not wanting to, but by now resigned to the idea that she would, until she was facing the door. This too was broken, the wood rotten and the hinges half-torn away so that it stood ajar, almost invitingly, like a door in a fairy-tale. Behind a cracked glass panel to her left, Alice could still read the names of the erstwhile tenants:

S..PPER 1
..SHLEY 2
..KIN 3
KEN...Y 4

371

The house had stood derelict and empty for over forty years. Alice looked around to check if there was anyone to see her go in, but the street was deserted. Then, taking a deep breath, she pushed the door and stepped forwards into the darkness.

The house was damp and stank of urine, mould and an under-smell of the circus. The nightwalkers were not the only ones to have used it as a hiding-place; on the ground floor Alice found traces of other visitors, sweet-wrappers and silver paper and plastic bags and empty tubes of glue. A box of broken toys had been dumped in one corner of the room, but dust covered it in a thick veil. Alice found herself wondering what had happened to those young trespassers, and she shivered.

The house was so silent and deserted that until she reached Rosemary's apartment she had almost begun to believe that she had been wrong, and that the nightwalkers had found some other place to hide; but as soon as she pushed the door to apartment 2 ASHLEY she knew that her instincts had been right.

There was a mattress in one corner, piled with blankets and a table and some chairs lined up against one of the smoke-blackened walls. Wine bottles littered the floor; a pack of cards had been left spilled across the rotten boards. A shoe-box containing syringes and silver paper on the window-ledge. Candles in empty wine-bottles. Tied to the door-handle, a white rag, cryptically marked with bloody hieroglyphs.

The atmosphere and the sense of predestination almost paralysed Alice. It seemed to her that there were ghosts in the very air she breathed, ghosts like fumes invading her lungs and her mind so that before long she was the one who felt unreal, powerless, unable to touch or to alter the giant, hallucinating actuality of Rosemary, the witch-goddess, absolute mistress of power and blood. Her sense of scale temporarily eluded her; she was infinitely tiny, helplessly huge, suspended in limbo, racing to oblivion faster than light. She was a puppet, jerking here and there on a cherry-coloured twist of string, dancing, choking, spinning as the air whistled from her lungs and she struggled to breathe . . .

Alice tore herself from the paralysis and ran to the window, gasping air. The ghosts and illusions dissipated, and she forced calm upon her fraught spirit, learning to breathe again, reassembling her fractured thoughts.

There could be no more cowardice, thought Alice fiercely to herself. No more hope of evading this commitment she had somehow accepted. When she had escaped from Joe, her breath a handful of needles in her throat, a hot stitch biting into her side as she ran down alleys and dodged under archways, every sound, every movement a renewed terror that he might have found her, she had somehow shed most of the burden of fear which had paralysed her. How it had happened she did not know; she simply knew that somewhere between Cambridge and Grantchester she had decided to *survive*, and that however ill equipped she might appear to bring down Rosemary and her friends, she would give whatever she had to do it.

For a moment, she was almost serene.

Then a sound jolted Alice out of her reverie, and she turned, the roots of her hair beginning to stiffen. In a single liquid movement (even Alice would have been amazed at her own grace if she had had time to consider the ease of that gesture) she had pulled out the knife and had turned to face the slight, grey figure which had detached itself from the shadows to speak to her.

'So you're here at last.'

Alice, the knife held out in front of her, adrenalin-charged blood singing in her ears, recognized the sparse grey hair, stubbly face, rheumy eyes and pink muffler; it was the tramp she had met the previous night. For a moment she hesitated, but, remembering Joe, held onto the knife anyway.

The old man nodded, almost covertly. He seemed sober now; maybe it was still too early in the evening for him to be really far gone.

'What are you doing here?' Her lips were dry, her throat was paper, and she looked at the old man with eyes which were sunken craters in her white face.

The old man nodded again.

'Same as you,' he said shortly. 'Just about. I reckoned you'd be here sooner or later.' His critical glance took in the knife, her pallor, the stubborn look behind her fear. Scared, he thought, but behind all that, there was an underlying toughness of which even she herself was not aware.

'Remember me?'

Alice nodded, still wary.

The old man smiled, not pleasantly.

'I'm not what you think,' he said. 'That's just a bad joke. Besides, it's a good way of getting people to leave me alone. If they can put a tag on me, they think I'm harmless, and the sillier the tag, the better.'

Alice stared at him, her eyes narrowed, re-assessing her earlier opinion.

'I remember you from the other night. Had a look to you, like you were planning something.'

The voice had changed subtly, had sharpened, the back was straighter, the eyes wily, less rheumy.

'I'm not sure I know what you're talking about,' said Alice.

The voice was crisp and very sane. 'Of course you know. I know what you saw in Grantchester that night, and I know you've read Daniel Holmes' book.' He took a step towards her, as if to punctuate what he was saying.

'Don't move.' Her eyes fixed his with a hard light, and the point of the knife rose a little. 'How did you know about that?'

The tramp shook his head with a little gesture of irritation.

'Put that down, girl, we don't have time.'

'Not a chance.' Alice's voice was cold. 'I've had that trick pulled on me once today already. Now if you want to talk—'

Suddenly, the old man's hand snaked out towards Alice. Before she had time to lash out, he had grabbed the hand which was carrying the knife and twisted it sharply. His fingers jabbed stiffly into the back of her hand. Alice jerked backwards instinctively, and found that he was holding the knife half an inch from her throat, his other hand locking her left arm firmly and agonizingly at the elbow and shoulder, the pain of the lock forcing her onto her toes. He held her for a couple of seconds longer, then released the hold.

'Here's your knife back,' he said shortly, holding it out by the handle. 'Next time you have to pull it on someone, use it to cover your body and keep them at arm's length. Don't just poke it at them like that.' His voice was amused and contemptuous. 'Now will you put it away?'

Alice pocketed the knife warily, still rubbing her aching shoulder.

'What do you want?'

'You'll want to hole up in the house for a while. If you go right up to the roof, you'll find there's a little room there with a stash of stuff, couple blankets, chocolate, flask of tea, all that. You can take what you want. You wait there till night comes. I've got some cans of petrol piled up there too, you'll know what they're for later. You—'

'Wait a minute,' said Alice, recovering from her astonishment. 'Who are you? What the hell are you doing here anyway?'

'I might well ask you the same thing,' he retorted. 'I've been watching you.'

'Why?'

'Because it's time you realized what you were up against,' he replied sharply. 'Time you let an old man tell you what he knows.' She looked at him, wondering for an instant whether he was as sober as he seemed. His red-rimmed eyes were bright and crazy as broken glass. He nodded.

'You're a bright girl. You know who I am,' he said.

Suddenly, Alice rather thought she did.

'I . . . yes. You're Inspector Turner, aren't you?' It wasn't even a question.

He smiled, showing a broken tooth.

'A lot of water under the bridge since there was any Inspector,' he said. 'The Inspector died when that girl came back from the dead. What's left is what you see. I'm Alec now, Alice, my girl, just Alec.' He shrugged. 'It's not so bad, you know,' he added.

'I thought . . .' Alice's voice cracked with disappointment. 'I thought maybe . . .'

'You thought I was Dick Barton? The undercover policeman come to save all at the last minute?' He rasped a phlegmy chuckle. 'No. If I were twenty years younger . . . and even then. I'm Alec, all right. Just an old drunk scrounging for money and making people laugh by making up bad verse. There was a time . . .' His voice trailed away. 'But that's all over. She killed me, like she killed Daniel Holmes. It's just taken a little longer, that's all.'

He sat down on the window-ledge, his back to the fading greenish light. 'He told me about the diary, you know,' he confided, 'before he went into Fulbourn. About leaving it in the church wall. He reckoned that if Rosemary ever came back, that would be where she came. He wanted to be cremated, so that she wouldn't be able to raise him. But he wanted the diary kept safe. Because he'd got it right, you see. Right for the first time yet, and too late for it to do him any good, but right enough for someone else to finish her off for

376

good, for ever. What we did in the flat, he and I . . . well
. . . it wasn't worth *that*. . .' Here he broke off and spat,
raspingly, like someone pulling Velcro. 'But he did have
the right idea. She can be killed, and kept buried, so
long as no one gets left to raise her. That was it. It was
that simple. I knew soon as I saw you that you were
going to be the one . . . you had that look on you. You've
got the power to do it, more power than we ever had.
I've been waiting for you for a long time. But now . . .'
He stopped again, clenched his blue-veined fists in their
fingerless gloves. 'You're not ready to deal with them,
Alice,' he said earnestly. 'You think they're going to
come like lambs? You've seen them; she'll come with
the others, the ones Holmes called nightwalkers.
You've never seen them at work. I came with you; came
ready. You think you'll do anything against all of them
at once?'

'I'm ready,' said Alice, not quite steadily. 'As ready as
I can be.'

'With that baby knife? Do you really think you'll use
it?'

Alice looked stubborn.

'I thought . . .'

'You didn't think,' he said acidly. 'There's more
important things for you to do than to get yourself
killed. You have to do what the old man missed; only
you can do that right. Leave me out there, in the alley
between the houses. I'll deal with the ones that come.'

He saw Alice's stare.

'You think I can't? You think that I'm an old drunk
with nothing left?' He reached into one of his pockets,
pulled something out.

'See this?' he said, holding the gun out to her. It
looked old to Alice, almost antique, but it was polished,
the wood of the butt oiled like a beloved cricket bat, and
the light filtering through the narrow window touched
its smooth burnished surface with a cool grey glow.

'I kept this all through the bad time,' he said, with

pride. 'When everything got sold, and my wife left me, and they tried to make out that I was crazy. While I got drunk and went on the wagon again. I kept it all the time. I knew that one day I might need it.' He gestured to her with the gun, grinning his broken, half-senile grin. 'Go back,' he said. 'I'll watch the street. No one suspects a wino, not in Cambridge, nowhere. I'll see them come. I'll stop them. You, just do what you have to do. You'll know what it is.' Then, as Alice hesitated, 'Go on! Time for talk later. I've known for years it would come to this; for years, and I've been waiting all this time, waiting and wondering whether I might get to die in peace before . . . but that doesn't matter much now. What matters is you and me doing the job in hand. Just be careful. The thing wants doing properly this time around. You don't want to leave anyone to bring her back. Not anyone.'

When Alice was upstairs in the little room Turner had told her about, she looked out of the window, and thought she saw him, hidden in the shadows, a darker smudge against the brownish stone of the alley, imagined him keeping watch against what might come.

She was a little way beneath the roof, in what must once have been an attic, and there was a tiny unbroken window through which she could see most of the street. It was cold by now, and she had taken one of Turner's blankets to wrap around her legs as she waited, because half the roof was open to the grey evening sky. She had found a flask of tea, which she drank in little gulps, savouring the warmth, and several bars of chocolate. When she had finished the food and drink she began to feel warmer, and by about ten o'clock she was beginning to feel almost drowsy.

Suddenly, as she drifted, her eye caught a movement below her, and instinctively she drew back, her heart hammering wildly. Very carefully, she came to the window again, and peered through the dusty pane. There. A kind of flicker in the shadows, as of a pale face turned furtively upwards to the light. Someone was watching the house.

Alice felt sick, adrenalin rushing to her head like alcohol on an empty stomach. Not now, she thought frantically; she wasn't ready. The reality of where she was flooded her; she was alone, unknown, in the nightwalkers' den, with only what she had brought to protect her. No one would know what had happened to her if she disappeared.

Mentally she shook herself. At least, she had the advantage of surprise over them, she thought. She would be ready for them before they even knew she was there. Daniel had done it, and in the same house. They could not know she was there. She was safe.

On the other hand, Ginny had her friends to help her, the very thought of which turned Alice to ice. She forced herself to look again. Yes, there it was, only visible to her searching, panic-sharpened gaze. It was watching.

She reached for the knife, felt its weight, somehow ridiculously alien, like a studio prop, in her hand. Despite everything, the weight was comforting, and the sick feeling abated, just a little. Alice began to try and force herself to move.

Very quietly, holding the knife before her, she began to creep down the stairs in the dark, her eyes straining against the brownish darkness. Inch by inch, she crept down the stairs, her tennis-shoes making no sound against the rotten floorboards, her blood a double bass-drum in her throat, every muscle tensed. She forced herself to breathe, though the temptation to listen, to stop breathing so as not to miss the slightest sound, was very great. One . . . Two . . . In . . . Out . . . Avoiding the steps which were unsafe, she concentrated on the breathing, on the pounding of her blood, and with those preoccupations uppermost in her mind, managed to reach the bottom of the stairs without flying off into the hysteria which threatened. There was no one else in the house.

Outside, then, thought Alice. She had seen one figure only, but there might be more. Should she go out to meet them? Every sense screamed no, but Alice, shaking with useless adrenalin and equally useless panic, knew that to delay the moment would only be to give the others a greater advantage when the final meeting came. If she could just creep out ... very quietly ... Maybe she would be able to catch them unawares. And Turner was there too, Turner with his gun. The thought that he was there, with his old service revolver tucked carefully under his woolly pink scarf partly reassured her and partly filled her with a kind of hysteria; what could they do, he and Alice, against Rosemary and her friends? A drunken, half-mad old man and a crazy painter, with no real faith in her own sanity?

She tried to hang onto the thought of Turner waiting in the shadows, tried not to think how old and frail he looked, concentrated on breathing. The knife felt hot and slippery in her hand, but in her head there was a sudden, merciful coldness. Why not? she thought, shifting the knife more comfortably in her hand so that it pointed at a sharp angle outwards into the night. Why not? she thought again, and stepped out into the alley.

The alley, just two feet or so wide, ran alongside the house. Originally it might have been a passage between the front and back of the terrace or a place to leave dustbins, but now it was partially blocked with old cans, pieces of charred wood and other rubbish. She stumbled as she made her way to the mouth of the alley, heard her feet crunch on some piece of debris and froze, her heart pounding with hysteria of its own. Pressing her back against the greasy side of the alley, she looked around her in a broad arc, the knife held out stiffly in front of her.

There was nobody there.

She moved closer to the alley's mouth, partly blocked by a parked car, dared herself to look into the street . . . braced herself for the sight of them, the nightwalkers, waiting for her above the bonnet . . . but she saw nothing. What now?

Carefully, she looked around again, daring herself to fail to see them. Her heart lurched uselessly, sickening her. She felt dizzy, remote, a spiralling fleck in the vastness of the night, of their absence, which even then filled the darkness with their names and their voices. She wondered whether she was going to faint.

Anxiously, she tried to stand upright, felt the world suddenly tilt and sideslip . . . caught herself just in time on the wall. Damn, she thought, with vicious hysteria. It was no time to be passing out like a sickly schoolgirl. She hauled herself upright, fighting for perspective, the sick feeling intensifying momentarily as her feet threatened to give way. For a horrifying instant, the world was a giant fishbowl, she the occupant, gasping under air which was suddenly as ripe and green as swamp-water, staring up into the curve of the sky at the monstrous eye which hovered there, distorted and amorphous, Rosemary's eye, axis of chaos. Then a hand grabbed her roughly by the arm, and she wheeled round, the world jumping back into place with a terrified lurch, the knife raking the air around her.

'Be quiet!' hissed Turner. 'Do you want them to hear you? Get down!' They both ducked back down beside the car, Alice flushing with anger and adrenalin, and crept back into the darkness of the alley.

'I saw someone,' whispered Alice.

Turner nodded. 'Stay here and be quiet,' he advised. 'Don't let them see you. I'll be all right.' And at that he turned and went back to the mouth of the alleyway and stepped out into the light of the street-lamp. Alice counted to ten and went back to the shelter of the parked car, looked carefully out into the street from beneath its rusty undercarriage. Her field of vision was limited and for a minute she saw nothing, but she was none the less certain that, this time, they were there. She felt them there, in the soles of her feet, in the dirt under her hands, the smell of old rubbish and corruption in the filthy alley. She knew they were there.

Somehow, the sight of them was not even a shock. Just a jolt from her heart as it revved up, that droning in her ears which always accompanied the adrenalin-boost. She forced herself to make sure. An unexpected voice in her head laughed and muttered (time gentlemen, please), then Alice took over again, the cool, practical Alice she had encountered in the fairground. No time for panic now, she thought, it's far too late for that now; and she watched for maybe a whole minute through the space under the car, as the nightwalkers came into sight.

They were all there except Ginny; she had expected something of the kind. Of course, Ginny would have stayed with Joe; only her minions would still be staying in the flat. She recognized Rafe by his fair hair, Java by his height and the little sounds she could hear from his motorcycle boots on the pavement. Sounds seemed to be magically amplified in the still night, and Alice thought she could hear all their footsteps, distinctly, individually, as she listened. Still watching she saw Elaine hanging back in the shadows, Anton at her side. The nightwalkers came closer, the light from the street-lamp touching their faces and their forms with a dull, uterine light. Java glanced around him, almost idly, and Alice flinched involuntarily, certain that, somehow, he had seen her.

Then she saw his gaze stop, snag abruptly as he saw something. Turner? She heard the old man's footsteps, audible now, in the street, and she pulled herself a few inches further under the car to watch. A furtive glance around one of the thick rubber-smelling tyres was all she dared try, but she retained an impression of a group of figures crowded around the street-lamp, not three feet from the house-door, discussing something.

Turner moved towards them with the shambling gait of the drunkard, muttering, seemingly to himself. Then he spoke more clearly, in his 'street' voice, loud and rasping; 'Hey! Spare a copper fr'a cuppa tea? Hey!'

Alice heard the other nightwalkers react, heard the sounds of movement as they turned to see who was coming. She recognized Java's voice, low and contemptuous.

'Old man,' he said quietly. 'Get on your way without delay.'

'Wassamatter?' complained Turner. 'Jussa copper fr'a cuppa tea. Ten pence. Jus' ten pence.'

'Look,' the voice was sharper now. 'Get out of the way.'

Alice guessed that Turner was near to them now, perhaps touching them, pushing. She could hear his voice complaining wordlessly.

'I'm warning you . . .' began Java, now out of Alice's field of vision. There was a scuffle, as of someone pushing someone else. A scrape of feet on the flagstones. Then she heard a shot. Someone screamed, the woman, guessed Alice. Then Turner fired again. More sounds, shuffling, running feet, two more shots in rapid succession. Cries. A crashing sound, a breaking of glass. In a couple of seconds, without stopping to think about the danger, she was on her feet, out of the alley and in the street, the knife ready. In the dim orange light she could not see very far, but retained the impression of Turner falling beside the parked car, almost in slow-motion, the pistol skidding out of his hands. Against the side of the car, Rafe was trying to stop himself from falling, his bloody hands printing smeary pentagrams on the glass. A sound at her left and Alice slashed out almost blindly with a wild cry of panic and felt the blade snag cloth. She leaped forwards at the figure she had touched, and at the edge of the light she glimpsed Anton and Zach, crouching back into the shadows, and she felt a brief, almost unbearable exhilaration (stitch that you bastards). Their eyes mirrored, like cats'; Anton hissed, showing his teeth. Then they were gone. A clink of metal from her right, across the road; (oh shit elaine and java wait a . . .) Java was almost invisible against the night, but she felt his eyes, saw a gleam of buckles and chains as he fled, heard his whisper like a psychic echo of her own thoughts (you wait bitch just you w . . .).

Footsteps disappearing into the distance.

Silence.

Alice endured the silence for a minute or so before she dared even think of relaxing. There was no sound; the street was derelict, and there was no one to come and investigate. Dizzy and drained with the surge of adrenalin, she forced herself to think, to assess and to gather the fragments of what had happened. For a moment, the world spun incomprehensibly, like a magic-lantern show.

Suddenly, a stray thought, on the heels of a spray of stars. (turner?)

'Turner!'

No reply.

'Turner!'

'Here.' The whisper was almost inaudible, coming from a patch of shadow beside the car. Alice sprinted towards him.

'Turner?' For a moment his face was a pale, unfocused blur in the sharp light of the street lamp, then she noticed the blood on his scarf, the side of his face. His hands went up to her face, twisted and crippled as old vines.

'Got two of the bastards,' he breathed. 'That woman. The blond kid. Think I hit the tall bastard. The other bastards got away.' His breath was a terrible croaking sound in his throat, where the blood bubbled out of the cut flesh as he spoke with a tiny dribbling sound.

'Don't worry,' she said hurriedly, 'I'll call the police. We'll get you to a hospital. Hang on. Here, let me put this scarf—'

He interrupted her with a gesture.

'No time.' He reached for the gun, which had been lost as he fell and was lying beside him on the road. 'Here. Take it before the others come back. Go on.'

Alice looked around; despite everything, the feeling of victory remained, a sick, uncontrolled exhilaration.

'I don't think they'll come back just yet. I—'

'Go on!' he insisted.

But Alice had already grabbed him under his arms, and was pulling him into the alley.

'Where you go, I go,' she muttered. 'Here. You'll be all right. Just hang on.'

In the semi-darkness of the house, Alice managed to light a candle, taken from the upstairs flat, and in its glow she inspected the damage. Turner was still conscious, but had lost blood; his frail old-man's body was shaking with cold and his eyes were bloodshot. The cut was not as deep as it had first seemed, and the knife (if it had been a knife) had missed the windpipe and the main artery.

Alice, whose knowledge of first-aid was rudimentary, could only try to staunch the flow of blood and pile blankets on the old man to try and keep him from the cold. The kitchen seemed like the warmest place on the bottom floor; there was an old mattress on which Turner could lie, wrapped up in blankets, and the windows were boarded up, so it wouldn't be too cold. She helped him to walk into the little room and settled him in. When she had done that, she went back into the street and picked up his gun, then, cautiously, she brought the bodies into the alley out of sight.

Elaine, with a bullet through the head, pale and almost beautiful; Rafe with three or four bullets in his chest, his thin arms spread, a splash of blood across his angelic child's face. They must have been killed almost instantly.

Back in the house, with their blood splashed on her arms and face, she began to review the situation. So far, Alice thought, things weren't looking good. The death of Elaine and Rafe still left her to deal with Java, Zach, Anton, and, of course, Rosemary. They would be forewarned, dangerous and hungry for revenge. Turner was still bleeding, for all she knew bleeding to death, and with no possibility of calling for help, and she had lost her element of surprise.

Alice did what she could; she brought the rest of the flask of tea, and some chocolate from Turner's hideout in the attic, took the gun from his shaking hand, and went into the wrecked lobby of the house to wait. If it was any comfort, she thought bleakly, she was certain they wouldn't be long.

Two

Cambridge, *April 1990*

Ginny seemed half asleep, her head tucked into the crook of his arm as he rocked her. The lamplight flickered onto her face and lit her hair like fireworks. The curve of her jaw was white, flawless, the baby hair at the back of her neck giving her pallor a golden bloom, like that of a fruit or a flower. She was wearing one of Joe's pullovers, a dark maroon, and the over-rich colour should not have suited her, but somehow it did, emphasizing her air of frailty, the clarity of her child's complexion. He shifted, carefully, not wanting to disturb her, but she opened her eyes and smiled up at him, stretching.

'Is it nearly time?' she asked, sitting up.

Joe shook his head. 'Nearly time. Do you want something to drink? Some chocolate? Something to eat?'

'I'm not hungry,' she said.

'Do you want to listen to the radio? I feel like some . . . rhythm.' His hands were nervous, moving to a quick complicated beat of their own against the arm of the chair. Ginny nodded and Joe flipped the switch to FM.

'I like this song,' said Ginny, and began to sing softly along to it in a clear child's voice;

'. . . Na na na.. Love Street, da-da-da-da Love Street . . .' Her eyes were closed and she was bobbing her

387

head to and fro to the rhythm, completely absorbed.

Joe smiled.

'I'm surprised you know it,' he said lightly. 'Don't suppose you were even born when this song came out. It takes an old fart like me to remember that far back.'

'I'm not that young.' Her tone was defiant. Joe tried to smile, but felt his headache intensify momentarily, a little point of light between his eyes. 'What's wrong, Joe?'

'Headache. Don't worry, it'll go away soon. I've taken some aspirin.' He glanced at his watch. 'Time for the snack, anyway.' From his pocket he brought out a packet of shortbread and opened the polythene package. 'I have to do this or I turn into a frog at midnight,' he said between mouthfuls of biscuit, but the joke was tired, weak as the rest of him. For a moment he thought he remembered something . . . something about Alice. Had he blown his top again? Had she . . .? He shook his head irritably. He couldn't remember. Suddenly the headache doubled, trebled. He felt ill, dizzy, his vision blanking over like a faulty TV screen, reception jumbled to a thousand points of light, jiving and spinning mercilessly before his eyes.

'Joe? Are you okay?' Ginny's voice sounded as if it had been put through a flanger, all distorted syllables, twists of sound in blackness. His own voice, endlessly remote, on a wind of white noise.

'Gin. . . go . . . fridge. Get the insulin . . . the needles . . .'

'Joe?' A thin edge of panic in her voice.

'Get it, quick . . .' He tried to keep the darkness from slipping over him as he listened to the sounds she was making, monstrously distorted, bubble-like in the veiled darkness; clinking of bottles in the fridge, patter of bare feet on the floor. An odd, dislocated feeling (shit this never happened before) as she put the ampoule and the syringe in his hand. Clumsily fitting them (thank god for practice), his hands working

388

almost automatically. The veil fell from his eyes; he pinched the fold of flesh just above his ribs and jabbed the needle in. The world began to come slowly back together (don't worry joey), the sickness to recede (what was that who was that?).

(just me joey remember me?) Joe took a deep breath and removed the drained syringe.

'Are you all right?' Ginny's face swam for a moment, then moved into focus, like something seen through glass. Joe nodded.

'. . . Must have missed this morning . . . maybe it was that couple of drinks I . . . yes. I'm OK.' He took another deep breath, and suddenly he *was* all right, with an abrupt surge of well-being and confidence. Energy exploded through him, and he stood up and picked Ginny right up from the floor and hugged her.

'Hey, that was pretty quick work, Doc. Good thing you were here.' He grinned again. 'This ought to happen more often; I feel great!' Then his face dropped, became older somehow, his eyes narrower. 'It must have been that bloody scene with Alice that set me off,' he decided. 'I was all right till that happened. She . . .' He broke off, his fingers beginning to tap the arm of the chair again.

(she really made a fool out of you this time joey)

'She got me so pissed off, saying all that stuff about you that I . . .' (right, and what did i do ginny what did i do) '. . . lost my rag completely. I should have . . .' (finished her off smashed her face in with the paperweight) '. . . tried to reason with her but by the time I realized that she'd already made a run for it.' He blinked and rubbed his eyes, thinking for a moment that maybe he didn't feel quite so good after all. 'She needs help, Gin,' he went on, 'because from what she said to me, your ex-friends have got a hold on her already. She's swallowed their story, hook, line and sinker. God knows what else they've told her.'

Ginny nodded.

'I know,' she said. 'There's no saying what hold they've got on her if she's at that house; you must get her out, by force if you have to, reason with her later, when she's out of there. Get her out of there, the sooner the better.'

Joe frowned, a memory chasing its tail in his mind, just out of reach of conscious recall.

(did i try i don't remember did i want to hurt you alice?)

(shh don't worry)

(but was i did i?)

'I don't want to do anything to hurt Alice,' he said pensively. 'Perhaps we should just call the police, after all. She—'

'She'll thank you for getting her involved in that, will she?' said Ginny sharply. 'I told you before, those people are selling drugs, they're making money from all kinds of petty crime. Do you think that the police will believe that Alice isn't involved? You have to get her away first, or you might as well report her for trafficking yourself.'

Joe sighed. 'I suppose you're right, Gin,' he said wearily. 'By now they'll be asleep, and it might be easier to take her unawares; but what if she won't come? I can't just . . .' his voice trailed off uncertainly and he looked at Ginny for reassurance. For a moment her image swam before his eyes like a magic-lantern show, her bright hair a spray of sparks. His vision blurred, the after-image of her hair printed on his retinas like neon. He shook his head to clear it, hearing his voice from a distance, muted, toneless.

'I really don't feel too clever, Gin,' he said. 'Maybe I should see a doctor. I don't think I'm in good enough shape to . . .'

'Trust me.'

She smiled up at Joe, like a happy child. 'We have to find Alice, remember? And it will be easy, I promise.' From her shoulder-bag she pulled out a little pouch, unzipped it and showed what was inside to Joe. A syringe, and four little ampoules of something straw-coloured.

Ginny saw Joe's expression and squeezed his hand reassuringly.

'It's all right,' she said. 'The hospital gave them to me when I got out. They're tranquillizers, that's all. Not big doses, either. One should make her sleepy and suggestible. If she's really aggressive, two should knock her out completely.'

'I don't think—' began Joe, but she interrupted him again.

'I'm just thinking about a last resort, Joe,' she said, pleadingly. 'They won't hurt her, I promise you that. Otherwise, you might find that she's hostile and she won't come with you. All she has to do is to yell once and all the rest of the crowd will come running. Unless you want to face them all . . .' her voice trailed off. She hesitated. 'If she's in that awful house, you have to get her out as soon as you can,' she added. 'You have no idea what it's like in there.' Joe frowned for a minute or so, then he relaxed and smiled.

('sright joey just lie back and)

'All right,' he said. 'OK. Just as a last resort, though. If nothing else works.'

Ginny smiled up at him. Her eyes were clear and innocent. She handed him the little pouch, carefully zipping it shut again.

'Here, Joe,' she told him. 'You take these.'

One

Grantchester

They were all there, in the flat; Rafe, Java, Anton, Zach, Elaine, all except Rosemary. I had told the others I wanted to hunt on my own, that they should not wait for me. They did not question my decision; they were used to my solitary habits by now, and Elaine, the only person who might have shown interest or suspicion, had ceased to talk since Rosemary had recalled her, and would only sit, speechless and dry-eyed in her corner, rocking herself like a frightened child. It was just after midnight. Since ten Turner and I had been hiding in the alley by the dustbins, watching, making certain that everything was going according to plan. At eleven Rosemary had come, and had gone again, passing so close to me that I caught a breath of her scent in the still air, imagined her heat beneath the black raincoat she was wearing. I almost reeled with the closeness of her, felt myself near to swooning, like a novice nun faced with the glory of the Host. She could twist perceptions, my Blessed Damozel, engender visions, awaken desires and appetites beyond imagining. But I held fast, Turner's arm trembling beneath my touch as he saw her, and I know he felt something too.

He was eager that night, brittle and fey with an excitement I knew was born not only of the wine we had both drunk to give us courage. For the first and last time, the monsters were not alone; instead, we revelled in our alienation, planned the unspeakable with winks and whispers, like schoolboys. I, who had never had a real childhood, experienced it all that night, the hysteria, the gleeful terror, the companionship, the dread and the unstoppable laughter which so few of us every really experience after the age of twelve. That night, I was happy.

At midnight, we crept up the stairs to the flat. I was calmer, Turner was twitching with anticipation and horror. I went to the door, opened it with my key and went in. I found them, as I had thought, in the bedroom, drinking wine. They had hunted, and they were drowsy, glutted and unsuspecting. Elaine was lying on the bed, her hair spread out onto the pillow like a mermaid's.

Tick . . . tick . . . tick . . .

I forced myself to sound normal, though my mouth was dry as salt, and my nerves like wires.

'Sorry I was so long,' I said, casually. 'Is there any of that wine left for me?'

Zach held out the bottle by the neck, grinning sleepily. He looked very young to me then, very alien. His beauty was almost more than I could bear, sublimated too by the fact that I knew I was going to kill him.

'I'll get a glass,' I said then, and went into the kitchen.

In the kitchen, I found the glass, and put it by the side of the sink. Then I disconnected the gas stove from the pipe in the wall and turned the mains on full, jamming the gas-tap on. From my pocket I took a little wrench and removed the tap, so that it could not be turned off again. Then, I left the tap in the sink on full so that it would sound as if there were still someone in the kitchen. I can't even say it was very hard to carry out; we had rehearsed it all every day that week. There was a jangling coldness in my mind as I forced myself to check that the window was shut. Very quietly, I left the flat, and with my key I locked it from the outside, plugging the keyhole with putty so that the door could not be opened. With bated breath we listened at the door, but heard only the muted sound of voices from the bedroom, where I knew the others were waiting, drinking wine and wondering vaguely why I did not come. Then, I took from my pocket a large roll of masking tape, of the kind you use for lagging pipes, and I taped all round the door. I cut the lengths of tape carefully, with a craft knife, trimming it neatly at the edges. I went round the door-frame twice, making sure no air could get in. Then we waited.

This was the critical point; the five minutes or so before the gas began to permeate every part of the flat. If someone had followed me into the kitchen and heard the gas hissing . . . We listened, Turner shaking silently, his eyes round as an owl's. No one came. The voices in the background sounded lethargic, casual; a meeting of nineteenth-century British poets discussing art.

I waited in the cold entropic spiral of my thoughts and my fear, suspended, like a fly in amber.

I could hear the ticking of my watch in my pocket, amplified as if under water, every second a step nearer to my salvation.

Tick . . . tick . . . tick . . .

Seconds

    are

      so

        huge.

One/Two

Grantchester

Alice stirred gently, then opened her eyes as the torchlight touched her face. Instinctively, she flinched, reached for her glasses. Cold and the cramped posture in which she had eventually dropped off to sleep had almost paralysed her, and she twisted round, trying to shake the cold from her limbs.

Joe caught himself thinking, irrelevantly, cloudily (cat's eyes you've got cat's eyes) of the fairground, of walking hand-in-hand with a younger Alice, neon stars in her eyes.

She stiffened as she saw Joe, sitting up abruptly, gracelessly, (oh god i went to sleep didn't i oh) drawing away from the light which blinded her.

'What're you doing here?' Her voice, still blurred by sleep, was wary, shrill with undisclosed hysteria; Joe thought he knew why. His gaze travelled to the corners of the room, taking in the bloodstained blankets, the filth, the silver paper and used syringes on the mouldy floorboards. Yes, he thought he understood.

'Don't worry,' he said over a wave of sudden nausea, forcing his voice to retain its gentleness.

Alice have a sharp, dry bark of laughter. Her own quick glance around the room had taken in the silhouette of Ginny, standing still and passive at the door; she spoke to Joe, but without taking her eyes off the girl.

'It's happened before, Joe,' she told him. 'The hard-luck stories, the little girl lost. She uses it as a cover, so that even if she's found out, some other poor sap will pay in her place. She's been doing it just about for ever. Feeding on people, taking their love and their life, making victims of some, monsters of the rest. Can't you see, Joe? Just look at her. It's in her face. There's destruction in her face. If you don't believe me, there are two dead bodies in the alley out there, and an old man next door who might be dead. I don't know.' Cautiously she was beginning to shift her weight onto her feet, ready to spring. Her hand was barely trembling on the butt of the pistol.

There was a silence, cold and blank as outer space.

Then Joe took a step forwards.

'Alice.' His face was unreadable, his hands, somehow threateningly, in his pockets. 'You're ill. I don't know what bullshit these people have been giving you, or what you've been taking, but you're ill and it shows. I want you to come back home with me today. I want you to see a doctor. Get some therapy.'

He took another step, and suddenly he was holding something in his hand (oh shit a needle isn't it?), something bright and dangerous. Alice must have seen something in Ginny's eyes which warned her, some subtle flash of triumph, or maybe the empathy between them was greater than she had previously imagined, because as Joe leaped at her, she stumbled backwards over the pile of blankets. Joe slipped, almost comically, on the greasy floorboards, and went down hard against the side of the wall, flailing at the air with the needle inches from Alice's face.

'What's in there?' demanded Alice sharply. 'Who gave you that?'

'It's just something to make you feel better,' he countered, swallowing his anger. 'A tranquillizer.

Look, I'm your friend, I'm Joe, remember? I wouldn't hurt you, would I?'

His voice was infuriatingly calm, silky, like someone talking to a wild animal.

Alice kept her eye on him. She jerked her chin towards Ginny.

'Did she give you that?'

Joe bristled. 'I'm not having you accuse her—'

'*Did* she?'

Joe nodded.

'And you never thought to disbelieve her,' spat Alice contemptuously. 'How could she lie?' She was backing now towards the door, her hunted gaze flicking from Ginny to Joe, and back again.

'Stay back!' she snapped at him. 'And as for you,' she told Ginny in a dangerous voice, 'you raise a finger and I'll blow you to hell.' Her hand went to her own pocket, gently lifting out the old service-pistol. 'Yes, it's loaded,' she said, and stifled a ridiculous urge to laugh. Wordlessly, Ginny moved aside, and Alice, still not taking her eyes from Joe and the girl, began to turn the door-handle. She was exultant now, the laughter barely restrained, shaking her at the seams. It was so comic, Alice with her antique gun, and Joe with that expression on his face, staring . . . despite herself, she grinned, half hysterically, but even the hysteria felt good.

Suddenly she froze, her ears pricking up. The laughter died and turned sour in her mouth. There were footsteps in the alley.

Wildly, she backed away from the door, fumbling now with the pistol, trying to work out how to fire it. Surely, there must be a safety-catch somewhere . . . hell, she didn't even know if there were any bullets left in it.

She was still fumbling when the door swung open, and the nightwalkers came in.

Even then, Alice was able to look at them coldly, and

was conscious of a savage glee as she remembered why Rafe and Elaine were missing.

'Joe,' she said tersely. 'Be careful.'

Java gave her a single glance of contempt and turned to Ginny. 'The other two are dead,' he told her. 'Shot by the old man.' He paused, hazarded another glance at Alice. 'I slit the old fool's throat,' he said venomously. 'He won't bother us again.'

Alice felt rather than saw Joe flinch by her side in the darkness as she backed away. She was aware of the three figures blocking her exit, and the slight form of Ginny standing at the door behind her; dammit, she should be able to cope with Ginny if it came to that. She moved towards the inner door, easing her steps over the broken glass, cans and rubbish which were scattered unevenly everywhere. To get to the back of the room Alice had to pass Joe, so close that she almost touched him, and remembering his attack on her in the house, and the fact that he still had a syringe which certainly didn't contain Lucozade, she edged past him with wary caution, her nerves razors skating on ice. But Joe was uncertain; she could feel his confusion as she brushed by him in the semi-darkness. He had dropped the torch, which now shone in a narrow arc against the doorway, lighting Java's boots and making giant shadowplay of the nightwalkers on the ceiling.

'Alice?' His voice rose waveringly, painfully adolescent. 'What old man? Alice! Where are you?' For an instant he reverted to the old Joe as he took a step forwards and half fell on some slippery debris. 'Shit! What the hell is all this?'

But no one was paying any attention to him. As he spoke, Alice made a dash for the inner door, pushing past Ginny to disappear into the dark passage. Java and Zach followed her, but not too quickly, their boots crunching the debris underfoot.

'She won't get very far,' said Java. 'Anton, watch the door. Zach, with me.'

400

Joe's voice, faint and thin, like that of a sick crone;
'Alice?'

A tunnel of blackness, a fathom deep, as Alice crashed her way through darkness to the stairs, the voices meaningless whistling on a black wind. Panic surged through her, spear-pointed, almost orgasmic in its intensity as she fled up the stairs. For a moment she could almost have believed herself to be flying against that wind, a wild witch with her hair in her eyes and a magic at her trembling fingertips which could at one gesture harness the wind to blow open all the secret dreadful doors of the world and launch her into a lightless slipstream of beyond-world, beyond-time.

(dammit what the hell was that?)

Alice slipped back into the jerky motion of panic with a conscious jolt. What had she been thinking? She seemed to remember, with an elusive visionary quality, a sensation of . . .

(destiny)

(rapture)

space, of speed, a feeling of being so much more than Alice that for an instant she had been beyond fear, had revelled in the death which pursued her, had almost welcomed it. She turned a corner of staircase, the palms of her hands slick around the butt of the pistol, pushed open a door at her back and stepped backwards into the dark, fighting the returned sensation with an almost physical effort. She had no power; all she had was her intelligence and the gun. The (rapture?) feelings were just illusions to confuse her. Suddenly the room seemed much bigger than she had expected; in the gloom Alice found that she could make out an unbroken window, the curtains drawn back to reveal a lighted square of window, moonlight reflections on a table, a candlestick, a pack of cards spilled across a patch of light as she pulled the door closed behind her. There were footsteps on the stairs by now; she could hear the sound of boots on the hollow wood, of voices remote, tinny, like the soundtrack of an old film. A snatch of music, half imagined on the rushing of the black wind, the wild jangle of a merry-go-round. A wheel turns against the sky; a wheel turns the sky under the façade of blue.

Footsteps on the landing; Alice levels the pistol. A slash of light underneath the door, bisected by the shadows of someone's feet.

Tick . . .

    tick . . .

        t . . .

        'Gas leak! Gas leak!'

Turner's voice had sufficient authority, even after what had happened, to rouse the few other residents from their beds; the smell of gas was enough to do the rest, and in a few minutes we had cleared the building, Turner making certain that no would-be heroes joined us in the deserted house as I took the petrol-can and sprayed the third floor liberally with its contents. I was taking no risks; there would be no recalling those charred bodies. No sound from the room, only a rushing emptiness, like a black wind, from behind the door, like the sea heard through a seashell. I mopped my handkerchief in the petrol, took out my lighter and turned to go down the stairs, my heart ticking away the strange momentum of my frozen thoughts like razor against stone. Sudden intensity of the black wind; a whisper, ice-cold music in a deserted gallery, long-dead minstrel with a lute of hair and bone sings songs of hate under a black moon. I knew she was there before I even saw her, my love, my lady, felt her wild breath in my ears as I spun to her measure and saw her face.

God, her face!

Her beauty damns me, her hungry, passionate, blessed beauty. For her I am crucified, my blood in the cup in her hand, my sweet white flesh consecrated by the touch of her lips. She has no defences but this rapture, my Beggar Maid, and through my twisted perceptions she shone like the sun, planets spinning their spirals around her.

Rapture.

> *Tick . . .*
>
> > *tick . . .*
> >
> > > *t . . .*

Joe staggers and puts his hand to the wall to steady himself, his night-vision slowly re-asserting itself above the lurid retinal glimmering of his mind's eye. For a moment he is still, allowing the world to stabilize, trying to think rationally. But thought is a sad outcast, himself a wailing infant on the fringes of a black desert, his voice a thin protest on the wind, his memories strangers.

(i cut the old fool's throat)

The silhouette of a beggar-child against the door, like a thin goblin sentinel, pale refracted light shining on his white face. Ginny, her hair freakishly incandescent in the dimness, staring into the dark with eyes like tunnels. To Joe she seems without substance, a statue of glass and smoke, pale and cold. He brushes her hand in the dark, but she does not respond. He understands dimly that wherever she is, she is not there. He feels cold, here at the end of all momentum, the energizing rhythm now stilled in his veins. For a cowardly moment all he wants to do is to lie down and sleep.

(i cut the old. . .)

He snaps the memory off as neatly as breaking a twig (no no no) but it returns, slicing the dark like a pendulum.

(. . . old fool's throat i cut the . . .)

'Ginny?' His cry is hoarse, almost inaudible. Ginny remains motionless, intent. With a terrible effort he forces his frozen body into motion again, the dark pressing on him like stone, his thoughts formless beckonings, terrifying. The child in him cries, cowering (it's dark don't want to go in there don't want to see the old man) but he moves nevertheless. A spike of panic drives through the soles of his feet as he passes the threshold and feels the cold breath of the beggar-child on his neck; but it has been left to guard the door, and though its hunger grins and gibbers at him it stays, obedient. The kitchen is cauldron-black, and he strains his eyes against the spangled dark as he feels his way between obstacles towards the huddle of blankets underneath the window. There is a fetid smell of old dust and mould and sickness, horrible sickness, sickness like the smell of the hospital where his grandpa died, like the smell of the old balloon-lady at the fair. An old terror, half-buried from childhood, takes him by the throat; he physically gags with the fear of it, begins to feel his throat tighten asthmatically. A dream, (no grandpa don't please) or the memory of a dream, comes back to him so clearly that for a moment he forgets who he is and where he is.

Tick . . .

tick . . .

t . . .

The door opens and Alice lifts the pistol, pausing only because she thinks it might be Joe. Light floods the room, a carnival light in a dozen bright acidic colours, pink, blue, yellow, green. A sharp hot scent in the air (and why had she thought it was cold? It's hot, hot), like peanuts and roasting apples and the slick sugary scent of candy-floss. For a second she forgets where she is, almost who she is; looks down at herself and sees (dirty jeans torn at the knees, blood in the creases in her palms, sweat-shirt grimed with soot, the gun held uneasily in a shaking hand) her clean Indian skirt, the ends of her flowing dark hair brushing her shoulders. The disorientation intensifies for a moment; Alice frowns, trying to remember . . . a hand falls on her shoulder, a kindly voice speaks.

(come on now alice it's all right you just freaked out for a minute)

(joe?)

He grins, pushing long hair out of his eyes.

'Who d'you think it is? Are you okay now? You were having your fortune told, and you must have passed out, or something. It must be the heat. Come on out here and I'll buy you an ice-cream.'

Alice frowns.

'Fortune?'

'Yes, don't you remember?'

She shakes her head. 'I . . .'

'You'll be all right in a moment or two,' the gipsy woman smiles, oddly young-looking in the bright light, the neon flickering metallic colours onto her red hair. Odd, that she should have red hair, thinks Alice vaguely; she thought that all gipsies were dark. A bird tattoo is etched starkly onto her left cheekbone, eerily lifelike.

'OK?' Joe's voice is concerned. 'Do you want to go home now?'

Alice shakes her head, forcing her eyes back into focus, manages a smile.

'No, it's all right,' she says, but even as she speaks she looks at Joe and wonders how, in the damp and muggy heat of this hot summer night, he can still be wearing that greatcoat.

Tick . . .

    tick . . .

        t . . .

Turner shifts uneasily under the filthy blanket, tasting the tinniness and slickness of his blood in his throat. His dreams fall away from him like thin snakeskins, bright tissue-like things with faery wings and sharp teeth.

In his dreams he has heard the nightwalkers come and go, shadowwalkers on the brink of sensation; for a moment he has almost touched Joe's hands as he reached out to him, but Joe is snatched away again into bright ether, and Turner smiles thinly through blood-crusted lips and drifts back (back go back if there's as much as a spark the whole place might go up in) . . . in (it's all right i'm a police officer everything's under control)

(back back).

Tick . . .

    tick . . .

        t . . .

She makes children of us all, I told you, children in the face of her, the glory of her. She revels in our fears, the scent of our childish terrors, and she feeds on them, on us – for what child does not fear being eaten? She is the witch in the gingerbread house, the ogress, the wicked queen, the ravening wolf, the monster in the cellar, the monster in the heart. This is her defence, this one rapture, shrinking us into children, wracked by children's fears, children's certainties. In the face of her deadly rapture I am not Daniel; I am you, I am me, I am the prince and princess, the wizard and the butterfly. I am the child in the cellar, afraid of the dark, and I am the man in the child, the woman in the man. I am the girl in the fairground, long hair flying across her face as she turns and sees her lover turn into a wolf and she runs, runs across the night sky starry with wheels and neon. I am the musician lost in the dark, following the bright notes of his playing into the night like fireflies. As I face her, the Blessed Damozel, essence of every dream and fairy-story and legend and fear I am filled with a rapture I cannot analyse; I am diminished and at the same time immeasurably increased. She laughs as she turns the wheel of the spinning-top but at last I know that I am ready for her. I run across the painted skyline, a perfect circle, spinning and sparkling for me alone. All around me rise the painted trees, the houses with windows painted on their bland red façades, the painted railway track humming as I hear the sound of the train, that hungry dragon from under the painted earth. I hear it, its voice like the apotheosis of all monsters, Rosemary at the wheel like a murderous out-of-control St Catherine grinning and beckoning and bearing down on me with its dragon's breath burning the world into ribbons. I, Rosemary's child, your child, your mother's child, screaming and laughing on a battlefield of paint and clockwork, suddenly realize that behind the terror and the nightmare we have *power*, a power great enough to break Rosemary's rapture. We are children; we wield the power of children, of magic, of vision. We believe. And with belief, with faith, if you like, we can destroy her. Children have the only true faith, not the stumbling faith of religions, those dim adult fairy-tales, but faith in magic, belief in rapture. Join hands with me and chant the rapture;

> *Tick . . .*
>
> *tick . . .*
>
> *t . . .*

Alice starts; for a moment she thought she was somewhere else, feels the hot breath of the night on her cheek. She looks at Joe as he grins, wolflike, (what big eyes you've got joe) she thinks, and draws a long black knife from the pocket of his greatcoat. Somewhere in the background, a merry-go-round the size of a spinning-top is playing; as she watches, the bird on the gipsy's face stirs and flies away.

> *Tick . . .*
>
> *tick . .*

For a moment she is taken off-balance and he strikes, the knife reaching her at a clumsy angle, slicing through the palm of her hand. She screams with rage and pain, the sound a clear bright lance in the rapturous air. The fairground dances around her like a carousel ride, scents assail her nostrils; blood and peanuts and the rank stink of animals. Zach claws at her, one earring swinging hypnotically; she feels his fingers jab agonizingly into the side of her neck, almost paralysing her. She kicks out at him sideways, taking him off-balance, her mind a cold rushing emptiness of (rapture?) silence. Her hands are almost someone else's hands as she finally lifts the pistol and fires.

For a moment time is suspended.

The shot surprises her even more than it does Zach.

It seems as if the gun has gone off entirely on its own, the sound a shower of multicoloured sparks, wrenching her shoulder badly as it does, leaping in her grasp like an angry cat. A second before the shock even registers, Alice sees the hole appear in Zach's chest, sees him stagger and fall back, sees him jerk again in mid-fall, and then the world is nothing but sound, sound and blackness, and Zach on the floor, reddish clouds before her eyes, and in slow motion and silently Java, his eyes narrowed slits of shadow, the black knife a slice of shadow in his hand, leaps towards her . . .

(rapture) The word is alien, like someone else's thought beamed by accident into Joe's mind. For a second he isn't even certain what it means, but as he hears its psychic echo the world snaps back into place with a sound like a breaking bone. The figure in front of him is vague, nebulous, giant one moment and small the next, dancing flamelike, shadowlike before him to some murderous choreography, the knife a blade of shadow slicing the air before him. His eyes drop to the needle in his hand; he has kept it all this time without even knowing that he had it, and a sudden (rapture) certainty invades him, a glorious self-knowledge, a rapturous rhythm like a bright wave to ride forever. For a startling moment he is Joey again, flying, riding the storm on a wave of impossible chords, pale air rippling magically before him; a sorcerer's apprentice conducting an orchestra of howling, screaming fantasies on the edge of a frozen dream. He leaps forwards into the wave with the syringe held high above his head.

The world comes back into sharp focus, but too late; Java is on her, crushing her windpipe. She swings her fist at him, still weighted with the pistol it strikes him on the side of the head, a messy blow which nevertheless loosens his grasp from her throat. The knife has fallen to the floor in the general mêlée, and Alice is almost sure she can feel the hilt of it under her ribs, digging into her back, but she cannot reach it. She feels Java's hand come back to her throat and twists to bite him, feeling her teeth against the cold flesh of his wrist. Almost gagging, she struggles to raise the pistol, but her hand is numb, trembling from loss of blood, her arm gloved in blood to the elbow; slick with blood and sweat, the pistol slides from her hand and falls by her side where she cannot reach it. She guesses Java's grin as he closes both hands around her throat and begins to tighten his grip.

(rapture)

With a cry of (rapture) savage elation I (he) fall upon her, fragments of her illusory glamour showering me (him) like glass. I (we) have broken out of the spinning-top at last, like a dragon eating himself up tail first. She can have no more power over me (us), I tell myself; I am free. We are free. I reach out to them over the years, to you, to him, to my figure reflected back over time like faces in a hall of mirrors. We are Daniel, you are Daniel, Daniel young and old, legions marching across the years for ever, grim joyful legions marching across the painted blue sky against the train, against the fevered call of the nightwalker. In this moment I can see you, clearly as in a camera obscura, I know you, know your face, your weaknesses and your passion, sense the flickering of your flame against hers. I know you and reach for your hand, here where all possibilities are true; I take your hand and give you (rapture) the power I know we have, the power of the circle of light, the feeble light, shining brief between two darknesses, the light of all things which die and suffer, all things which love and yearn for the unattainable. God help me, in this endless, sacred moment I feel redeemed, I feel *blessed* with all the brave

410

certainty for which I will grieve in vain in later, darker years. Maybe it is the gas, the hunger, shock, or maybe, as I choose to believe, the divine re-asserting itself in the striving of my tortured soul, but for a brief longed-for instant, I feel that despite Rosemary I have at last glimpsed God. As I struggle with the nightwalker, feeling her cool flesh beneath my fever, my glasses fall to the floor, my heel grinds the glass to dust. I feel (the needle in my hand) her bones beneath my hands, the hollow of her throat give way under the pressure (the syringe empties i can feel its response to flesh, to muscles). Her sweet flesh yields reluctantly; for a moment all illusions are stripped away, and we see her face as it really is, the childish features cut away to reveal the demon, the rage and the glory and the everlasting boundless hatred of the nightwalker unmasked. In that instant she speaks to me without words, promises worlds and lifetimes, but she is weakened, ebbing like a bloodtide, waning, shrinking. The face of the demon becomes a burning rose . . . the cup passes over.

Alice's face is nothing but a bubble of blood, the pressure agonizing, unbearable, a single degree of pressure away from death. Both her eyes have blacked with the pressure, and her nose is bleeding thickly. Her right arm is almost completely paralysed now, and both she and Java are struggling in a growing puddle of sludge made of blood and dust. Her thoughts are terrifying, simple patterns, (oh shit oh shit oh shit) unaware even that they are thoughts. Suddenly she feels him flinch, his thoughts assailing her with a blast of unexplained panic, his hands going from her throat. For a second she fears that she will not be able to move, but she finds that she can, a powerful jerk of the hips sending him forwards, out of control onto his knees over her head. At the same time she grabs his knife, falling towards him with one fluid movement,

411

her mind a triumphant anthem of rapture. His thoughts are clear to her as she hits him cleanly for once, just below the ribs . . .

(god ginny it's ginny it's ginny it's . . .) Joe's mind circles in a broken loop of thought as he stares in shock at the red-haired girl. In the faint glow from the broken window she is a jumble of light and shade, hair the faintest nimbus of rose in a stark and violent monochrome. The syringe is planted in her neck, just below the jugular, and as he reaches to draw it out, the girl twists round to bite him, hissing, her eyes rabid crescents of white, her teeth brushing his wrist. She thrashes, snakelike, flamelike, a burning rose; as he reaches to take her in his arms she rakes his face with her fingernails, hissing in a deep, choked voice just beyond the audible register; but the psychic echoes of her rage are enough to half stun him, sending him to his knees with his hands shielding his face as she burns.

(god the light!!)

Something terrible is happening to Ginny; her face twists and shifts, her image splitting apart into fragments of spectrum like breaking crystal in the sunlight. For a moment she is infinite, a zillion shiftings from ultra-violet to infra-red, every one unique, unforgettable; she is a child gathering flowers, a half-grown teenage girl running through a moonlit field, a red-haired sculptress caressing dream lovers into spectral life, a drowned virgin, a shameless whore.

Joe reels before the force of the visions, cringing back against the wall as they spin around him like souls of the damned. Half obscured by the shiftings of the light against his retinas he is still aware of the figure of Ginny kneeling on the floor, hissing and raking at the air with her fingernails, and though he can hardly see her real body, he seems to see behind the veils of rapturous flesh a formless thing, tearing at

412

its own face, at the rags of its red hair to reveal something black, lightless and pitiless, something which echoes already in his own wailing child's soul, reaching out its long cold fingers towards him to touch despair into his heart. She screams in rage and hatred as she strips the flesh from her bones, Joe's own cry lost in the black throat of the nightwalker. The illusions stripping away from Ginny's body circle him as he retreats to a foetal position, his eyes closed like the door to his mind. Black flowers bloom behind his eyelids, black flowers, brown flowers, red flowers. For a moment he is mesmerized, all sensation receding mercifully at the end of a tunnel of light. Going back to a soundless world, world beyond memory.

(bye bye)

(wait)

(no no no)

(i said wait)

The voice has authority, and automatically he obeys, turning in confusion as the accents coalesce into a figure, a face he does not recognize; a young man about his age with thin, academic features and old-fashioned half-moon glasses.

(who are you?)

(don't worry about that you've got to listen to me i haven't very much time)

(what do you want?)

(you have to set fire to the house make sure it's completely destroyed then you have to burn the bodies)

(ginny oh gin)

(don't say her name don't mention her you have to forget her no grave no funeral nothing do you understand?)

(i. . .)

(it's terribly important you have to forget her if you don't do as i say you'll call her back)

(. . .i)

'Daniel?'

Alice stumbled and almost fell at the foot of the steps, and in the strange flickering light she thought she saw a figure standing in the room, a young man in an old overcoat, grey eyes obscured by thick glasses, thinning hair hidden by a brown felt hat, but when she regained her balance he had gone, and her consciousness was flickering before her eyes like an old black-and-white film, the light a million motes in the night's eye.

Joe was lying on the floor beside Ginny, and Alice was still alert enough to know a stab of panic at the sight of the girl, circling the body carefully before she realized that Ginny was dead. The syringe lay beside her body, crushed to powder and wire, but she could see the mark it had made, the bruise and the single drop of blood on the white throat. For a sudden, absurd moment, she was reminded of the Sleeping Beauty. She took Ginny's wrist in trembling fingers, searched for the pulse, but found nothing. Just the rushing nothingness of the sea in an empty shell. She found the ampoule a few yards away where it had been thrown in the violence of the struggle, picked it up almost idly, wondering in the vacuum of her dislocated thoughts what Ginny had intended for her, then her foot touched something in the dark and she jerked her foot away, trembling with pure reaction. Something moved slightly, and she heard a sound, half-sigh, half-groan, almost a voice.

'Ginnyyyy. . .'

'Joe?' In an instant she was on her knees beside him, pulling him up. 'Are you okay?'

'Al?' He sat up abruptly, and Alice thought she could *feel* the fever in his body through his clothes. His voice was brittle, almost sharp, and his movements were quick and febrile. She guessed that he might be in shock.

'Where's Gin?' He stood up, still with that false

briskness, and Alice wondered at how strangely *normal* his voice seemed, his gestures miracles of precision in the narrow, surreal circle of her own perception. She supposed that she too was in shock, but for now the sensation was pleasant, even euphoric. Even the blood, which was still trickling sluggishly down her arm and the whole of her left side, seemed to belong to someone else.

'Ginny's dead.' Her voice felt remote, her mouth slack, as if she had just come out of anaesthetic.

'What?' He was hardly paying attention. Two strides took him to where Ginny was lying, and he patted the dead girl's face gently for a moment. 'Gin. Wake up. come on, Gin. She's fainted. There was something in the air. Drugged incense or something. I passed out too. Ginny!'

'She's dead,' repeated Alice quietly.

'Gin? Wake up, Gin.'

'Joe. I said she's dead. You injected her with the syringe she gave you for me. She meant you to kill me all along.'

'No!' He shook her, more violently this time. 'Ginny!' He turned to Alice. 'She's not breathing. We need an ambulance. Ginny!' He began to try to pump air into the girl's lifeless body by force, sobbing with the strain, the precision of his movements corrupted into a violent trembling which seemed to pull his muscles and tendons in opposite directions like cruel wires.

'Ginny! Wake up! Gin!'

'It's no good,' said Alice. 'Whatever was in that syringe wasn't a tranquillizer. She wanted me out of the way. That's why she told you—'

'*No!*' He was crying now, still pumping air into the girl's body, calling her name, swearing and crying, a thin stream of bloody spittle trickling from the corner of his mouth; 'Wait! Ginny! I love you! I love you!'

And it wasn't the blood, or the shock, or even the

relief of thinking it was all over. It was hearing him say that to Ginny, to Rosemary, even after everything which had happened, that made her lose control. The world sideslipped, half dissolved in tears and bitterness. Her stomach flipped over, everything strong in her collapsed, and with that last 'I love you' in her memory's ear (so much sharper than reality), she began to throw up.

Some time later she found Turner's petrol and divined its use. For all its damp, the house burned fairly well.

One

Fulbourn Hospital, Cambridge, *May 1978*

The radio's on somewhere in the building; I can hear it playing weird dream-notes through the walls, some kind of modern music, I suppose. I don't much like the modern scene; I expect it's because I'm too much of a purist. I never even liked jazz. But somehow, these notes, odd, semi-discordant resonances rarefied into almost-nothing through the thickness of the walls . . . they compel me, somehow. I can hear the voice of the singer, low, almost atonal, a kind of lament; I can even hear the words:

> Remember me, for I am not gone away.
> I am in the air you breathe—
> I am in every part of you.

No, I never heard that. I must be making that up.

> Remember me when shines the sun;
> I am a statue made of glass—
> The sun shines through me.

How strange, that my subconscious should speak to me through rock music.

> Remember me when comes the night;
> I'll haunt your dreams.

Two

Cambridge, *May 1990*

It is raining, and the tiny sounds of the rain against the window tick against the glass like time going by. Alice remembers the cup of tea by her elbow and tastes it; it is cold. Moggy is sitting on her knee, quiet for a change, paws tucked neatly under her body. Alice forces her eyes back into focus and re-reads the letter, crumpled by the weight of the cat. There are cat-hairs clinging to the smooth paper; it is moulting season. The hairs are brindled, like the cat. For a minute or two, the hairs are more clear than the writing.

A phrase catches her eye, holds it almost magically;
'*Something inside me remembers. . .*'
(oh joe)
. . .*and I'll never forget.*
Never.
She brushes the surface of the paper, absently, begins to read again; she knows the words almost by heart, but still she re-reads them, as if to discover some undisclosed secret in the close-written lines.

Cambridge, May 1990
Dear Alice,
    I have arranged the funeral in Grantchester for the 21st of May. Nothing elaborate, but I wanted to make sure that she wasn't just forgotten.

I'd like you to come. First, I think it would do you good, and would get you to see things in a proper perspective. Second, I need to talk to you about Ginny. I can't believe what you told me last time I saw you; I can't and won't. I love Ginny, and she loved me, I can swear to that. I think she was still disturbed; I'm willing to believe she was an addict, and after the result of the inquest I think that you're right in thinking that she intended to give you a drug overdose. Perhaps she even knew it was an overdose. At least none of that had to come out in court; they all assumed that she'd done it herself. In as much as I can feel gratitude in any of this rotten business, I'm grateful for that; because I know she was innocent. As for the rest, I'm convinced that what I thought I saw in the house was a kind of hallucination caused by drugs; it's the only explanation I can accept. It would be better for you if you'd accept it too.

I don't know what I'll do without her; I'm writing this to you and wondering when I'll start feeling the pain ... in a way, the most terrible grief would be better than this empty, sterile mourning. I've left the band; I found I couldn't take any interest in what was going on any more, and I didn't think it was fair on the others to drag them down just when they were beginning to get somewhere. Maybe I'll get going again some day; I don't know, but every time I pick up my guitar I just keep remembering Ginny.

I need you, Alice. You're the only person who knew her that I can talk to. I need to know all about her, to make her live again for me. Don't try to make me forget her; I can't. Something inside me still remembers her, and I'll never forget. Never. I've had my bit of love now, and I won't have it again. But she can live again, in me, in my thoughts and dreams. God, sometimes I feel her so close that I can almost touch her. Please come to the funeral; no one else will. I've ordered white flowers.

Alice stops reading.

In her mind's eye she sees a carnival wheel, still and black against the white sky. She walks across the deserted fairground towards it, as it looms dinosaur-like, dragon-like, above her. For a moment she glimpses the intricacies of its inner workings, red with rust and black with oil, hears the voices of birds calling in the still pale air. Then a sound, faint and whispery at first, then beginning to gather momentum ... the sound of the beast's intestines at work. A grating, creaking sound, a grinding of metal on rust, metal on metal. A sound like the machinery that turns the world on its axis like a roundabout, keeps the blue sky's circle in place. Slowly, but with the inevitablility of Fate, or Faith, the wheels begin to turn.

Epilogue

Fulbourn Hospital, *1 April 1991*

No More Twist.

The Tailor of Gloucester: Beatrix Potter

I held out for as long as I could; it took me this long to realize that after all, this was where I needed to be. It's quiet here, tranquil; every day a new kind of serenity. I sit at the window and comb my hair into the sunlight, like Mariana, and I wonder whether death will come today. It comes to me in the mornings, almost gently, with the sun, and somehow with its coming I begin to understand Daniel better than ever before. We remember, Daniel and I: we remember and we know that it's only a question of waiting. A wheel turns, a clock ticks, a girl rides a roundabout through a carousel of dreams to come full circle again under the same sky which turned for Daniel's little train in his spinning-top all those years ago.

I haven't seen Joe in a long time; now that I come to think about it, didn't I see something in his eyes, that last visit, something bright and desperate, almost like hate? Almost like hope?

Poor Joe. I should have known better than to

imagine that he could have forgotten her for my sake; I, after all, am still alive, whereas she now has the advantage, on top of all her other attractions, of being definitively inaccessible. She is not dead, she has simply withdrawn into another kind of mystery, beyond the coarse realities of the flesh into the etheric, limitless refinements of the spirit. Every little death brings her back, stronger and more beautiful in the minds of those men who have loved her, and who have never ceased to love her; Rosemary Virginia, reborn a thousand times, child of a thousand desires. I think he recalled her; I remember him at the funeral (yes, I was there, trying to prove to myself that we had won), dry-eyed and somehow unfocused, his little bunch of lily-of-the-valley clutched so tightly in his hands that the knuckles showed white under the skin; and sometimes his hands shifted slightly, nervously, and I saw the marks his fingers had left on the delicate leaves, bruising them into transparency. No one else came; no friends, not the family she had said she had; no one, and yet all Grantchester seemed to welcome her back, mutely, with the ease of long understanding.

Yes, it must have been then that he called her; perhaps when he dropped the crushed flowers into the grave and felt the dark, fragrant call of the earth below his feet; perhaps he saw her standing by the hawthorn-tree in blossom, all in white, like a novice. Sometimes I wonder whether he saw her looking at me. But he called her, I'm sure of it; as sure as I know the air I breathe. The wheel has come round again, and she is coming. April, come she will . . . this morning I thought I saw her in my mirror, looking out from her haunted underwater eyes. Did I see her? Or did Joe see her one clear grey morning, staring out at him from his mirror like a drowned girl, opening her arms? Was she holding a noose? April . . . come she will. It almost sounds like a promise. Something inside her remembers . . . and come she will. I don't think I can be like

424